ACKNOWLEDGMENTS

Thanks to Kim Whalen of The Whalen Agency for all of your support over all of these years. Because of you, I can bandy around the word "novelist" at parties.

Thanks to Dannie Festa for suggesting the title of this book.

All of my love to my Cerga! Those related by blood and marriage: Jenn, Rob, Haley, Declan, Maibre, Brian, Alex, Mom, Janis, and all of the Gruenenfelders, Campbells and Smiths.

And those related by love, especially my Girlfriend Cerga: Dorothy, Missy, Gaylyn, Nancy, Jen, Carolyn, Lila, London, Ysabela, Francesca, Quinn, Faa, Laurie, Suzi, Sarah, Miracle and Dania. And the boys, too: Bob, Jeff, Brian, Cormac, Dave, Dan, Patrick, Blake, Chris and Bev.

And to any Ex who may have bought this book: If you're actually reading this, then no, I did not write about you. Unless you like it, in which case, yes, you're totally in there.

My Ex's Wedding

ALSO BY KIM GRUENENFELDER

Hangovers & Hot Flashes

Love the Wine You're With

Keep Calm and Carry a Big Drink

There's Cake in My Future

Misery Loves Cabernet

A Total Waste of Makeup

My Ex's Wedding

KIM GRUENENFELDER

MY EX'S WEDDING. Copyright © 2020 Kim Gruenenfelder

ISBN: 978-1-735-58050-0

First Edition: August 2020

10 9 8 7 6 5 4 3 2 1

To Brian, my favorite Ex. Twenty years and one kid later,
I think we're doing pretty well.

And to Alex – you're the kid. Be grateful people give each other
second chances.

1998

Great sex can only last for two years.

I don't mean good sex; I'm told you can have that for decades. I'm talking about once in a lifetime, really great sex. Phenomenal, multiple orgasm, *you can think about it ten years later and still climax* sex. Let's face it, we only really get that kind of sex once in our lives, usually in our 20s, and only with one person. That one guy who we were so completely, madly, and deeply in love with that... well... it was a sickness really. We were genuinely crazy. There were hormones involved.

I've actually read about this. The hormones are called oxytocin, vasopressin and dopamine. You secrete a combination of them when you're in love. That, and an opioid similar to heroin. Heroin, people. This Molotov cocktail of hormones is what makes you deliriously happy when your boyfriend is around (hormones secreted in your blood: happy, happy, happy), and insanely depressed when he's not (hormones gone: major drug withdrawal. Only instead of the shakes and rehab, you get weeping and eating an entire cake over a "Must See TV" Thursday block of shows).

Your body stops secreting this mindfucking concoction after about two years.

And, usually, the two of you go your separate ways. It might be after college, on your 25th birthday, or when he announces that he's (inexplicably) moving to Japan for work, and you are secretly relieved.

Or not. Point is, he's gone. That part of your life is over. Moving on...

Unless...

1

Cut to a "just hit my 30s" dilemma: Let's say you are confronted with that one man from your past whose body your body was *literally* addicted to. The one who gave you phenomenally great sex. You know the guy – we all have one: that asshole who broke your heart.

At least twice.

Now, let's say your present guy is amazing. You and he have everything in common: you love the same things, have the same goals. You're *nice* to each other. In the old relationship, you had to win the fight. In your present relationship, you're on the same team, so making a point isn't nearly as important as making sure you're both happy.

And you are happy. You've both been through all of the hideous prerequisite courses of mating and dating: *Romantic Obsession 101*, *Mindfucking 102*, *Gaydar 103* to live happily ever after.

Happily Ever After. There's a sentence loaded with all six bullets, designed to make you want to shoot yourself in the head.

But it is what most of us strive for, wish for, and dream about at night: to live happily ever after.

So the question is who do you pick? The guy who will, once again, give you phenomenal sex for two years, followed by a lifetime of heartache? Or the one you want to raise kids with, travel with, laugh with, and grow old with?

Do you choose the person you were so in love with that you couldn't see straight, or the man you love so much that you can't imagine *not* waking up to him every morning for the rest of your life?

Do you choose the one you know – YOU KNOW – will accidentally hurt you time and again, just for the promise of all those addictive hormones that last only two years? Or do you choose the one who is perfect for you? The one whose name always makes you smile when you read it on your cell phone.

Who do you choose? The one you're with or the one who got away?

The question is deceptively simple.

Or, at least I would have thought that two weeks ago...

One

I'd like to think that we all have regrets in life.

Sure, we all know someone who says, "I don't have any regrets, because if I had done anything differently, I wouldn't be the person I am today."

But I'd like to think that person is mired in self-delusion.

I finish reading the passage aloud, and look up from my notebook to see Vanessa Waters, the former voluptuous bombshell from the 1960s and fabulous diva from the dishy prime time soap in the 1980s, pouring herself a glass of champagne. "That's wonderful!" Vanessa says with the enthusiasm of Auntie Mame. "Much better than what I said. By the way, what did I say?"

I look down at my notebook to read her words verbatim. "I don't care how many failed relationships Marlon Brando has had, or how viciously he battles with a box of donuts, I'd still pin him to a wall and show him who's boss."

"Ahhh... he does and I would," Vanessa says dreamily, handing me a glass of Bollinger champagne as she takes a seat on the plush sofa across from me. "As a matter of fact, I heard a rumor he's in a bungalow here for the next few days. Care to snoop around?"

I take the champagne and put it down on a highly polished coffee table without drinking any. "I'm not skulking around the Beverly Hills Hotel with one of the most famous women in the world looking for sex," I say firmly. "Again," I add under my breath.

"You're no fun," Vanessa says, mock pouting. "Okay, back to my other story. You haven't lived until you've been done by a drag queen in Vegas."

"Impersonated," I say as I transcribe a few of her earlier thoughts into my notebook.

Vanessa takes a sip of champagne. "What?" she asks.

I look up from my notebook. "Impersonated. It's not, 'Until you've been *done* by a drag queen.' It's, 'Until you've been *impersonated* by a drag queen.' *Done* implies you had sex with him."

"I did."

I purse my lips and look at her suspiciously. "You had sex with a drag queen?"

She shrugs. "Well, it *was* the 70s."

"Well, it *was* a drag queen."

"Sweetie, they're not all gay."

I let my jaw drop just enough to let her know that I think she's nuts. She leans back on the couch. "Okay. Fine. Impersonated," Vanessa concedes. "But once you said it, I thought having sex with a drag queen sounded so much more interesting."

"How many times do we have to go over this?" I ask, sighing. "You're not supposed to lie in your own autobiography. You've had a very interesting life. Met everyone, done everything..."

"I haven't done a drag queen," Vanessa points out.

"No, but you've been impersonated by one," I counter.

"Are you going to drink that?" Vanessa asks, pointing to my champagne, and using a tone of voice like she's my mother trying to force me to eat my Brussels sprouts.

"Maybe," I lie, even though I have no intentions of drinking while I'm working.

Vanessa glances at her diamond Patek Phillipe watch. "My God. It's four o'clock already," she gasps, seemingly shocked at how the time got away from her. She turns off my tape recorder. "We've been slaving away all day. No wonder I'm so tired."

I've been here for all of two hours. Trying to get this woman to help me write her "autobiography" is about as productive as trying to wrestle a kitten into a new pair of Manolo Blahniks.

I turn my tape recorder back on. "So, you want to tell me more about the men you slept with in the 1970s?"

"Boring. They may have been hot at the time, but back then they never called the next day. And now they're all old with paunches, thirtysomething wives, and toddlers running around. And they still don't call the next day." Vanessa spreads some caviar on a toast point, and sniffs it. "Does this smell right to you?" she asks, thrusting the fish eggs in my face.

I take a whiff. "Smells heavenly to me."

Vanessa looks at it, makes a face, then hands it to me. "Here, you eat it. I must be missing something."

I take the caviar, just as I have every day since we began writing her memoirs. I practically inhale it and it's ridiculously good. "You know," I say with my mouth full, "You could just order champagne without the caviar."

"Then I'd look like an alcoholic," Vanessa nearly shrieks. "What do you think the waiters would say about a woman who orders champagne for lunch and nothing else? It's hard enough to wait until two o'clock for the stuff."

"You don't wake up until two," I point out, scooping up some more of the delicious spheres, and spreading them on another toast point.

"That's only because I can't have champagne until then. Otherwise, I'd get up at noon."

She says that like if it weren't for the champagne problem, she'd be up at dawn and jogging.

Vanessa is currently staying in a one bedroom bungalow at the Beverly Hills Hotel, while her home in Bel Air is being renovated for the fifth time in as many years. Every day, we go through the same routine: In the late morning, I head out to work and make my way to her hotel. Around noon, I get to her bungalow, pound on her door, and try to roust her out of bed. Vanessa always takes at least five minutes to answer, finally opening the door wearing one of the hotel's signature pink robes, and looking like death warmed over. Vanessa then asks me to please come back at one, she's so sorry, but she had a late night and isn't quite ready to entertain yet. Then she tells me to go to the Fountain Coffee Shop and have a cup of coffee, charge it to her room, and work on whatever she dictated to me the day before.

I do.

By one o'clock, it only takes her two minutes to answer the door. I assume this is because she fell back asleep on the couch, which is only a few feet from the door. Vanessa then insists she needs a shower, and asks me to go have lunch and charge it to her room.

I do, and I have to say the Polo Lounge's burgers are fantastic.

At two o'clock, I bang on Vanessa's door one final time, and she emerges, her hair dry and flying in all directions because she never took that shower, never made it past that nap-inducing couch.

This time, Vanessa looks delighted to see me, gives me a kiss on each cheek, welcomes me into her oasis, and orders room service: a bottle of Bollinger champagne for her, a pot of black coffee for me, and caviar with all the accouterment.

"You know, you could just order several bottles of champagne at night, then keep one bottle in the fridge for breakfast, and no one would be the wiser," I suggest.

"Yes, but then they wouldn't bring it to me chilled in a silver ice bucket. So much of the pleasure of champagne is presentation."

I write that down. Don't know where I'm going to put that in her book, but it's the most interesting thing she's said all day.

I'm a ghostwriter who specializes in celebrity "autobiographies." You know those memoirs "written" by celebrities that reach the best seller lists their first week out? I write those.

Really, I'm a novelist. Well, okay, not really. But I have written a novel. A completed one and everything: one hundred and ten thousand words. Seven drafts. It's called *The Edict of Edith*. And while *Edith* may not have been published (yet), it was good enough to get me an agent, who got me my first job ghostwriting celebrity "autobiographies." And while it slightly saddens me that I have yet to see the words "by Samantha Evans" on a book jacket, I love seeing the words "Pay to the Order of Sam Evans" on my paychecks.

There are three types of celebrities who use ghostwriters. The first are people such as politicians or CEOs who barely have enough time to meet with a ghostwriter, much less the countless hours needed to pen a whole book. They lack time. The second type can't string a sentence together to save their lives. (I'll go out on a limb and say think anyone who has ever starred on MTV's *The Real World*.) So they lack intelligence.

The final type is Vanessa Waters. She's got time. She's got nothing but actually, having shot her last movie back in 1989. She's got brains. Went to Princeton before she became America's Sex Bomb in the 1960s. Unfortunately, Vanessa lacks the third quality necessary to write a book: she has no discipline.

About two months ago, Vanessa agreed to write her memoirs for my employer, Sideways Publishing. In exchange for a guaranteed best seller, Amy Sideways, the owner of the company, gave Vanessa a five hundred thousand dollar advance.

And me.

Since I began working on Vanessa's book, *Oh, To Hell With It!*, I have been scuba diving, shoe shopping, parasailing, and accompanying Vanessa to various cocktail and dinner parties about town. I have not, however, been writing much.

"You know where the sales are really phenomenal this time of year?" Vanessa asks me excitedly. "London! Let's just hop on a plane and go."

"I am not hopping on a plane with you just so you can avoid writing," I say firmly. "Again," I mumble under my breath.

It wasn't London, but I let her take me to Paris a few weeks ago for New Year's Eve. She didn't have a date, and my boyfriend Eric, who's an E.R. doctor, was working that weekend. So I figured that rather than sit around watching *Mary Tyler Moore* reruns and being depressed about being thirty and not married, I'd go to glamorous Paris.

Where, it turns out, Vanessa and I watched *Mary Tyler Moore* reruns in French ("Je deteste spunk!") and got depressed about being thirty, and sixty, and not married.

The snails were good though.

"Why don't you tell me more about your ex-husbands?" I suggest.

Vanessa shrugs. "They're all old with paunches, married to thirtysomethings…"

"I'm sensing a trend here," I say, rubbing my forehead in exasperation. "Let's try something new. Some people say that you are one of the sexiest women of the twentieth century. How do you respond to that?"

She squints her eyes at me suspiciously. "Who says that?"

"People."

"What people?"

"Well, male people."

"Hmm," she says pensively, mulling over my statement. She taps her index finger on her chin. "Do they mean Sophia Loren sexy, or Pamela Anderson sexy?"

"I don't know. What difference does it make?"

"Because my response would be different depending on who it is. If it's Sophia Loren sexy, well, hey, get me names and get me phone numbers. Sophia Loren is 'love at first sight' sexy. Men would die for her. Pamela Anderson is 'She's hot. I'd like to bone her' sexy. Men don't want to marry that kind of sexy, they want to have it and move on. That would be an insult."

I think about her statement. "You can't fall in love with someone at first sight. It takes months or even years to…"

"Sure you can," Vanessa says emphatically. "People do it all the time."

"People divorce all the time, too," I remind her.

"That doesn't mean they weren't in love. It just means they fucked it up later."

I shrug, pretending to agree with her. Vanessa watches me, then cocks her head as she studies me, observing me like Jane Goodall studies the behavior of a chimp.

"You did," she says slowly, suddenly realizing this about me for the first time.

I look up from my notes. "I did…what?" I ask, dubious of where this is going.

"You fell in love at first sight," she says definitively. "And you fucked it up."

Two

I should have remembered that, as an actress, Vanessa studies people for a living. It's her job. She might as well be a psychiatrist.

Because the truth is, Vanessa is one hundred percent right. I did fall in love at first sight. When I was twenty. David Stevens. I saw him at a fraternity party the first week of my junior year at UCLA. He was sitting on a beat-up green couch, drinking beer from a red Solo cup, and laughing as he talked to some random red headed girl.

And I could barely breathe. I'd never had a reaction like that before. It was like every cell in my body went into overdrive the second I laid eyes on him. He was just...there was just something about him.

I mean, I could describe him physically: brown hair, cut short, greenish brown eyes, runner's build, 6'1" and oh-so-cute. But that doesn't describe the way my heart leapt into my throat every time I saw him. It doesn't describe how I was so nervous and in love that I felt like I'd throw up every time he knocked on my door for the next few years. It doesn't describe how empty I felt when he wasn't around. Or why I succumbed to all of the silly things young and in love couples do around each other: the making out in public, the speaking in soft baby talk to each other, our staying on the phone all night, then me leaving it off the hook and on my pillow, so I could hear him breathing while I fell asleep.

Those few years in college were perfect, and I was convinced at that time that everything for the rest of our lives would be perfect. Dave was a guitar player for a band, and I was an English major studying pre-law. I thought that I would get into Harvard Law

School, and he would get a record contract, and we would get married and stay madly in love forever.

That's almost what happened.

I did indeed get into Harvard. And Dave and his band, Almost 70, did get a record deal. We got married the week after college graduation, in front of friends and family who secretly thought it wouldn't last, but didn't say anything at the time.

At twenty-two, I didn't realize that I would hate law school. I didn't realize that a recording contract meant Dave would be touring around the country constantly, leaving his new wife to stay at home and worry about all of those female fans he was meeting, all of whom would have slept with him in a heartbeat.

But, mostly, I didn't realize that that random redhead he had talked to all those years ago on the couch, the one who was also the backup singer of his band, would one day steal him away from me.

Men suck.

Anyway, after boring Vanessa with all of the details of my failed love life so many years ago, and absolutely refusing to troll around the hotel in search of Marlon Brando, I packed up my stuff for the weekend, and slogged through Friday traffic to my abode.

I live in a fantastic home. A cozy two-bedroom sanctuary on the Valley side of the Hollywood Hills that looks like a mountain cabin tucked away in the middle of nowhere. Of course to pay the rent on a place like this, I need a roommate. Fortunately, I have Liz, the best roommate in the world.

I met Liz a lifetime ago, when we shared a dorm as Freshman at UCLA.

My first day at school would have been a disaster if it wasn't for her. I had recently lost my mother to cancer, and my father was in Europe on a book tour the day I drove my beat up 1973 Buick Apollo to Hedrick Hall, ready to begin my new life.

I checked in with the folks in the lobby, got my room number, and trudged two large suitcases and a duffle bag up to Room 503. I opened the door to a stunningly beautiful 5'10" Chinese American girl with a body that would tempt Barbie to do more sit ups. She was with her 4'11" Chinese American mother, and her 6'4" Swedish father, and the three of them looked like the perfect family to me.

There's a word I heard at a party once. Cerga. I think it might be Turkish? Anyway, I don't know what the exact translation is, someone told me "tent" then another said "circus folk" but to me the word means the family you've picked, not the family you were born with. Liz and her parents quickly became my Cerga.

Liz and I are a household of writers, not such a rare occurrence in L.A. Liz is a greeting card writer. (Yes, there are people who actually do that. I wouldn't have thought so either. And there are people who name lipsticks, and people who eat ice cream... for a living! Life's not fair.) She used to write these sappy greeting cards I couldn't stand: A picture of a dog with the caption, "I Ruff You!" or a lion with the caption, "I ain't lion – I love you." Blech!

Back then, Liz was madly in love with her fiancé Fred, and luxuriating in an incredible storybook courtship which was quickly becoming the storybook wedding for a storybook marriage. Until one night, about six months ago, when Liz came home early to find Fred in bed with one of her co-workers.

Did I mention men suck?

Liz moved in with me and began the typical healing process of a heartbroken woman: crying one day, reading self-help books the next. Swearing off men one night, dragging me out to a hot new bar or club the next.

Her career has taken an odd turn for the better, however. At first, her job was suffering. Instead of seeing a cartoon of Cupid with his arrow, and writing crap like, "I quiver when I think of you," when she saw the drawing, she'd write, "Back in Roman times, Cupid was a toddler, and a bow and arrow was a weapon. Imagine your three-year-old nephew with an AK 47, shooting people at random. Love sucks. Get over him."

And a whole new line of greeting cards, called the "Get Over Him" series, was born. Apparently, at some point in our lives, all of us need a card that says, "He's a dickhead. Love sucks. Your girlfriends still love you."

As I enter the house, I see Liz leaning against our living room doorway, still wearing her T-shirt and pajamas from this morning, and calmly observing two people running around our living room. The first person is an ancient Chinese man with a long white beard, carrying a compass, and speaking what appears to be Mandarin to Liz's mother Lauren, nursing a cigarette and writing down notes on a clipboard.

I walk under the arched doorway, stand next to Liz, and watch the scene unfold. Then I ask, "Why do we have an old bearded man running around our house carrying a compass and speaking Mandarin to your mother?"

"If I had a nickel for every time I got asked that question..." Liz deadpans. Then she explains, "My grandmother offered to have our place Feng Shuied. I figured meh, how can it hurt?"

"Your grandmother who lives in Xiamen?" I whisper/ask Liz.

Liz nods, then leads me into our living room, where the man stands at the window, staring out at our yard, then eyeing his compass.

"Oh, hey Sam!" Lauren says brightly to me. "This is Mr. Li. He is a Feng Shui master." She says something to Methuselah in Chinese. The old man turns to me, smiles, and bows politely. I self-consciously bow back. Lauren gives me a quick hug, then continues. "Last time she visited, my mother begged Liz and me to Feng Shui our houses. If this was being done by a Beverly Hills con artist, it would cost thousands, but Mom got a real guy and a good deal."

The man runs up to our couch, looks down at his compass, and continues with his Mandarin monologue of advice. "Huh." Lauren says, almost to herself as she dutifully jots down a note on her clipboard, then says something to Mr. Li in Chinese.

"What did he say?" I ask.

"That the couch is a place of relaxation," Lauren answers.

"Of course it's a place of relaxation," Liz mutters, handing her mom an ashtray. "It's a couch."

"Okay, so not all of his comments can be gems."

Mr. Li smiles at me warmly. "I look at your bedroom. Very good room for marriage."

"Wait, you saw my room?" I repeat to the Feng Shui master, and now I'm a little excited. "Am I getting married soon?" I ask, hope seeping into my voice.

The man smiles at me, then looks to Lauren to translate what I said into Chinese. She does. He answers her with a smile in Chinese, then Lauren tells me in English, "This year you are going to marry the man who makes you want to throw up." She furrows her brow and thinks. "Wait, that doesn't sound right."

"Pretty sure he means puts butterflies in her stomach," Liz surmises. "Although I want to steal that nausea comment for a new greeting card."

My face lights up. "He means Eric!" I tell them, then excitedly tell Mr. Li, "That's the man I'm dating. So I'm going to marry him?"

The man nods. "Yes. Room very good for marriage."

SCORE! (I know women my age shouldn't be so into weddings. But I am so into weddings.)

As Mr. Li walks to our kitchen, Lauren following close behind, I look over at Liz brightly. "So what else have we learned?"

"That I hate men and don't want to get married anytime soon. Oh! And that I desperately need to get laid," Liz tells me.

My eyes bug out in amazement. "He knew all of that from your bedroom?"

Liz shrugs. "No, I'm just saying..."

"Girls, we need you in here," Lauren yells from the kitchen.

The two of us walk into our kitchen/dining room/desks thrown in there because we have no space for a home office. As Lauren grabs a bottle of beer from the refrigerator, Mr. Li tells her something in Chinese.

"He says you should move your desks closer to the window," Lauren translates. "More creativity there." She looks around at the stacks of papers scattered about the room, interspersed with dirty dishes. "And get a maid."

Mr. Li taps his finger on Liz's desk. More Mandarin. Lauren translates. "The most passionate work in the house is done right here. A lot of passion..."

"That's my desk," Liz says proudly.

"...All of it negative," Lauren continues, shooting a warning look at her daughter.

Liz crosses her arms and narrows her eyes at her mother. "Mom, what's Chinese for 'Bite Me'?"

Three

After another half hour of learning all about real Feng Shui, as opposed to the interior decorating and furniture trend most Americans think of as Feng Shui, we were assured that our house would be ninety percent lucky for the next five years, and our guests left us to get ready for our dates that evening.

As I walk into Liz's bedroom to get her opinion on the little black dress I plan to wear tonight, I see Liz lying on her bed, still dressed in her flannel pajamas, madly scribbling down words on a yellow legal pad.

"Does this look dress make me look slutty?" I ask.

Liz looks up from her work to examine my outfit. "For a third date, no. But you're meeting an old friend of Eric's, right?"

I nod.

"Change," she says unequivocally.

I nod again, then walk over to her closet to see if I can borrow something of hers. As I do, Liz reads from her legal pad. "Okay, how about this? No man starts out perfect. Each one's like a cube steak. He must be seasoned with love, then pounded into submission."

I shake my head, smiling. "I'm surprised you didn't add, 'Then grilled over an open flame'."

"Oooohhh, that's even better," Liz says, furiously adding my words to her own. "Now how about this one? A toast for women everywhere: We could drink to the men we love, we could drink to the men who love us. But the men we love will never love us, so fuck them! Here's to us!"

I nod appreciatively. "Not bad."

I watch Liz draw a star next to her toast, then throw her pad down on the bed and collapse into a heap. "Well, I'm drained."

"You're drained?" I ask, trying not to sound too incredulous. "What the hell did you do all day besides watch *Oprah, CNN,* and reruns of *Murphy Brown?*"

"Hey, I specifically live with another writer so I don't have to defend my creative process," Liz counters.

"Can you explain to me how watching TV all day is part of your creative process?" I ask.

Liz smiles at me. "Glad to. One day, I saw a Starbucks ad during a *Mad About You* commercial break, and the muse came to visit. That's how I created my, 'I like my men the way I like my coffee...' series."

Actually, those were pretty funny. They included the punch lines, "Dark and Bitter." "Liquefied." And "Wait, I forget. How do you make stupid coffee?"

"Which, by the way, you probably shouldn't brag about tonight," I gently remind Liz. "The last thing a guy needs on a blind date is a woman proudly talking about how her job is to write that men are best served with scalded milk."

"What would you prefer I say? That they should be ground up and have hot water poured over them?"

"Fair enough," I concede as I flip through hanger after hanger of Liz's clothes. I stop at a respectable, long beige skirt from Banana Republic, and put it up to my waist. "When's he picking you up?"

Liz looks at her digital clock. "Oh, shit. In seven minutes."

"I don't understand why you're not more excited," I say as I watch Liz whip off her work clothes – and by that I mean her flannel plaid pajamas. "Mike sounds like a nice guy..."

Liz tosses her PJs onto the floor, then shimmies into a pair of black leather pants already laid out on her bed. "Please," she says dryly. "He's an accountant who owns a house in Calabasas. I'm not exactly all tingly with anticipation, I'm just doing this as a favor for a friend."

"Why go in with that attitude? For all you know, this guy could be the one."

"The one what?" Liz asks, eyeing me suspiciously as she sucks in her gut and zips the pants.

"You know," I say as I pull off my short dress to try on her beige skirt. "The one who changes your life. The one who puts butterflies in your stomach. The one who gives you babies."

"Oh Good Christ," Liz blurts out, rolling her eyes as she takes off her pajama top. "Fred gave me butterflies, and look how that turned out."

"Fred was an asshole," I point out.

Liz throws her blouse over her head. "Apparently, he was. Which is why I'm specifically looking for a guy who doesn't have that kind of power over me. Besides, that whole *Butterflies in the stomach. Oh my God, I missed you so much* thing. That's so college. Thirty year olds don't fall for crap like that."

"You are so cynical."

"I prefer the term *realistic*," Liz retorts, slipping on a pair of black stilettos. "And by the way, you lied to that Feng Shui guy when you said you had butterflies when you met Eric."

"I totally got butterflies! Eric is insanely hot and I couldn't believe he was actually talking to me."

"Yeah, but come on. You may have been excited to meet Eric, but did you really feel like you were going to throw up? You seem too smart for that."

"Not *nausea* butterflies," I correct. "Gawd. No one over the age of twenty-five should get that *Oh my God, how did I ever live without him?* feeling right away. But yes, butterflies."

"Then you're an idiot," Liz declares. "Butterflies are Exhibit A in the alphabet of crap from my youth I am happy to leave behind. Don't you remember all those stories we heard about during the rollercoaster years of college relationships? The girl whose boyfriend of two years inexplicably broke up on their anniversary, saying he needed to "explore his options." Or the girl who learned her boyfriend of three months boinked her sorority sister and vowed never to love again… only to go back to him and be cheated on again the following month. Let's not forget the girl whose man just suddenly stopped calling and never returned any of her calls, which eventually drove her to go to his house at two in the morning in a confused rage. Not to mention what Fred did to me or what Dave did to you. Isn't it glorious to know we'll never be that hurt and stupid again?"

I'm silent for a moment, thinking about what Liz just said. Isn't it weird how some heartbreaks can still stab you out of nowhere years later?

"Ooh," Liz says, happily reaching for her pad and jotting down a phrase.

"What did you think of?" I ask.

"A card for every twentysomething," Liz says, reading her latest bon mot to me. "You used to want to give him butterflies in his stomach. Now you want to give him a punch in his kidneys."

Liz looks up at me, beaming with pride at her new creation.

I slowly shake my head. "I begged you to stay on the Paxil."

Four

Liz leaves with her date about ten minutes later, leaving me to my dress dilemma.

She also leaves me with a box of Twinkies. I'm not sure if I love her or hate her for that, because I keep stressing about my outfit, then grabbing as individually wrapped slice of heaven, and wolfing it down before trying on another dress. What is up with that vicious circle of trying on clothes that make us feel fat, which makes us turn to distress eating, which actually makes us fat?

And why don't men go through it?

Back to the task at hand. I am very excited about my date tonight. And not just because the Feng Shui master told me that I am marrying Eric, my incredibly hot, sexy, and wonderful boyfriend. But because tonight I am meeting his childhood friend Libby, who he has known since they were babies. This is a big deal because his family is back in Houston, and she will be the closest thing to a family member I will have met so far.

An honor which is leaving me to obsess about how much leg is still showing in the more modest black dress I've just changed into, whether I am wearing the wrong shade of lipstick, and if, when trying to seduce a man through scent, you're supposed to spritz the perfume on your wrists, then rub the wrists on your neck, or if you're supposed to spray it in the air, then run through the mist.

Running through the mist always seems like a waste of perfume, so I choose to spritz.

Tonight I go with Joy, even though I'm usually more of a Chanel No. 5 girl. In college, I wore Coco by Chanel. But in law school, that scent came to symbolize my ex-husband, my naiveté towards marriage, and all the pain that that led to, so I switched scents when I switched apartments, jobs, states and mates. I haven't looked back, although for some reason I still have a box of Coco scented powder I can't bear to throw away, but will never use.

Eric gave me the Joy perfume as a one month anniversary gift, and I've been wearing it ever since.

Ah, Eric. I've been dating him for about three months, and he is my reward for the freak show that was my dating life the previous five years. I met him one night while taking Liz to the Emergency Room. She had stomach pains and vomiting that she was attributing to her breakup. Thinking it might be appendicitis, I drove her to the hospital.

And I met my Prince Charming.

He was amazing: 32, tall, tan, gorgeous, sexy as hell. When he walked up to us, I was short of breath and couldn't speak. Then he started asking Liz medical questions, and I couldn't stop babbling.

I made a lame joke about the show "ER" and he laughed. We got to talking, and he surprised me by asking me to dinner.

That night, Liz got an appendectomy and I got a boyfriend.

And I have been deliriously happy ever since.

Tonight, we're going to the Polo Lounge because Libby, his good friend from grade school, is staying at the Beverly Hills Hotel. I'm a little nervous about meeting her, which is probably why I keep changing my lipstick. Like she's really going to notice my lipstick. But he keeps saying she's practically family, so I want to look my best, and make a good first impression.

The doorbell rings. "Coming!" I yell, then run out of my bathroom, through my bedroom, and towards the front door.

I race to the door and open it to find Eric, looking James Bond handsome in a dark green Armani suit and holding a bouquet of dark red roses.

My shoulders fall. "I forgot our anniversary, didn't I?" I realize guiltily. Dammit.

Eric shrugs. "Don't worry about it. I only remembered because my computer calendar reminded me." He hands me the roses. "Why don't we just pretend I brought you roses just because I love you?"

"They're beautiful," I say, smiling as I give him a kiss. "Do I have time to put them in a vase before we leave?"

"Yeah. Libby says she's on her way from the airport, so we don't need to be there for another half hour. You look beautiful."

"You think?" I ask insecurely, glancing down at my shoes. "I'm thinking I should have gone with a lower heel. And maybe a dress that doesn't show my knees. I don't want your friend to think I look like a slut."

"You're perfect," Eric says lasciviously, rubbing my leg then giving me a deep kiss. Man, he is an amazing kisser. Should have gotten a varsity letter for it in high school. "And as long as we have half an hour…"

I pull away and joke, "If you think I'm going to chance being late to this dinner and making a bad impression on your friend, you've got another think coming. But I promise to make it up to you later."

"How?" He asks seductively, wrapping his arms around my waist, and pulling me in for another kiss.

"Well, you'll just have to follow me home later to find out," I say coyly before giving into temptation for another minute.

Yup. I've found someone to pretend to be coy with. Life is good.

Eventually, we stop our smoochfest, and Eric follows me into the kitchen, where I grab a vase, and fill it with water. "I have something else for you," he says, pulling a key out of his pocket. "Had this made today."

"You made me a key?" I ask, audibly flabbergasted. I quickly throw the flowers into the vase to grab the key and inspect it.

"You sound surprised."

"Well, it's just... No one has ever made me a key before," I say, turning it back and forth in the light like you would an engagement ring. "I mean, I guess my ex-husband did, but that wasn't until we were moving in together. Oh my God. I love it!"

"Good. I was wondering since I'm in New York next week, maybe I could ask you to water my plants, mmph..." his sentence is cut off as I grab him and kiss him hard on the lips, nearly knocking him over.

I pull away to repeat, "I really love it!"

Eric seems almost amused by my level of enthusiasm. He smiles. "Hmm. Had I known a four dollar item would have made you so happy, I might have brought the flowers a different day."

A thought suddenly occurs to me. "You need a key," I say, then quickly head to my bedroom.

Eric follows me. He leans in the doorway as I rifle through my top drawer, trying to find my spare key. "You don't have to give me a key just because I gave you one," he says, amused.

"No, no," I insist. "You gave me a key. Quid pro quo."

"Ah, what man doesn't yearn to hear those three romantic words from his girlfriend: quid pro quo. Makes me all warm and gooey inside."

"Sorry," I say, yanking out various lingerie from my top drawer, and flinging them onto my bed. "The failed lawyer in me talking."

Eric picks up a black lace teddy from the top of the pile and inspects it. "If you can't find a key, maybe you could give me this. With you in it."

I slam shut my top drawer and try my jewelry box. "Here we are!" I say sing-songily, infinitely pleased with myself. I hand him the key. "It's kind of old, but it should get you in the door."

"What's going to get you into this?" Eric asks, holding up the teddy, and pulling me onto the bed to kiss him.

We start making out. "I'm not kidding," I say, giggling and still necking with him. "We don't want to be late…"

And a minute later: "Don't do that," I say, only half meaning it. "You're going to run my nylons…"

And a minute later: "Hey, you're wrinkling the dress."

And a minute after that: "Okay, but we only have ten minutes. I really don't want to be late."

Forty-five minutes later, we are late, and racing through the Beverly Hills Hotel lobby, on our way to meet his friend Libby.

I now wear an even more modest black dress — not so much because the last one was slutty as because it had makeup smeared all over it after Eric pulled it over my head. Which meant, in actuality, I was slutty, but I didn't want his friend to know that.

I also had to wear my FM pumps, as I broke a heel when… All right, just needless to say, there was a costume change.

"Meet me in the Polo Lounge," I say, breaking away and heading towards the ladies room. "I need to go powder my nose."

Eric grabs my hand and tries to pull me towards the restaurant. "You look fine."

"I look like I've just had sex," I counter.

"You did just have sex…" he says, still dragging me in the direction of the Polo Lounge.

I yank my hand away from him. "That's not the point. I need to powder down this afterglow, and redo my lipstick. Besides, this will give you a minute to see Libby and talk me up."

"But…"

"Just go. I'll be right there," I say, then hurry into the ladies room.

The Ladies Room at the Beverly Hills Hotel is like all of the other rooms here: ridiculously posh. Sparkling white and pink marble everywhere, a large, well lit makeup area in a different room from the stalls.

I walk over to the makeup area, sit down at one of the pink chairs, stare at the large mirror, and try to figure out what to do with my face. I have a big smear on my cheek from where my foundation completely rubbed off, and some redness from my skin bursts through. Great. I pull out my Mac foundation and powder and get to work.

About a minute later, I am back to looking fairly coifed. I pull out two lipsticks. One is bright red, stunning, and not my style at all. I'm sheepish. I go for the purply beige *you can't even tell I'm wearing lipstick* lipstick, and begin applying.

Wimp.

Suddenly, an exquisite Latina with a body to make J. Lo envious charges through the doors like a bat out of Hell. "Why the fuck did I ever give you a job?!" she screams, making me jump.

I turn away from my reflection to look at the woman and am surprised to see, up close and personal, Isabella De Leon.

Like, THE Isabella De Leon. Singer/movie star/internationally known diva.

Holy Shit.

Another beautiful Latina, maybe even prettier than Isabella, but in a more natural and understated way, follows her in quietly. The girl rolls her eyes before saying quietly, "If you would just calm down for a minute so I could explain..."

Isabella whips around to her, waving a perfectly manicured finger in her face. "Don't you EVER tell me to calm down! Do you know how many people would kill for your job? I could have you replaced in the morning. Hell, I could have you replaced just by calling the concierge, and asking him to send over a monkey."

The poor girl jumps a bit at the tirade, then pushes her tongue around in her mouth while she tries to decide on an adequate response. "Right."

Isabella's eyes bug out, and her jaw drops a bit at the girl's dismissive tone. "I could put an ad in the *Reporter*, and have a thousand people begging for your job."

"If you say so," the girl says dryly.

"Don't you use that tone of voice with me," Isabella snarls. She walks up to the bathroom mirror next to me, opens her large Hermes bag, and pulls out her Bobbi Brown powder compact. "I asked for red roses throughout my bungalow, not ranunculus! What do you think I am, an idiot? You think I wouldn't notice?!"

Frankly, I wouldn't have noticed. The only reason I even know the word *ranunculus* is because I ghostwrote a book for an internationally known party planner a few years back. I think they look like really big roses.

Isabella begins powdering her flawless, poreless, golden skin. "And before that, you told the pilot we could be late taking off. I am paying tens of thousands of dollars an hour for a private jet, and you can't make sure they leave on time?"

Her assistant narrows her eyes and glares as she responds. "Well, unfortunately Air Force One…you know, the President's plane…"

"Shut up," Isabella snaps. "And to top it off, I specifically asked you to tell the hotel to send up 1992 Dom Perignon, and they send me Clos du Mesnil (which she pronounces Kloss duh Mesnull). I've never even heard of the stuff. What am I, a redneck?"

I try to avert my eyes, but can't help being mesmerized by Isabella's reflection. She is exquisite: 5'6" with hourglass curves, lustrous black hair, glowing skin, and clear hazel eyes perfectly framed by lush dark eyelashes.

But her beauty is clearly only on the outside. On the inside, she's a monster, and I feel sorry for her assistant.

Isabella flips around to face the girl. "Answer me! Do you think I'm a redneck?!"

The girl looks Isabella dead in the face. "Redneck's not the first word I'd use to describe you, no. And you didn't ask for Dom Perignon. You asked for Krug."

Isabella misses the veiled insult. "Fine. Then it's your fault. Why the hell did you tell them to send me a Kloss duh Mesnull?!"

"Because you and D..." the assistant begins. Then she gives a defeated, "You know what? Never mind."

For several seconds no one says anything.

"It's pronounced Cloh due Mehnee," I finally say.

Isabella turns to look at me as though she's just realized someone else is in the room. Or in the universe for that matter. I continue, "It's made by Krug. Its vintages are some of the most expensive in the world."

Did I mention that one of the more useless things I've been doing since beginning Vanessa's book is learning all about different champagnes? For some people, alcoholism is a disease. For Vanessa, it's a hobby.

Isabella looks like she's going to punch me. Finally, she gives a tut sound as she throws her compact into her bag. "Well, I've never heard of it. And I only drink Cristal and Dom Perignon."

I shrug, consciously brushing her off the way she's trying to brush me off. "Music videos sure have done a lot to mess up the champagne industry," I mutter, proud of myself for standing up to the little princess.

Isabella's eyes widen. I suspect no one has spoken to her like that in many moons. She looks like she's going to bite me. Bitchypoo gives me a once over, concludes I'm not worth her time, then turns on her heel to leave.

"I still need those ranunculus out of my bungalow by the time my fiancé gets here," she says to her beaten down assistant. "And make sure Eduardo is in my suite by ten tomorrow morning. I haven't had color therapy in a week, and I'm starting to get constipated."

And with that, the one and only Isabella De Leon tears out of the ladies room.

After she leaves, the young assistant and I wait to make sure she's not coming back. Then the girl looks at me and her face breaks into a grin. "You are my new best friend," she jokes as she runs up to me. "I'm not sure if I was more worried she was going to fire me, or put a hit out on me. My name's Britney."

"Sam, and no problem," I say back. "I have to ask: what is color therapy, and what does it have to do with regularity?"

Britney deliberately closes one eye to signal the answer is so stupid, she won't bother to utter it aloud. "In all fairness, she's not normally this crazy. She got engaged on New Year's Eve, and she's suddenly planning this big wedding Valentine's Day weekend, so she's massively stressed out. Plus, she feels like she has to act like this perfectly calm, nice person when she's around her fiancé, so when he's not around, there are all these mini-explosions. I'm surprised her head hasn't exploded from the stress of that charade."

"She's planning a wedding in less than two months? Baby on the way?"

Britney shakes her head. "No, that's not it. Isabella's kind of famous, or notorious depending on who you ask, for both her fabulous weddings and her disastrous breakups. She's been engaged five times before this one. Each time, she spent months planning elaborate weddings, and each time the marriages didn't take. Four ex-husbands, married to most less than a year, and a broken engagement on the eve of the wedding. Now she's got it in her head that if everything is different from the other weddings, the marriage be different too. So she needs it to go perfectly."

I bug out my eyes a bit and blow out a sigh. "Man, a perfect wedding. Spotting a unicorn is more likely."

"She got one of those for wedding three. Wait, no. Two." Britney looks to her side for a second thinking. "Yeah, it was wedding two. I remember the Loch Ness monster kept trying to get out of the pool."

"Yikes! Well, good luck."

"Thanks. I'll need it."

We say goodbye, and I make my way back to Eric.

When I get to the dining room, I wave to the host and make a beeline for Eric, already seated at a table for four. He looks relaxed in one of the restaurant's signature green chairs as he speaks to a woman across the table from him, her back to me. I race up to him excitedly. "You wouldn't believe who I just saw in the ladies room acting like a raving b…"

I suddenly realize the woman sitting across from him is none other than Isabella.

"Beauty," I finish. Then I nod weakly. "Yup, a raving beauty."

A what? Worst save ever. That doesn't even make sense.

She doesn't seem to notice my ramblings. Instead, she smiles at me sweetly, as though she's never seen me before, and puts out her hand. "Hi. I'm Isabella De Leon."

"Samantha Evans," I say awkwardly, shaking her hand.

"Eric has told me so much about you," she says, smiling her perfectly capped smile.

I look at Eric in utter confusion. "I wish I could say the same," I say, slowly taking a seat.

"I told you she was a singer," Eric says with a slightly defensive tone.

"You told me her name was *Libby*," I answer, trying to keep my shit together.

"Oh, that's just my nickname," Isabella says cheerfully, completely unaware that her friend and I are now having our first fight. "First it was Isabella, then Belle, then Liberty Bell, then Libby."

"Huh," is all that comes out of my mouth. Because, wait a minute: my boyfriend's childhood friend is one of the most famous women in the world, and that has not come up in conversation? Even once? Will we be having dessert with George Clooney after this?

Steve, our waiter, walks up to us. "Hey, Sam," he says casually.

"Hey, Steve," I say distractedly, not taking my eyes off Eric.

"Can I get you guys started with some drinks?" Steve asks.

Before I can speak, Isabella orders. "A bottle of Clos du Mesnil for the table," she says, pronouncing it perfectly.

"Great choice," Steve says, writing it down. "Do you have a particular year in mind?"

Isabella gives him a sexy smile. "Surprise me."

He grins at her. "Perfect." Then he turns to me. "Shall we start you off with that Beluga caviar you like so much?"

Eric and Isabella both look at me in surprise. "It's not what you think," I tell them. "I'm writing a book for someone staying at the hotel and she orders a lot of caviar."

Isabella bristles, I'm not sure why. She turns to Steve. "Please bring us two orders of caviar then."

I try to stop her. "You really don't have to..."

"No, no," she interrupts. "I want you to have what makes you happy." She says that last word so sweetly I may get a toothache.

After Steve leaves, Isabella asks, once again in the sweetest tone, "Who exactly are you friends with at the hotel?"

"Actually," I begin awkwardly, "I'm a ghostwriter. And this person is a client I'm helping to write a book."

"What's her name?" Isabella asks.

"I'm afraid I'm not at liberty to say."

"Vanessa Waters," Eric tells her proudly. "Sam is the most amazing writer. You should read her, she can always capture exactly how you're feeling in just a few words. Reading her stuff is part of what made me fall in love with her."

"Really?" Isabella says, now appearing to be impressed. (Although with this lunatic, who can tell?) "Have you written anything I may have read?"

"No," I say at the same time Eric answers, "Absolutely."

I kick him under the table. Then I glare at him as I tell Isabella. "Again, I'm not at liberty to say who I write for."

"You know, I've always thought about writing a book. I'd like to write one about how to plan the perfect wedding."

"From what I understand, you've had some experience with that," I say.

Did I just say that out loud? Shit. "I mean, Eric tells me you're getting married in a few weeks."

Eric looks at me in confusion, what with him having not mentioned that and all. It seems to be one of a long list of things he forgot to mention to me about his childhood friend. Little things like her name, her marital history, the fact that she is one of the sexiest women alive…

"Oh, yes," Isabella beams. "This wedding is going to be the wedding to end all weddings. You see, I've planned five before, but they weren't quite what I wanted. So, you know what they say, sixth time's a charm."

As Isabella begins babbling about her fiancé, whom she's known for all of four months, "...which in Hollywood is more like twenty-eight months anywhere else..." I look up to see a man in the doorway looking around for his party. My God, in this light he looks almost exactly like...

"Shit!" I exclaim, standing up involuntarily, and hitting the table with my leg. "Ow," I yelp, grabbing my knee.

"Are you all right?" Eric asks, startled.

"I'm fine," I stammer as I rub my leg and sit back down. "I just thought I saw someone I knew..."

I try to regain my composure by asking Isabella, "You were saying something about how in Hollywood, dating a guy for four months is as good as dog years."

"Yes. Hollywood relationships aren't like normal relationships. So much happens, they need to be measured in dog years," Isabella surmises. "I mean, there's nothing to do in Iowa, so you might as well get to know your fiancé there. But in New York and L.A., there are so many distractions, if a man can hold your attention for four months, you might as well keep him."

"Sam?" I hear a familiar voice ask. I look up, and there he is. Dave. My ex-husband. Standing there in a blue Prada suit he wouldn't have been caught dead in six years ago. Dave smiles awkwardly. "Hey. How are you?"

You know, I'm not saying I *want* the Earth to swallow me whole, but...

Actually, yes. I am saying that. And now would be the perfect time.

Five

"I'm good," I say to Dave, my voice barely audible. "You?"

Dave slips his hands into his pockets, clearly ill at ease. "Good," he stumbles. "I see you've met my fiancée."

I look over to Isabella, who glows as she smiles up at him.

Isabella is engaged to Dave? This just gets better and better. You'd think God would just have a sense of humor about my hair. But no, now he's just fucking with me.

Isabella stands up, puts her arms around Dave's neck, then purrs, "Oh, baby, I missed you so much this week." sounding like she's going to have an orgasm just from giving him a hug. Then she French kisses my husband right in front of me.

Ex-husband, whatever.

When they finally break apart from each other, Dave puts out his hand to shake Eric's. "Hi, I'm Dave."

"Eric. And I guess you already know my girlfriend Sam."

Dave looks at me and smiles a noncommittal smile as he takes a seat. "Sam. Yes, we're old friends."

We're what????

"Oh. So where do you and Dave know each other?" Eric asks me, his tone pleasant and cheerful.

"Oh, we go way back," Dave answers for me. "I think college..."

While Isabella smiles and nods at his answer, my jaw drops slightly, and I glare at him. "Are ya kidding me?" I ask, putting out the palms of my hands to pantomime "*What the fuck?*"

Dave bugs his eyes out at me, trying to signal me to shut up. "We might have gone on a date or two," he concedes.

I roll my eyes. "Yeah, that's it. A date or two," I say, crossing my arms and pouting.

Isabella's face lights up. "Oh, then you simply must come to the wedding. I've already invited about six hundred people, but Dave has given me less than a hundred names so far. It'll be good to pad the groom's side a bit."

Rather than state the obvious, "No, I will not be attending my ex's wedding." I decided to roll with the blessing that this woman can't read a room to save her life, and lie, "That sounds like fun." Then I change the subject. "So, have you decided where you're getting married?"

"I have a home in Malibu I've never used for a wedding. We're going be married right on the beach. Dave's never been married at the beach before. Right, honey?"

Dave gives me a nervous look. "No, I haven't. My last wedding was in a church."

"I think I went to that," I say, snapping my fingers a few times, as though trying to jog my memory. "It was so long ago... Let me see. I think it was in Brentwood...or Westwood. And you got married to...your college sweetheart, wasn't it?"

Dave purses his lips and stares daggers at me. "You could call her that. It was a long time ago."

I tap my chin and look up at the ceiling, trying to recall. "Help me out here Dave. What was her name? Sadie? Sue? Siddhartha? Something with an S..."

Dave gives me his best Elvis Presley snarl. "All right. Forgive me for not wanting to make everyone uncomfortable." Then he turns to Isabella. "Sam is my ex-wife."

Isabella is visibly stunned. "Oh!" she says, turning to me, then back to Dave. "But you said she was beautiful."

Ouch. "No, no," Isabella says quickly to me. "I just meant that he said you were very *aristocratically* beautiful."

I squint my eyes, trying to figure out how that clarification makes her statement any less insulting.

Eric quickly takes my hand and smiles warmly. "I agree with you, Dave. Sam is absolutely, aristocratically beautiful. I've never thought to use that word before, but it describes her perfectly."

And now, since two men at the table have called *me* beautiful and not her, Isabella perseveres with her not so veiled insult. "I just meant that Dave always talks about how earthy I am. How my beauty is very approachable. Apparently, Sam was never very approachable."

I'd like to approach her with a...

"Champagne!" Steve announces cheerfully, appearing out of nowhere. He shows us the Clos du Mesnil label as another waiter places four champagne flutes on our table.

"Perfect," Isabella beams.

Steve opens the champagne with the requisite near silent pop of the cork, then pours a small bit for Isabella. As he hands it to her she waves him off. "My fiancé knows so much more about... well, everything. Honey, would you like to taste?"

"Huh? Oh. Sure." He does. "That's great. Load us up."

Steve pours us each a glass, then disappears again. Dave is about to take another sip when Isabella lightly touches his wrist. "Baby?"

"Right. Sorry," Dave says quickly. Then he raises his glass for a toast, looking right at me. "To old friends," he says, his tone of voice apologetic.

"Here, here," Eric says. And we all toast.

Isabella notices the fact that Dave is paying attention to anyone other than her, and quickly raises her glass for a second toast, "And to younger friends, too."

We all toast again, then three of us take another sip. Isabella demurs, instead asking me, "How old are you again?"

I choke on my champagne.

"Libby," Eric exclaims.

"What?" Isabella asks innocently. "Dave said his ex-wife was older than him. I just want to know by how much."

"You told her that?!" I half-ask, half-yell.

"Well, you are," Dave says, defensively.

"By six months," I counter. "Oh wait, I forgot. In Hollywood, that's forty two months, isn't it?"

Dave shakes his head. "What the hell are you talking about?"

"Are you ready to order?" Steve says, silently reappearing. Damn, I need to put a bell on that guy.

"I think we're going to need another minute," Dave says, quickly opening his dark green menu, and welcoming the much-needed break in conversation.

The three of us follow his lead, burying our heads in our menus.

I scan the offerings. Filet mignon, salmon, their famous steak tartare…yeah, whatever. Who the hell can concentrate?

"What do you mean I'm not approachable?" I say to Dave.

Dave looks up from his menu, confused. "What?"

"Isabella said you told her I was never very approachable."

Dave looks down at his menu, acting like I'm a crazy homeless person screaming epithets at him on the street, and he's going to pretend that I don't exist. "Don't cause a scene, Sam."

"Don't treat me like I'm gum on your shoe you can barely bring yourself to acknowledge. I hate it when you do that. Also, I approached *you* the first time we met."

Dave looks up from his menu again. Now he looks irritated. "You know, you have a really bad habit of remembering things whether they happened or not."

"I approached you at your fraternity party."

Dave throws down his menu, ready to prove a point. "You want to go there, fine. No, you didn't. You were at the party for at least an hour before *Joe* went up to talk to *Liz*, and you and I eventually wound up talking."

"We're doing everything in red this time," Isabella says happily, completely oblivious to our fight.

Huh?

She continues, "You see, I've been engaged five times, six including this one. Once the wedding didn't happen, and four times the groom and I didn't make it to our second anniversary. So I've decided this wedding needs to be different from all of the other weddings I've planned. I've never had red and white as my wedding colors."

I try to think of a clever response, but I got nothin'. Finally, I force a smile. "Well, it sounds like you've given this a lot of thought."

"Yes. First I had seashell pink, then dark purple, then neon pink with neon green, then powder blue, then this sort of medium pink, but I should have known it wasn't going to work out, because it just kept looking like Spam to me."

I have to hand it to her – she has rendered the table speechless.

I see Steve walking by and throw my arm out like a crossing guard to stop him. "Steve, can I get the chicken please?" I ask, handing Steve my menu.

"Good choice," he says, writing my order down on his pad. "And can I get you anything to drink with dinner?"

"A glass of Cabernet," I growl.

"Any particular label?" he asks.

"The house is fine," I say.

"House wine?!" Isabella nearly spits out. "Sweetie, it's on us tonight. Please let me get you something decent." I want to say the house wine is quite decent, but before I can, she turns to the waiter and demands, "Have the sommelier get us an Opus One. An older one."

"Perfect. Are we celebrating anything tonight?"

"I'm always celebrating," Isabella says, but in this weird submissive tone. She waves him off. "Eric order before me. I want to collect my thoughts."

Yeah, like she has thoughts...

"I'll have the New York steak. Medium rare," Eric says, flipping his menu shut and handing it to Steve. "And a glass of what the table is having."

"Very good. And for you sir?" Steve asks Dave.

"I'll have the filet mignon," Dave says. "Rare. And..." He looks at Isabella. "Why don't we get a different Cabernet? You don't need to waste five hundred dollars on a bottle..."

"Why don't we just have them get us a box of Inglenook, and we can put it on the table?" Isabella counters derisively. "Honey, please don't embarrass me by showing our guests your blue collar side."

Dave clearly doesn't know how to take that. He doesn't look embarrassed, which the old Dave would have been, or pissed, which I would have been. Instead he just kind of... shrugs it off.

Isabella reads from her menu. "I'll have the Pad Thai, with Green Mussels, and a nonfat vanilla milkshake."

"Very good," Steve says as he takes her menu.

I'm confused. As Steve leaves, I say to Isabella, "I didn't see that on the menu. Do they make Thai food here?"

"They make whatever I want," Isabella says, taking a sip of champagne. "So, how did you and Dave break up?"

She asks that question the way some people would ask how you met.

Dave opens his mouth to speak, but I beat him to it. "He lied to me, he cheated on me, he left me."

Dave makes a tsk sound. "You know, it's funny, but I distinctly remember your name on the divorce petition."

"Yeah. What a bitch I was, divorcing a man who was sleeping with another woman."

Dave leans into the table, angrily whispering, "I did not sleep with her, I had a crush on her…"

"Crush?" I say in a clear voice. "Hmm, is that the euphemism you musicians use nowadays? Crush? How many times did you crush her before you finally admitted…"

Dave raises his voice to interrupt me. "I told you the truth about that. I said I had a crush on Stephanie. I never said I was going to sleep with Stephanie, or that I was going to divorce you over her, I merely said…"

"That you loved talking to her…" I spit out, angrily.

"Oh, for God's sake!" Dave exclaims, turning away from me.

"Is Stephanie the one we hate?" Isabella asks Dave.

"Yes," Dave and I answer in unison.

I'm surprised by this. "Wait. Why do we hate her?" I ask Isabella.

She flashes Dave a brief look of disgust as she tells me, "Because he slept with her once to get over you, and she's been acting like his ex-girlfriend ever since." Isabella then notices a server wheeling a tray of caviar towards us, and immediately brightens. "Appetizers! Yay!"

You know how one new piece of information can suddenly change how you remember a story? Dave didn't sleep with her until after we divorced? Really? I was positive Stephanie and Dave had been at it for months before we split up. The only thing that gave me the courage to go to the courthouse and file the paperwork was the fact that I was sure they were sleeping together. The only thing that got me through the divorce was the rage I felt at being dismissed in that way.

Huh.

The server makes a big show of presenting the caviar with all the accoutrements, gives us each a small plate, then disappears.

"Isabella tells me you're a video director," Eric says to Dave, trying to lead the conversation back to something vaguely resembling civility.

"Yeah. I did the video for her song *Shopping Around*," Dave says.

Dave glances over at me, then does a double take. "What was *that* look?" he demands, looking like he's about to chew my head off.

I react, startled. "What look?"

"That rolling your eyes, *Oh, Dave is an idiot* look."

"I don't know what you're talking about," I say so innocently I could be batting my eyelashes.

Because, yeah, I totally rolled my eyes.

"Don't give me that tone," Dave demands.

"What tone? There's no tone," I insist (even though of course there's a tone. I practically invented the tone).

"I'm having my dress decorated in rubies," Isabella boasts, rubbing Dave's arm lovingly as she addresses me.

I furrow my brow at her. "What is it like to have the whole world revolve around you?" I ask her harshly.

She smiles, hugging Dave's arm. "It's wonderful," she says dreamily.

I'll bet it is. I decide to spend the rest of dinner in a state of sulky silence.

Six

After finishing our dinners in less than an hour, followed by a decisive pass on dessert, Dave and Isabella walks us out to the valet, and we say our goodbyes.

Anyone who's ever been part of a couple knows what happens next: the moment after the valet shut both car doors, the gloves come off.

"What the fuck was that about?" Eric asks me angrily as he drives away from the hotel.

I cross my arms and stare out my window. "I *really* wouldn't talk to me right now."

Eric asks dryly, "Okay, so you can embarrass me by causing a scene, but I'm not allowed to talk?"

I refuse to answer him, and the two of us spend the next few minutes listening to traffic as we head up Coldwater Canyon.

I break first. "You had your chance to talk. For months. Maybe I wouldn't have caused a scene if you hadn't lied to me about who your friend was, or who she was marrying. You made me look ridiculous."

"I made you..." Eric begins. He clutches the steering wheel tightly, then takes a deep breath. "They are getting married in a little over two weeks, and I'm in the wedding, which means we'll be seeing a lot of them. So please get your shit together and start acting like a grownup."

"So how many times have you fucked her?" I ask/accuse him.

Eric looks over at me warningly, then shakes his head "no" refusing to take the bait. We both spend the rest of trip to my house stewing in silence.

When Eric pulls into my driveway, he stops the car, but keeps the motor running.

I'm furious. Yet I don't want him to leave. My mind races ahead to our inevitable breakup caused by my insecurity this evening. I turn to Eric. "Do you want to stay over?"

Eric stares straight ahead. "I need to be at work early."

I nod silently.

But I don't get out of the car. "I'm sorry I caused a scene tonight," I force myself to say. "I haven't seen Dave since the divorce...and coupled with you springing Isabella on me..."

"Okay, I was wrong to do that," Eric concedes, although I can tell his apology is also forced. "It's just...she has such a bad reputation in the press and I didn't want you judging her before you actually met her. And I had no way of knowing your Dave was her Dave. I mean, you've never even showed me a picture of him."

"Because I cut him out of my life completely," I say angrily. Then I calm myself down, and shrug. "Anyway, I'm sorry."

We're both silent again. Eric hasn't turned off his car, so I guess he's still going home.

Which makes me want to cry. "You sure you don't want to stay tonight?" I ask him again.

"I'm sure," Eric says, although his voice softens.

"Okay," I say weakly, opening my door to get out.

Even though I know he's still mad at me he asks, "Do you still want to drive me to the airport tomorrow night?"

I nod. At least some form of truce has been forged.

"Okay," Eric says with a little more love in his voice. "I'll be off work tomorrow at six. My flight's not until eleven. Maybe we can grab dinner before I leave."

I nod my head again. Eric will be in New York for all of next week. Yet another reason to burst into tears. "I love you, you know," I say in a tone that's less of a statement, more of a *Do you love me too?* question.

"I love you too," he answers stiffly. Then he leans over to give me a quick kiss goodnight. A decidedly unromantic kiss.

As I get out of the car, I give him one last "I love you" and get the compulsory "I love you too" back. Eric watches me make my way up the walkway, get my keys out and unlock my door. He doesn't drive away until he knows I'm safely inside.

I wave goodbye, watch him drive off, then shut the door.

"Anyone home?!" I yell out.

Silence.

Damn. Well, I suppose it's only ten o'clock. You don't come home from a date at ten o'clock unless it's going really badly.

I stand in the entryway, thinking.

And feeling swirls of anger, sadness and embarrassment pump through my body.

I'm embarrassed for several reasons. One, all through dinner I was mentally comparing my life to Dave's, and he was way ahead of me: great career, great apartment in New York, getting married before me. Two, despite my bravado, I'm also embarrassed about my behavior in front of Eric. I'm supposed to not care what Dave thinks anymore: why did I spend the whole evening feeling weird around him and starting a fight?

I'm also a little sad. Sad because this isn't how I pictured my life at thirty. Sad that Dave's not around anymore. Sad that I was ever stupid enough to get married and want him in my life in the first place.

And, finally, I'm angry. At Dave. I can't quite explain it - it's irrational. I shouldn't care who my ex-husband dates. But *this* is the girl Dave chose to replace me with? This is the type of woman he chooses to marry? Am I in that category? Self-involved, stupid, and nasty? And he's known her for all of four months. What the hell is he thinking?

I walk into my room, turn on the light, and look over at my closet.

Dave is wrong. I think to myself. *I approached him. I'm sure of it.*

I walk to my closet, climb behind my hanging clothes, and open up a small cardboard box. In it are my old diaries.

There aren't very many of them. I'm not organized enough to write in a journal every night. As a matter of fact, I haven't written in one in years.

There are four of them in the box, assorted colors. The blue one was from high school. I started the journal for an English class. Wrote for a few months, then got bogged down studying for AP tests one May, and didn't get back to it for a few years. The red one was from my sophomore year and junior year of college, the year I met Dave. I didn't write every day – only wrote when I had news, or needed to write about a problem I was sick of talking to my friends about.

The brown leather one was from my senior year of college, when I got into Harvard law, and Dave got his record deal. And I wrote for an hour the night Dave proposed.

I hadn't looked at the brown one in a long time. I never wanted to remember how happy we were back then, because then it would make me sad, mourning the life I thought I would have.

The black one ended up being apropos for our divorce. I started writing it towards the end of my first year of law school. I hated school so much, and because Dave's band was touring the country, he was never around to talk to, so I wrote and wrote and wrote.

I wrote about our fight when I told him at the end of my first year that I was quitting, that I didn't want to be a lawyer after all. I wrote about our fight when he guilt tripped me into going back for my second year. I wrote about the night I thought I was pregnant, then the night I was heartbroken to realize that I wasn't. I wrote about the night I told him I had quit law school, this time for good, and that I wanted us to move back to L.A. The same night he told me he had a crush on Stephanie.

During my divorce, I would read a few passages from that black book over and over again to remind myself of why I left him.

But right now, for the first time in years, I pull out the red one.

I take it to the kitchen, grab a bottle of Pinot Noir from the wine rack, pour myself a glass, then go back to my room, where I flop on my bed, open my red journal, and start reading.

September 24th
Dear Diary,

Today I met the man I'm going to spend the rest of my life with. I know that sounds weird at 20, but this is the one, I've never felt this way before. Liz dragged me to fraternity rush tonight...

"Just go over there and talk to him," Liz says, taking a sip of beer from a large red Solo cup.

"What on Earth would I say?" I ask nervously, eyeing the gorgeous guy on the green couch.

"Hi, I'm Sam, and I'm the mother of your future children," Liz jokes.

"Yeah. That always works at a fraternity party. Talk about future. Guys love that," I respond sarcastically.

"How about just 'Hi'?" Liz suggests.

I look at her and nod. We've been at Delta Sigma Phi, one of the fraternities on campus, for the past hour. The past fifty-eight minutes of which I have spent trying to figure out how to talk to the extremely hot guy sitting on the green couch.

So far I have failed.

"You're right. I should just walk up to him, and say hello," I say, determined to take destiny into my own hands. I pull down the bottom of my miniskirt, which has been creeping up my thighs for the last fifteen minutes, square back my shoulders, and prepare for the ten-foot walk across the room.

"What are you?" Liz asks (only mocking me the tiniest bit).

"I am a woman of action," I say firmly. Then I march five feet over, realize I'm about to make a fool of myself, and turn around and race back to Liz, teetering on my four-inch pumps as I go.

"Liquid courage, liquid courage," I say, downing the rest of my beer.

I regroup for a minute. "Okay, I have a better plan," I say, pointing to Liz. "You go up to one of his friends, chat him up for awhile, then introduce me to him."

"What makes you think I have a better shot at talking to a guy than you do?" Liz asks.

"Because you're gorgeous?" I upspeak.

"Shut up. That's not true. Quit saying that," Liz says, scrunching up her shoulders and crossing her arms. She does that anytime someone compliments her on her looks. I don't get it. If I looked like Liz, I'd be at a party every night, just perusing the guys: "No... No... Maybe if he got a haircut... No..."

"Hello, ladies," I hear from behind me.

I turn around to see what would be the best looking man I've ever seen in my life – if it weren't for all the tattoos, and his dyed jet black hair. He is holding a tray of little paper mouthwash cups filled with multi-colored Jell-O shots. "Can I interest you in a beverage?"

"I'm not..." I begin.

"Oh, I don't know if I should," Liz says, giving him her best doe eyed look. "I get so drunk from those, and my friend wants to go soon."

"The two most beautiful women in the room leaving? Why, I won't hear of it," Tattoo Guy says to us, smarmy to the nth degree. He puts his tray of shots down on a side table. "I'm Joe," he says, putting out his hand for me to shake.

"Sam," I say, putting out my hand to shake. Joe surprises me by raising my hand to his lips, and kissing it. "Charmed."

All right, I don't know how he did it, but he effortlessly moved from smarmy to charming.

Liz delicately puts out her hand to be kissed. "Elizabeth."

"Enchanted," Joe says, then plants a kiss on her hand. "So, Elizabeth, how do you feel about a house, two kids, and a new car every other year?"

Liz shuts him down. "Gonna need a lot of Jell-O shots to be talked into that. Seriously dude, has that line *ever* worked?"

Joe doesn't miss a beat. "Not in the slightest. But it usually gets a laugh." He takes two red shots from the tray, then hands one to Liz, and one to me. "A toast," he says, taking a red shot for himself, and raising it high in the air. "To new friends!"

We raise our paper cups and toast. Normally, I don't do shots, but I notice hot guy on the couch watching me, and I don't want to look anti-social.

Liz crumples the paper to get every last bit of Jell-O into her mouth, tosses it in a trashcan, then says, "It was nice meeting you, Joe. But we have to go."

"Boyfriend to get to?" Joe asks.

"Best friend," Liz answers, gesturing to me. "Poor Sam is so shy. And she doesn't know any guys here, so we're going to head over to the Lambda house."

"Lambdas? Give me one minute to change your mind," Joe says, turning to me. "Samolina, what's your type?"

I ping pong my eyes from Liz to Joe. "What? Me? I don't really have…"

"She likes the Tom Cruise type," Liz says. Then she pretends to look around the room. "Kind of like…him," she says, pointing to the guy on the couch.

"Dave?" Joe says. "Dude, Dave's my best friend. Let me introduce you."

And like the dog that I'm sure he is, Joe heads over to the couch to fetch me the man of my dreams.

I glare at Liz. "You know that guy Joe is going to want to sleep with you."

"Well, of course he wants to sleep with me. I'd be offended if he didn't."

Joe walks back, dragging his friend with him. "Ladies, this is Dave. Dave, the beautiful and talented Elizabeth, and her delicious friend Sam."

"Hi," Dave says, smiling shyly. He looks ill at ease, and I could kill Liz for having him dragged over to me.

"Hi," I stammer back, my heart leaping into my throat. I'm so nervous, I can barely breathe.

Joe takes Liz's hand. "Dave, can you take care of Sam for a few minutes? I want to show Liz around the house."

"Oh, I can go too," I say, a bit worried Liz is going to get in over her head.

"You can. But you may not," Liz says, smiling at me and winking as she walks off with Joe.

Dave and I exchange nervous glances and several awkward moments. "Can I get you a beer?" he asks.

I notice the redhead he was with is now talking to someone else on the couch.

"I should probably let you get back to your girlfriend," I say, fishing.

"Huh?" Dave asks, confused. Then he turns to follow my line of vision. "Oh, no, she's not my girlfriend. I don't have a girlfriend. She's the backup singer in our band."

Mental note: no girlfriend.

"You have a band?" I ask, grateful to have a topic to ask him about.

"Yeah. Well, it's Joe's band actually. He's the lead singer and bass player. I play guitar."

"Wow. Cool," I say, nodding. "What's your band's name?"

"Almost 70. We're playing at Red Herring tomorrow night if you want to come by."

I smile. I like him. I really like him. "I'd like that."

He walked me home, and we talked until sunrise, and he's perfect.

And, all right, so no, he didn't kiss me or anything. But I'm seeing him tomorrow night. And I figure, if I play my cards right, he will.

I stare at my diary. My God, was I ever capable of being that stupidly head over heels infatuated? After one night?

I walk back to the kitchen to pour myself another glass of wine.

As I pour, our home phone rings. I read the caller I.D.: Private Caller. This time of night, that means Vanessa calling me with some new hare brained scheme.

I pick up the phone and emphatically state, "I'm not going to London with you at the end of January. It will be fucking freezing."

There's silence on the other end of the phone. Finally, I hear Dave joke, "What about Sheboygan? I hear it's positively balmy there this time of year."

I laugh quietly. "Wisconsin in winter. Hard pass," I take a sip of wine. "How'd you get my number?"

"Called 411," Dave answers casually. "Now, I know I shouldn't care. It doesn't really matter what you think of my artistic endeavors... But...why did you roll your eyes at dinner? Did you even watch Belle's video?"

I look out my window and debate whether or not to tell my ex-husband the truth. Yeah, right. Just admit that I rolled my eyes because on top of being engaged to one of the most beautiful women in the world, he also has an amazing career and an amazing life, and I'm jealous as hell? Admit that he's so far ahead of me in every area of life that I can't stand it?

Not so much.

"It was uneven," I finally say.

"Uneven?" Dave repeats defensively.

"You had a story line that was very strong, mixed with some weak dance scenes that detract from your overall theme."

Silence on the other end of the line. "You're absolutely right," Dave finally admits, a smile in his voice. "The label insisted we put in some dance numbers. Belle can dance, and I edited them in as best I could, but... yeah, it sucked."

I laugh. "I miss you," I blurt out, surprising myself.

"I miss you, too," Dave says quietly, a little nostalgically. Then, "It was good to see you."

We're both silent for a bit. "I should probably let you get back to your fiancée," I say.

"Oh, she's at her new club, Cirque, making an appearance," Dave tells me. "But I'm sure Eric wouldn't want me taking up any more of your evening."

I scratch my neck self-consciously. "Actually, Eric went home."

"Oh?" Dave asks, surprised. "It wasn't because of anything Isabella or I did, was it?"

"Of course not. He just had to be at work early tomorrow, and he didn't have the right clothes here."

More silence. "I called Joe," Dave says, changing the subject. "He says we're both full of shit, that he introduced us, and that neither of us were particularly approachable."

I smile. "You called Joe? What else did he say?"

"He wanted to know if you've seen him on TV since he went solo, or bought either of his solo albums."

I laugh. Figures. Joe was the lead singer of Almost 70 until four years ago, when the band broke up and he went solo. "Typical," I say. "Well, he's right. I just read my old diary. Joe did indeed introduce us."

"Oooo, the diaries," Dave teases knowingly. "Did you just read the red one? Or did you read the black one too so you can remember how much you hate me?"

"I don't hate you," I say, taking a sip of wine. "Truth be told, I kind of miss you. It'd be nice to have you back in my life."

I'm almost sure I can hear him smiling over the phone. "I'd like that too. What's your day looking like tomorrow?"

I'm a little surprised by the invitation. Then I surprise myself even more by answering, "I'm open."

"You want to meet at Red Herring for lunch?" he asks.

He did not just ask me to the place where we had our first kiss.

"How about Gladstones?" I ask him. "Great views. Good food."

"How about Red Herring? No view, terrible food, and there's usually a really loud band drowning out any chance of conversation."

"I'm not sure how comfortable I'd be…"

"Oh shit! That's not what I meant," Dave interrupts. "No, I'm scouting it as a location for my next video, and I'm going tomorrow. I thought you'd get a kick out of it."

"Um… I mean… maybe?"

I hear my front door unlock, then Eric's voice. "Sam?!"

"Oh shoot. Eric's here. I gotta go."

I can hear Eric walking towards my bedroom. "Sam?"

"I'm in here!" I yell from the kitchen.

"What about Red Herring tomorrow?" Dave asks.

The last thing I want Eric to hear is me on the phone with my ex. "Fine," I say to Dave, lowering my voice. "What time?"

"Noon?"

"I'll be there. Gotta go."

And I click off the phone, putting it back onto its base about five seconds before Eric appears in the doorway. "What are you doing here?" I ask him, still nervous that he heard me on the phone.

Eric shrugs. "I'm gonna be gone for a week. I don't want to fight. Can we just go to bed, and forget this night ever happened?"

And we're back. "I'd like that." I say, smiling. Then I walk over to him, throw my arms around his neck and give him a kiss. Followed by a longer, deeper kiss.

Later that night, Eric fell asleep before me, and I lied in the crook of his arm feeling so lucky. Because when you crawl into bed with the man you love and cuddle in silence, divas and ex-husbands and insecurities seem to magically dissolve away.

Even if that might be a red herring.

Seven

Around six in the morning, after a blissful session of makeup sex, Eric left to go to work. I promptly fell back asleep. The last thing I remember was a lovely dream featuring me, Johnny Depp, and a room full of chocolate: when I am rudely awakened by Liz screaming, "A dog needs a hat as much as Mariah Carey needs a library card!"

Must be Saturday morning. I drag my ass out of bed and open my bedroom door to see Liz at the front door, arguing with her ex-fiancé Fred over their dog.

They have joint custody of a beagle. Don't get me started...

"And what the hell possessed Jill to put him in a sweater," Liz yells, still wearing her pajamas and madly trying to wrangle a pink sweater off of her dog Zac.

"Jill knew you'd have a problem with it," Fred says with the same superior tone he's used ever since she caught him in bed with her bridesmaid. "Let's face it, you don't have a problem with the sweater. You have a problem with the fact that I've moved on and you haven't."

"I have a problem with the fact that no matter how many bad thoughts I put out into the universe, your brakes still work," Liz mutters. "Raise your paws," she says to Zac the beagle.

Zac raises his front paws, much like a three-year-old raises his arms to let his Mom take off his shirt.

"What would you prefer Jill and I do?" Fred asks smugly. "We go on hikes every morning. He'll catch his death of cold out there."

"He's a dog. He has a fur coat. That's how they're made. And what the f..." Liz grabs Zac's collar and reads his shiny new tag. "Fluffy?" she reads in horror. "You renamed the dog Fluffy?!"

"Jill didn't like the name Prozac," Fred explains. "She thought it was negative and humiliating."

"But a pink sweater and a hat, that's positive and life affirming."

Fred makes a "tsk" sound. He furrows his brow, and pretends to sound like he's actually concerned about Liz's well being. "You know, I worry about you, staying home all day, writing all those man hating cards, no one around to love you. You don't want to go into your old age bitter just because you weren't good enough for me."

"Fuck you, Fred."

Fred puts his arm around her shoulder, and softens his voice. "Look, baby, we had some good times. If you still miss me, maybe I could help you get over the breakup."

Liz starts to shake, she's so angry. "What?"

Fred leans in, trying to sound sexy. "Baby, you know you could call me anytime if you want to rekindle things."

Liz squints her eyes at him. "What?" she asks again in disbelief.

"Look, Jill and I are engaged now. You could me my mistress. The sex would be way hot." Fred notices me, now glaring at him in disgust. He gives me a shrug, then turns back to Liz. "I know you're not going to admit you want me in front of your roommate. But come on, we both know the real reason you're not dating yet is because you can't get over me. I'm just trying to help out. A little hair of the dog…"

Liz stares at him in stunned silence. Finally, she grabs the newspaper from our front table, rolls it up and smacks Fred on the nose.

Fred shakes his head. "Whatev. I'll see you Monday." And he's out the door.

Liz is now shaking. I walk over and give her a hug. Her eyes start watering up, like they do every time Fred shows up. But no actual tears fall down her cheeks. And in the world of breakups, this is progress. Up until a few months ago, every dog drop off was accompanied by hours of hysterical crying. Then an hour of quieter crying. Then twenty minutes. And now her eyes only well up.

Eventually, Liz and I walk to the breakfast table, Zac tagging along behind us.

Liz grabs a pad of paper as she takes her seat. "What's another word for moron?"

"Idiot," I suggest as I putter over to the coffee maker.

"I already used that."

"Halfwit?"

Liz debates. "Mmmm…"

As I pull out the old coffee filter and replace it with a fresh one, I begin ticking more off. "Imbecile, numskull, male member of the species…"

"That's it!" Liz exclaims, raising her pen in the air, then quickly writing.

"Onto a more positive subject: How did your date go?" I ask while I make coffee.

"He's still attached to his ex-girlfriend," Liz tells me distractedly, still writing.

"That's kind of normal at our age," I point out. "Pretty much anyone could be in the final stages of a breakup. That's not to say…"

"He brought her on our date."

I give her a "Yikes" look.

She shrugs. "Part of the pursuit of happiness is learning what you don't want. How'd your big 'meeting the almost family' thing with Eric go? Did Libby like your dress?"

"You mean Isabella?"

Liz looks confused. I point to her. "Yeah, that was pretty much my reaction. Turns out Libby is just a nickname. Her real name is Isabella. As in Isabella De Leon."

Liz's eyes bug out. "Isabella De Leon like… the diva?" she asks, throwing down her notepad to give me her full attention.

"The one and the same."

"Is she the complete bitch everyone says she is?"

"Oh, she's worse. But that's not the worst part…"

"Oh my God. I heard she's getting married again for, like, the seventh time," Liz interrupts. "To some nobody, just like she did that third time."

Liz had read about the engagement. That sort of sparks my interest. "This will actually only be her sixth wedding and her fifth husband, but who's counting? So what do you know about the fiancé?"

Liz looks up at the ceiling, trying to remember. "Um, I think I read he's a photographer. Wait, no, Maybe a director?"

"Catch his name?" I ask, leading the witness.

"Dan, I think?" Liz guesses. "Maybe David? No one we've ever heard of."

Boy, are you way off. "David Stevens?" I ask.

Liz's face lights up. "Yeah, that's it!" She says, pointing to me. "Yeah, he's…" Then her face drops. "Nooooooo…"

I force a tight smirk and throw up my hands.

"Your David Stevens?"

"Not mine anymore. *Very clearly* not mine anymore," I say, clenching my teeth together as I fake a smile. "I got to have dinner with the happy couple last night."

"How'd he look?" Liz asks. "No, wait. How'd she look?"

"Why do you care how *she* looked?"

"Because if you're going to steal Dave away from her, the first thing we need to do is size up the competition. So what do you know about her? Does she have a drinking problem? Maybe a drug problem?"

"Are you out of your fucking mind? I'm not stupid enough to fall for that jerk again. He's a cheater."

Liz crosses her arms, and eyes me suspiciously. I meet her gaze. "What?"

Liz waits for more. I give her nothing. She shakes head. "At the risk of sounding like a character in a bad action movie, this is me you're talking to."

"Trust me – there's nothing there anymore. Dinner was a complete disaster."

She narrows his eyes at me. "So he didn't ask for your number at the end of the night or anything?"

"Of course not," I answer defensively. Then I reconsider. "He didn't need to. I'm listed in the phone book. He may have called me last night after dinner. But that was just to call a truce, which is great. I have Eric, he has Isabella. We're both in a good place, and I'm ready to be friends with him again. But just friends."

Liz continues to give me *the look*. "Seriously," I insist. "We're meeting for lunch today and everything's fine. I feel no more romantically about him than I would any other old friend."

Liz watches me in silent disbelief. I stare back defiantly.

"Okay," Liz concedes.

"Okay," I repeat resolutely, "I have been down that road before, and it's a giant dead end. I'm not twenty anymore. Thank God."

A thought pops into Liz's head. "When's your lunch?"

"Noon. Why?"

Liz smirks. "Fred was late this morning. It's 11:25."

"Crap!" I mutter, bolting out of the kitchen. "I've got ten minutes to lose eight pounds!"

I race into my bedroom, Liz tailing me.

"Oh, no. You don't still like this guy," Liz says sarcastically, lying down on my bed.

"I don't!" I yell from my closet. "But I need to look better than him. Otherwise, he wins!" I emerge from the closet, carrying two miniskirts. "Red or black?"

"Neither," Liz says. "Both look like you're trying too hard."

I toss them on the bed, then run back into my closet.

"Ann Taylor, Abercrombie…" I say, quickly pushing each hanger to the left. "What about a long flowy skirt?" I ask loudly from my closet.

"If it's Ann Taylor, it's going to look too officey."

I emerge from my closet with a long skirt I like. "How about Banana Republic?"

"Meh. Where are you meeting?"

"Red Herring," I answer as I throw off my pajama bottoms.

Liz's eyes widen as though she's seen a ghost.

"It's not like that," I say defensively. "He's on a location scout and wanted to meet up for lunch."

"At the place where you first kissed."

"At the place his band played throughout college." I counter. "Anyway, stop psychoanalyzing me for a minute and help me pick an outfit. Baby doll dress and boots?"

"Jeans. Tight ones that make your butt look good."

"Thank you," I say, pulling a pair of Diesel jeans from of my dresser drawer. "Strappy sandals?"

"With jeans?" Liz states dismissively in the form of a question. Then she abruptly walks out of the room. "Are you gonna wear a Wonderbra?!" she yells.

"Not for my ex-husband, no!" I yell back.

"Probably a good call. He's already seen you naked, and when you end up in bed together it'll be embarrassing when you have to take off your bra!"

"We're not going to end up in bed together because it's…"

"Not a date!" Liz finishes with me from the other room.

"It's not!" I yell back. "I just need to look smoking hot so that he knows that I am doing way better than him since the divorce!"

"Because people always try to look 'Smoking hot' when they're not on a date," Liz says sarcastically as she walks back in, carrying a bottle of Coco perfume. "Let me know if he doesn't kiss you while you're not out on a date."

She hands me the bottle of perfume, but I don't take it. I can feel my shoulders tense up as I remind her. "I don't wear that anymore."

What I really mean is not just *I don't wear that perfume anymore.* It's also *I'm not in college anymore. I'm not in love with him anymore.*

Liz keeps her arm outstretched.

"All right. Fine," I say, grabbing the bottle, and spraying a bit on my wrists.

The scent immediately takes me back to college, and being wildly in love and wildly happy.

I walk to the bathroom and wash it off.

Eight

After my scrub down, I change into the Diesel jeans and an old T with the band's *Almost 70* logo on it, slip on some sparkly flip flops, then grab my car keys and head over to Red Herring.

I haven't been in my car two minutes when my cell phone rings. I check the caller ID. It's Amy, my boss at Sideways Publishing, and also the owner of the company. I put on my headset, and pick up the phone. "Hey, Amy."

"Great news!" Amy says, her voice exploding over the phone. "Guess who we just got to commit to an autobiography for next Christmas? Isabella De Leon."

I already don't like where this is going.

"And guess who she *specifically* asked to be her ghostwriter?" Amy continues.

Dead silence on my end. If I hang up right now...

"I can barely hear you," Amy says. "Are you in a canyon?"

"Huh," I say, almost to myself. "How do you think it feels to have a blood vessel burst in your brain? Do you think it's like a dull headache, or a blinding shot behind the eye?"

Amy ignores me. "I need you to go meet her right now at her Malibu home. The address is..." she gives me the address from the 22000 block of the Pacific Coast Highway. Then, "I'll need the final draft turned in by June 15th in time for the Christmas season, so you'll really have to..."

"I can't." I interrupt.

"What you mean you can't?" Amy asks. "I'm afraid I don't hear that word very often in my position."

"Neither does Isabella. Which is one of a plethora of reasons for why I can't work with her. I'm sorry, but we wouldn't be a good fit."

My boss does not sound pleased. "Why do you think that?"

"Well, I'm a magna cum laude graduate with some significant post graduate study. And she's an idiot."

Amy takes a second to absorb my argument. Then, "Maybe so. But she's an idiot who's going to write a book."

"Great. She'll be one of the few authors in history who's written more books than she's read."

"You're being awfully snarky this morning."

"I'm sorry. It's just that that woman rubs me the wrong way. Anyway, I'm not available. I'm already working on Vanessa's book."

"Don't be silly. Lots of ghosts have two clients at once. Besides, it's not a problem. I talked to Vanessa and asked her if you could take on a second client while you were finishing her book, and she couldn't have been more hospitable."

"You talked to Vanessa?" I ask, unable to conceal my shock. "This morning?"

"You sound surprised."

"Well, it's just that the last time she was up in the morning was in 1984. How did you manage that?"

"I sent her a magnum of Cristal at eleven, then called her at eleven-oh-five."

Brilliant.

Back to the matter at hand. "I'm sorry," I repeat. "But I still have a lot of work to do for Vanessa. I can't stretch myself too thin. Vanessa's book would suffer."

Amy sighs loudly. "I understand what you're saying, and I totally respect you and your artistic integrity."

"Thank you," I begin.

"Now let me explain to you my problem. Isabella will only write the book if you're her ghostwriter. She's having it put in her contract. So I kind of need you on this."

Crap.

"I'll throw in some royalties," Amy adds.

I'm still silent. Not enough money in the…

"And we'll buy your novel," she continues. "What's it called? *Edict of Edith?*"

My novel. My dream. The book that took me three years to write, a year to rewrite, and another three years trying to find a publisher for. A publisher I still haven't found.

My life's work. Bought and paid for. If I sell my soul.

My phone beeps. I look at the Caller ID to see it's Dave.

"Can I call you back?" I ask Amy.

"Of course," Amy says cheerfully, then adds. "But you're doing the book or you're fired. Love ya, hon!"

Only Amy Sideways could threaten to fire someone in the same sentence she says she loves them.

I click over. "I'm on my way…"

"No, you're not. Wanna shoot for dinner?"

I let out a heavy sigh. "You heard."

"Isabella just called me. Apparently she read some articles you wrote for *Cosmopolitan* magazine and loved them. Plus she really wants to write a book. Has for a long time."

Once again, I sigh. "I freelanced for *Cosmo* years ago. How did she even figure out…"

"I may have mentioned that you used to write for them."

"Fantastic."

"She keeps a copy of everything she has ever been on the cover of, so she had their October 1995 issue. She read the article where you wrote about Sex with…"

"I remember what I wrote, thank you very much," I quickly interrupt.

"Sorry," Dave says. Then he adds brightly, "But she loved it and you're a great writer. Or she wouldn't have offered you the job."

"I'm not writing my ex-husband's future wife's book."

"I'll admit, your relationship is a bit tense…"

"No. Celebrating Christmas with my Dad, his ex-wives, his current wife and his current mistress is tense. This is just weird." My phone beeps again. I see it's UCLA Med Center. "That's Eric. I gotta go."

"Okay, but take the job," Dave insists. "Let me take you dinner tonight and we'll talk more."

"I can't tonight. I'm taking Eric to the airport. How about lunch tomorrow?"

"Perfect. Still want to go to Red Herring?"

"Sure. One o'clock?"

"Great," he says, and I can his voice relax a bit. "Good luck."

"Thanks. I'll need it." I click over. "Hello?"

"You were so sexy this morning," Eric growls sexily to me.

I smile. "So were you," I say, my voice softening immediately. I really do love him. "I'm going to need your help with something to do with Isabella. I'm completely freaking out."

"I get it," Eric says sympathetically. "I know you don't want to go to the wedding, but it won't be that bad. So your ex is getting married first. Big deal. It's not like everyone's going to be looking at you and thinking *She still isn't married? Why isn't she married?*"

"Oh! My! God!" I yell as three different sentences into the phone.

"What's wrong? Wasn't that why you were freaking out?" Eric asks.

"It wasn't before. Now it is! Oh! My! God!" I yell again, pulling over to the curb. "I think I'm hyperventilating."

"Sorry. I didn't mean to make things worse. What's wrong?"

"What's wrong is that your friend Isabella just signed on with my publisher to write her memoirs, and she specifically asked for me to be her ghostwriter."

Eric is silent a moment. "Sam, I really don't think that's a good idea."

"No Shit, Sherlock!" I exclaim, dropping my head between my knees. "Unfortunately my boss made a deal with Isabella's people this morning. She's insisted on me, and if I don't do it, I'm fired. You put your head between your legs to keep from blacking out, right?"

"You're not going to black out. You're overexaggerating."

"Wrong. I'm exaggerating exactly enough for my current situation."

"Let me call Libby and get you out of this."

"What are you going to say?" I ask, bringing my head back up, and accidentally slamming it against the steering wheel. I rub my head. "If she thinks I don't want to do it, I could lose my job, and I can't afford to lose my job."

"Just leave it up to me. I love you. Bye."

I start to say, "I love you too," but he's already gone.

I rub my head again, then stare out the windshield. Watching the wind slowly blow around the trees, I try to think of something to bring me solace in this situation.

A hike to clear my head? Yoga? Meditation?

I pull my car back on the road, and head to the store for a Sara Lee cheesecake.

Nine

"Hemppllo," I say into my cell phone, my mouth full.

"Is that the cheesecake talking?" Liz asks. "Or have you hit the chocolate fudge pop tarts?"

I look over at my passenger's seat, where an open box of chocolate fudge pop tarts keeps an open bag of potato chips company. "Actually, they were out of cheesecake. I'm eating a tube of cookie dough."

"Chocolate chip?"

"Peanut butter wouldn't have the same effect," I say, swallowing. "Do you know they actually tell you on the package not to eat them until they're baked. Yeah, like I have that kind of time."

"I blame the lawyers."

"Wait," I realize. "How come you know I'm pigging out?"

"Oh, we've had a variety of interesting phone calls in the past twenty minutes on our answering machine. Amy called to say congratulations, you got a new job – working for Isabella De Leon. Dave called to warn you of the same thing and try to reschedule you for dinner. And Isabella's assistant Britney called to ask if you could come meet Isabella at her compound in Malibu. Naturally, I was concerned. So what the Hell is going on?"

I read the plastic cookie dough tube. "Did you know there are only six grams of fat in a slice of cookie dough?"

"Did you know there are twelve slices per package?"

I read the label further. "Crap. How did you know that?"

"Wild guess. So, are you all right?"

"I hope so. Eric is talking to Isabella now. Hopefully, he'll be able to get me out of this."

My phone beeps. "That's him. Hold on a sec." I click over to Eric. "How'd it go?"

"I'm not sure," Eric says, sounding torn. "You didn't tell me you're not the ghost writer, you're the co-writer with your name on the cover, and that she got you a hundred thousand dollar advance."

I am stunned. I sit in the convenience store parking lot and stare through the window at the turbaned cashier reading a paperback of *Men are from Mars, Women are from Venus.*

A hundred thousand dollars. A co-writing credit. (Isabella and my book would easily hit the Top 10 of every publishing list in the country that first week. Hello, *New York Times* bestselling author!) And Amy will buy my first novel.

"It turns out," I say to Eric. "I am a poor man's Demi Moore."

"What does that mean?"

"It means that unlike her character in *Indecent Proposal*, my price is a tenth of that. I have to go to Malibu to meet with my new co-writer."

Ten

I call Amy to officially accept my new job, then Liz to scream, "One hundred thousand dollars!" in my most girlish squeal. Then I throw a sweater over my Almost 70 T-shirt, and head out to Malibu.

Forty-five minutes later, I pull off of the PCH, drive up to the gate of Isabella's compound, and press the intercom. A small TV screen flickers on to show me a burly uniformed guard, looking angry. "Can I help you?"

"I'm Sam Evans to see Isabella De Leon."

I watch him read from a clipboard. "You're not on the list."

I really can't stand it when high school dropouts act like this. But I will probably have to pass this guy's checkpoint several more times in the next few months, so I try to be polite. "Well, I'm sure that's an oversight," I say cheerfully. "Could you check with Britney, please?"

The guard crosses his arms. "You're not on the list."

Looking at the camera above the TV screen, I know he can see me as well or better than I can see him. I pull out my tape recorder, turn it on, and put the microphone towards the camera. "I'm sorry. And what is your name again?"

His face registers a flicker of either anger or fear. "That's none of your business."

"That's none of your business, *ma'am*," I correct him. "Try to remember, your conduct reflects how people will feel about Miss De Leon, possibly for decades. Now, I have an appointment with Miss De Leon. The name is Sam Evans. I suggest you announce me."

I watch him pick up the phone, make a call, and hang up. "Forgive the error," he says without a hint of remorse in his voice. "Britney will meet you at the front entrance."

The gate slowly swings open. I drive down a long, gravel driveway and up to an all-white palace. Britney comes charging out of the house, carrying a pile of files, and waving to me frantically. "Park over there!" she yells, pointing to her right.

On Britney's right is a twelve-car garage housing two Bentleys, a Hummer, a Porsche, a Ferrari, and a Lamborghini. I pull my Honda Civic next to one of the Bentleys, and wonder at what point a person looks in their garage and thinks, "My life would be so much happier if only I had another Bentley."

I grab my briefcase, purse and tape recorder, then get out of the car as Britney rushes up to me. "I'm so sorry your name wasn't at the gate. Isabella's been a complete pain in the ass today. The wedding planner is here touring the place, and I'm a bit behind schedule."

"No problem," I say, putting out my hand. "I'm Sam. We actually met last night in the ladies room. I'm going to be working on a project with Miss De Leon."

She shakes. "The ghostwriter. I know, she told me all about you. Used to be married to husband number… Jesus, I've lost count. I'm Britney. Isabella's beck and call girl. Follow me."

I follow Britney to the front of the house, which has been built to look like a smaller version of the Taj Mahal.

"Isabella has me reading the wedding book you ghostwrote," Britney tells me as she opens the leaded glass front door. "You're really good."

"Thank you. What does Isabella think of it?"

"Ha!" Britney snarks. "Izzie doesn't read."

We walk through the front door and into an ornate white marble front hallway. On the left, I see a painting that looks dangerously like...

"Is that a Warhol?" I ask, walking up to the painting to inspect the signature.

"Indeed. She won it in divorce settlement #2."

"I just don't understand why the unwashed masses are allowed on *my* beach," I hear Isabella scream from upstairs. She races down the stairs, her four-inch Gianni Versace heels clicking against the marble. "I didn't pay twenty million dollars for a Malibu compound just so any Tom, Dick and Harry can watch my wedding wearing a pair swim trunks and rubber flippers."

A very hot, very gay, African American man follows Isabella into the room. He throws her a dismissive look she doesn't notice. "Maybe you can arrange for the tide to be in for the entire afternoon," Paul deadpans.

I smile.

Paul. Dave's old band mate and my old friend from college.

Upon seeing me, Paul's jaw drops and his face lights up. "The prodigal wife returns!" He runs up to me and wraps me into a big hug. "You look amazing. How are you?"

I hug him back. "I'm good," I say. Then I pull away to get a good look at him. "My God, you look exactly the same as you did in college."

Paul waves his hand around dismissively. "Girl, I've put on ten pounds and my hairline is receding. I look more like my mother every day. You're the one who still looks twenty-two. I think the last time I saw you was..."

Paul quickly backtracks. The last time he saw me was the day I asked him to pick up the divorce papers from me so that he could officially serve them to Dave. I didn't want a stranger to do it, and at that point Paul was the closest thing we had to a mutual friend. We had divided everyone else up in the divorce.

"Your Dad's wedding," Paul says, interrupting my thoughts.

"Wow. I totally forgot you planned that," I say, putting my hand up to my mouth, and grinning. Man, just being around Paul feels like...home. And at that moment I realize just how much I missed him. How do we get so distracted by our day-to-day lives that we let our closest friendships melt away into the past?

Isabella crosses her arms, clearly pissed off. "Ah-hem!" she coughs loudly, pretending to clear her throat. "Speaking of weddings, let's get back to mine. I need to have the beach below cordoned off."

"Sweetie," Paul says calmly, "all California beaches are public. You don't want to be seen like that asshole David Geffen trying to claim a public beach as your own. Just have the ceremony on the cliffs, overlooking the water."

Isabella looks over at me. "Has Dave ever been married on a cliff?"

"No. But he once compared marriage to jumping off of one," I joke.

Isabella ignores my nasty remark, and turns to Paul. "Okay, fine. We'll do it on the cliff." She looks at Britney. "You there, do you still work for me?"

"Girl, you are working my last nerve," Britney retorts.

Isabella visibly flinches, then quickly regains her composure. "Get us some cappuccinos. We'll be in the backyard." She turns back to Paul. "Now, explain to me why we can't cover this foyer completely in snow."

"Because snow is made of water, and it will melt."

Isabella sighs loudly. "Okay, but I need carolers. Lots of them. I need to immerse my guests with the feeling of a magical Christmas."

"You're doing a Christmas theme on Valentine's Day?" I ask, confused.

"Oh, I'm not limiting myself to Christmas. I don't believe in ever putting limits on myself. Oh," she starts waving her index finger at me. "Write that down. I want that as a chapter title in my book. *Don't Limit Yourself*. In it, I want to talk about all of my jewelry." Isabella turns on her heel, clickety clacks away from Paul and me, and heads outside. Paul and I quickly follow Isabella out to her backyard, a stunning oasis dripping with an abundance of roses and calla lilies, and located on a cliff overlooking the Pacific.

"We're doing a Winter Wonderland theme, highlighting all of the great things about winter," Isabella continues. "I want cupids, carolers and a Christmas tree. Maybe I'll have a ball drop too. Sam, for my book, I want to do a women's empowerment theme, but with lots of details about how to catch and keep a man."

Isabella turns to Paul as she points to a rose garden ornate enough to rival the Garden of Eden. "Paul, I'm going to need a seventy foot Christmas tree here, with full decorations. I want it to look like the one at Rockefeller Center, only on a grander scale." Then she turns to me. "Sam, I think we should concentrate on the fact that I'm just a down home girl, true to my roots, and let the reader know there's nothing flashy or fake about me." And she turns back to Paul. "Paul, I don't care what you say about it melting, we need to get real snow out here, not that fake soapy stuff they use at Disneyland. Get some snow cone machines and wind blowers... I don't know, just make it work. The ice rink will be," she points to her left, where a dark blue marble pool sparkles in the cool winter sun. "Here. See if you can get Nancy Kerrigan to perform some twirls or something. Oh, yeah, and speaking of performances, see if Barbra Streisand is available for weddings."

I write a note about what she wants to say in her autobiography as I mention, "Dave can't stand Barbra Streisand."

"This is my wedding, not his. Oh, speaking of Dave... Paul, will you make sure he's wearing a Savile Row tuxedo. He's going to try and get away with a nice suit that day, and I won't have it. Now, Sam, another thing I want to emphasize in my book is how to truly listen to a man. Many women think that I got my men because I'm incredibly sexy, when in reality it's because I hang on a man's every word."

Then she points to me accusingly. "You look like you eat cake."

"I'm sorry?" I ask, startled.

"Paul says I have to pick a cake baker and flavors. I can't do it, because I'm on a diet until my wedding day. But you look like you eat cake."

I probably should take that as an insult. But I do eat cake. Lots of it. She might as well have said, "You look like you pet puppies."

Isabella puts her hands together in a prayer and begs, "Could you be a love and pick the bakery and flavors for my cake?"

"Maybe Dave would prefer..."

"Samples are in the fridge. Five bakeries, and they've each sent over ten cake flavors and twelve fillings. Have fun with it." She points at Paul. "Paul, Sweetie, let's continue our discussion in the car. Sam, I have to go. *E!* is doing a story on my club tonight, and I need to get to my stylist for the final fitting of the dress I'm wearing for the opening. Let Britney know if you need anything."

She dashes off, so I yell in her direction, "Uh, when would you like to begin your interviews?"

Isabella stops dead in her tracks, then turns around. "My what?"

"Your interviews. I need to interview you for the book so I can start writing."

"The book?" Isabella asks absentmindedly. "Oh. That. Well, just work on what you have so far. We'll talk more later. Tah!"

Eleven

Five minutes later, I'm sitting in the middle of Isabella's Sub Zero kitchen, staring at a plethora of cakes and fillings taking up almost every inch of her oversized marble counter. I take a bite of moist dark chocolate cake that I've spread with a chocolate mousse filling. I'm in heaven. Next, I spread vanilla chip filling on a square of yellow cake and pop that in my mouth. Oh. My. God. Culinary orgasm. If I could afford to, I'd camp out at this bakery and eat until I looked like Jabba the Hutt. I take a white cake square, and debate whether to top it with strawberry cream cheese or dark chocolate fudge.

"Do you need some coffee?" Britney asks me while putting three very thick, white damask covered photo albums down next to me.

"No, thank you. These cappuccinos are amazing," I say, referring to the three cappuccinos Isabella ordered her to make before she left. "Do you want one? Or some cake?"

"Thanks, but I've already had three double espressos this morning just to keep up with Isabella. Who wants you to go through these, and come up with some questions for her."

I look at the stack of photo albums. "What are they pictures of?"

Britney points to the photo album at the top of the pile. "These are Isabella's press clippings, divided up by weddings. The first book, that's the ecru one, has all of her magazine clippings from her first marriage to Blake Minor, the movie director, including the engagement and the wedding. The second book, the cream colored one, concentrates on her second marriage to Jerry Bach, and her first record album. The third album, the ivory one, includes both her disaster third wedding and her broken engagement. FYI, he left her the day of the wedding, so she has some pretty strong thoughts on him."

I'll bet.

Britney pushes the three books over to me. "Let me run up and get you the other three."

Britney takes off upstairs, and I look through the first book. Blake Minor.

Shit.

I pull out my cell phone and dial Vanessa's private number, expecting to leave a message. Instead, she picks up. "Sam, darling. I woke up under the most charming young man this morning, and we're off on an adventure. I'll call you when I come up for air."

"Real quick," I say, staring at a picture of a very young Isabella with a man old enough to make Hugh Hefner look spry. "Blake Minor."

"Old with a paunch, thirtysomething wife, toddler running around…"

"Yeah, I know that part. Weren't you married to him?"

"Yes."

Vanessa says nothing else. I pause, waiting for her to say more. She doesn't. Finally I ask, "Any hard feelings when you divorced?"

"You mean because the asshole cheated on me with some teenaged slut, then was stupid enough to leave me for her?"

"That might be a reason, yes."

"No."

"No?" I stammer, incredulous.

"If a man wants to leave, there's not a damn thing you can do about it."

"But he left you for a conniving, self centered bitch who only used him to further her career!"

"Well, dear, they don't tend to leave you for virgins who have respect for the institution of marriage. Besides, he got what he deserved. She left him the second her career took off. It's called Karma."

"But doesn't it piss you off that Karma hasn't come after *her* yet with a machete or a two by four? And that society keeps rewarding her for her atrocious behavior? This woman just steamrolls over everyone around her, and nothing! She gets no comeuppance, just a lot of million dollar weddings! I mean, how can you stand knowing that a woman like that..."

"I take it Isabella De Leon is your new client," Vanessa interrupts.

"How'd you know?"

"That shrill tone of voice you have right now? She has that effect on women."

"I wouldn't have taken this job had I known she was Blake's second wife."

"Darling, she was Blake's fourth wife. Some people are not meant to be truly loved. Blake's one of those people. Isabella's one of those people. Let it go. Write the book, collect the paycheck, and be done with it."

"But..."

"Now I'll be entertaining for the next few days in Cabo. There are some valium in my hotel room if she drives you to them. Just take the pinks. The blues'll have you on the floor. Love you sweetie!"

And she's gone. I stare at the phone, then click it off. I open the first photo album. The first picture is the cover of Star magazine, with Isabella looking perfect in a wedding gown, and a small picture of Vanessa looking old, angry, and abandoned. Makes me wonder why people buy this crap. Could the average housewife really be gleeful that a young woman stole an older woman's husband?

Britney walks back in. "The off-white one covers wedding #4 and her movies from that year. The sand one covers wedding #5, which ended disastrously, she didn't know peacocks attacked people. And the white one covers her life until now, including when she met Dave."

I look at the albums in front of me. "Aren't they *all* white?" I ask Britney.

"You're preaching to the choir. But what do I know, I was a chemistry major in college. I've got to run some errands. Are you gonna be okay here by yourself?"

I look around. "By myself? There are three guards, two maids, and a pool cleaner here."

"You forgot Hans the masseuse," Britney half-jokes.

I laugh. "How could I forget the masseuse? Hey, can I ask you a question?"

"Always."

"How come you took this job? I mean, you seem so annoyed with Isabella. And I'm sure you're way too qualified to be here."

Britney leans in to me. "Can you keep a secret?"

I nod.

"Isabella's my sister," Britney admits. "She had this big fight last month with Dave because he said she couldn't keep an assistant for more than a month. So she called me and begged me to work for her for the next few months just to prove she could."

"Wow. You're a good sister."

"I'm the best. Now if you'll excuse me, I need to go buy something called a TiVo."

Britney takes her leave and I start to pore over Isabella's clippings.

Okay, well, mostly I eat cake. A lot of cake. Wonderful cake. Sinful cake. Chocolate, cheese, butter, yellow, white, carrot...wait, how did that get in there? I push the carrot cake to the side of the table so I don't accidentally eat it again.

After about ten minutes of gastronomical heaven, Dave pops his head around the corner. "Still eat when you're stressed?" he jokes.

My mouth is filled with vanilla cheesecake as I retort, "Mmph mmph, mm-mm-mph."

Dave furrows his brow, amused. "What?"

I hold up my index finger to tell him to give me a second, then I swallow. "Hey – mess with me, and you'll be eating carrot cake with lemon filling at your wedding."

Dave smiles. "Duly noted. I ran into Brit outside. She said Isabella was having you pick out our cake."

"Indeed. Apparently, and I'm quoting your fiancée verbatim," I imitate Isabella perfectly, "You look like you eat cake."

I make it clear from my tone of voice that I got the insult.

"She didn't mean it that way," Dave apologizes.

"Of course she did," I counter.

Dave takes a deep breath, then asks, "You don't like her very much, do you?"

"I didn't say that," I say, taking a bite of yellow cake so perfect I want to burrow into it and move in.

"You didn't have to. I know what people say about her, she's a diva, she's demanding..."

"She'd eat her young..." I continue.

Dave tilts his head, then gives me an enigmatic smile. "So said the Vanity Fair writer." He takes my fork from me, snags a bite from one of the chocolate cake samples, then hands me back my fork. "I don't see her that way. I see a woman who knows exactly what she wants in life and goes after it. She's very determined. I admire that a lot. She just needs to soften up a bit, and I'm working on that. I think the security of a good marriage will help her with that."

I take a bite of white cake. "People don't change when they get married, Dave."

"Not true. We both changed."

I look away from him, feeling inexplicably stung.

"Hey, it's a good thing," Dave adds. "If we hadn't changed back then, we wouldn't be able to be friends now. And I really miss having you as my friend."

We're both silent a moment, but it's a comfortable silence. Dave changes the subject. "So, what's on your agenda for the rest of the day?"

"Well, I have to eat about three more pounds of cake. You want to grab a fork and help me?"

Dave looks down at all of the samples. "Did you know that you can sum up the differences between men and women just by how they look at pizza?"

Dave always had all these theories about the differences between men and women. They were frequently amusing and usually had a grain of truth to them. "Okay, I'll bite," I say. "How can the differences between men and women be summed up in terms of pizza?"

"You call a woman and say, 'I'm bringing over a pizza.' Her response is, 'What are you putting on it? Where are you getting it from? What size is it? Is the crust fat free? Is the cheese fat free?' You tell a guy you're bringing over pizza, he says, 'Cool.'"

I chuckle. "So you don't care at all about your wedding cake?"

"Nah. There will be cake, and that will be cool. Besides, this wedding is her thing. I said Vegas."

"No, you didn't," I say, laughing a little as I remember planning our own wedding. "You hate Vegas. You associate it with playing to drunks. You wanted to get married in Kauai."

"Yes!" Dave agrees, putting up his arms in mock exasperation. "Why don't any of you women want to get married in Kauai? It's only the most beautiful place on Earth. And you can just call a hotel and have the wedding plans done in half an hour."

"True," I concede. Then I give him a smile and joke, "But then the hotel gets to pick out the cake."

"Again: There's cake? Cool."

I laugh. "Well, in retrospect, I'm sorry we didn't get married in Kauai. It would have been a lot less stressful. Do you still want to retire there?"

Dave has wanted to retire in Kauai ever since his parents took him to Princeville, on the northern part of the island, when he was twelve. When the band was still touring, they even took a gig there for next to no money just so that we could spend New Year's Eve in Kauai. It was a magical week. We spent those seven days sleeping in, snorkeling on the North Shore and looking at houses while we dreamt of where we were going to spend our golden years.

It was our last New Year's Eve together.

"You want to go ice skating with me?" Dave asks, ignoring my question.

"Now?" I ask, confused.

"Yeah. Belle's having an ice rink put in for the wedding, and she wants us to skate around with the guests. I haven't been on the ice since you and I went to Rockefeller Center six years ago, so I thought I better brush up on my skating skills. There's a rink in Calabasas, about half an hour from here. I figure we can go for a few hours, then grab a late lunch."

"I wish I could, but I have to go through all of these albums before I see Isabella again."

"Isabella is swamped with other work right now. You'll be lucky to see her again by next week. Grab the albums, let's go skating, and you can go through all that stuff later."

I look at the albums and debate. A day skating with Dave versus a day reading about his narcissistic bride and trying to find a way to make her look good to her adoring public. Oh, gosh, what's next? Choosing between a spa day and a gynecologist appointment?

I flip the white book shut. "You got yourself a date."

Twelve

There are several things that always sound really romantic before you actually do them. Covering your bed in rose petals. Making love on the beach. Ice skating.

In reality, when you cover your bed with rose petals, they quickly get squished, wet and cold, so you get cold, wet and messy. Making love on the beach usually involves an ocean, thereby making you cold, wet and messy (and sandy). And, as for ice skating? I've already fallen on my ass twice, making me cold, wet and messy. And cranky.

Dave, on the other hand, played ice hockey as a kid, so he's gliding around like Mario Lemieux.

"Is it time for hot chocolate yet?" I ask, clutching the side of the rink for dear life. "Preferably with some bourbon in it."

"We've been here for all of ten minutes," Dave points out, effortlessly gliding in a u shape around me.

"That's about eight minutes more than it turns out I needed."

"Do you need me to help you?"

"No! I'm not a child," I huff. Then I push myself off the rink wall, whisk past Dave, swerve to avoid a six year old, and land on my butt.

Dave's eyes widen.

"I'm fine," I assure him quickly. "I didn't need my coccyx anyway."

"Interesting," Dave says, skating around me. "I try to use my coccyx every day."

He stands behind me, donuts his arms around my waist, and hoists me back up.

Once again, in theory this would be romantic. But it's not. I can't skate. I grew up in Southern California: learning to ice skate here has about as much point as learning to surf in Montreal. This is why other cities' hockey teams have menacing names: Bruins, Sharks, Panthers. Here in Southern California we have Ducks. How intimidated are you watching a mallard waddle by?

Dave takes my left hand in his right. "All you have to do is glide your left foot out, then lift your right foot, then glide your right foot out, then lift your left foot."

I slowly glide my left foot out. Okay, focus, don't fall, glide the right foot, lift left foot...maybe I'm getting this...

Dave smoothly switches his right hand with his left, then leans back and puts his right hand around my back to steady me. "There...see?"

We skate in unison for a bit. Move my foot to the left, move my foot to the right, left, right...

"So tell me how you met Eric," Dave asks, still holding onto my hand.

"No," I say firmly.

"What do you mean 'no'?"

"Look, I can either skate with you or I can talk to you. I can't do both, I need to keep my focus."

"Didn't you say that once when we were having sex?"

"Ha-ha," I deadpan.

Dave lets go of my hand and puts his hands behind his back, easily skating beside me while I try not to look like an idiot. "Seriously. He seems like a good guy. How'd you guys meet?"

"No talking! I need to focus."

"You're doing great," Dave says. "Will you be skating at the wedding?"

The wedding. Interesting. Not *my* wedding, not *our* wedding. *The* wedding. But maybe I'm just reading into something here.

"We met at the Emergency Room," I answer. "I had to take Liz in. Turned out she had appendicitis."

"Really?" Dave says, smiling at a private joke from years past. "So am I to understand someone passed the Liz test?"

Ah, the Liz test. Dave always made fun of me for this. "The Liz Test" was what I used on guys from school, and later in my twenties. It was pretty straightforward. Basically, if a guy met Liz and me at the same time, he usually picked Liz. If he met her *after* beginning to date me, I still lost him to the *idea* of her about thirty percent of the time. Only two men ever passed the test. "He did. With flying colors."

"Cool," Dave says approvingly. "A man with taste."

"Not really," I say, making light of it. "After all, Liz was vomiting and unable to walk when he saw her."

"Good to know you've still got your rocket high self-esteem," Dave teases.

"I try."

"You love him?" Dave asks.

"Abso-fuckin'-lutely. He's the type of guy I could see myself in Kauai with."

The slightest wave of pain crosses Dave's face, then disappears just as quickly. Or maybe I just imagined it.

"But I may be jumping the gun a bit," I admit. "It's only been a few months."

Dave doesn't respond. I can tell from his breathing my statement put him in a bad mood. Damn it. We were having such a relaxed time. I decide to change the subject. "So how on Earth did Paul go from your drummer to a famous wedding planner?"

Dave's face brightens. "Oh, that's a funny story. Remember how we once opened for "Carlyle"? Well, their lead singer was getting married and Paul helped her plan it. Suddenly, the wedding's on the cover of *People*, *OK!*, and *Us*, and Paul is being heralded as the 'Wedding Planner to the Stars'."

"Really? Huh, that's quite a 180. How long has he been doing it?"

"About five years. He quit the band so that he could devote his life to it full time. In some ways, I think that was the beginning of the end for our group."

"Were you okay with that?" I ask.

"What? Him leaving?"

I shrug. "Well, you just said it marked the beginning of the end of the group. Some people would hate him for breaking up the gang."

"Nah. We were kind of done. I mean, being in the band was like college. I wouldn't change my experiences for the world: I had fun, I learned a lot about what was important and not so important in my life… I mean, I don't know, so many people freak out about turning thirty. I liked it. I wouldn't want to be twenty-five again."

Dave suddenly stops talking. Hard to speak when your foot is in your mouth. We were finalizing our divorce when he turned twenty-five.

Once again: I change the subject. "So, you said you talked to Joe last night. How's he doing?"

"He's finishing up a small tour in the Northeast. Two more dates. Then he's coming into town next week. He says 'Hi', by the way."

"Hi back. And what's Greg up to these days?" I ask, referring to their keyboard player.

Dave chuckles. "Get this: he reunited with his high school sweetheart, moved back to Texas, and has a beautiful daughter and another on the way."

"No," I say, smiling in disbelief. "Man, one of us has kids."

We skate around, listening to an old Madonna song play on the outdated sound system. I look over at Dave, and he steals an awkward glance at me. There's only one band member I haven't asked about yet. "How's Stephanie?"

Dave furrows his brow, taking a second to answer. "She's good. Owns a restaurant in Hoboken, dating a decent guy..."

Dave's voice trails off. If this were a movie, this would be the point where I apologize for falsely accusing him of having an affair, or where I realize I no longer have animosity for this woman who intentionally hurt me so many years ago. I'd be the better person, having moved on with my life and let go of all that hate. Treated it like a balloon, and let it blow away.

This so isn't a movie.

I wish I could say those things or feel that way. Maybe when I'm forty. Maybe there really does come a time in your life when you make peace with your past.

I'm just not there yet.

My cell phone rings, rescuing me from the past. I look down to read, "Isabella Stevens."

She took Dave's last name already? Puke.

I hit the "send" button to talk. "Hello?"

"Drop what you're doing," Isabella says, her tone rushed. "I've just had a Tiffany's."

I jolt my head back. "A what? You mean you're *at* Tiffany's?"

"No. Although that's a good idea, maybe we can go later. No, I had a Tiffany's. You know, a brilliant idea?"

I look at Dave, watching me, clearly wondering who I'm on the phone with. I turn away from him to concentrate. "You mean an epiphany?"

"Right. See, now that's why you're the writer. Anyway, I have a wonderful idea for a chapter -- How to Throw an Unforgettable Wedding for over a Million Dollars."

I turn to Dave. I can tell he has figured out it's his future wife. "Don't you mean under?" I ask.

"I'm sorry?"

"Under," I repeat. "Don't you mean 'How to Throw a Wedding for Under a Million Dollars'?"

"No. Anyone can do that. I'm at the Vittorio Valpicelli Salon in Beverly Hills. Can you come meet me?"

"Um…sure," I say awkwardly.

"Great! I'll put your name on the list. Oh, and I have another idea for a chapter: How to Seduce a Man in Five Easy Lessons. The chapter should only be a page long, so we'll knock it out while you're here."

Thirteen

After a quick goodbye to Dave (nice hug, nothing weird) I make my way to the Vittorio Valpicelli Salon in Beverly Hills. The showroom for celebrity designer Vittorio Valpicelli, it is considered the most exclusive bridal salon in the city, possibly the country. You have to make an appointment just to look at the gowns, and I doubt you can get out of the place for less than ten thousand dollars. Probably more like twenty-five.

I park my Civic next to Isabella's bright red Ferrari F355 in one of the salon's parking spaces in the back, grab my tape recorder, notepad and purse, walk around to the front of the building, and try to open the salon's gold leafed double doors. Locked. I press the intercom button to my right (what is it with Isabella and places with intercom buttons?) Then I wait.

"How may I be of service?" a polite English woman's voice liltingly asks me over the intercom.

"I'm Sam Evans. I'm here to see Isabella."

Suddenly I hear cameras clicking away behind me. I turn around to see three men who have appeared out of nowhere to take my picture.

I smile self-consciously and wave to them.

"Ah, Miss Evans, we've been expecting you," the woman tells me, her voice brightening, as though my arrival has made her day. The door buzzes, and I let myself in.

The plush salon inside is so stunningly beautiful, it makes me want to be a bride again. The floors of the entryway are white marble, polished to a sparkle. The white carpet ahead of me looks like powdered sugar, and I'm tempted to take my shoes off to see if it feels as good as it looks. Surrounding me are mannequins wearing the most exquisite white dresses I've ever seen: ball gowns, sheaths, A-lines, V lines. I walk up to scrutinize a strapless gown that flares out at the bottom.

Back when I was engaged and subscribed to every bridal magazine in existence, I learned that this style was called "mermaid." And now I understand why: unless you are as skinny as Darryl Hannah in the movie *Splash*, it will look like crap on you. I mean, what sadist sat with his sketchpad one day and thought, "I need to make the bride paranoid about how large her thighs are by making the dress skin tight, then have it burst out over the feet in a big triangle shape so that no one can see she has decent ankles." Must have been the same moron who came up with the idea of bell bottoms.

But it sure looks good on the size zero mannequin with the D cups.

"Lovely, isn't it?" I hear behind me.

I turn around to see a well-dressed, middle-aged woman in a beige Coco Chanel suit smiling at me. I smile back. "It's breathtaking," I agree.

"Not half as breathtaking as your friend is going to be on her special day," the woman tells me in her proper British accent. "Come with me."

As she walks me across the showroom of gowns, she introduces herself. "I'm Edna. Can I get you anything? A glass of champagne, a spot of tea perhaps?"

They just *give* you champagne here? Back in the day, I hit the Filene's bi-annual basement sale for my gown. All it gave me was a headache. "I'd love a cup of coffee," I say, maintaining my habit of never drinking while I work.

"Cappuccino?"

"Plain coffee — black."

"I'll get that for you right away," Edna tells me, leading me to a frosted glass door. "She's right in here."

Edna opens the door, and I walk in to see Isabella standing on a pedestal in the center of the room, surrounded by floor to ceiling mirrors. She is dressed in a strapless white satin ball gown that is covered in red and white crystals. It's the most beautiful dress I've ever seen.

And I don't mean to be, but I'm jealous. I found my dress at a vintage shop for thirty bucks. I mean, I loved it: a 20s style flapper dress with a drop waist and a tiny bit of sparkle.

But, oh, to have been able to wear a dress like Isabella's on my big day. It's like a ball gown for Cinderella if Cinderella loved bling and her Fairy Godmother had ever seen Elsa Klensch.

Isabella is scrutinizing her reflection in the mirror. "How much is the dress costing me so far?" she asks the handsome man standing behind her.

"This one's almost half a million," the 6'2" male model says to her in a sexy Italian accent.

Isabella sighs, staring at her reflection unhappily. Then her face lights up. "Ooh! What if we got an authentic pair of Dorothy's ruby red slippers from The Wizard of Oz? That would drive up the cost."

"Judy Garland was a size five," Italy tells her. "They would never fit. You would look like...uh...how you say...? like Cinderella's wicked stepsister."

"Sam!" Isabella exclaims, just noticing me. "I'm so glad you're here." She lifts her dress, climbs off the pedestal, and heads over to me. She gestures to the handsome Italian. "This is Vittorio. He designed my dress. Vittorio, Sam."

Wow. Do designers look like that?

"Charmed," Vittorio drawls seductively, taking my hand to lightly graze it with a kiss.

"Vittorio, can you describe the dress for Sam?" Isabella asks him excitedly. "She's the author of the book I'm writing."

Vittorio gives me an alluring smile (I wonder how many future brides he's bedded with that smile) as he describes the dress in his sexy accent, "It is a strapless ball gown made of duchess satin. Here we have a princess bodice with a dropped waist, which emphasizes the future Mrs. Stevens' tiny waistline. Then, in addition to the intricate embroidery embellishing the skirt, we have added real gemstones throughout. See these red stones? These aren't Swarovski crystals. Anyone can do that. They're genuine rubies. And some of the clear crystals are diamonds."

"Isn't that cool?" Isabella says, beaming. "I'm going to need a bodyguard to follow me around at my own wedding. It's going to be just like the Oscars, only without that hideous Joan Rivers."

"The ball gown is floor length," Vittorio continues, "with a ten foot detachable cathedral length train."

"Oh, that's another cool part," Isabella says gleefully. "They have a special woman they send from the shop whose only job for the day is to detach my train. She costs seven hundred and fifty dollars. Isn't that awesome?"

Wow. There's an actual job out there called "train detacher," and it makes seven hundred and fifty dollars a day! How does one land that job? Back in my twenties, such employment would have kept me from regularly rummaging through my couch, looking for spare change to pay my electric bill.

"Let me show you the other wedding dresses," Isabella tells me, spinning around and heading towards a dressing room.

"Other wedding dresses?" I ask.

"Well, you didn't think I'd wear the same dress all day did you? What am I? Amish? This dress is for the ceremony. I also have a silk mermaid dress for the nighttime reception beaded with aquamarines and pearls..."

Of course she does.

"...then I have my going away outfit for when we leave the wedding. Oh, and I have the cutest skating outfit for the afternoon reception..."

"She's going to be covered from head to toe in fur," Vittorio tells me.

"Right," Isabella tells me proudly. Then she turns to Vittorio. "By the way, what can we do that's fur but doesn't piss off PETA?"

Vittorio leans in to her conspiratorially. "What do you think of white Fox?"

And Isabella's face lights up. "To match the invitations! Vittorio, you're a genius!"

He waves her off. "It's a gift. But if I were truly a genius, I would have landed you."

Pukepukepukepukepuke. And also, how does fox fur not piss off PETA?

"Oh, that reminds me," she says, walking over to her Hermes bag. She pulls out a tiny fur coat on a hanger. "Ta-da!" she exclaims, handing it to me.

I take the tiny white fur coat and examine it. It looks like it was designed for a Cabbage Patch Doll.

"I used real fur," Isabella says proudly. "And each note was hand calligraphed. Is that a word? Anyway, open it."

I open the coat. Inside is a wedding invitation: In gold calligraphy it reads:

*The honour of your presence
is requested
at the marriage of
Miss Isabella Josephine De Leon
to
Mr. David William Stevens
On Saturday, the fourteenth of February*

Followed by various wedding information.

As read, this weird sense of unhealed wounds flows over me.

Which makes no sense, because I never wanted Dave back. I guess I just wanted, at some point in our lives, for him to admit he was wrong. Not just about Stephanie, but about all the fights we had about law school, and priorities, and...well, everything towards the end there. I guess I thought if we became friends again, I wouldn't feel like I was still fighting a war in my head that I lost years ago.

But he has moved on, and I need to move on too. I just need to get these interviews over with, get the book written ASAP, and get on with my life.

Wounds healed (or scarred over anyway). Moving on!

I hear Isabella's cell phone ringing her latest Top 40 hit. "I have to get that," she says, pulling a small jeweled phone out of her bag and reading the caller ID. "Hello?" she says, then listens to the other caller. "No, no!" she whines, her voice going up two octaves. "I have your dress right here. You're going to look perfect..."

Isabella's voice trails off and her face falls as she listens to the person on the other end. "But you said you'd be in it. You promised me!"

I can hear the muffled sound of the person explaining herself as Isabella's face darkens. "Oh, don't be ridiculous. You'll have plenty of time... But this is my wedding! ... Fine. I'll do it without you! But I never want to see you again!"

Isabella hits the "end" button, throws the phone across the room, then throws herself down on the ground. She starts pounding her fists into the white carpet. "No, no, no, no!" she yells, kicking and screaming like a two year old having a temper tantrum. "No, no, no!"

I lean down to her. "Something happen?" I ask carefully, kind of wanting to give her a hug, but afraid to touch her.

Isabella sits up, her eyes starting to water. "My friend Kristina just backed out of my wedding! Apparently, her C-section is scheduled for the Monday before, and she won't be out of the hospital in time. Why does everything always happen to me?!"

I search for something comforting to say. "I can understand why you're disappointed. But there will be other weddings."

Isabella looks at me, cocking her head.

Backpedal. Sam. "What I meant was, other events. Anniversaries... Christenings... Funerals. Plenty of chances for you to show the world what great friends you still are."

Suddenly, Isabella gets a dangerous glint in her eye.

I don't like that look. My eyes dart back and forth, scanning the room, looking for the quickest way out. Maybe if I drop to the floor and crawl along the carpet with my elbows...

Isabella starts waving her hands up and down like a hummingbird. "Oh my God. You *totally* should be my bridesmaid!"

The mind boggles. I close my eyes and shake my head for a moment, trying to wake myself from this nightmare.

No good. I open my eyes, and I'm still here. Okay, stay calm. "I don't think that would be very appropriate."

"Don't be silly," Isabella says, her mood immediately stabilized as she stands back up. "In the last few hours, you've become one of my closest friends. It would blasphemy not to put you in my wedding."

"First of all, it's not really blasphem… sorry. Gonna stay on point. I'm pretty sure it's bad luck to see the groom…'s ex-wife before the wedding."

"You're going to look super cute!" Isabella exclaims as she grabs my wrists and shakes them enthusiastically. "I am dressing all of the bridesmaids to look like Cupid. Vittorio, go get her the dress!"

As he leaves for the backroom, I pray to the Gods of fashion that he'll come back with a bow and arrow, so I can shoot her in the…

Vittorio reemerges, holding the tiniest dress I've ever seen. But on the plus side, it's totally hideous. A bright red mini-dress with bright red sequins and bright red fur trim.

"Do you love it?! Tell me you love it!" Isabella enthuses as she grabs the dress from Vittorio and hands it to me. "Try it on. Lisa was a size eight, just like you."

A nine month pregnant woman was a size eight? Only in LA.

"Isabella…" I begin.

"Call me Libby…"

"Libby. You don't pick people for your wedding based on how they fit the dress. I'm not Johnny Bravo. I shouldn't get the job because I fit the outfit."

"So you'll do it," Isabella declares, hugging me. "Thank you, thank you, thank you! I love you so much." She pulls away from me. "I'm going to change into my evening reception dress while you try on your dress."

And with that, she races to the back room to change. I look at Vittorio, and narrow my eyes as I hold up the dress. "How could you?"

"Do not look at me," Vittorio tells me in his sexy accent. "She designed it. I just charged her ten thousand dollars each to make it."

I furrow my brow, turn around and hold the dress up to myself in the mirror. "What on Earth could make this dress cost ten thousand dollars?"

"What can I say?" he asks breezily, gesturing with his hands. "It is fashion." Vittorio makes a point of checking out my ass. "For you, I throw in the matching underwear for free."

I shake my head slowly. "Are you supposed to wear underwear with an outfit like this?"

A few minutes later, I am staring at myself in a full length mirror, wearing nothing but a tight little red cocktail dress, and five-inch heels so gaudy they would make a hooker reconsider her career options. Every time I think I've hit a new low in my life, Isabella drags me down a notch further.

Isabella makes her second entrance of the day wearing a gorgeous white, silk satin, beaded V-neck, floor length gown. "So what tiara do you think should go with... Oh my God! You look perfect!"

Perfect for what? Finding a traveling businessman in Vegas?

Isabella trots over to me, furrowing her brow as she scrutinizes my dress. "Vittorio, where are the Ostrich feathers?"

"We had to have them shipped in from Africa. They'll be here tomorrow."

I start pulling an imaginary thread from the dress. I know I'm going to regret asking this, but like a moth to a flame... "Exactly where will the feathers go?"

"On the left shoulder and on the butt," Isabella answers, beaming. "This is exactly how I pictured my bridesmaids would look."

Like giant blood clots?

"Like giant hearts," she continues, tearing up with emotion. "But hearts hot enough to be showgirls."

"Holy shit," I hear Dave mutter behind me. I turn around.

"Baby," Isabella exclaims, rushing over to give him a big kiss. A really long, wet... did I mention annoyingly long? kiss. With tongue and moaning.

I start tapping my fingers... Should be over any minute...

"I missed you so much" Isabella announces in baby talk once they finally break apart to come up for air. She points to me. "Isn't she stunning?"

Dave shakes his head slowly. "Please tell me that's just the top."

"Yeah, could you tell me that too?" I ask, even though I'm not sure I can afford another ten thousand dollars for a skirt.

"I told you I was going for something completely different," Isabella reminds Dave.

"When you said something completely different, I didn't think you meant you would imitate a Monty Python routine," Dave says, a tinge of anger creeping into his voice. "You expect my sister to squeeze into that?"

Isabella thrusts her head back. "Of course. It's the perfect dress for a larger woman. It's flirty, it's fun. It screams confident!"

"It screams, 'It's your money honey. My meter's running,'" Dave quips, raising his voice more as he points to me. "Sam can't even pull off that dress. Your cousin Wendy doesn't have a chance in hell."

"Don't be silly," Isabella says, waving him off. "I wore a blue dress just like this in my last movie, and it looked fabulous."

Dave rubs the side of his right temple, a headache coming on. "Belle, you have the perfect body. You get paid millions of dollars every year because your body is so good. Some women are not as fortunate."

Isabella crosses her arms. "You once told me all women are beautiful."

Dave takes another glance at me. "I stand corrected. Not in that dress, they're not."

"You know, I *am* in the room," I remind him huffily.

"Sam is going to look great," Isabella insists. "She's got two weeks to start running, get her legs in shape, and hit some Pilates classes. Then watch out!"

"Yeah? Where's she going to find boobs in the next two weeks?" Dave asks angrily, pointing to my chest.

I smack him on the arm. *Asshole.*

Dave puts up the palms of his hands. "No offense, Sam, I'm just trying to make a point."

"Offense taken. And as long as we're talking about things that could be a little bigger…"

"I'll buy her boobs, if that's your problem," Isabella says to Dave, then turns to me. "You don't have a problem getting a boob job in the next two weeks, right?"

Before I can answer, Dave yells/asks, "And what the hell are you wearing on your feet?!"

I realize he's looking at me, not Isabella.

"Oh, I'm supposed to answer that," I say quickly. "Umm… these are…" I look down at the red sparkly strappy heels Vittorio gave me to wear with the dress. "Um, well, I know they're *not* the ruby red slippers from the Wizard of Oz."

Dave tilts his head, narrowing his eyes at me. "I don't even know what that means."

My cell phone rings. As Dave and Isabella continue bickering, I walk over to my purse and pull out my phone. Eric. "Hey," I say quietly into the phone. "Let me get a little privacy."

I walk out of the showroom and into a silent hall, then whisper, "I miss you more than you know."

"Are you with Isabella?" Eric asks, concerned. "Is she making you nuts?"

"All I can say is that I need chocolate and sex tonight, and not necessarily in that order."

"I warned you she was a little high maintenance," Eric says apologetically. "Speaking of... she called to say you couldn't take me to the airport tonight. How come?"

"She what?!" I say, raising my voice two octaves. I walk back into the showroom. "Isabella, why did you..."

"Why would you even have the caterer do lobster mac and cheese when you know I'm allergic to shellfish?" Dave asks Isabella in exasperation.

"First of all, nobody eats at their own wedding. Second, lobster isn't a shellfish. It's a crustacean..."

"Why did you tell Eric I couldn't take him to the airport tonight?" I interrupt to ask Isabella.

They both turn to me. "Oh, Sam. Hi. I didn't see you there," Isabella says cheerfully. "There will be a bunch of reporters at my club Cirque tonight. I want them to interview you about our book. Dress trendy. Or like a clown. Up to you."

I open my mouth, ready to stand up for myself.

"She has to take her boyfriend to the airport tonight," Dave tells her. "Honestly, how can you be so self-centered?"

"Me? Self centered?" Isabella asks, incredulous. "Is that why I not only arranged for a limo to take Eric to the airport, but also for a limo to take Sam to my club? Is that why I told the reporter from

E! all about Sam's novel, *Edict of Edith*, so that it gets lots of publicity and sells millions of copies, so she never has to work as a ghostwriter again?"

Dave and I (and Eric on the other end of the phone) are all silent.

"How did you know I wrote a novel?" I ask Isabella, staring at her suspiciously.

"Eric told me," Isabella happily tells me as I hear Eric concurrently say under his breath, "Oh shit."

Oh shit indeed. "Isabella..." I begin.

"Call me Libby..."

"Okay, Libby... *Edict of Edith* isn't done yet...and I can't sell something that isn't done yet."

"Don't be silly. I sold my book before you wrote a word. Oh! Speaking of my book," Isabella says distractedly, noticing her backside in the mirror and suddenly finding it much more fascinating than either her fiancé or this conversation. "My contract from Sideways came. My lawyer said it was all wrong."

"You've rewritten *Edith* sixteen times. Put a fork in it," Eric suggests to me.

"If I were you, I'd be very quiet right now," I warn him over the phone.

"I wish I could be," Isabella says, thinking I'm speaking to her. "But my mind just keeps racing. My intelligence is a gift and a curse. Anyway, I told them you're the co-author. They gave me a half million dollar advance, but you only got a fifth of that. I told my lawyer you're supposed to get half. I mean, you're the one writing the book. She'll have it fixed by tomorrow."

I stare at my new boss in silence.

This is over. I can not be bought. I mean, yes, it's a lot of money. But what am I? Some beck and call girl who's supposed to drop everything every time this little maniac…

"So I'll pick up a sandwich on my way to the airport," Eric asks knowingly.

"I've never loved you more than I love you right now," I quickly tell him.

I mean, come on, it's a quarter of a million dollars. I'm catching up to Demi Moore's character, and it's only four o'clock.

Fourteen

An hour later, after allowing Isabella to exact a promise from me that I would be at Cirque at 7:30, I head back to my house carrying a large gold Vittorio Valpicelli box under one arm.

"Remind me again of why I do my job," I ask loudly as I unlock the door and make my way into the house.

"Two words," Liz says from the kitchen. "Coal Miner." I walk in to see Liz at our kitchen table tossing three pennies down on the table, Zac curled up by her feet. She examines the coins, proclaims, "Tails, tails, heads." then jots down a broken line on a lavender legal pad.

"Can I ask a stupid question?"

"When I was twenty one, and no, not to Joe," Liz deadpans, tossing the pennies onto the table again, then writing again. "Tails, tails, heads. Seriously, again?"

"Going to ask about that in a minute." I say, referring to the coins. "But since today I hit a new low in life, me first." I put the Vittorio Valpicelli box in the middle of the table.

Liz's face becomes electric. "Vittorio Valpicelli? That is so cool!" She says, practically ripping open the box. As she pulls out the bright red dress she begins excitedly, "Oh my God, this is so…"

And her face freezes in horror. "Soooo…" she repeats, holding up the dress to inspect it. Noticing the insanely short hem, she paws through the box in search of more dress. As she realizes there is nothing else hiding in the white tissue paper, she searches for some polite words. "It's very…um… I mean, with the right accessories you could…" Then she gives up. "This is the ugliest thing you've bought since the Kangol hat. Did you keep the receipt?"

"I didn't have to. I won't be returning it. I have agreed to be a bridesmaid in Isabella's wedding. This is my, and I use the term liberally, dress."

Liz's eyes widen at my news.

"Wait. It gets better," I continue, taking the dress back. "The dyed to match Ostrich feathers are coming tomorrow. I am going to look like a freakish slutty mascot for the Cardinals."

"I was thinking Big Bird's hooker...."

I toss the dress back into the box and fall down into a chair. "And that's not the end of my complete humiliation in the name of furthering my career. I am also missing taking Eric to the airport tonight because I have to be at Isabella's new club Cirque at 7:30."

Liz immediately perks up. "Wait? You got invited to Cirque? Do you get to go to the VIP lounge?"

"Not only that, but she's sending a limo..." I say, sighing. "Which means there's no way to get out of it because the driver will just politely knock on our door until I succumb in defeat..." It's then that I notice a very wicked glint in my best friend's eye. "Don't look at me like that. You know that look scares me."

"How can you not appreciate the gift the universe has just bestowed upon us?" Liz says, gleefully hitting my arm.

"People to make fun of..." I mutter under my breath as Liz joyfully declares in unison, "People to make fun of!" Then Liz adds, "Does she call it a bar-slash-lounge."

I nod. Liz happily claps in machine gun rapid-fire. "Perfection. Oh, I hope some music executives show up. I love making fun of music executives. Tell me it's in the seediest part of Hollywood."

"Silverlake."

She throws up her hands like she just heard the most inspirational sermon in church. "Even better. A bunch of Westsiders acting like they're slumming and edgy as they talk about cheese shops over cocktails 'crafted by mixologists.' I'm creaming in my jeans right now."

I smile, because at least one of us is seeing the humor in all of this. "Fine. You can go."

Liz points at me. "You will NOT regret this. Maybe I'll get a few hedge fund managers drunkenly ask me if I'm the girl who played Julie on *Friends*."

"You crack me up," I say, shaking my head. Then I acknowledge the pennies, the Chinese characters she seems to be drawing, and a book on the table. "Okay, I give up. What are you doing?"

"I'm consulting with the I Ching."

I stare at Liz blankly. "It's an augury," she clarifies.

Still no recognition from my side of the table.

"It's a fortune telling book," Liz explains. "Well, it's also supposed to be a book of advice. You write down a question, then toss three pennies on a table six times. Depending on how the pennies land: three heads, three tails, or a combination of the two, you write down solid or broken lines from bottom to top. The six lines form a hexagram, or symbol, that should answer your question. If you get all heads or all tails for any of the six lines, the line changes from solid to broken, or vice versa, thereby giving you two hexagrams: the first hexagram represents what's currently going on in your life, the other will tell you the 'coming tendencies' which basically just means advice about to handle your problem."

"Hold on, let me get a donut," I say, running into the kitchen, grabbing a day old chocolate Entenmann's, then running back. "I'm in. What was your question?"

"I asked, *'What will happen with me romantically in the next few months?'*" Liz throws the coins again. "Heads, heads, tails."

"Why is it whenever women have a chance to ask a fortune teller about their future, they always ask about their love lives?" I ask.

"Because the only women who have the time and money to consult fortunetellers have no love lives," Liz states, throwing the coins a final time. "Tails, tails, tails."

Liz starts making notes and consulting the book. "Okay, the sixth line changes. So, we have the trigram Sun over K'un, that means number 20. Then we have K'an over K'un, that's 8."

"What do the numbers mean?" I ask, craning my neck to look at the book.

"The numbers refer to a hexagram. There are 64 in the book," Liz says, flipping through the book to the number 20. "The number 20 means *Contemplating*."

She starts reading. "Basically it means I am currently thinking, or in my case obsessing over, stuff going on in my life. Now, my future is..." Liz flips back in the book to number 8. "The symbol for *Unity*."

Liz continues reading. "Something's coming up romantically in the near future," she reads, "I will soon be able to see myself as part of a whole, which will allow me both to amplify my individuality, and annihilate it..."

"Annihilate it?" I ask. "That sounds ominous."

Liz shrugs. "I think it's just telling me that's I'm ready to be part of a couple again." She flips to the front of the book, then hands me the pad of paper she's been writing her questions on. "Okay, you're next."

I take the pad.

"What will happen with my job with Isabella?" I ask aloud as I write the question down.

"Wait. You're not going to ask about Eric or Dave?"

"Of course not. I already know my futures with both of them." I say, then toss the coins. Each of the six times, it either comes up two tails, one heads, or two heads, one tail. "That can't be good," I say. "I only got one symbol."

"Actually only getting one symbol can be a really good thing," Liz tells me. "It means your past, present and future are all in sync." She consults her chart, translating. "Let's see trigram K'an over K'an...that means you're number 29," Liz flips through the book, and gasps. "Oh."

I look over at the book, and the 29th symbol:

DANGER.

Fifteen

An hour later, Liz and I are in a stretch limo, pulling up to Cirque. "I can't believe you're not freaked out by the danger symbol," she announces for the millionth time.

"Liz, it's a fortune telling book, not an almanac. It's going to give me about as much insight into my life as the yoga you're making me do tomorrow morning."

Our limousine pulls up to a plain brick building with no sign in front to tell us the name of the club. Not that we need one: based on the beefy doorman standing at attention next to the gold doors, and the paparazzi huddling on the left waiting for their next hundred thousand dollar shaved crotch shot, we're in the right place.

Our driver walks around and opens our door. The moment we emerge from our limo and head into the club, photographers scream at us and jockey for position against each other as they madly snap our picture.

"Oh, Toto, I don't think we're in Kansas anymore," Liz jokes as flashes go off, and I hear men scream, "You're beautiful" and "Look this way" in a variety of languages.

"Who do they think we are?" I whisper to her, confused.

Liz, wearing a sparkly red leotard, sparkly red pumps, and little else, happily waves to them. "I have no idea. But how fun would it be to end up in the Enquirer? I hope they say I'm JFK Jr's mistress."

"I still can't believe you had a knife thrower's assistant's leotard hanging in your closet."

"That was one strange summer in Montreal," she says, waving at the paparazzi. "But at least I got to keep the jewelry."

"Turn around!" One guy yells at Liz. "Let's see that great ass!"

Liz turns around to show her backside, throws her hands on her hips, then swivels her head around to flash a sexy smile to the horde.

The stunningly handsome doorman standing by the gold double doors nods politely to us and opens the door. As we walk through the doorway, I whisper to Liz, "How cool is that? It's like he just knew we were on the list."

"It's 7:30," Liz reminds me. "No one's on a list at 7:30."

We walk in to an over the top (over the big top?) three ring circus, complete with side shows. As an old dance mix of Isabella's song *Candy Girl* pulsates in the background, I watch a scantily clad woman "tamer," complete with whip, "train" a male swimsuit model who is covered in makeup from head to toe to look like a lion. The trainer opens her mouth, shows her lion a little bit of tongue, then smacks the whip down so fast it causes Liz and I to jump. The lion immediately drops to his knees in submission, looking up at her crotch.

"I wonder if she can also train a guy made up as a wolf," Liz begins.

"Please don't make a doggie style joke," I beg.

"You're right. I'm better than that. How about what that cat is going to do to that pussy?"

As I make a show of rolling my eyes, a beautiful African American girl who looks exactly like a model I've seen in Vogue approaches us. She is dressed as a ringmaster who forgot to finish dressing, sporting a black top hat and overcoat over a lacy black bra, panties and garter belt. "Welcome to Cirque. I'm Vivienne, your ringmaster. What can I do to make you feel amazing?"

"I wonder if any men here tonight will use that as a pickup line," Liz ponders aloud. "I mean, you gotta admit, as pick up lines go, that's a solid six. Seven if you're drunk."

I elbow Liz lightly in the stomach as I smile at the hostess. "Hi. I'm Sam Evans. I'm here to meet with Isabella De Leon."

"Oh, Miss Evans, we've been expecting you," Vivienne says. She takes two very large red and gold menus from a podium, then says. "Follow me."

Liz and I follow Vivienne past several couples eating dinner in various side show booths. The first couple is clearly on their first date, judging from the coquettish looks and pent up energy from lack of touching: she pulls down her dress hem so as not to show too much thigh, he nervously leans in to talk to her. Next, we pass a couple on their third date: she feeds him a forkful of her pasta, then they kiss. Finally, we pass a fortysomething couple on their bazillionth date: she's got a ring the size of a doorknob, and both are focused more on their dinner than each other.

"Miss De Leon has been unexpectedly detained," Vivienne informs me as we walk. "She'd like you to enjoy dinner and drinks compliments of the management."

Vivienne walks us upstairs to the VIP area, which has a perfect view of a ring in the center of the restaurant, currently featuring a stilt walker with no shirt having his world mock-rocked by a sexy clown pretending to fellate him. "Huh," Liz comments. "So that's how you'd go down on a stilt walker: you stay exactly where you are."

I widen my eyes at her in warning as Vivienne stops at a bright red leather booth. "Steve will be catering to your every whim this evening. And we hope you enjoy the greatest show on Earth on your greatest night on Earth."

Liz practically jumps in an arc into the booth. "We'd like some carpaccio to start, and the crab cakes," she orders happily.

"Great choices," Vivienne says, handing Liz and me our menus. "I'll let Steve know immediately."

As Vivienne walks away, I slide in next to Liz. "How did you know they had crab cakes and carpaccio here?"

"All places like this have crab cakes and carpaccio," she says, a big smile spreading across her face as she reads her menu. "Cool. I just ordered forty dollars worth of stuff, and we haven't even ordered drinks yet."

I throw my notebook and purse onto the table and take a seat in the booth as a good looking man dressed as an elephant, and by "dressed" I mean wearing full gray body makeup, and nothing but a gray Speedo with his trunk between his legs, brings over a silver tray with two martini glasses filled with purple drinks. "Good evening ladies. I'm Steve, and I'll be taking care of you." As he puts the purple martinis in front of us, he lets us know, "I'm starting you both with a Pussy Galore, our signature drink. Enjoy!"

Liz smiles at Steve and asks, "Steve, what are my chances I could trade that in for a beer?"

Steve smiles. "100%. We have twenty seven beers on tap."

"Steve, will you marry me?" Liz deadpans.

Steve laughs. "What type of beer can I tempt you with?"

"I like my beer the way I like my men: dark, a little sweet, and definitely something that can be tapped all night."

Steve returns her smile. "Okay. How dark and sweet? Are we dreaming of a brown ale?"

"I'll date a brown ale, but I won't marry a brown ale."

He laughs again. "I think I've got just the beer for you. It's a Vanilla Porter from a new microbrewery. Let me get you a squinch, and I'll also get your appetizers started."

He walks away as Liz looks at his backside lasciviously. "Wow. Almost motivates me to rejoin a gym." She grabs my notebook. "What do you think of a, 'I like my men the way I like my beer...' series?"

"Well, it would allow you to use your 'first thing in the morning' punch line again," I reason.

"Bonus!" Liz says, happily writing down an idea.

I look around the club for signs of Dave or Isabella. "I can't believe Isabella made me miss Eric just so she could be late."

"Chill out. She'll be here," Liz says distractedly. "How do you spell *Pasteurized?*"

"E-U," I say, pulling out my phone and pressing my speed dial for Eric. I get his voicemail. "Hi, this is Eric. Please leave a message." Beep.

"Hi, it's me. I just want you to know how much I love you, and how much I'm going to miss you this week, and how grateful I am that you were so understanding about my not being able to take you to the airport... Okay. I love you. Have a good trip. I love you. Bye."

I press the "End" button, and stare at the phone. "Rats."

"He's a doctor. Why don't you page him?" Liz suggests.

"Because I don't want to be one of those clingy girlfriends that needs to be reassured every three minutes," I say, dialing *86 to check my voicemail. "You have two new messages," the automated voice tells me.

I punch in my secret code: Dave's birthday. I really should get around to changing that.

"Message number one," I hear the automated voice tell me. Then, "Darling, it's Vanessa. I called your house earlier. I have a wonderful idea for a chapter: *Pool Boys, Tennis Pros and Yoga Instructors: How to Get One, Keep One and Convince Your Husband that*

You Need One. I spoke with your roommate Liz about it...she sounds delightful... Love you, sweetie." Beep.

"Message number two," the voice tells me. "Hey, baby it's Eric," he says softly. "My battery's about to die, so I have to turn my phone off. But I want you to know how much I love you, how proud I am of you, and to tell you that you're going to do great with Libby's book. And *Edict of Edith* is awesome, I can't wait to see it in bookstores." He pauses, like he's debating saying something else. "All right, well, obviously you're not picking up, it's a cell phone." Another pause. "I miss you already. Love you, bye."

"Damn!" I say, hitting seven on my phone so I can save Eric's message. "I missed him." I check my received calls list. "He must have called when we were in a canyon."

Isabella's song fades out, replaced by a dance mix of Spice Girls' *Wannabe*. I look around the room again. "How long do you think she's going to be?"

"I hope she takes at least an hour," Liz says, happily perusing her menu. "Starving artists like me never get to eat this well. $50 for a lobster? I am so getting the lobster. Wait no... they have a filet mignon with Stilton cheese stuffed inside. Can you get that, and we'll switch halfway through?"

Steve walks back to us, carrying a single shot glass of beer on a silver tray. "Madame," he says, handing Liz her beer, "your squinch."

"Thank you," Liz says, then downs the shot. "Perfect. Keep 'em coming until they kick me out with a peacock feather on my head."

"Don't you mean lampshade?" I ask. Liz points to a dancer dressed like a peacock spinning around what can only be described as a silk curtain.

I emit a confused, "Huh." just as my phone rings.

I pick up on the first ring, assuming it's Eric. "I miss you already," I purr in a slightly baby talk voice.

"I…uh… miss you too," Dave stammers. "Are you there yet?"

Yikes! "We got here a little bit ago," I say, immediately returning to my normal voice. "Where are you guys?"

"I'm back at the hotel. Belle is having her dress altered. She should be back anytime, and we'll be there half an hour after that. I'm just about to start your book."

I jolt at that. "What book?"

"Uh… *Edict of Edith*. Wait, how many books do you have?"

I try not to let panic seep into the question, "How did you get my book?"

"The Sideways offices in Beverly Hills messengered several of your manuscripts to Belle. Britney says this one had her hooked from page one. She made me a copy. So what's it about?"

A different waiter, this one dressed as a Speedo tiger, brings us our crab cakes and carpaccio. Liz is already grabbing the first crab cake before he can put the plates down. "Um…it's about a stand up comedienne who has to go to Maine to take care of her dying grandmother and take over her Timber farm. But it's not done yet. I still have to rewrite it. Sideways shouldn't have sent it out."

"Is it a comedy?" Dave asks.

"Um…sort of?" I answer nervously.

"Great," Dave says, oblivious to the awkwardness in my voice. "You've always been really funny. I can't wait to read it. See you soon."

"No, wait…" I begin.

And he's gone. I turn off my phone and throw it into my bag. "Shit."

Liz dips the crab cake in sauce, then takes a huge bite. "What's wrong?" She says through a full mouth. "They're late?"

"Yes, but it's worse than that. Dave got a copy of *Edict of Edith*, and he's about to start reading it."

"So? It's an awesome book. He's going to be floored."

I glare at Liz. "And how do you think he's going to react to the ex-husband character?"

Liz winces. "Oh. Shit. He's not still named Dave in the book, is he?"

"I figured I'd change all the character names before it got published!" I say, weakly defending myself.

Liz looks pained *for* me. She looks around for our waiter. "Steve!" she yells, getting his attention by holding up her hand and waving. "We're going to need a few more Pussy Galores over here!"

Sixteen

Liz and I spend the next three hours dining on lobster, crab, prime beef, and something called a molten chocolate lava cake. Which would have been wonderful, if I hadn't been obsessing about Dave reading my book the entire time.

The music volume has gone up with every song for the last hour, so Liz and I have to scream over the music just to have a conversation.

"Brad Pitt or George Clooney?!" Liz yells to me.

I take a moment to think about her question. "I still think Johnny Depp is a perennial!" I yell back, downing the rest of my purple Pussy Galore and signaling to Steve that I need another drink.

"Take it easy, sailor!" Liz loudly tells me, referring to my empty glass. "You never know! She may show up, and you may have to work tonight!"

"It's almost eleven!" I yell back. "She's not coming. And even if she did, she'd be coming with Dave, who's reading my book, and I'm going to need to be pretty loaded for that!"

Two smarmy looking men in thousand dollar suits walk up to us. "Good evening ladies," one begins.

Liz turns to me. "What do you think?!" she yells. "Investment bankers?!"

"I'm going to go with lawyers!" I project, giving the men the once over.

They turn to each other, confused.

Liz then asks me, "What do you think?! Twelve o'clock boys?!"

"Nope," I answer, acting as though they're not there. "Not enough booze in the world!"

Liz smiles at the first guy. "I'm sorry! That's a hard pass! But thanks for playing!"

The first guy begins, "But all we said was..."

"Just being your winggirl here!" Liz interrupts. "It's almost eleven. You've only got another hour to make a Love Connection before your choices get severely limited. Don't waste time talking to us!" She searches the room. "See those two girls in the miniskirts? I guarantee at least one of them would love to get a right home tonight in your Porsche!"

"How did you know I drive..."

"Chop! Chop! Time's a wastin'."

The guys look over at the women Liz pointed to, give her a thumbs up, then leave to bother them.

I smile at Liz, shaking my head. "How do you always manage to do that?"

"Do what?"

"Reject men without them calling you a bitch?"

"The trick is to be honest without being disrespectful. Usually it works. And if a guy insists that he's not looking to get laid and wants to talk to me, then I see it as an opportunity to make him defend his entire sex and all of their foibles for the rest of the night. So for me, it's a win-win."

Steve appears, handing me another drink and Liz another beer just as, finally, Isabella makes her appearance.

You can tell when a big celebrity enters the room: first the crowd suddenly hushes, then everyone starts quietly gossiping and trying not to look.

She is flawless in a stunning blue dress that highlights her tan perfectly. And holding her hand is Dave, wearing a gray suit and a fake smile as she talks to a reporter from E!.

Noticing the E! reporter and film crew, I stumble to get out of the booth. Liz stops me. "What are you doing?"

"Going to see Isabella," I say, missing a step and falling back into the booth.

"Sweetie, you can't go over there like that. You're drunk."

"But the whole point of my being here tonight was so that Isabella and I could publicize *Edict of Edith*," I say, trying to stand up again.

"Why don't we let *her* do that," Liz says, gently pushing me back down. "You've had a lot to drink. If you go over there now, you're going to make a fool of yourself on national TV."

I hate it when she's right. I stare at Isabella and Dave, the picture perfect couple, beaming as they talk about their perfect life. As Isabella talks to the reporter, I watch Dave look around the room, see Liz and me, then break into a big smile. He excuses himself from Isabella and her entourage, then quickly makes his way through the crowd and upstairs to us.

"Liz!" he exclaims as Liz stands up to pull him into a bear hug. "My God. You look great!"

"Hard living will do that to a girl," she jokes, clearly happy to see him. "And you're late," she teases.

I love her for pointing that out to him without being accusatory.

"I know," Dave says, clearly not offended. He pulls away from the hug, and slides into the space between the two of us. "I am so sorry. Isabella took forever. Because there was going to be press tonight, she brought in her hair and makeup people, and they took over two hours to get her ready."

"She spent two hours getting ready and she looks *that* natural?" Liz asks, taking a seat.

"Two hours and six thousand dollars," Dave answers.

"Six thousand dollars?" Liz repeats. "How is that a thing?"

Dave smiles, shaking his head slowly. "Her hair person has a day rate of twenty five hundred, her makeup guy thirty five hundred. That's nothing. On the video I did for her, she had so many people buzzing around her that we spent over twenty five thousand dollars a day on hair and makeup."

Even I, who have dealt with celebrities for years, am stunned by that amount. "Isn't that the video where she gets out of bed at the beginning and her hair's flying everywhere?"

Dave smiles. "Yup. Took 'em four hours to get her ready for that setup." He looks around the room. "Where's your waiter?"

"Steve!" Liz yells. Steve walks up to us. "Good evening, Mr. Stevens. What can I get you?"

"It's Dave, not Mr. Stevens. Can I get that one from the Kona Brewing Company?"

"I'll be right back with it. Do you ladies need anything?"

"Just some water," I say meekly.

Okay Sam, sober up, sober up, sober up...

As Steve heads towards the bar, Dave turns to me. "On the plus side, Isabella's getting ready for the ball gave me enough time to I read the first few chapters of your book."

I'm about to barrage him with questions when Isabella races up to us. "Sam, I have the perfect title for my book: Weddings, Cake and Pussy Galore."

Liz chokes on her beer.

Isabella looks at us proudly. "What do those things have in common? They're all necessary for a great life."

Dave tilts his head and squints at her. "You want to tell people that you need Pussy Galore for a great life?"

"Oh. That's a good point," Isabella admits. She thinks for a moment. "How about Weddings, Cake and Cosmos?"

"But you don't drink Cosmos," Dave points out. "And you don't eat cake."

"But the public doesn't know that. And, frankly, it's none of their business."

"Hey, there's your title!" Liz deadpans, taking another sip of her beer. " *My Life: It's None of Your Business.*"

Isabella turns to Liz. "I'm sorry. And you are?"

Liz smirks. "I'm an orbiting planet in your universe."

Isabella looks confused.

"This is Liz," Dave says. "She's an old friend from college."

"Oh," Isabella says suspiciously, scrutinizing Liz with a jealous eye. "Did you sleep with her?"

Dave smiles, inexplicably amused by his future wife's possessiveness. "No, she was just a friend."

Isabella immediately breaks into a smile and gushes to Liz. "Oh, then you simply *must* come to our wedding."

Isabella's publicist walks up to her. "Miss De Leon, I've got *ET* here. Can you come with me please?"

As Isabella allows her publicist to take her hand and drag her away, she turns her head back, and says over her shoulder to Liz, "Give Sam your address. We can't wait to see you at the wedding."

And she's gone.

"Excellent!" Liz says. "I get to go to a big fancy wedding and I don't even have to dress like a giant blood clot."

A man comes to our table dressed like an acrobat. "Elizabeth?" he asks in an accent I can't quite place.

"Jean Claude!" she beams. "Tell me you have a trapeze for me to play with."

"Mais oui. And, more importantly, a net."

"Fun!" Liz exclaims, sliding out of her seat, grabbing one of the acrobat's hands, and leading him away. "Back soon guys!"

Dave and I watch her and the trapezist walk to a platform. "I didn't know Liz could…"

"Me neither." I say as we take a moment to watch the acrobat put Liz in a safety belt, then fly around with her.

And then, silence. Awkward, gut wrenching silence.

Steve appears with Dave's beer and my water. They have a quick conversation while I look around, avoiding eye contact. Once Steve leaves, Dave rests his chin onto his left hand. "Why do you look so nervous?" he asks, sounding amused.

"I'm not nervous," I insist.

I grab my water and down it in one gulp.

He doesn't call me out. "Okay, you're not nervous. So what's up?"

I sigh. Also rest my chin on my left palm. Then I awkwardly begin, "Not that I should care… But what do you think of the book?"

"It's really good," Dave says, suddenly animated.

"You sound surprised," I say.

"No, it's just…well, the stuff you ghostwrite for other people…most of it is so trite. But *Edith*… Why aren't you writing stuff like *Edith* all the time?"

"Because *Edith* won't be a bestseller and *Edith* won't pay my bills."

"I think you're selling yourself short," Dave argues. "Literary books break through all the time."

I shrug, not knowing how to take his statement. I nervously look around the room, unable to think of an adequate response. Dave takes a sip of his beer and watches me.

The pregnant pause lasts about as long as an elephant's pregnancy.

"Were we really that bad?" Dave finally asks, his voice serious.

I wince. "You did get to Chapter Six."

Dave nods.

I think about how to diplomatically answer him. "We had our moments."

Dave looks saddened by my answer. And I feel bad. So I lean in conspiratorially to confide, "I'll let you in on a little secret. She gets back together with her ex-husband in the end."

"Well, good," Dave says, leaning in to continue the mock secrecy, "because I think that Dave character has some good qualities."

I cringe. "I'm sorry. I'll change the character names. I promise."

"Nah, I like being in a book," Dave says. "Proof I existed on this planet." Then he asks me a pointed question. "So, will the Dad still be named Jim?"

"No," I state firmly. "I'm planning to just call him fuckhead."

Dave knows he hit a nerve, but continues anyway. "So what does your Dad think of the book?"

"I have no intentions of telling him about it."

"Sam, I'm not the guy's biggest fan, but don't you think…"

"He can find out about it the day it hits bookstores, along with everyone else," I state angrily, ready to start a fight.

Dave puts up his hands in surrender. "All right. Paws up. He's *your* Dad."

"Yeah. He is," I nearly spit. *Do not poke the bear, Dave.*

Dave wisely decides to change the subject. "I liked that word you used, Cerga," he says, pronouncing it SIR-guh, "to describe her friends from Boston."

"Thanks," I say. "Actually, it's pronounced CHAIR-guh. It's one of my favorite new words."

"CHAIR-guh. Good word. What language is it?"

"I don't know," I say, thinking I should look that up. "The word came from a friend of Liz's who's Yugoslavian, so I guess it would be Serbian or Croatian?"

"Do you elaborate more on it in *Edith*?"

"Yeah, it's sort of one of the themes in the book, the idea that you can choose your family, that people have to earn the right to be a part of a family, that blood isn't everything."

"That's a good theme," Dave says, leaning back to relax. "I mean, I get along really well with my family, but I'd like to think I have a Cerga too."

I follow his lead, leaning back to make a concentrated effort to relax.

"So, you think there's any way we can be part of each other's Cerga again?" he asks.

"Um…" I begin, a little startled by the question. "Sure. I mean… yeah."

Dave smiles. "Good. I like that."

And I smile back. Awkwardly at first, but then… I don't know. For a brief second, we have this moment. It feels like how I used to feel at our old apartment so many years ago. Nothing sexual, just super comfortable. Relaxed. Effortless.

I haven't felt this relaxed in awhile actually.

"That idiot reporter just asked me if I read the book my latest movie is based on," Isabella says, suddenly appearing like a jump scare and causing me to jolt out of my reverie. "Why would I read the book when the script is so much shorter?"

Apparently the question is rhetorical, because before anyone can answer, she turns to Dave and croons in her sexiest voice, "Baby, we have to go." Then normally to me, "Sam, everything's been comped, have fun with the limo. Can we meet Monday at the hotel? Say around ten?"

"Sure," I say.

"Perfect. We're in the Presidential Bungalow. It has its own pool and Jacuzzi, so bring a suit," she says, taking Dave's hand as he stands up to leave. "Oh, and I have this "Blow Me" List I need you to help me with."

I scrunch down my brows, confused. "I'm sorry. A what?"

"A "Blow Me" List. It's for this magazine that has celebrities write a top ten list of things they hate. I already wrote a bunch, but I need your help narrowing it down to ten."

"Um…okay."

Isabella takes Dave's arm and forcefully puts it around her waist. "So, ten o'clock Monday?"

"Absolutely. I'll see you then."

Dave gives me an apologetic look, waving goodbye as his fiancée pulls him away.

And for the first time in years, I'm a little sad to see him leave.

At which time, Liz's hands appear to descend from the sky, and she descends above my table. "It's actually all in the wrist," she yells to me happily. "Kind of like…"

"Please don't finish that sentence!"

Seventeen

Liz decides to hit a coffee shop with her Montreal Circus folk, so the limo drops me off around two, then they continue on without me.

I unlock the door, greet Zac the beagle, then head over to my bedroom to pass out.

I fall onto my bed, fully clothed. Zac jumps up, spins around a few times, then plops down next to me, his eyes asking me how my night went.

I pet him and he wags his tail vigorously. I pull my cell from my purse and dial Eric. His flight should have landed by now.

I get his voicemail, then the beep. "Hey, it's me. Tonight was fun, I guess," I lie. "Isabella is very nice and I'm excited to work with her," I lie some more. "But I wish you had been there, and I wish you were here. Call me when you land and your phone is charged and you're in bed so I can here your sleepy voice."

I realize I'm pausing to wait for him to pick up, something I still do out of habit from years of answering machines. Finally I say, "That's right, this is voicemail, not a machine. You can't hear me. Okay, well, I love you. Call me."

And I press the red button to hang up.

Damn.

I look at Zac, who is already curled up and asleep.

"You know why dogs can sleep so soundly?" I ask him quietly. He pops his eyes open to hear my answer. "Because they don't worry so much. You like a dog, you mount the dog, you move on. You don't worry about what that dog thinks about your novel. You don't start worrying about what a dog you've mounted thinks about your life choices. You don't worry about whether or not

125

someone will ever love you enough to have puppies. You don't worry about having a legacy, and you certainly don't debate whether or not to finish the bag of cookies on the kitchen counter."

Zac eyes me hopefully. "Seriously, I'm so still so full from dinner, I just can't."

Zac closes his eyes again. I stare at the ceiling, debating whether or not to wash off my makeup and get ready for bed or admit to myself that I'm wide awake.

I glance across the room and see the red diary on my desk.

Why do we save diaries? What's our intent? Is it a psychic footprint we secretly hope some great granddaughter will find a hundred years from now, maybe tucked away in an attic, ready for her to dust off and make us a little less forgotten? Do we keep them to make our past selves less forgotten to our current selves? What is this compulsion some of us have to climb into a moment from our past and relive it over and over again?

Maybe that compulsion comes because those moments are few and far between once you hit a certain age. I've had some phenomenal first kisses. But each one came with a price. A few cost me a lot long term, some had but a small price to pay. But there's always a price. Which is probably why some of us like to relive our memories through diaries: there's no price to pay. No three-hundred-dollar ticket to a sold-out concert. No exhausting twelve-hour flight to Paris with a stopover in North Carolina and a middle seat. No emotional scars. Just the bliss of remembering your favorite song played live, your adrenalin surging at seeing the Eiffel Tower for the first time, or that feeling of utter euphoria that swoops through your body when the guy you love thinks you're amazing.

I bring the diary over to my bed and open it to a page that is way more dog-eared than I remember.

And I am once again whisked away to a simpler time.

October 9ʰ

Dear Diary,

He kissed me! I went to the Red Herring tonight (again) to hear his band play (again). It's been over two weeks since we met and I was beginning to think he wasn't interested...

I'm sitting at the bar at Red Herring, sipping really cheap white wine and wanting to hide under a table. Almost 70 has just finished their set, and the band is packing up their gear. Dave looked at me several times during their songs. But is that because he thinks I'm cute or because there are all of twelve fans who showed up tonight?

I can't decide if I should slither out in embarrassment or throw up. Neither option really moves me closer to my goal.

"For all that is good and holy and pure, just grab him and kiss him," Liz says to me in exasperation.

"I can't. I don't want to look easy."

"For fuck's sake, you're a twenty year old virgin. No one thinks you're easy," Liz insists, sipping a Long Island Iced Tea from a giant tumbler. "And you guys have been together every night for weeks. Dave's got to put up or shut up."

"Do you think Dave's cute?" I ask her as we watch Joe and him walk off the stage with the last of their equipment.

"I *do* think Dave's cute," Liz confirms. "I also think that the point of spending every waking hour with someone is to have sex on tap. And if he ain't flowing, it's time to tap another keg."

"How enlightened," I mutter.

"I need another drink," Liz says, unfazed by my sarcasm. "Josh," she yells to the bartender, "can I get four shots of Sex on the

Beaches?" She turns to me and squints. "Sex on the Beaches? Or is the plural of beach, beach?"

"Why do you need four shots?" I ask her suspiciously.

"Time to find out if that keg can be tapped," she declares, raising her eyebrows up and down just as the boys get to us.

Josh leaves to make our drinks as the song *Point of No Return,* by Exposé, gets turned up louder over the speakers.

"Who the hell put on Expose?" Joe complains, walking up to us.

"What?" Liz asks sarcastically. "You don't think it's the ideal follow-up to your romantic ode to the world, *Fuck Me Baby?*"

"I told you that wasn't gonna go over well with the women in the audience," Dave says to Joe, shaking his head.

"You win," Joe concedes. "Next week, we'll change it to *Do Me Baby*."

"*Love Me Baby*," Dave pushes.

Joe shoulders fall. "Awwww...you mean every time I think 'fuck' I have to say 'love'? That's just so wrong."

"Shots all around," Josh says, placing the four purple shots on the bar. (Ah, God Bless fake IDs)

Liz hands a shot to each of us. "Joe, maybe you can help us out here. See that blonde guy in the green shirt in the corner."

Joe and Dave turn to see whom she's referring to. "I *might* have the hots for him," Liz continues. "Haven't decided yet. Now, Joe, pretend you're a nice guy. What could a girl say to you to show that she's interested, but not slutty?"

Joe sighs loudly. "What do you mean what would a girl say? Did any of you actually listen to the lyrics of *Fuck Me Baby?*"

"*Love Me Baby*," Dave corrects.

"Dude, I'm not a New Kid on the Block," Joe protests, taking his shot glass and downing the purple concoction. Then he returns his attention to Liz. "Love of my life, if you listened to the words in my song, you would know that all a woman has to do is walk up to a guy and say 'Hi.' If we're interested, we'll do the rest."

"Duly noted. But I'm not asking what a guy would do. How would a guy *feel* if the girl made the first move?" Liz asks, giving me a pointed look. "Would he assume the girl was easy?"

Dave shakes his head as Joe shrugs. "No./Yeah."

Dave turns to Joe. "It's amazing to me that your number is fifteen."

"Night's young," Joe says, smiling. "Liz, can I buy you another cocktail?"

Point of No Return fades out. A few seconds later we hear the first chords of *We Don't Have to Take our Clothes Off* by Jermaine Stewart waft from the speakers.

"This again?" Joe asks incredulously. "Okay, who's been messing with the jukebox?" he pulls out his wallet. "Does anyone have ones or quarters? We need to get some real music playing."

"We'll take care of it," Dave says, taking my hand, interlocking his fingers in mine, and gently leading me to the jukebox.

"Something in a Zeppelin or a Queen," Joe yells to us as we walk away.

Dave's holding my hand. Yay! I want to just stare at the floor and giggle coquettishly.

But what does it mean?

"Honestly, Jermaine Stewart?" Dave says to me under his breath. "Why poke the bear?"

"How do you know it was me?" I ask.

"I've seen your CD collection. So what did you choose as your third selection?

Please tell me you didn't pick Huey Lewis and the News," Dave jokes.

"No," I say defiantly. Then I self-consciously shrug my shoulders and turn my eyes away. "*Against All Odds.*"

I hear a loud sigh escape Dave's lips. "Cheese."

"Well, now we know why your number's way below fifteen," I tease.

Dave's eyes widen and his jaw drops. "What is *that* supposed to mean?" he asks, I think flirtatiously?

"That song is what we women would call a *closer.*"

"Oh please," Dave argues. "How can you think that? The lyrics are sappy…"

"Well I'll admit, it doesn't have the romance of, say, *Fuck Me Baby.*"

Dave pulls a one-dollar bill from his pocket and slips it into the jukebox dollar slot. "I can guarantee you that I can find three songs on this jukebox more romantic than *Against All Odds.* And none with the cheese factor."

I pull my hand away from his and lean against the jukebox flirtatiously, pretty much daring him to kiss me. "Go ahead."

He smiles and raises one eyebrow. The look makes me want to melt into a puddle. Then, he slowly brushes me aside. "Will you move, please?"

I do. Dave begins pressing the button to flip through the catalogue of CDs. He stops at a U2 cover.

"I can't stand U2. Move along."

"You don't like U2?! Everyone likes U2."

"I'd rather hear a cat mating than Bono's voice."

"You picked Moon Unit Zappa last night."

"*Valley Girl* is hysterical. I stand by my choice."

He flips through to the Beatles. "*In My Life,*" he says, then turns to me and smirks. "Is that acceptable to her ladyship?"

"I can live with that one," I say coyly.

My God, he's so cute. So cute! God, I just want to pin him to a wall and...

"How about *You're My Best Friend* by Queen?"

"Don't know it," I admit.

"You don't know... Man, I have so much to teach you."

I wish. And I wish he'd start teaching me right now.

Dave continues perusing the CDs. "All right. *Unchained Melody* by the Righteous Brothers." He presses the buttons for the final selection, then turns to me. "I have now officially found three songs with lyrics more romantic than *Against All Odds.*"

I shrug playfully as I look into his ocean blue eyes. "We'll see."

We have that moment where we're staring into each other's eyes, smiling, and waiting for the first kiss.

And then it doesn't happen.

"Come on," Dave says, taking my hand. He leads me to the dance floor, where a few couples fast dance to Jermaine. As the song ends, Dave gently takes my right hand in his left, places his arm around my waist, then waits.

In the silence that follows between songs, my body zings with electricity. He's touching me. He's dancing with me. He's practically hugging me.

"Maybe since I'm the last one who put in money, it'll start playing one of my songs next," he whispers in my ear.

"Don't count on it," I whisper back.

The first few bars of *Against All Odds* begins.

We dance anyway. Or should I say, we hug and dance. And he does everything right: when the drums crash he leads me around the dance floor quickly. Then, at the very end, when it's just the piano, he slowly dips me, staring into my eyes. "Take a look at me now," he croons.

And he kisses me. Right there in the dip. And he doesn't stop kissing me as he pulls me back up. And he doesn't stop kissing me during *In My Life*. And he doesn't stop kissing me during *You're My Best Friend*. And he only stops once, during *Unchained Melody*, to look me in the eye and say, "I've been wanting to do that for weeks."

I close the diary. Huh. I forgot how deliriously happy I was that night. How hopeful about my future. And there is a small part of me: like, nothing really... a few dreamy brain cells scattered in a cranium of reality... But there is a small part of me that wishes we had gotten past all the crap that happened years later. We did love each other once. Very much. There were moments in my life when he was everything to me and I was deliriously happy because, somehow, I was everything to him too. That's rare. Why didn't I hold on to that?

Why do we move away from our dreams just because the day-to-day work of keeping them gets hard?

Eighteen

That night, I couldn't sleep. Thoughts swirling around my head making me crazy. Not just about Dave and Eric, but also about being thirty, and how my life doesn't look the way I thought it would by now. You know, all the usual midlife crisis stuff we think about at four in the morning when it's silent out. (Maybe not midlife – I do hope to live past 60.)

Around dawn, I give up and decide to drive to the beach to go for a walk to clear my head.

Instead I wind up at the Beverly Hills Hotel, pounding on Vanessa's door. I need a little advice from an elder. (Although I would never call her that to her face.)

After a few minutes, she opens the door with her hair flying in all directions and wearing the signature pink robe with nothing underneath.

Vanessa says by rote, "Lovely to see you, dear. Can you please come back at one? I'm so sorry, but I had a late night and I'm not quite ready to begin the day yet. Why don't you go get yourself some coffee, and..."

"Thanks, but I'm going to need something stronger than that," I say, pushing past her with a sense of urgency she's never seen in me.

I walk to the middle of her living room, then stop dead in my tracks. I look around to see five different bottles of champagne in five ice buckets, and a bunch of banana peels flung around the room. "What happened here?"

Vanessa closes the door, then walks over to me. "Well, Darling, it was the strangest thing..."

"You know what? You can tell me later. Right now, I need your help," I say, going to one of the open bottles, and pouring myself a glass. "Why do people date their exes?"

"Easy prey?" Vanessa surmises. "Bored on a Tuesday night. Need someone to accompany you to a charity event. The guy can make your clitoris rocket to the moon just by…"

"Let me rephrase," I interrupt. "You married one of your exes twice. Why?"

"Oh. To get back at the bitch who stole him," Vanessa answers easily.

I open my mouth to ask another question, but Vanessa raises her index finger to silence me, then looks over my shoulder and says in baby talk, "Well, look who's up."

I turn to see a chimpanzee emerge from her bedroom, walk over to Vanessa, then climb into her arms. She holds him the way a mother would hold her two year old.

Normally, this would pique my interest, but I'm on a mission. "Why do people fall for their exes?"

Before she can answer, I continue, speaking in rapid fire, "For some inexplicable reason, I've been up all night thinking about my ex husband. And I'm freaked out. Does that mean I want him again? I mean, probably not. Probably I'm just holding on to some childhood dream that doesn't exist, right? But why? Why now? What the hell is wrong with me?"

Suddenly Drew Stanton, the hot young guy from that action movie last year with Tom Cruise, walks out of Vanessa's bedroom, fully dressed but a bit disheveled. "I owe you," he says to her, taking the chimp and giving her a kiss on the cheek. "I'll call you."

"No you won't, Darling. But I'll call you," she says sweetly, patting him on the cheek as the chimp climbs into his arms.

Drew notices me and says, "Hi," with a megawatt smile that shows me the guy is going to be a megastar.

I wave nervously as he and the chimp leave, closing the door behind them.

I don't get starstruck easily, but... Wow he is pretty! I turn to Vanessa. "I take it when you stay up all night it's not to think about your ex-husband."

"Oh, him?" she asks, waving off the door where Drew just left and making herself comfortable on the sofa. "A dear friend in need of a small favor. Your story's much more interesting. Now I'm going to need more information on the ex. Dave, is it? Is he a breast man, or a leg man?"

"I don't want him back. I want to stop thinking about him."

Vanessa makes a show of turning to look at my ass. "I'm guessing leg man."

"Actually, yes. But that's not my point. Even if I were interested in him, which I'm not, he's getting married in less than two weeks. Do you think this sudden obsession has something to do with my relationship with Eric getting more serious?"

Vanessa considers this. "Possibly. Did he divorce you or did you divorce him?"

"I divorced him."

"Oh!" She exclaims, brightening. "Then it has nothing to do with him. Your life is great, but you're not twenty anymore, and you're thinking back to the road less travelled. He reminds you of that time in your life when everything was shiny and new and hopeful. I wouldn't overthink this. Just pretend he's dead and move on."

"Kind of hard to do that. I'm ghostwriting his fiancée's autobiography."

Vanessa looks flummoxed. "I don't understand. The only two women you're writing for are me and ooooohhhh noooo... He's engaged to that whore?"

I nod, wincing.

Vanessa takes a deep breath. "Then I take back everything I said. You are totally in love with this man and we need to get him back. Preferably at the wedding. And in front of paparazzi."

"You're not helping."

She glances to her left, a wicked smile creeping onto her face to rival *The Grinch Who Stole Christmas*. "You'll name your first born Karma. Or Vanessa, if it's a girl."

We hear a knock on her door. Vanessa stands to answer it, by I'm closer so I open it. Isabella charges in, wearing workout shorts so tight I can see a tampon tucked into her teeny front pocket. "Sam, I need you to... Ah!" She throws her hands up to her face. "Don't hit me!" she screams in terror at Vanessa.

Vanessa stares at her with preternatural calm. "Why would I do that, dear?"

Isabella looks confused. She puts her hands down and answers, "Because I slept with your husband, stole him from you, then embarrassed you publicly by being photographed with a giant engagement ring on my finger the day your separation was announced?"

"Well, yes, dear. I'll admit that would make social engagements between us rather awkward."

"Isabella, what are you doing here?" I ask.

"I was out jogging and saw you come in. I thought I'd come over and see if you wanted to start that *Blow Me List* now, instead of waiting until Monday."

Isabella turns to Vanessa, clearly scared of her. "I'm really sorry about your husband. Please don't hurt me."

Vanessa looks past her to me, gets an evil look on her face again, then answers Isabella. "Darling, that's all water under the bridge. Do you know what would really soothe my ego? If you could have the honor of my presence at your wedding."

My eyes nearly pop out of their sockets.

Vanessa smiles. "I hear your new love is absolutely perfect for you and I would be honored to be able to dance at your wedding."

Isabella is so excited, she starts flapping her arms up and down like a bird. "Oh my God! Do you know what would be even better? You should totally be one of my bridesmaids!"

Oh, for Christ's sake...

"Sam's also one of my bridesmaids. You could be twinsies!" I throw up my hands in exasperation as Isabella continues, "Vittorio Valpicelli is doing the dresses. They're maroon red, and I know he could make one for you that would be make you look utterly spectacular!"

I need to put a stop to this now. "Vanessa, you don't have to..."

Vanessa waves me off. "What fun!" she exclaims to Isabella, "I simply can not wait to see what confection he creates for me. Now, I'm afraid Sam and I were right in the middle of a chapter I am writing: *How to Break into Hollywood Without Sleeping Your Way to the Top*. It's an absolutely revolutionary idea for some women."

"Oh," Isabella says innocently, missing the insult completely. "Would it be possible for me to meet with Sam later, around nine o'clock?"

"Well, of course I'm not her social secretary," Vanessa says, then turns to me. "How's your morning looking dear?"

"I don't think that's a good idea," I say to Isabella, "I haven't slept and I'm a bit worse for wear..."

"Perfect! Meet me at the Presidential Bungalow at nine. And bring your swimsuit." She turns to Vanessa. "I can't wait to put you into a bridesmaid's gown. Tell me, do you like feathers?"

"Not even on a chicken, dear," Vanessa says, subtly pushing Isabella out the door.

Vanessa closes the door behind her, then turns to me with a devilish gleam in her eye. "I haven't busted up a wedding in ages," she says, rubbing her hands together in fiendish glee.

Then she looks me up and down. "Don't take this the wrong way, but if you're going to compete with that body, you might want to take up jogging."

Nineteen

Two hours and three Red Bulls later, I head to the gift shop, buy the magazine with the latest "Blow Me" List, then knock on the door of the Presidential Bungalow.

Isabella answers, looking like a Bond girl in a gold lame bikini and matching gold heels. "Great! You're here! Why don't you get changed and I'll meet you out by the pool?"

I don't have the self-confidence to wear a bikini in a Macy's dressing room, so I certainly will not be wearing a bathing suit next to sex personified. I have rehearsed my cop out, "Since I can't really write and swim at the same time, I think it would be best if I just stay dressed the way I am."

Isabella shrugs. "I wish I had the self confidence to wear what you wear. To possess the inner peace to not care what society thinks."

As we walk out to her pool area, I decide to ignore the barb and subtly look around for Dave. "Is Dave here?"

Isabella slips off her heels and climbs into her private pool. "He's still in bed. It's like if he doesn't sleep at least five hours, he's Oscar the Grouch all day. Okay, so this is supposed to be the top ten things that make you want to say, 'Blow Me.' I have some thoughts."

As Isabella closes her eyes and relaxes, I take a seat at the glass table next to her. "Great," I begin, holding out the magazine to her. "I got a copy of the 'Blow Me' list published this month, just so we have an idea of what they're looking for…"

"I'm too tired to read," Isabella says dreamily, not opening her eyes. "Just take this down: Number 1. Valets who park my Ferrari out of sight."

So I'm not even a writer now, I'm a stenographer. Fantastic. "Hold on," I say, tossing down the magazine and pulling out a pen and notepad I snagged from the front desk. "Valets... Ferrari... got it."

"Number 2. Chefs who refuse to let me go off menu."

Just write it up Evans. Think quarter of a million dollars. "Done."

"Number 3. Valets who park my Lamborghini out of sight."

I shake my head ever so subtly as I continue to write. "Little bit of a duplicate..."

"Number 4. Cats."

I look up. "The musical?"

"The animal. Love me unconditionally or get the Fuck out."

"Hmm," I say. "You actually might be onto something there."

"Number 5. Valets who park my Rolls..."

"Okay," I interrupt. "I think you might be missing the theme of this list."

Isabella opens her eyes. "The theme is annoyance, right? It's supposed to be things that annoy me."

"True, but I think the editor wants things that annoy everyone," I say, opening the magazine, and showing her Page 32. "This 'Blow Me' list that includes things like fat free ice cream and Star Trek junkies."

Isabella squints at me. "What's fat free ice cream?"

"It's the stuff you eat when you want to binge on ice cream, because the guy you had the great first date with still hasn't called, but you don't want to eat too much and gain weight, in case he does call."

She looks at me blankly. "Do men do that?"

"Do what?"

"Say they're going to call and then not?"

"Some do."

"Well, that's awful!" Isabella cries out. "That's like when a casting director says you have a call back and then your agent never hears from them again."

"Exactly!" I say, pointing at her.

"Okay. Number 5. People who say they'll call and don't?"

I smile. "Awesome. Let's call that Number 1."

"No. At least Number 2. I need to keep Cats."

"Although I love your point, millions of people have cats."

"Millions of people have leggings too. They're wrong."

"How about number 2. People who can't love unconditionally?"

"I want cats."

"Fine. Number 3. Cats."

"Yay," Isabella says, clapping like a preschooler. "4. Women who wear chipped heels."

My shoulders slump. "I'm still not sure your getting the gist of this assignment..."

Isabella moves her lips towards her left ear, a la Elizabeth Montgomery in *Bewitched*. "People who shop at Walmart?"

"Why don't we try a new approach? As a ghostwriter, I can take your ideas and organize them in a way that the average reader might find either relatable or funny. Give me a person you don't like."

"Puff Daddy."

"Okay, I could see that. He's controversial. Why don't you like Puff Daddy?"

"He thinks I can't sing. Said he'd have to Auto-Tune me just to produce anything."

He's probably not wrong, but...

"Great! How's this? Number 4: Friends who don't support each other. Next."

"Donald Trump."

"Soooo…do you want to go with people with money but no class? Men who cheat on their wives? Toddlers who need to see their name on everything? Liars?"

Isabella thinks about it. "That last one."

I write it down. "Liars. An excellent Number 5. Next."

"Ashley," Isabella says, clearly irritated.

I look over at her. "Who?"

"She's this eighteen year old at Neiman's who's always trying to sell me eye cream. She calls me ma'am. But when she says ma'am, she says it like, 'Old Bitch, get out my way. I'm the center of attention now. And I will steal your man.'"

I think about a way to spin that. "Number 6. Eighteen year olds who call me ma'am. I think most women will relate to that."

Isabella's face lights up. "Oooo, can you do a few that make me sound smart?"

I take a deep breath. "Um…sure. Smart in what way?"

"You know like in that article you wrote about how people use words wrong."

My face lights up. "Oh…you mean like *literally*," I cheerfully write, "Number 7. People who use the word *literally* when they mean *absolutely*, or *very*, or *quickly*. 'Her face *literally* lit up'? If that were true, that poor girl's face would be on fire."

"Are people going to understand that?"

"Wait, I'm on a roll. Number 8. People who use the word *utilize* when they mean *use*."

"What's utilize mean?" Isabella asks, confused.

"Use. Number 9. People who don't know the members of the Supreme Court, but can recite every Seinfeld episode by heart."

"Now you're making me sound *too* smart. Pick one of those, and throw the other two out."

Damn! I was really getting into a groove. She has a point, though. God forbid I should make her sound too smart. I cross out numbers eight and nine. "All right. But I'm keeping *literally*. Who's next?"

"People who confuse me with Salma Hayek."

Yeah, I'm sure the average woman would really hate that.

"How about we rephrase that to, People who don't see the real me," I suggest. "What else?"

"Bill Cosby!"

I stop writing. "America's favorite Dad. Can I ask why?"

"I get a sick sense around him."

"You mean a sixth sense."

"No, I mean sick. But I might have just eaten a bad clam."

"I really don't think you want to take on America's Favorite Dad."

She shrugs. "Your call. Oh! The Golden Raspberry Awards!"

"Why?"

She frowns. "Because I keep winning."

Fair enough. "How about: Number 9. The voting members for the Golden Raspberry Awards. I'm sorry I did *The Bodyguard 2*. Get over it."

"Perfect. And Number 10. Howard Stern."

"Why?" I ask.

Isabella shakes her head. "Oh, he knows."

Mm...kay. "How about this?" I suggest. "Number 10. People who are so boring, they have to quote Howard Stern at parties."

"Great! We're done!" Isabella exclaims. "So what are you doing later today?"

Before I can answer, I hear Dave yell from inside, "God damn it, Belle! What's the matter with you?"

He suddenly appears in the doorway, wearing nothing but dark blue silk boxers.

"The Hotel Ritz in Paris left us a message..." he begins, angrily. Then he sees me and forces himself to calm down. "Oh, hi. What are you doing here?"

I force a smile and give him a small wave. "Helping Isabella with her 'Blow Me' list."

"Oh," he says distractedly, then looks at Isabella, and with gritted teeth asks, "Sweetheart, can I see you inside for a moment?"

I see a look I haven't seen on Isabella's face before: worry. "Well, Sam and I were just..."

"Now," Dave growls, turning on his heel and disappearing inside.

Yikes! I've seen that look before.

I do NOT miss that look.

Isabella quickly gets out of the pool and throws on a bathrobe. "Let's meet at noon tomorrow for book stuff. You can see yourself out."

And she nervously runs inside.

I look at my watch. 9:05. I'd say it's time for bed.

Twenty

Of course during the five minutes I was with Isabella and Dave, I missed Eric's call. "Got your message. Calling from the hotel, which may have shown up as a private number, which might be why you're not picking up... Anyway, my day is packed. Conference meeting, plus my phone seems to be dead, so I need to hit a Nokia Store and get it fixed, plus the flight was awful, so I need to sleep. But I love you and will definitely call you later... Oh, and also, I'm really glad you and Libby are getting along... Okay, love you. Bye."

It's now eleven in the morning, and I still can't sleep. I toss and turn, bouncing my thoughts between missing Eric and thinking about Dave. I hate myself for noticing, but he looked good in those boxers. Like, "Yet another example of how he's way ahead of me in life since our divorce" good.

He always had a hot body. Athletic, but not gross Arnold Schwarzenegger *more muscles that I know what to do with* athletic. More like runner's athletic.

Which stands to reason, because Dave is a runner.

Back when we were dating, then married, I frequently got annoyed with the running. Dave woke up every morning to run. This wouldn't have been a problem, except that every few months he would try to get me to join him. At six in the morning. Sometimes in the rain. When we moved to Boston, sometimes in the snow.

Getting me to wake up at six in the morning in order to jog is a little like trying to teach a pig to sing: it ain't gonna work, and you're just going to annoy the pig.

It would always go the same way. The night before, Dave would tell me how great it was going to be for us to go running together. I would always agree: visions of myself as a size two dancing in my head. It would be fun! We would bond and talk while we ran. And after a vigorous workout, we would get cappuccinos, then take a shower together, then have sex. It always worked the same way in my mind: Heaven. And it always worked the same way the following morning: Hell.

I mean, just the first ring of Hell: not awful, but no one wants to be there.

Dave would wake me at 5:55, and I would look at the clock, then in irritation remind him that it's not six yet. He'd then wake me at six. And six-fifteen. And six-thirty. After five or ten more minutes of my refusing to leave my warm and toasty bed, he would yell from the living room, "Okay, I'm going to go without you!" And I would finally jump out of bed, throw on jogging clothes, and begin our little adventure.

I'd spend the first few blocks running as hard as I could just to keep up with him. Even in zero degree weather, I would be sweating rivulets. Dave would look over. "You're not winded yet, are you?" he'd always ask.

"No," I would always pant.

"Good. Let's pick up the pace."

And then he'd run ahead of me. And then he'd turn around and make fun of me for being out of shape, which would lead to an argument that usually included me yelling, "Well, what the hell's the matter with you that the only way you can think of to get hot and sweaty in the morning is by running?"

And then I'd turn around and limp home while he finished his run.

Then he'd come home, we'd apologize to each other profusely, and we'd agree never to try to run together again.

Until a month or two later.

But I gotta admit, clearly it works for him. Who knew that to have a twenty year old's body at thirty all you had to do was run?

Hmmm.

The house is dead silent. I tiptoe over to Liz's room, and knock on the door quietly.

No response.

I knock louder.

Still nothing.

I open the door and silently walk in. Liz is out cold in her bed, wearing pajamas, Zac curled up beside her.

"Wake up," I whisper.

Liz moans a little, then rolls over, turning her back to me.

"Are you awake?" I say a little louder.

She's dead to me.

Finally, I pull out the big guns. "I think I hear Fred coming for the dog."

"I have custody until Monday?!" Liz yells, bolting upright in bed. She looks around, confused.

"Did I wake you?" I ask.

She glares at me.

"Want to go running?" I ask, a hopeful smile plastered on my face.

At this, Zac jumps up and start running around the room excitedly. Liz sighs in exasperation. "What time is it?"

"Eleven o'clock. I'm taking up running again."

"What on Earth for?"

"I figure if I lose one pound a day for the next thirteen days, I should look pretty good in my bridesmaid's dress. But I can't do that without running. Besides, I just saw Dave this morning in nothing but silk boxers and…"

"Stop," Liz commands, putting up the palm of her hand. Then she puts her hands on my shoulders and looks me dead in the face. "I'm going to pass down some advice my mother gave me, and her mother gave her: No man is worth running for."

"Eric is, and I want to look great for the wedding," I tell her, my voice jacking up to rapid fire. "I figure today we'll run the first mile, walk the next three, then finish off with a one mile run. Tomorrow, we'll alternate between three miles running and two of walking. If I increase the run by a mile a day for the next twelve days…"

"My God, I'm exhausted just listening to you. How much coffee have you had?"

"Two pots… And two Red Bulls. So can we go?"

Liz sighs loudly. "I hate you so much right now."

That means yes.

Five minutes later, I am suited up in a dark blue sweat suit and ready to begin my new life as a lithe runner. As Liz, Zac and I leave the house, I race down the driveway. Hunh, Hunh, Hunh… I hear myself breathing.

"You're going too fast!" I hear Liz yell behind me.

"No such thing!" I yell back, thrilled with myself for having the fortitude to do this.

And for about four minutes, I kind of missed running. The wind rushing through my hair, my heart pumping, knowing my thighs are getting smaller with every step I take. I don't know why I ever quit running. I am woman, hear me…

I roar in pain from a leg cramp.

A little sooner than I thought, but it's fine. Discomfort is good. No pain, no gain and all that. Well, no lose, whatever, the point is...

My throat is starting to burn. Should have brought some water with me. Can I feel my lungs?

Forget about that – push through the pain! I too can look like Isabella! I can have the trim waist, sculpted calves, perfect butt. All I need to do is work at it. Rome was not built in a day, and if I push through...

Oh, good Christ, I've never wanted water so much in my life, and my right calf just seized out from under me. I stop abruptly, grabbing my stomach. I'm breathing so hard it hurts. Ignoring the leg cramps, I start up again, running for a few more steps...

Until I get to the next street and fall over from exhaustion. I'm breathing so hard, I think I'm going to have a stroke.

Liz and Zac slowly saunter up to me. "Half a mile. Congratulations, Flo-Jo."

"Get away from me," I pant, waving my hands frantically. "You're hogging all of my oxygen."

Liz sits down next to me. She hands me her thirty-two ounce water bottle. I take it and gulp greedily.

Then I spit it out. "That's not water."

"Nah, it's a mimosa. I figured with all this physical exertion we should reward ourselves with a drink."

"I'm gonna die," I say, panting for breath. "I think I see my Great Aunt Mary calling me to the light."

Liz looks up at the street sign. "Let's see. You made it to Carrington. So, if you increase your training by one mile every day for the next twelve days..."

"I'll have a heart attack by Tuesday," I pant.

"That's pretty much what I'm thinking, yeah," Liz agrees, taking her mimosa bottle from me and taking a sip.

Liz and I take a moment to rest. I bask in the silence up here in the hills.

"So are you ready to admit you have a crush on him?" Liz finally asks.

"I'm not doing this for Dave. I'm doing it for Eric. Wait! No! Myself! I'm doing it for myself."

"Sure. Why not?" Liz says, standing up and putting out her hand to me. "Now, do you need help up?"

"No. I'm okay," I say, standing up. At first, my knees are shaky. Then they just give out. "Nope! Not okay! Charlie horse! Charlie horse!"

Liz puts my arm around her shoulder, lets me lean on her, then helps me limp home.

Twenty-one

Once home, I take a quick shower and pass out. I fell asleep around two, but not before picking up the red diary, and reading myself to sleep...

January 9th
Dear Diary,
Yesterday, I finally became a woman. Okay, well maybe not, but I did have sex...

"Do you want to turn around?" Dave asks me.

"Nooo," I say, sighing and crossing my arms. "We've gone this far, might as well get to where we're going."

Dave and I are in his 1979 Honda Accord, driving to Las Vegas. This is supposed to be our "romantic getaway weekend," and by that I mean the weekend I lose my virginity.

There's a weird stigma about being a virgin at my age. Guys think it's cool you're a virgin, until you hit a certain birthday. Problem is, no one has agreed on which birthday that is. Nineteen? Twenty? Thirty? Most people seem to think that if you have sex at fifteen, you're a slut (unless, of course, you're a guy, in which case you're a stud). But anytime after that has people debating. And while they may agree that a forty-year old virgin would be an oddity, at what age does society decide you're going to be a spinster?

Dave and I had "the conversation" about five weeks into our relationship. We had been making out like crazy, ever since that wonderful night in October, and had been circling around some bases. Then one night, Liz headed out on a date, leaving Dave and me alone in our apartment. On the way out the door, Liz joked, "Remember, save it for the Four Seasons."

And the conversation began: "What did she mean by that?" "Well, I'm a virgin." "But you had a boyfriend in high school." "Yeah, but I thought that would make me a slut." "Okay, but your boyfriend freshman year…" "Gay." "Sophomore year?" "All the guys I dated were for less than three months." "Wait, we have to wait three months?" Blah, blah, blah.

Tonight is officially our three month anniversary. And his father had a free weekend at Caesar's Palace that he gave to Dave, so that's where we were headed.

That Friday, we headed out to Vegas. Of course, we didn't realize that on Friday afternoon, everyone in L.A. leaves town, so after four hours we were barely out of the California mountain area.

Then an hour after that, just outside of Barstow, we got a flat tire. Dave managed to get us to a Costco, to get the tire changed, but that meant waiting around another few hours, and caused our romantic three-month anniversary meal to be a slice of Costco pizza and a fountain drink.

Now we are on our way again, but it's dark, and I'm cranky, and I just want to go home.

So when he asks, "Do you want to turn around?" Naturally I answer honestly, "Nooo. We've gone this far, might as well get to where we're going."

It's pitch black and getting cold. I turn on the heater.

"Doesn't work," Dave apologizes.

I force a smile. "No problem."

"I mean, we live in California, so I never bothered to fix it."

"That makes sense," I say, silently cursing him in my mind.

"I'm really sorry," Dave says.

"You've been saying you're sorry for the last five hours. It's fine," I say, although really I don't mean it, and I don't even vaguely want to have sex with him tonight.

"Yeah. It's fine," Dave repeats sarcastically. "That's why you have that look on your face."

"I do not have a look on my face."

"And the tone…"

"I have no tone. There is no tone," I insist, just now hearing the tone of my voice to realize there is a tone. And then, "What the hell is that?"

Dave cranes his neck forward to look through the windshield at white pieces of paper fluttering at us. "I don't know. There must be a truck ahead of us or something."

He turns on his high beams to get a better look. "Shit," I say, panic creeping into my voice. "That's snow."

"No," Dave assures me calmly. "We're in the middle of the desert. It doesn't snow in the desert."

I open the window and put my hand out. "You wanna bet?" I ask, bringing my hand in to show him the melting snowflakes. "This is snow."

Dave eyes widen as he looks at my hand. "Oh crap." He focuses on the road, suddenly looking a little scared. "I don't have snow chains. Okay, Primm is in twelve miles. There are hotels there."

Now I'm scared. "Are we going to make it twelve miles?"

"We'll be fine," Dave says, reaching over to hold my hand. "This is a light snow. We'll be fine."

By the time we get to Primm, we are in the middle of a full-blown blizzard, with visibility of about zero. We make a left into the parking lot, parking in front of a cheap replica of a Medieval Castle.

As we get out of the car, a fierce wind blows my car door shut before I can get out. I push my door open again, this time using my legs, quickly get out, and let the car door slam shut a second time while I race with Dave into the hotel lobby.

When Dave opens the door to the lobby, tobacco smoke billows out. We go in anyway.

I can hear coins crashing down into metal containers and the sounds of electronic "pings" as people play slots. Dave and I shiver as we make our way through a casino to the front desk, where a woman wearing a polyester shirt and the name tag "Tammy" taps away on her computer. "Welcome to…!" and she tells us the hotel name. "Have you seen the Bonnie and Clyde death car?"

The what now?

"Not yet," Dave answers through chattering teeth. "Can we get a room please?"

"Yes, sir," Tammy answers cheerfully. As she begins the process of checking us in, I turn to more closely examine the casino. I have never been in a casino before, and somehow I was imagining something not quite so…sad. A man in a wheelchair holds a large plastic cup with the hotel's name on it while he pulls a slot machine arm over and over again. Next to him is a large older woman with a bleached blonde beehive and plastic earrings. She holds a beer in one hand and a cigarette in the other, has a look on her face that I can only describe as "comatose."

I sigh. This is my big romantic weekend? This is what I've saved myself for?

"I'll be back in a second," I say, walking to the roulette wheel. Huh – it appears you really can bet on 00. Something to be said for those numbers: kind of how my day is going.

Dave appears next to me. "I got us a deluxe room. Why don't you stay here and I'll go get the bags?"

About five minutes later we are in our "deluxe room," which features two queen beds covered with cheap bedspreads, a stained carpet worn out in places, and a smell so overwhelming it might kill a goat. I go to the window heater to crank it up as high as it will go as Dave tosses our suitcases onto one of the beds. He sniffs the room. "It smells like cigarettes. I wonder if we could ask for another room."

I put my hands over the hot vents. "It has heat and it's dry. I say we don't mess with an already fucked up day."

I notice something through the open space of the curtains. I pull back a curtain to see, "Huh. There's a pool."

Dave walks over and looks out the window. He smiles. "Wow. I wonder if it's a shallow pool?"

"Why?"

He flashes me a smile. "Then we could go skating."

That smile is everything, and I melt, happy to be with him despite everything. But still a little sad. Dave puts his arms around me. "So, are you hungry?"

"Not really," I say.

"Wanna go get a drink?"

I shrug. "Um…we could. Do you want to get a drink?"

"Well, I did see a sixty year old woman singer in the lounge crooning 'Having my Baby.' Hard to resist that."

I force a smile.

"You look sad," Dave says.

I shrug. "No, I'm fine."

He rubs my shoulder and gently asks, "What's wrong? Talk to me."

I shrug again. "Well, it's just…" I look around the room. "I mean, I love you, and I know you tried really hard, and I love you, but…" I sigh. "I just didn't picture losing my virginity in a place like this. This isn't my dream of how the night would go."

Dave kisses me on the forehead and pulls me into a hug. "No one said we had to do anything tonight."

"Come on," I say, pulling out of the hug. "Three month rule. I know you've been waiting."

I walk away from him because even though we've been together three months, I still get nervous around him. I point to my suitcase. "I even bought new lingerie…"

"Well, if you bought new lingerie, I guess we're gonna *have* to do it tonight," Dave jokes.

"You know what I mean," I continue. "I'm going to feel like I'm disappointing you if we don't tonight. But I'm gonna feel like this is all wrong if we do."

Dave squints his eyes and puckers his lips, thinking. Then he grabs my hand. "Let's go," he says.

I let him pull me to the door. "Where are we going?"

"You're right, tonight is not the night. Your first time should be perfect. But we're having a perfectly imperfect day, so let's go with that. First stop: the worst greasy food we can find."

And he brings me down to the lobby, to a coffee shop that serves up a cheap shrimp cocktail, then a plate of steak and eggs that costs less than five dollars. (Both surprisingly good).

And I spend the next hour laughing. Because no matter what is going on, Dave can always make me laugh. At one point, I laugh so hard, I have tears streaming down my face.

Next, we make our way to the lounge, where a bad singer with frosted hair sings, "Baby Don't Get Hooked on Me" by Mac Davis, then "What's New Pussycat" by Tom Jones. And we drink cheap champagne, and dance to Dave's request: *Against All Odds* by Phil Collins.

And later that night, in an overheated hotel room, in a queen size hotel bed with a cheap bedspread, next to a nightstand with two plastic cups filled with cheap champagne, and a view of a silent snowstorm outside, I made love to my boyfriend for the first time.

And it was perfect.

I close the red diary. Weird thing about dreams – every once in awhile, if you're lucky, reality is just so much better.

Twenty-two

I wake up at seven the next morning. Geez, I knew I was tired, but I didn't realize I was *that* tired. I grab my cell phone from the nightstand to check my messages.

Nine messages. Shit.

The first one is from Eric. "Hey there! Okay, first round of meetings over and I have a new cell phone. A normal phone. They showed me one with a keyboard. So weird, who would need that? Anyway, call me back or page me. I have a dinner, but I can sneak away for a few minutes. Wish you were here — you'd love this hotel. Love you."

Beep. "Hi Sam, it's Libby. I have to go out of town for a retreat tomorrow for a few days, and I need you to come with me. I'll pick you up around ten. Bye."

Beep. "Darling, it's me," Vanessa says. "Listen, fabulous gossip. That ex of yours just stopped by to see if you were here. He is yummy. And I'm pretty sure he just had a fight with his future betrothed. Call me."

Beep. "Hey, it's me," Dave says, sounding dejected. "Listen, I'm kind of embarrassed that you saw that. It's just..." He pauses. "You know what? It's fine. Forget it happened. Love you, bye."

Did he just say, I love you?

Beep. "Me again." Dave. "That last thing I said was habit. Don't read into it, okay? I mean, not that you would... Never mind, I'm not making sense. Okay, Bye."

Beep. "It's Libby again. Did Dave happen to call you? Just wondering. See you tomorrow at ten. Bye."

Beep. "Me again, darling." Vanessa. "Fab news. Isabella just came by to drop off this hideous bridesmaid's dress and to make

158

sure she could steal you from me for a couple of days while she's out of town on some retreat. I said fine. Anyway, I got her talking, and it turns out that she had this huge fight with Dave because he wanted to go to Kauai on their honeymoon and she wanted to go to Europe. Apparently, she just went ahead and booked the hotels and flights to Europe without telling him, and he flipped out, and they ended up fighting about the whole wedding. He called her a Bridezilla. Isn't that a fabulous name? Should be the title of a movie. Anyway, FYI."

Beep. "Hey there," Eric says sleepily. "I called Isabella to see if you were with her, and she said you were up all night, so I assume you're out cold." I hear him yawn loudly. "Just wanted to say good night. Talk to you tomorrow. Love you."

Beep. "Goood morning!" Happy Eric. "Actually, it's five a.m. there, but my meetings are about to start, so I figured I'd try you one last time. I'll call you later."

Beep.

I erase all of my messages, play phone tag with Eric once again, then realize I have a caffeine headache. Ow, ow, ow...

I walk out of my room to see Liz at the doorway fighting with Fred. "Fine. You're getting married. What the hell do you want me to say?" she almost spits at him.

Fred oozes his usual narcissistic smarm. "Well, I'd like you to admit that it's killing you inside."

"Oh. My. God. What did I ever see in you?"

As I walk pass by them, Liz says to me, "Dave called our landline twice yesterday. I told him you were asleep both times."

"Thank you," I say, ignoring their fight to head into the kitchen...

I putter over to the cupboard, pull out my "Frasier" mug, and pour myself a cup of coffee.

"Sam?" Isabella says, putting her hand on my shoulder.

"Ah!" I yell, nearly spilling my coffee. "Isabella, what are you doing here? How'd you get in here?"

"Your roommate let me in. I had a fight with Dave and I need some private time. I'm going on a retreat to collect my thoughts and rejuvenate my spirit, and I want you to come with me. My Ferrari's outside."

I stare at her, dumbfounded. "Isabella, it's seven o'clock in the morning. You said you were coming at ten. I haven't even had my coffee yet."

"I understand. But it was an emergency."

A spa emergency?

"Isabella..." I begin.

"You know what? Can you hold that thought?" she says, patting me on the shoulder. "Something's really bugging me."

She turns around, her four-inch heels clicking across our wooden entryway until she gets to Liz and Fred. I follow her in my bunny slippers.

Liz is in mid-yell. "No, you can not have the dog for your honeymoon! And what kind of person honeymoons in Pittsburgh?"

Isabella taps Liz on the shoulder. "Excuse me, Sweetie, but I am really good at reading men. Can I say one quick thing to your ex?"

Fred and Liz stop talking. "Yes," Fred says, eyeing her lecherously.

Isabella turns to Fred. "I've been listening to Liz talking, and I've been listening to you talking, and I think that what you're trying to say is that you're still in love with her, you really want to be with her, and these engagement theatrics are just your way of hurting her so that she realizes how much she misses you and loves you. Am I right?"

Fred is stunned by Isabella's psychoanalyses. "Wow. I mean… maybe."

Isabella continues. "And your only flaw is that you like to sleep with other women. And you don't think that you should be punished for that. Because you're such a catch, what woman *wouldn't* understand that she has to share you?"

"Yes!" Fred says, excited to have a woman finally understand him for the first time.

Isabella turns to Liz. "And Liz, I think what you've been trying to say to him is this…"

And Isabella smacks Fred dead in the face.

As Fred goes flying backwards and out the open front door, Isabella turns to Liz. "That was what you were trying to say to him, wasn't it?"

"You're dead on, Girl," Liz tells her in admiration.

Fred, flat on his ass, puts his hand up to his mouth, looking for blood. He stands up, looking at Isabella in shock. "I could sue you."

"You *could*," Isabella agrees. "But I'm five two and a hundred pounds soaking wet, so no one would believe you. And, of course, I have three eye witnesses who would denounce you for the terrible liar that you are."

Fred looks through the doorway at me and Liz. And he starts to walk menacingly back inside. "I only see two other bitches…"

"Oh, Ron!" Isabella sings out sweetly.

A large hand suddenly smacks down on Fred's shoulder. Fred immediately switched from angry to scared.

"Have you met Ron?" Isabella asks Fred, as though she's introducing them at a cocktail party.

Fred looks up to see a six foot seven former football player glare menacingly at him.

"Ron's been my bodyguard for years. I ask him to stay invisible, try to blend in. But sometimes he senses I'm being threatened. And Ron gets very protective when I'm threatened."

Ron gives Fred the benefit of a low guttural sound, and Fred cowers.

It's a fantastic thing to watch. Makes me all warm and runny inside.

Isabella picks up Zac se she puckers up her lips. "Who's the best dog?" she says in baby talk, smothering Zac in kisses. "You're the best dog. Yes, you are."

Isabella hands the dog to Fred. "Now, you are going to take the dog, shut the hell up, and go home. When you bring back the dog, you are going to drop off the dog, shut the hell up, and go home. If Liz or the dog tell me that you've behaved like a bad boy, I'm going to have to sic Ron on you." And with that, Isabella gives Fred a bright smile. "Are we clear?"

Fred takes a second glance at Ron, gulps, then says grudgingly, "Yeah, we're clear."

"Perfect! Ron… down boy."

And Ron takes his hand off of Fred's shoulder just as Isabella closes the door in Fred's face.

She turns to us and exhales a happy breath. "Ah, I feel so much better now. Seeing men act like assholes is like being in a room completely decorated in beige. I just have to get up and do something."

Liz and I stand in stunned silence, recovering from the aftermath of Tornado Isabella.

Isabella points to me. "You're still not dressed."

Twenty-three

Five minutes, one huge cup of coffee, and two aspirin later, I throw an overnight bag and my work stuff into the tiny back seat of Isabella's bright red Ferrari F355, hop into the passenger seat and watch her tear out of my driveway.

"You might want to slow down," I warn her. "There's a cop who waits on Coldwater this time of day for speeders."

"Jim," Isabella says knowingly.

She stops at the stop sign at the corner of our street and Coldwater, waiting for a break in the morning commuter traffic.

Or not. Isabella lets a small Mercedes pass, then slams on the accelerator to cut off a Lexus SUV, who honks his horn at her in anger.

"Don't SUVs piss you off?" she asks me nonchalantly. "They act like they own the whole road."

She tailgates the Mercedes as we take Coldwater over the hill, heading towards the valley.

"I guess you're wondering what Dave and I fought about," Isabella says as she drives.

"Actually, all I'm wondering right now is where the nearest Starbucks is," I mumble, rubbing my temple and wishing I wasn't so addicted to coffee that I get a splitting headache every time I go without the stuff for more than eight hours.

"Ventura Boulevard," Isabella says. "As long as you're going, get me a venti half caf latte with three pumps of vanilla, two of mint and a flower on top."

Twenty minutes later, venti lattes in our hands, Isabella pulls her car onto the 101 freeway, going West.

"I have a new idea for a chapter," Isabella says. "Honeymoons: How to do Europe, the Tropics or Hawaii on ten thousand dollars a day. The first trick is to find the best hotel in the area. For example, Dave and I are honeymooning in Europe..."

Isabella's cell phone rings. She pulls out her jeweled Motorola, adorned with real rubies, and looks at the caller ID. "Asshole!" she yells, throwing the phone into the compartment between our seats.

Then her face immediately relaxes. "So, back to Europe. We're beginning our trip in Paris, so naturally we'll stay at the Hotel Ritz. That's where Princess Diana stayed before she died..."

Her phone rings again. This time she answers it with a matter-of-fact, "I'm not talking to you right now. I need time to think." I can't hear the other end of the conversation, but it sounds like someone apologizing. "Well, if you feel that way, maybe we shouldn't get married." And she hangs up the phone.

Say what now?

Isabella smiles. "Back to Paris. Now the suite I like there is only about two thousand dollars a night. If you can economize like that, you'll have lots of money left over for things like making your own perfume at Creed, shopping at Hermes or eating at that place. You know, the one with the potatoes?" She turns to me. I gotta figure I look shocked by her phone call. Is the wedding off?

"Shouldn't you be taking notes?" she asks me.

"Huh?" I ask, thrust back into reality. "Oh, right." I unzip my notebook to grab my notepad and tape recorder. I turn on the tape recorder and say, "Okay. Paris. Go," just as her phone rings again.

Isabella turns the phone off. "Recap: Hotel Ritz. Two thousand a night. Creed, Hermes, Potato place. Now the villa I like in Italy is forty thousand a week. More expensive, but there's less shopping to do around there..."

Then my cell phone rings. "Is that Dave?" Isabella says, trying to sound breezy, but clearly alarmed.

I pull out my phone. "Private Caller. Probably Vanessa. Do you mind?"

She shakes her head "no," so I pick up. "Hello."

"Hey, it's me," Dave says, sounding depressed. "Do you have time for breakfast?"

"I can't. I'm afraid I'm working with a client for the next few days," I say carefully, hoping he'll figure out my code.

"Oh. Shit. So she not only left me in a huff, she's kidnapped you. I don't fucking believe it."

"Who is it?" Isabella asks.

"Just a friend from my writer's group," I lie.

"Man or woman?" Isabella asks.

"Man," I say, just in case she hears a male's voice on the other end of the phone.

"Does he want to go to my wedding?" she asks.

"I hate it when she storms off like this," Dave continues. "Where are you guys going?"

"I don't know," I say with forced cheer. "Can I call you later?"

"Sure. I lo... I'll talk to you soon," Dave says, then hangs up.

"For the South of France, I like the Hotel du Cap..."

"Can I stop you for a minute?" I ask her.

Isabella stops talking.

"So this fight with Dave," I begin carefully. "Want to tell me what happened?"

"He's just ruining everything!" she whines like a two year old. Then she waves her hand in the air to dismiss her last comment. "I don't want to talk about it. It just expends needless energy towards others and their crazy making behaviors. I'd much rather be with a close friend at a spiritual retreat where we can focus our energies on that which is positive and spiritually fulfilling."

Close friend? Okay…

"So where is this spiritual retreat?" I ask.

"Santa Barbara. Now, when you're travelling to England, it's important to hit the theaters in the West End, but it's also important to hit Savile Row…"

"I feel like this fight is weighing on your mind," I push gently.

Isabella turns to me, then looks back to the road. "Have you ever had an avocado-citrus body wrap?"

A what now? I'm not sure which would be worse: someone rubbing me all over with an orange, or with an avocado. My phone rings again. I look at the Caller ID. "It's Dave," I say, as Dave has now unblocked his number.

Isabella takes a deep breath. "Answer it."

I do. "Hello."

"Put Belle on the phone," Dave commands.

I hand her my phone. "He wants to talk to you."

Isabella glares at the phone. "Tell him if he wanted to talk to me he shouldn't have left yesterday morning, then not come home last night."

"You did what?!" I gasp into the phone.

"I needed time to think," Dave explains.

"That is *just* like you," I say, my voice rising. "I'll bet you didn't call to tell her where you were either."

"Did he used to do that to you?" Isabella asks me.

"Oh my God," I exclaim in exasperation. "Like, five different times I can think of off the top of my head. He knew I would always jump to the conclusion that the relationship was over, and then I'd be so relieved when he came back, he'd win the argument."

"Okay, that is so not what happened," Dave utters in disgust. "Can you put my fiancée on the phone please?"

I hand her the phone. "He still wants to talk to you."

She still refuses to take it, shaking her head. ·

I put the phone back up to my ear. "She's indisposed at the moment."

All I hear is a heavy sigh. "Tell her to take the goddamn phone or this is going to get ugly."

I put my phone back out to Isabella. "He says, and I quote, Take the goddamn phone or this is going to get ugly.'"

She determinedly keeps her eyes on the road and keeps driving.

After about twenty seconds of silence, I put the phone back to my ear. "I think you might want to give her a little extra time."

"Oh, for God's sake... Fine. Where are you guys going? I'll just come see her."

"If he asks where we're going, don't tell him," Isabella warns.

I wince. "I'm afraid I can't tell you," I answer sympathetically.

"Of course you can," he says softly. "You can tell me anything."

Why did my heart just flutter?

"Well..." I begin coyly.

"Did he ever tell you he thinks you're selfish in bed?" Isabella blurts out.

That takes a moment to sink in. "You said what?" I say through gritted teeth into the phone.

"That was totally taken out of context," Dave answers.

"Really? And what would that context be? Sam was the best thing that ever happened to me, I particularly liked how selfish she was in bed?"

"And he said you were bad with money," Isabella continues.

"Once again, out of context," Dave counters.

"And that you never followed through on anything. That anytime anything ever got difficult, you quit," Isabella finishes.

Dead silence. Silence in the car. Silence on the phone. "Anything else?" I ask both Isabella and Dave.

"No," Isabella answers, "That was pretty much it."

"Well," I say to Dave, "This conversation has become very difficult, so I guess it's time for me to quit."

And I hang up on him.

Isabella gets back to business. "Okay, now when you go to Spain…"

"Who was your first love?" I ask her, collecting my thoughts.

"Excuse me?" she asks, startled.

"Sorry. Just thinking out loud." I turn to her. "If you want to include chapters on your million dollar weddings and your lavish honeymoons, that's fine, I'll write them. But as a reader, what I would want to know about is who was your first love? Who was your second? Who do you love now? Because what you buy doesn't define you. Who you love does."

Isabella considers my question. Then, "You know a great place to spend ten thousand dollars a day? New York."

Twenty-four

Two hours later, I am standing in the middle of a beautiful hotel room at the Biltmore Hotel in Santa Barbara. My room has the same stunningly beautiful architecture as the hotel itself, built in the same classic Spanish Colonial style of red roof tiles, ivory adobe walls, and terra cotta floors. My room is decorated in rich golds and greens, with a king size bed and a cozy fireplace. The Spanish tile bathroom is sparklingly clean and flawless, complete with a rain shower and deep tub. I have a dazzling view of the hotel gardens. The place is perfect. I'm meeting Isabella in twenty minutes at the hotel's spa for an eighty minute massage, then a body wrap, then a facial. One could not ask for a more relaxing way to spend a day.

I'm a nervous wreck.

The moment I am out of Isabella's universe, I call Eric on his cell. He picks up on the first ring.

"Finally!" he says cheerfully. "I've been thinking about you all day. You would love this hotel. It's right next to Central Park. Next time I come here, I'm bringing you. We can take a horse drawn carriage ride, take in a show…"

"How come you never dated Isabella?" I interrupt.

"Whyyyy…?" Eric asks me, dragging out the word to let me know he thinks it's a ridiculous question.

"You mean, 'Why do I want to know why you've never dated her?' or, 'Why would you have ever dated her?'"

Eric is silent a moment. "I guess the second one?"

"Why would you have ever dated her? Well, let's see: she's got a perfect body…"

"She didn't in first grade," Eric quips.

"She's stunningly beautiful…" I continue.

"And expects everyone in the room to notice it…"

"She's ridiculously successful…"

"And has acquired her success through dubious means…"

"She's rich, she's famous…"

"She's spoiled, self-centered, and totally high maintenance," Eric finishes.

I think about his last statement. "I'm sorry. Then why are you friends again?"

Eric laughs. "Look, I love Libby. Very much. But there's a reason I only see her once or twice a year. She's just too…" Eric drags out the word, looking for an adjective. "Much. She's too much. She's like really dense ice cream. Wonderful every once in awhile. But you don't want to eat it every day."

That is absolutely the wrong thing to say to me. If I could wolf down a pint of Ben & Jerry's every day for the rest of my life, I would feel like the Genie granted me my biggest wish.

"If we went to Broadway what would you want to see?" Eric asks. "Or maybe off Broadway? There's this…"

"Am I selfish in bed?" I blurt out.

"What? No. Who told you that?"

"Dave."

"When did you sleep with Dave?"

"Six years ago," I answer, my voice getting higher, louder and more stressed out.

"You're with Isabella right now, aren't you?" Eric asks calmly.

"Actually, she's a few doors down. Wait, how did you know that?"

"That tone of voice you have right now? She has that effect on women."

My phone beeps. "That's Liz," I say to Eric. "Can you hold a sec?"

"I actually slipped out of a lecture to pick up. Do you want me to call you later?"

"Yeah. I'm at the Biltmore in Santa Barbara."

Eric starts laughing.

"What?" I ask.

"Nothing," he says, still chuckling. "Let me guess: Isabella's spineless groom finally stood up for himself in some way, shape, or form, and now she's punishing him by disappearing for a few days and not telling him where she is."

A part of me is happy that Eric called Dave spineless. I'm not sure why. "How did you know that?"

"I've known her since we were kids. I've been through all of her weddings. I'll probably go through several more. You can't be surprised when the snake eventually eats the mouse in her cage. I love you."

"I love you more."

"That's mathematically impossible. Bye."

He clicks off. I exhale a long breath, feeling much more relaxed. Eric always does that for me.

And ha! I may be selfish in bed, but at least I'm not a spineless groom.

My phone beeps. Liz. I pick up.

"I just got off the phone with Dave. Boy, does he sound wonky," Liz says in a gossipy tone. "He called to say disregard all those messages he left in your box on our home machine in the middle of the night last night. I'm now dying to press '3' so I can hear them."

"First of all, define wonky," I say, just noticing the hotel room's minibar for the first time. I open it to see a giant Hershey Bar and grab it. Mine.

"So can I play them?" Liz asks excitedly. "CanIcanIhuh?

"You probably shouldn't…" I say, debating, and feeling a little wonky myself. I rip open the Hershey Bar wrapper and take a big bite. "Besides, don't you have more interesting things going on with your life that you don't have to live vicariously through mine?"

"Hardly. I just paused *The Brady Bunch* for this. Hit 'play'?"

I take another bite of candy. "You said he called to say to disregard them. We should probably just delete them."

"No!" Liz shrieks. "What if he called to say that he was driving around directionless, much like his life, and that he has realized in the past few days that you are his one true love and that you should be together for eternity?"

"When, in the course of human events, has a man ever uttered those words aloud?"

"Fair enough. But let's play the messages and find out if a man ever will."

"I thought you said that when he called you told him I was asleep," I tell her.

"Apparently he called again after both of us had gone to bed. I'm hitting play."

"But…"

"You have four messages," the automated male voice tells us. "Message one: Message left on Sunday, eleven fifty-four p.m.: "Hey, it's me," Dave says, sounding completely sober and completely depressed. "I know it's really late, but Liz said you were sleeping several hours ago, so I'm hoping you're up… I was kind of wondering if I could stop by and talk. Call me when you get this." BEEP.

I take another huge bite of chocolate.

Message two: Message left on Sunday, one fifty-one a.m.: "Hey, me again. I wish I knew where you lived. I think I'd just pound on your door until someone let me in… I had this big fight with Belle earlier today, you heard part of it. It started with a fight about our honeymoon that led to a fight about everything else." He exhales a big breath. "I've been driving around for hours, and I don't know who to call. I called Joe, but he's in Boston and you know how he gets," Dave lowers his voice to imitate his friend. 'You fucked up. Go home.'… So I'm calling you again. Call me on my cell when you get this, no matter how late." BEEP.

I grab a Pringles can, rip off the paper top, and dig in.

"Message three: message left on Sunday, three-oh-two a.m.: "One of these hours you're bound to wake up… Do you think I'm too controlling?" BEEP.

Message four: message left on Sunday, four-fifteen a.m. "Wanted to give you one more shout out, in case you were up… Look, I…if you have time tomorrow…maybe we could go get breakfast. I love you. Good night."

BEEP.

I slowly sit down on the plush hotel bed, stunned. "Did he just say I love you?" I ask Liz.

"He did!" Liz confirms gleefully. "Want me to play that last one again?"

"No. Delete it," I begin firmly. "Delete all of them. He said to ignore them." Then I stand up, reconsidering. "Wait, no, don't delete them, maybe I'll want to hear them later," Then I begin pacing. "No. Delete them. What am I going to do with them? Listen to them twelve times and drive myself crazy?"

"I'm gonna go with 'yes'," Liz says. "Because that's totally what I would do."

"No. Del…"

Suddenly, I hear pounding on my door. "Sam, I have my Raindrop massage in fifteen minutes!"

"Just a minute!" I yell towards the door. Then I whisper into my cell. "Don't delete them yet. I'll call you later." And I hang up.

I run over to the door and yank it open. Isabella stands there wearing tiny shorts, a babydoll T, and sparkly Manolo high heels. "The spa just called. Did you want the hot stone massage or the rainbow massage?"

"Give me one sec," I say, quickly grabbing my phone, then heading out the door. "I don't know," I say as we walk through the hotel's lush gardens and over to the Spa. "Either one will be fine. What's a raindrop massage?"

"They drop these essential oils on your spine from a height of about six inches," Isabella explains to me.

"Why would they do that?" I ask.

"I don't know. Something about electrons or magnets...I didn't understand the brochure."

"What's the hot stone massage?"

"They take hot stones, and put them on your body while they massage you."

Hot rocks on my body? On purpose? I'll pass.

"Don't they have a regular massage?" I ask.

"Yeah, but that's so pediatric," Isabella says.

I try to decipher what she meant. "Pedestrian?"

"Oh, no. I don't think we want a massage while we're walking."

Twenty-five

Five minutes later, we change into the spa's superplush robes, and wait for our massages in the Spa's Relaxation Lounge. An attendant offers us herbal tea, which I take to wash down the half pound of candy and potato chips I just ate.

As I sip my tea, I look out the open window at the ocean view, listen to the waves, and smell the perfume from the rose garden flowers as a gentle wind wafts in. I close my eyes and try to relax. I should be totally at peace. Instead, I'm trying to figure out what Dave meant when he said he loved me.

"Do you think I should do a diet chapter?" Isabella asks me, jolting me back to reality.

I open my eyes. "You could. What would you say in it?"

She sips her tea. "Have lots of sex. The more of it, the better."

Oh, gag me.

"And occasionally sneak a cigarette. Oh, and water."

An attendant walks out. "Miss De Leon."

Isabella silently follows her to a treatment room.

And I immediately begin obsessing again: What did Dave mean when he said he loved me?

Another attendant comes out to greet me. "Miss Evans?"

I bolt out of my seat. "Can you excuse me for two minutes?" I ask her.

I race out of the Relaxation Lounge and into the women's locker room.

"But your massage..." the attendant begins.

I put up my fingers in a V shape. "Two minutes. Stay right there."

I run into the locker room, press the code on my keyless locker, grab my cell phone, and dial.

"Hey," Dave answers.

"We're staying at the Biltmore in Santa Barbara," I whisper into the phone, worried that the walls have ears.

"I know," he says, and I hear a smile in his voice. "But thanks for telling me."

I look around the empty locker room, still worried I'm going to get caught. "You *know*?"

"Yeah. Isabella has LoJack on all of her cars. I had Britney call them."

I smile. "That's brilliant," I say. Then I get more serious. "Listen, I'm really sorry I didn't just tell you where we were. She said some stuff that triggered twentysomething me. It was dumb and I'm sorry."

"Thanks," Dave says. Then, "I'm sorry that after our fights I would leave and not tell you where I was going. That was really shitty of me."

I take a moment to let that soak in. "Thank you," I whisper, still looking around the locker room in paranoid delusion. "Um...I really have to go. Can I call you later?"

"Yeah. I'll be around. Enjoy the hotel. Bye."

"Bye."

I turn off my phone and head back out to the Relaxation Lounge.

And I am immediately not only more relaxed, but happy. It should not matter anymore, but twentysomething me *finally* winning that argument, finally being heard, after all of these years, makes me downright jubilant.

Twenty-six

I spent an hour and a half getting massaged (your basic "pediatric" Swedish), another hour getting a facial, and another hour getting something called a "Salt Glow."

At that point, I was so relaxed I was ready for bed.

Unfortunately, all of this invigorated Isabella, who had quite the day planned for us.

"We've been invited to a friend's party tonight," Isabella tells me as we walk back to our rooms. "It starts at eight, so I want us to get there around nine."

Which, if her schedule at Cirque is any indication, means we'll be there around eleven.

"It's an A-list party, so we'll need new dresses and new shoes. I'm having the concierge send up a selection for us. I noticed you had an I Ching book on your dining room table. Is that what you usually use?"

As we walk, I squint my eyes at her, confused. "Use for what?"

"Your augury."

"Why would I need a…"

"Hold on," Isabella says, abruptly stopping in her tracks. She closes her eyes tight. "Should we start with Celtic Runes or I Ching?" she asks aloud to no one in particular.

She pulls a large plastic eight ball from her purse, shakes it wildly, and reads the plastic pyramid inside the inky water. "It's telling me we should start with Celtic Runes. We'll do those first. Then some I-Ching, then Tarot cards."

Half an hour later, Isabella and I are driving up the hills of Santa Barbara, through a suburb that looks like it was built in the 1980s. "Our first fortune teller is named Fiona. According to the concierge, she's the best reader of Celtic runes in all of Santa Barbara."

Isabella parks her Ferrari in front of a chewing gum colored house that looks exactly like all of the other chewing gum colored houses in the neighborhood. Not exactly what I imagine when I think of a fortuneteller's home. Somehow, I pictured a shack on the beach, or a walkup in Chinatown.

As Isabella and I get out of the car, a thirty-something woman opens the door, carrying a baby on one hip. "Isabella?" she asks, walking out to us. "I'm Fiona."

Once again, not what I pictured. Somehow the word *fortuneteller* for me conjures up images of an older, large lady with even bigger hair wearing a muumuu and lots of cheap necklaces. But this one's a thin, young, pretty mom.

We exchange pleasantries, then Fiona leads us into her house.

It looks like Toys R Us exploded in here. Baby toys litter the living and dining rooms. "I'm sorry the place is such a mess," Fiona says, putting the baby in one of those new "travel yards" that you can't call a playpen anymore. "I wasn't expecting you for another hour."

"Oh, we're on a tight schedule, so I figured we'd just pop by," Isabella says. She opens her huge Hermes purse and pulls out her wallet. "It's five hundred, right?"

"Yes," Fiona says, leading us to her dining room. She takes a seat at the head of the table. "Please sit to my left. Now, do you have your own runes?"

"I do," Isabella says proudly, pulling a velvet pouch from her purse as she sits next to Fiona. "They're amethyst with solid gold lettering."

"Perfect. Now, you understand you're only supposed to ask one question per day, correct?"

I sit down next to Isabella. Five hundred dollars for one question? I thought Isabella was overpaid.

"Yup," Isabella says confidently, shaking her velvet bag. "I've got my question."

"And which cast would you like to use?"

"Which kind will give me the best fortune?" Isabella asks.

"No. It doesn't work like that. Your fortune is your fortune. I see what I see. The cast doesn't matter."

"Oh," Isabella says, disappointed. "Okay, well, what kinds do you have?"

"Celtic, Planetary, Odin's, Thor's, Tree of Life..."

"I just want to know how things are going to go with my wedding to Dave. Which one is that?"

Fiona considers her question for a moment. "Loving Cup."

"How many stones do I need for that one?" Isabella asks.

"Runes. And nine."

Isabella pulls nine purple rocks out of her bag. Fiona places the stones in a "Y' shape, then stares silently at them, as if in a trance.

After a minute or two that feels like twenty, I start drumming my fingers on my knee and look around distractedly. The baby cheerfully plays with a plastic light-up elephant. I wish something that simple could make me that happy.

Fiona moves the bottom stone to center it. "Is your wedding coming up?" Fiona asks, looking troubled, like a doctor about to tell a patient they have a month to live.

"In less than two weeks," Isabella says proudly.

Fiona lets out a heavy sigh. "You need to go through with it, but it's not going to go how you planned."

Oh Fiona... For five hundred dollars, how hard is it to tell a bride she's going to have the perfect wedding day?

"What does *that* mean?" Isabella asks, her voice rising in panic.

Fiona points to one of the stones. "There's someone else in the marriage. Are you in love with another man?"

"What? No!"

Fiona grimaces. "Well, I can only tell you what I see. There's another person here, and they're – pardon my French – fucking up your wedding."

Uh-oh. Is that me? Please don't let that be me.

Isabella swoops up the stones and shoves them back into the velvet bag. "That's ridiculous. Let's try again."

Isabella madly shakes the stones in her bag as Fiona reminds her, "I'm afraid you only get one question a day."

"This is the same question," Isabella reasons. "Which one of those casts has the most runes?"

"Celtic."

"How many?"

"Ten."

Isabella starts madly pulling out stones and handing them to Fiona, who places them into another shape: an arrow pointing up, a Z, and a line. All of the stones have a different symbol painted on them, but I have no idea what any of the symbols mean. After the tenth stone is picked and placed, Isabella once again asks, "How will things go with my upcoming marriage?"

Fiona reads the stones. "Well, this cast is better..." she concedes. She adjusts one of the stones, making an H shape with one extra stone on the left. "The marriage is going to be good, I see babies, but I still see trouble on your actual wedding day..."

"You mean, like rain?" Isabella asks hopefully.

Fiona shrugs. "Possibly?"

Isabella quickly stands, swoops up the runes up, and throws them back into the pouch. "Thank you so much for your time. Sam, lets go!" And she's out the door like a bat out of Hell.

I thank Fiona for her time, then quickly run out to Isabella's car. She's already inside and starting the car as I get in.

"Are you all right?" I ask gently.

"I didn't pay that bitch five hundred dollars to be told I'm getting rained on," Isabella practically spits. "Let's hit the I Ching."

We drive for forty-five minutes to the next fortune teller. His home looks more like how I pictured a clairvoyant's home: a small ramshackle house on the outskirts of the city, located across the street from an empty beach.

Isabella parks out front. "We're seeing Mr. Wei," she says as we get out of the car, and head up the walkway to the house. "He also did the Feng Shui for my Malibu home. Doesn't speak much English."

Isabella knocks on the door. A petite Asian girl answers, wearing jeans and a UCSB T shirt. "Isabella," she exclaims, her face brightening.

"Heather," Isabella says, giving her a hug, then handing her a stuffed envelope. "Here's his gift."

"Thanks," Heather says, taking the envelope. "Grandpa is expecting you. Take off your shoes and we'll join you in the dining room in a moment." Heather then leaves us as we take off our shoes and put them by the door.

"What did you just give her?" I whisper to Isabella as she takes off her tiny Barbie doll high heel shoes.

"You can't pay the master for his services," Isabella tells me. "But you can give him gifts. Mine was a thousand in cash."

Wow — how do I get into the psychic business?

We head into the dining room, which again challenges my assumptions: it's a classic dark cherry table with six chairs around it and a large book resting at the head of the table. On the wall are several pictures of a family, and one U.C. Santa Barbara pennant.

"Heather goes to UC Santa Barbara," Isabella tells me, pointing to the pennant as she sits on the chair to the left of the head of the table. "She translates for her grandfather."

As I sit down to the left of Isabella, an ancient Chinese man walks into the room, followed by Heather. As Heather takes a seat on her grandfather's right, Isabella pulls out six pennies. "Now these are my special I-Ching coins. Only I touch them."

Heather translates for her grandfather, who smiles pleasantly as he nods to Isabella.

"My question is, how is my wedding and marriage to Dave going to turn out?" She throws the pennies down six times. The first three throws turn up all heads or all tails, the next three are a combination of the two.

Mr. Wei draws two symbols on a note pad, putting a right facing arrow between them. He frowns, deep in thought. Then he opens the book, and I see the number "29" above the first symbol. Damn it, that's the same symbol I got when Liz read the I-Ching for me.

Danger.

Isabella leans in to Mr. Wei to look at the symbol in the book, but nothing registers with her because the text is in Chinese.

After reading the first page, Mr. Wei flips the book to the symbol numbered "63." I don't know what that is, but I memorize it, just in case I want to read Liz's I Ching later.

Mr. Wei looks at me, gives me an odd look, then studies Isabella for a moment. He turns to Heather, speaking to her in Chinese. She cocks her head at him, then looks at me.

I don't like how this is going.

Heather turns to Isabella. "Your first symbol is *Danger*. These next few weeks are going to be very tumultuous. You need to be very careful at this time."

Mr. Wei speaks to his granddaughter, who responds in Chinese.

Heather turns back to Isabella, addressing her in English. "Your future symbol is *After the End*. That is very good for your question. Everything turns out happy for you. But remember, relationships take work. The ecstasy you feel the day that you finally marry your true love won't last. One can not stay ecstatic forever. Eventually, your soul mate becomes the guy who leaves his socks on the floor and forgets to pick up a quart of milk on the way home."

"Perfect!" Isabella exclaims, quickly standing up. "Sam, let's go!"

Mr. Wei gently puts his hand on Isabella's, but says in a warning tone in English, "A wedding lasts for just one day. A marriage lasts a lifetime."

Well, for some people it does anyway, I think to myself.

Isabella puts her hands on her hips, frowning at Mr. Wei. "So what are you saying? That my marriage is doomed?"

Mr. Wei turns to Heather, who translates Isabella's question. Mr. Wei answers in Chinese. Heather then tells Isabella, "Fortunes are malleable. They can change based on your actions. My grandfather is just reminding you to be nice to those around you. Particularly your groom. Otherwise, he could be lost to you forever."

Twenty-seven

Five minutes later, Isabella is clutching her steering wheel so tightly she looks like she's trying to strangle it. "How dare that man take a thousand dollars from me just to tell me my marriage is doomed."

I clench my hands against the seat as we go at least ninety in a fifty-five zone, with Isabella whipping her Ferrari around little old ladies going forty five. "He didn't say your marriage was doomed. He just suggested that you to be nicer to those around you."

"I can't do that. I'm a movie star. What would people think?"

She speeds her Ferrari around a snail pacing Toyota Tercel, then cuts him off with less than ten feet to spare, and I wonder if People Magazine will mention me in their cover story about Isabella's and my untimely death.

"How far is State Street?" she asks. "I need to find a Tarot card reader."

Soon Isabella is slowly driving down State Street, a tourist favorite. Beginning at the Pacific Ocean and ending in neighboring Goleta, the street oozes old town charm, and is home to shops, restaurants, two different Starbucks, and one tarot card reader.

After Isabella parks, I head into Starbucks to get a venti latte for myself, and a Grande decaf latte filled two thirds of the way up with four pumps toffee-nut flavored syrup for the crazy nit.

I was shocked to see it only took them two minutes to get our order ready.

I grab the two cups of coffee, take a big ol' sip of mine immediately, and walk one block over to a small brick building with signs for an insurance company, an accounting firm, and Lady Victoria – Tarot Card Reader.

I open the door to the fortuneteller's office to see Isabella sitting across a table from the Lady Victoria, crying hysterically.

Lady Victoria shrugs.

Fifteen minutes after that, Isabella and I walk into a Turkish coffeehouse we pass on State Street. Isabella wipes her eyes and blows her nose loudly. "It's doomed! And I...I..." She bursts into tears again. "I even got a groundhog for the reception!"

A young, dark-complected woman wearing a black skirt, white shirt, and red apron walks up to us. "Hi. I am Ana," she says brightly in an accent I don't recognize (I'm going with Turkish) as she hands us menus. "Do you know what you'd like today?"

"Yes. To have my life not be over!" Isabella whines, throwing her face into a silk handkerchief. "I'll have a martini, two olives."

"I'm afraid we don't serve alcohol," Ana tells her. "But we have wonderfully strong Turkish coffee and pastries, including Baklava."

"We'd like two coffees," I say. "And Baklava sounds awesome."

Ana smiles and leaves us to get our order.

"I don't like Turkish coffee. I like French press," Isabella mopes to me.

"Then why did you walk into a Turkish coffeehouse?" I ask.

"I thought it was a perfume store. I figure maybe if I smell different, my life will be different."

I sigh. "What did Lady Victoria say?"

"I...I..." Isabella bursts into tears again, shaking her head to signal she can't even talk about it.

Moments later, Ana comes back with two cups of coffee and a rectangle of Baklava. She places everything on the table. "The baklava is pistachio. My mother made it. You'll love it."

And Isabella keeps sobbing.

"May I ask what is wrong?" Ana asks delicately.

Unable to speak, Isabella shakes her head, hunches over, and wails into her handkerchief.

"My friend just went to a Tarot Card reader named Lady Victoria," I tell our waitress. "I'm guessing she told her not to get married."

"Ugh," Ana exclaims, waving her hand in the air dismissively. "That woman is a fraud. You want a real fortune told, I'll read your grounds."

That stops the tears immediately. "Say what now?" Isabella says, looking up at Ana.

Ana points to Isabella's small cup. "Drink your coffee, then I'll read your grounds at the bottom of the cup and tell you your fortune."

Isabella looks down at the cup. "But I don't like..." She stops, looks up at me, then looks down to talk to the cup. "How will my marriage to Dave go?"

Then she pushes the cup towards me. "Drink this."

"What?"

"I don't like Turkish coffee. But you do. Drink it and then she can read my fortune."

"That's not how it works. If she drinks the coffee, then the grounds will show her fortune," Ana tells Isabella.

Isabella frowns. She takes her cup back, pinches her nose and takes a sip, acting like a three year old trying to swallow her Brussels sprouts.

I take a sip of my coffee and it's heaven on a cup. I don't know what that woman's problem is.

Isabella finishes her coffee in one graceless gulp. "How much do you charge?"

"You can pay me what you think I'm worth."

Isabella opens her purse, pulls out a wad of hundreds, and peels off ten of them. "Is that enough?"

The girl's eyes nearly bug out of her head.

Isabella hands her cup to Ana. "How will my marriage to Dave go?"

Ana focuses on the bottom of Isabella's cup and smiles. "You marry the love of your life," she pronounces. Then she looks up and warns, "But be nice to your groom. He's thinking about marrying you right now, but he's not sure. While he thinks mostly of you, when you're not nice to him, he thinks of another."

A customer at another table says something to Ana in Turkish. She turns to him, says something back, then turns back to us. "I have to help other customers. Please let me know if you need anything else."

And she walks away. I shouldn't care, but I feel a pit forming in my stomach. Dave and Isabella are going to be happily married. Which saddens me, but not because I have feelings for Dave, but because she's awful.

Then I remember: this is all bullshit. Fortunetellers aren't real. What kind of a moron would really believe you can see your future at the bottom of a coffee cup?

"Let's go home," Isabella says.

"You mean hotel home, or home home?" I ask.

"Home home. I have a wedding to plan."

Twenty-eight

I spend the next three days getting Isabella to open up about her childhood, her career, and her ex-husbands. And by open up, I mean getting her to admit that everything was always everyone else's fault. Except the good stuff, which she did completely on her own with no help.

It's now Thursday night, and Liz and I have been invited to Cirque for me to schmooze with entertainment reporters and for Liz to get a comped a lobster dinner and a free trapeze ride.

Once again, Isabella sends a limo. Once again, we are greeted with frenzied paparazzi snapping away, this time yelling "Sofia! Sofia!"

As Liz waves and smiles, she leans into me and whispers. "Who's Sofia? And why are they taking so many pictures?"

"They think you're that supermodel dating Leonardo DiCaprio?" I guess as the first doorman opens the first set of doors.

"Excellent!" Liz beams. And as we walk through the doors, Liz turns around and says, "No drinking tonight, boys! I'm having Leo's baby!"

And the cameras flash like mad as the doors close.

The hostess brings us to our assigned booth in the VIP area, and within moments our waiter Steve has brought Liz her favorite beer and me a Pussy Galore cocktail, and taken our food order: we start with the Carpaccio, Crab Cakes, and Escargot, followed by main course of Lobster and Duck.

"It's amazing how hungry you get when the food is free," I deadpan to Liz.

"Isabella said we can order whatever we want. I'm just following a long line of minions who follow her every command," Liz happily tells me.

We spend the next hour eating our fabulous meals, with Liz slurping down free beer as I mostly sip sparkling water, waiting for Isabella and Dave to show up with the press.

They don't. Liz and I look around at the other patrons.

"Anyone look good to you?" Liz asks.

"I have a boyfriend," I answer, irked.

"Who I notice you haven't spoken to much this week. As opposed to Dave…"

"Dave and I haven't seen each other this week either."

"No, but you were on the phone with him last night," Liz says, glancing at me like she's caught me having an affair.

"I've been on the phone with him every night. I'm writing a book for his wife and I'm in his wedding, it would be weird if we weren't talking."

"Have you talked about how you want to throw him down and make him remember why he's a man?" she asks cheerfully.

I roll my eyes. "I have a boyfriend," I repeat to Liz. "And he has a fiancée."

"You forget: I hear how your voice changes when you're on the phone with hm. How long do you think before you kiss again?"

"All right, that's enough," I warn her.

"I'm gonna go with the rehearsal dinner," Liz decides. "As usual, you'll procrastinate, like you do with your writing, but then it'll be put up or shut up. So you'll put up."

"I'm not listening," I say sing-songily.

"You do like a deadline," she responds in the same sing-song manner.

Dave and Isabella walk in, surrounded by several members of the press. "They're here," I say, then turn to face Liz. "How do I look?"

Liz smirks. "But you don't care about Dave."

"I meant how do I look for the cameras. I'm supposed to be promoting my novel tonight, remember?"

She crosses their arms, looking at me dubiously.

I stare back at her. "Okay, fine. There is also a *small* part of me that wants to look good for Dave. But not because I want to kiss him."

"You know what I think the problem is? You've had mostly water all night. Maybe if you could blame it on the booze, you'd get farther with him."

"Sam! Over here!" Isabella yells to me, waving me over.

I make my way through the crowd to Isabella, dressed head to toe in Prada and looking perfect, and Dave, looking slightly uncomfortable in a dark blue suit.

Dave in a suit? Twice in a week? How did Isabella pull that off? This is the same man who refused to wear a tuxedo to our wedding, because he insisted, "I don't want to look like a waiter." The same guy who had to be wrangled into a jacket and tie for the big day, with him complaining the entire time that if we had eloped in Hawaii he could be jacketless, tieless, and maybe even shoeless on the beach.

I had said at the time that if he insisted on eloping, he'd also be ringless.

I always knew he'd look amazing all dressed up. I just never knew how to get him to dress like that for me. Which makes me a little sad.

Isabella walks away from Dave to talk to a middle aged, frumpy woman with badly dyed, frizzy brown hair. I grab my opportunity to see Dave alone, practically running over to him.

"Wow, I never thought I'd see you in Prada," I say to him.

"You still haven't," he says. "This is Armani."

He slowly leans in to give me a kiss on the cheek, then whispers, "I hate it with a passion."

I don't think he meant to, but he accidentally blew into my ear. Pretty sure an electrical charge just raced from my ear down to my...

Nah, he probably didn't mean to.

"Well, you look good," I say.

"So do you," Dave returns, smiling. "I notice you wore my favorite skirt."

At this, I turn away from him. He noticed. The skirt he is referring to is floor length, but has one slit that goes up the side, enough to reveal a hint of leg as I walk. It was his favorite article of clothing in my closet. And that included the "wedding trousseau" that I spent three hundred bucks on, only to have it hit the floor four minutes after it made its much-ballyhooed debut.

"Sam," Isabella says, appearing out of nowhere to grab me by the hand. "Listen, I'm really sorry, but apparently it's going to be all bridal magazines tonight, so I won't be able to talk about your book. But I promise sometime soon. Meanwhile, enjoy the dinner and drinks. Dave and I will catch up with you guys later."

She tries to pull Dave away, but he stays firmly planted in his spot. She pulls again. "Come on baby, let's go," she purrs.

I have to learn how to purr. Do they teach classes in that?

"I think I'm going to stay with Sam for a minute," Dave tells her.

A look crosses Isabella's face of a woman scorned. "But sweetie," she says pointedly, "We have guests we need to see."

"Noooo," he corrects. "*I* have *guests* I need to see. You have *reporters*. There's a difference."

Isabella appears stunned by the rebuff. "Ohhhh...Kay. I'll go do some interviews by myself."

She turns away from us to walk towards the reporters, then turns back. "Does this have to do with..."

"No," he insists, calmly but firmly.

And she slinks away. She looks so sad, I almost feel sorry for her.

Almost.

I'm confused. "What was that all about?"

"Nothing. I'll go find her in a minute. She's upset because I'm meeting a friend tonight," Dave says.

"What fr..."

"Samolina!" I hear from behind me.

I visibly wince. *Oh, Dear God, No...*

I turn around to see Joe, Dave's best man and his best friend since high school. And the lead singer of his band. And the former bane of my existence. Never have I met a man with such a huge ego and such low self-esteem in my life. Imagine a guy who would be the best looking man you've ever seen... if he never opened his fucking mouth.

Joe grabs me and hugs me so hard, I worry he will crack my rib. "How are you, baby? You look good!" He lets go of me, then walks around to check out my backside. "Lookin' very good."

Puke.

"I read that article you wrote for *Cosmopolitan* about dating rules," Joe says, finishing off a beer. "And you totally screwed the pooch with number six."

Yup. Hasn't seen me in five years and the first thing out of his mouth is designed to start an argument.

"You wrote about dating rules?" Dave asks me, surprised.

"Schyeah," Joe says. "She wrote this bullshit about how women should ask men on dates and to dance and stuff."

I cross my arms and glare at him. "I'm shocked to learn that you disagree with my assessment. Shocked."

Joe smiles, refusing to acknowledge my animosity in the least. "At the Playboy mansion one night, this centerfold asked me to dance. I said no. She said she'd kiss me if I danced. So I joke, 'Where?' And she looks down at my crotch and says, 'Wherever you want.' I meant the grotto. Hard pass. We men can smell desperation, even if it's packaged in a pretty bunny."

"Okay, but that's not the same as..."

"Ended up going home with an MIT graduate who at the beginning of the night wouldn't give me the time of day."

"How did you get an MIT... never mind. I don't want to know."

My cell phone rings. It's Liz. I pick up. "Yes?"

"Are you making out with him?" Liz asks.

"No!" I answer back.

"Good. Then get drinks. I can't find Steve."

"I think maybe you've had a little too much... Hello?" It's then that I realize she's hung up on me. "What is it about this place?" I mutter to myself.

"Liz is here!" Dave tells Joe.

"No fucking way!" Joe beams. "Where is she?"

Dave points to our booth upstairs just as Isabella walks up to us. "Sweetie..."

Upon seeing Joe, her face deadens. "Joe. You made it."

"Miss De Leon," Joe says formally, then grabs her face in both hands, and plants a big kiss full on her mouth.

When he pulls away, Isabella just looks confused. Dave laughs, shaking his head at his "zany" friend. Oh, yes, what a laugh riot. Isabella shakes her head to clear the cobwebs, then looks at Dave. "The reporter from *Brides* is here. They're doing a story on our wedding and they want to ask you some questions."

"Didn't I already talk to the reporter from *Brides?*"

"No, that was for *Modern Bride*. This is *Brides*."

She takes his hand and pulls him away from us. Dave makes a joke of it, smiling as he is led away. "I'm off for an interview."

I watch Isabella pull him into the crowd and away from me.

And a tiny part of me… just a sliver really… misses him.

"Did you know that Bonobo chimps are the only animals other than man that perform oral sex on each other to the point of orgasm?"

I slowly turn my head towards Joe, then stare at him. I blink several times. Joe stares back at me, grinning, waiting for my response. Finally, I give him one. "In the entire time you've known me, has there ever been anything I've ever said or done to make you think I would be even remotely interested in knowing that fact?"

I leave him to head to the bar. Then I try to get the bartender's attention. "Excuse me?" I say loudly, but politely. The bartender doesn't hear me.

Joe continues with his monologue. "Back to Bonobo chimps. They also practice homosexuality, including mutual masturbation…"

As the bartender walks towards me, carrying drinks for other patrons, I yell/ask, "Pardon me, when you get a chance…?" But he walks right past me.

"Wouldn't that be cool, if women just routinely practiced mutual masturbation on each other?" Joe continues.

"Excuse me?" I say to another bartender walking past us. Ignored again. Sigh.

"Yo! Adam!" Joe yells, startling me.

Adam the bartender immediately walks over to us. "Good evening, Mr. Robinson. What can I get you?"

"It's not for me. It's for the lady."

Adam turns to me and I force a smile. I hate these places. "Can I get a bottle of Cabernet and two glasses?"

"Do you want to see the wine list?" Adam asks.

"Oh! And they have public sex too," Joe tells me excitedly. "Wouldn't it be awesome if women could just perform oral sex on each other, in public, whenever they felt like it?"

"Women *can* perform oral sex on each other in public whenever they feel like it," I say, ready to lose it. "And you've still never seen any of them do it. Do the math."

I turn my attention back to Adam. "I would like something in the sixty dollar range," I say, then point to Joe, "and put it on his tab."

The bartender leaves us to get a bottle as Joe smiles appreciatively. "Good one, Samolina," he says, grabbing my shoulders and shaking me. "God, I've missed you!" he pulls me into another rib crunching hug. Then pulls away. "Adam, can you also get me a pint of whatever dark beer you've got on tap? And three shots of Sex on the Beach on a tray."

Within moments, Adam presents us with an uncorked bottle of Cabernet, two glasses, a pint of beer and three shots on a silver tray for Joe. I grab the bottle and glasses, then turn to Joe. "Well, I'm sure you have gobs and gobs of other women to offend so…off you go!"

I walk through the crowd, and up to our booth. Joe follows me with his beer and his tray of shots, magically managing to weave his way through the crowd without spilling a drop. "You know what else Bonobo chimps do? They practice *casual* sex. You've never heard a female Bonobo chimp complaining the next day to her friends..." Joe raises his voice three octaves, pretending to be a woman. "Why didn't he call? How could he have had sex with me without feelings? I'm telling all of the other Bonobo chimps I know not to have sex with him, because he's an asshole."

As we make our way through the throngs of young, hip people and up the stairs, I am convinced that I must look like Meg Ryan in "When Harry Met Sally" when she is forced to listen to Billy Crystal monologue about why men and women can't be friends.

"We should totally be like a Bonobo chimp society," Joe continues. "Think about it: We could regularly practice casual sex and public sex. Wouldn't life be better if you could have sex with anyone you wanted whenever you felt like it, no questions asked? The chimps have the right idea: no marriage, no monogamy. Speaking of, so what are you packing for Dave's bachelor party?"

I turn to him and seethe, "You know, you have a very bad habit of confusing being rude with being charming. Making people feel uncomfortable does not make them respect you more or like you more. It makes you unable to visit your male friends when they get married..."

And then it hits me. "Wait a minute. What do you mean what am I packing for Dave's bachelor party? There's no way I'm going to his bachelor party."

"EE-ee. EE-ee," Joe screeches like a chimp.

I turn around to walk away from him. He continues to follow me. "Seriously, Dave needs to get laid one more time by a woman who doesn't make him wear Armani to get a blow job, don't you think?"

I shake my head slowly. "I can't..." I begin, stuttering, "I'm not...you can't really..."

When I get to Liz, I must look stunned. "What happened?" Liz asks. "You look like you just saw a ghost."

I point to Joe. "He...I...It..." I start rubbing my temples, feeling a headache coming on. "The mind boggles."

"Hey!" Liz says, her face lighting up.

Joe just stares at her, suddenly transformed into a lovesick schoolboy. "Liz. Wow, you look...amazing."

Liz furrows her brow, joking, "How much have you had to drink?"

As Joe places his tray of shots on our table, Liz stands up, looking to bring it in for a hug. Instead, she smacks Joe lightly on the back of his head. "Be nice to her. Don't make me go Three Stooges on your ass." Then she hugs him.

"May I sit with you ladies?" Joe asks, in a tone of voice so polite that, I swear, if he had a hat, it would be in his hands right now.

"Of course./No. Go away."

You can guess who made which statement.

"Have a seat," Liz says to Joe.

I droop my shoulders and start to pout. "Oh, come on... Make the bad man go away."

As the two of them slide into our booth, I put the bottle of cabernet on the table and slide in, placing Liz between Joe and me. Liz's face falls when she sees the bottle. "You got wine? I hate wine. I wanted a real drink."

"Yeah, well, after the crap I went through with the bartenders, you're getting wine," I snarl. "I wasn't about to spill beer on my clothes trying to maneuver a full pint through this crowd."

As I begin pouring the wine, Joe proudly hands Liz one of the purple shots. "One real drink, coming up!"

Liz stares at the shot glass in confusion. "Ummm. Thank you?"

"It's a Sex on the Beach," Joe says, clearly thinking he's making inroads with the beverage.

Now she looks offended. "Are you making fun of me?" Liz asks, waiting to be the punch line of a big Joe joke (though that seems to be my exclusive domain).

"No," he says genuinely. "You said you wanted a real drink."

Liz shakes her head. "A real drink is a martini, a beer, maybe a scotch. It's not a...what the hare in these things anyway?"

"I'll be right back," Joe says, standing up and racing (and I mean racing) back to the bar.

"You know what would be great?" I say to Liz as I hand her a glass of wine. "If you could just have him run away to switch drinks for you all night. Then I wouldn't have to deal with him." I take a sip of wine. "Although, I must begrudgingly admit, it's kind of cute that the guy hasn't seen you in forever and yet he still remembers your favorite drink from college."

Liz looks up at the ceiling. "Oh, yeah, that was my favorite drink back then, wasn't it?" She shrugs. "Well, Bon Jovi was once my favorite band, so what the hell did I know?"

A few minutes later, Joe returns carrying a huge tray of drinks. He places them in front of Liz, allowing her to choose her favorite. "Okay, we've got a Scotch, neat..." he begins, pointing to the first drink. "Then a scotch on the rocks, then a martini, I didn't know if you wanted Gin or Vodka, so I got you both..." He points to several pint glasses. "I didn't know what kind of beer you wanted, but I figured you wanted it on tap, so I got you a Hefeweizen, a lager, a pale ale, a stout, and a bock."

Liz looks at the group of drinks in front of her, then turns to me. "I just got an idea for a new line of greeting cards: *I like my men the way I like my cocktails: the more of them the better.*"

"Change *cocktail* to *drink*," I suggest.

"No, because I plan to write some cock jokes."

Joe slides back into the booth. "Can we talk about Dave's bachelor party now?"

Liz's ears perk up as she grabs the vodka martini. "Wait, Dave's having a Bachelor party?"

"Yeah. And I want Sam to go. But she's in a huff about it."

Liz turns to me. "So what's the problem?"

"What the problem?!" I nearly shriek. "It's bad enough that I have to be in Dave's wedding. I am not going to sit around watching a bunch of aging rockers eat too much meat, drink too much, reminisce about the good old days and lament about their pot bellies and receding hairlines."

"I'm only thirty-two," Joe points out, unconsciously putting his hand on his (not receding) hairline.

"I think that one was directed at her Dad and his last bachelor party," Liz surmises.

"Possibly," I concede. "I still don't want to waste an evening…"

"Weekend," Joe interrupts.

"Gawd. Even worse."

Joe takes one of the Sex on the Beach shots and downs it, then explains to Liz, "We're going to Waikiki for the weekend. We leave tomorrow morning."

"Hawaii for a whole weekend?" Liz turns to me. "You could nail him if you had a whole weekend."

"Me?" Joe asks, clearly startled.

"No. Dave," Liz corrects.

He relaxes. "Yeah, that makes more sense."

"No, it doesn't! What are you two smoking?"

"Oooo…" Liz coos, turning to Joe. "Are you holding?"

As he nods, I continue my point. "Eric comes home Saturday. I would like to spend time with my loving boyfriend, who I have not seen in a week. Not kill my weekend just to see a bunch of guys throw twenties at strippers, then tell me they have a genuine connection."

"Hookers," Joe interrupts.

"Hookers," I say firmly, making my point. Then, shocked. "There will be hookers?"

He smiles. "If there were, would that make you more or less likely to go?"

I huff a weird noise, then tell Liz, "Smack him."

"On it," Liz says casually as she raises her palm to smack Joe upside the head again.

Joe puts out his palms in surrender. "Okay, paws up. You don't want to go. Fine."

Dave and Isabella walk up to us, holding hands and looking adorable.

I hate them.

"So, what are we talking about?" Dave asks uneasily, staring at Joe.

"I was just talking to Sam about your bachelor party," Joe says happily.

Isabella's face lights up. "Oh, you're going?" she asks me. "I'm so relieved to hear that. Now I know he won't come home with anything."

I pretend to be crushed to give the news. "I'm afraid I can't. Eric will be home Saturday night and I have to pick him up from the airport."

"Isabella can pick him up," Joe offers cheerfully.

This time I reach around Liz to smack Joe on the back of the head myself.

"No, he's right," Isabella says quickly. "I'll do it. It'll give us a chance to catch up before the wedding guests start coming into town."

Think, Sam. Think.

"Well," I say, stalling for time, "I also have a lot of work to do on your book. I really don't have the time to…"

"Can't you bring that with you?" Liz asks innocently.

I glare at her. "I could, except that some of the work I have to do this weekend is to get another interview with Isabella. And I can't do that unless I'm in town."

"Sure you can," Joe says in an upbeat tone. "You can call her between strip clubs."

If looks could kill, he'd be six feet under.

"I'm sorry," Joe concedes. "Gentlemen's clubs."

"I'm not going…" I say to Joe under my breath in a sing-songy voice.

"Yes, you are…" Joe counters in that same sing-songy voice. Then he does his best Vince Vaughn from *Swingers*. "Samolina, baby…"

"Quit calling me that!" I yell, losing it. "If you think I'm going to be responsible for Dave getting drunk, then getting another tattoo to piss off another wife, you're even dumber than you look."

I watch Dave visibly wince as Isabella glares at Joe and cross her arms. "That's *your* fault?" she asks venomously.

"No, that's *Dave's* fault. I was merely there to suggest a pattern."

The pattern was the cartoon of Elizabeth Montgomery from the beginning of *Bewitched*. Samantha Stevens. Get it? Yeah, like I hadn't heard *that* one seventeen times before and after we were married.

That tattoo became the bane of our marriage. I thought it was tacky. Not to mention a constant reminder of Joe's complete lack of decorum and complete disregard for my feelings, which constantly seemed to rub off on my soon-to-be husband. The only saving grace was that the tattoo was small, and Dave had it tattooed on his ankle, so at least if he wore socks, no one ever saw it.

Isabella puts her hands on her hips. "We had it removed," she says, staring daggers at Joe. "And if he comes home with another one, you two might not get to play together anymore."

Joe stares at Isabella, stunned. I'm not sure if it's because she's just proved that her relationship with Dave trumps his or because she threatened him so openly.

Joe looks at Dave in mock horror. "You had it removed???"

Dave nods, appearing rather sheepish as he turns away from his best friend.

Isabella smiles wide as she focuses on me. "Sam, please tell me you'll go to Hawaii with them and make sure they don't do anything stupid."

"Now would your definition of stupid include Bonobo chimps?" Joe asks Isabella.

Isabella tries to furrow her botoxed brow in confusion. "What?"

"You mean Bonobos," Liz says to Joe, talking to him like he's an idiot.

I turn to Liz suspiciously. "Excuse me?"

"They're not Bonobo *chimps*, they're just Bonobos. They have longer legs and smaller heads. Plus chimps tend to be governed by aggression and an alpha male. Bonobos are governed by females and sex."

Sometimes I worry about her.

"What do Bonobo chimps have to do with Dave's bachelor party?" Isabella asks.

Joe's face lights up. "Glad you asked. Did you know that Bonobo mmmph…"

That's the sound of me covering his mouth.

"Will you excuse us for a moment?" I say, forcing a smile as I drag Joe out of his seat. "I need another drink. Anyone else need drinks?"

Isabella sees the massive tray of drinks on the table. "But there are…"

"I've got a hankering for a Diet Coke. We'll be right back."

I pretend to drag him to the bar, but once we're downstairs and out of everyone's sight, I make a swift turn to a dark corner. "What the hell are you doing?"

Joe puts his hand on the wall next to me, leaning in as though he's going kiss me. "Come on. You know you want to," he says seductively. "We'll pick you up at ten. Pack slinky."

"Now you're just creeping me out."

Joe immediately backs up, flashing his boyish smile. "Look, you know you're going. So you can either admit you're going now and still salvage part of the evening with your friends and enjoy clowns and stiltwalkers, or you can spend the rest of the night with me following you around to talk you into going. Which means you'll also have to listen to me talk about Bonobos, my latest sexual escapades and Flipper the dolphin."

"What does Flipper…"

"I don't think you want to go there."

I put up my index finger and shake it in Joe's face. "There is no way I am going. Do NOT fuck with me about this. You know who wins when you fuck with me."

Twenty-nine

There's a term used in Hollywood scripts: SMASH CUT TO. Basically, it's written for comedy scripts. The character says, "Absolutely, positively, the kids and the dog are not coming with us on our honeymoon!" SMASH CUT TO: Three kids in the back seat, the new wife in the passenger seat, the dog on the lap of the new husband who just made the pronouncement, who sulks while he drives.

Smash cut to me the next day being driven to the Van Nuys airport so that I can be whisked away with Dave and his buddies on a private jet headed for Waikiki.

Actually, let's go back ten minutes. Back to when I was out cold, having a delicious dream about Cary Grant and a castle in Bordeaux. Which is a fine way to sleep off a hangover.

Cary leans down to kiss me, then whispers in my ear, "Wakey! Wakey!" in a woman's voice.

That can't be right.

"Wakey, wakey," I hear Vanessa croon in a motherly voice.

I open my eyes and look around in confusion. I'm in my room at home, yet here she is.

"What time is it?" I ask, my voice crackly and pained.

"Nine forty-five."

"What day is it?"

"Friday, dear. Care for a hair of the dog that bit you?"

I try to sit up. Oh God, the nausea is already starting. "I don't think it bit me. I think it mauled me and chewed out my liver."

"Liz says that you were drinking something called a Pussy Galore," Vanessa says, loudly shaking a metal cocktail shaker. "Five

204

different kinds of alcohol in one glass. What were you thinking dear, mixing grains like that?"

I grab my head. "Never ask someone with a hangover what they were thinking the night before. It's like asking a guy why he bought red pants or asking a girl why she permed her hair at two in the morning. There's never a good answer." I rub my eyes, trying to get the mascara gunk out of them. "What are you doing here?"

"You called me this morning to ask me to come over and help you pack."

"I did?" I say, struggling to remember the rest of my night.

Okay, think. It turned out I didn't have press to impress, so I stopped drinking water and started drinking wine. Then Joe kept talking about this damn bachelor party, and I switched to Pussy Galores. A lot of them. Then I started alternating the Pussy Galores with shots of Sex on the Beach...

Yeah, Sam, drink when you get uncomfortable. That always makes the night end on a high note.

"Wait. I called you this morning and you woke up?" I ask Vanessa as she hands me the purple drink.

"Well, it was five this morning, so I was just heading off to bed. But you sounded so desperate, I thought I better pull an all-nighter and do some shopping. The car's coming in less than fifteen minutes. Go wash your face."

Shopping? Car? "I'm sorry. I'm a little fuzzy on last night," I say as I sniff the drink. Ugh, the smell of it is going to make me hurl. "Why were you shopping and what car are you talking about?"

"You called me in a panic. Kept talking about love and commitment and *Chair-guh*, whatever that means. It was so obvious that this was your way of saying you needed my help seducing your ex."

"I doubt I meant that," I say, rubbing my temple. "Cerga is a word I use to mean the family you choose, as opposed to the family you're born with. I'm sure I was talking about Eric."

"Darling, no woman is up at five in the morning obsessing over how to seduce a man she's already sleeping with."

Before I can ask her to elaborate on last night's conversation, the doorbell rings. "That's probably the driver!" Vanessa says, jumping up, grabbing two pieces of my black luggage, then heading out of my room. "I'll answer the door and give the driver your bags, which are already packed. You clean up and change."

I drag my ass out of bed, and try to piece together my night.

At one in the morning, after arguing for hours with everyone at Cirque about the bachelor party, Isabella handed me her cell phone. I answered to hear Eric's very sleepy voice. If memory serves, he told me that Isabella desperately wanted me to go and make sure Joe didn't let Dave "do anything stupid." I drunkenly argued about how much I missed him, how much I loved him, blah, blah, blah. Then he said how he loved me enough to see me Sunday night instead, blah, blah, blah. Then he said something about the books and the money waiting for me when I got back.

And somehow, at the behest of my boyfriend, I agreed to go.

Yuck. A long weekend with seven guys, including Dave, his former band mates Joe and Greg, and four other guys I have yet to meet. And no one around to help me dampen the "bro" festivities. Dave's bandmate Paul had to stay behind with Isabella, since he's planning their wedding. Which is a shame, because I know Paul well enough to know he'd spend the weekend trying to get them to turn off whatever sports event was on during the day, then give them a running commentary on the stripper's shoes at night.

Okay, that mystery is solved. But why did I call Vanessa at five in the morning?

As I try to jog my memory, I quickly wash my face, throw on a baby blue track suit, and pull my unbrushed hair into a ponytail. I grab my laptop computer and all of my notes from my desk and stuff everything into my briefcase. Maybe I can at least get some work done during this weekend of Bacchanalia.

I head over to Liz's room and open her door to see Liz out cold in her bed.

I nudge her gently. "Liz. Wake up."

She opens one eye. "Hmm?"

"What happened last night?"

She opens her eyes. "I think Joe tried to kiss me. I moved my head away, he kissed my cheek. We went home."

"Um...well, I guess that's not surprising."

Liz closes her eyes and drifts back to asleep.

"I don't mean to sound self-centered... But what happened with me?"

She starts snoring lightly.

"Honey, the car is waiting!" Vanessa yells from outside.

I give up, let Liz sleep it off, and head out.

A black stretch limousine idles out front, a uniformed driver standing by the open back door. Vanessa stands next to him.

If I were four, I'd throw myself down on the ground and scream, "No! No! No! I don't wanna go!"

Vanessa walks up to me and rubs my shoulders. "You'll be fine. I put your makeup bag in the back. Do something about the bags under your eyes before you see Dave, and for goodness sakes brush your hair. Also drink plenty of water. Good luck dear."

She gives me a kiss and hug, then sends me into the car.

Dead woman riding.

I keep my briefcase with me, as I plan on getting some writing done en route. I give Vanessa one last wave, then climb into the limo to see Joe, leaning back against his seat and smiling, a flute of champagne in his hand.

Now would be the perfect time to throw up. On him.

Joe hands me one of the flutes. "Cristal?" he offers brightly.

"No thank you," I say. I open my briefcase and pull out a notebook. "If you'll excuse me, I have a lot of work to get done."

Joe happily grabs my notebook, tosses it to the side, then scoots next to me. "Okay, so here's what I'm thinking. We check into our hotel, drop off our stuff, and immediately slip away from the rest of the crowd for a little private time."

I try to disguise the fear in my voice with repugnance. "Excuse me?"

"We start at the salon: kick it off with some mani/pedis. Then I go get my roots touched up while you head for a bikini wax. What do you like? Brazilian? Charlie Chaplain? Personally, I prefer a bikini on women. Anything less than that looks prepubescent to me, but I seem to be in a minority these days. Oh," he pulls out a pair of tweezers from his pocket. "I'm assuming you'll want to tweeze your breast hairs yourself. These are the best."

I don't take the tweezers. "You have someone dye your hair?"

"No, I don't have someone *dye* my hair. I have it rinsed. What? You think someone with my skin tone naturally has jet black hair?"

"No, I just always assumed you colored it yourself. I mean, it always looks so…What's the word I'm looking for?"

"Cheap?" Joe asks.

"I was going more for 'tacky' or 'completely lacking in style''. But 'cheap', that's a good word."

"Hey, I may have been able to look like a sexy nineteen year old who just fell out of bed when I was nineteen. But at my age, it takes some maintenance. You have no idea how much money I pay a stylist to keep me looking like a penniless teenager with a bottle of generic hair dye and a dream."

"Fair enough," I say. Then I climb over him to retrieve my notebook. "But I'm not going anywhere with you. I have a lot of work to do and I plan to hide in my room all weekend while you guys do whatever it is guys do at bachelor parties."

Joe smiles. "Wait a minute. You're not even going to *attempt* to seduce Dave with witty repartee and double entendres before knocking boots tomorrow night?"

"What is with everyone?!" I snap. "I'm not going to have sex with Dave. I have a boyfriend."

"Please... I've had sex with lots of girls who have boyfriends."

"And he has a fiancée."

"Yeah, and she has Got! To! Go!"

Maybe. But as I am obligated to point out to Joe, "Well, she's giving me a life changing amount of money and getting my novel published. So she doesn't have to go this weekend."

"Okay," Joe says, shrugging.

I open my notebook, and begin reading my last interview. Joe pushes the flute of champagne between me and the page. "Have a drink with me."

"No, thank you," I say, gently pushing the glass back to him.

"If you do, we can talk about whatever you want," he offers.

"No."

"Because otherwise, I'm just going to babble on and on about whatever I consider socially acceptable dialogue."

I stare intently at my notebook. "Babble away."

"Have I ever told you about the mating rituals of dolphins?"

"Not listening."

"Or how my friend last night was babbling about red diaries?"

I look up, eyes wide. Grab the glass. "You win. What did I say?"

"What do you think you said?"

I shake my head. "Nope."

"That you'd been talking to him all week, and you worried you may have feelings for him again."

Damn it. "I said that?"

"Yup. And you were also talking about how you needed a runner's body and how you hated fortune tellers, and how I was in your chair. And then you threw up."

"I threw up on you?"

"No. You threw up in the restroom. I had to hold your hair."

"You were in the ladies room?"

"No. The woman who sits there with the breath mints and gum wouldn't let me in. You were in the men's room."

"This just gets better and better. Where was Liz?"

"Silks."

"I'm sorry."

"You know the acrobatic thing, silks? She was doing that. You told me not to tell her you threw up. Then we went home."

"Huh," I say, almost to myself. I take a sip of champagne. "Well thank you for taking care of me."

Joe stops with his snappy and annoying dialogue for a moment, and tells me in all seriousness, "It was my privilege."

We're both silent for a bit. We listen to the silence and sip our champagne. Finally, I ask, "Did I say anything else about Dave?"

"Whether you did or didn't doesn't really matter. What matters is that you're honest with yourself, without needing to get so hammered someone you don't even like has to hold up your hair."

Joe lets me take a minute to collect my thoughts.

"I don't know," I finally blurt out weakly. Joe looks at me, eyes soft, really listening. "I don't know how I feel about Dave. I think about him all the time. Ever since I saw him a few weeks ago. But I love Eric. Dave is just new. Or old. Or maybe I'm sad he's really gone this time. I don't know. I don't know why I'm thinking about him. And I really wish I wasn't."

Joe waits for me to continue. But I'm done. Finally he says, "Okay."

"Don't say that! I'm not even making sense. So I'm thinking about him. So what? If I really wanted him back, I could have called him a million times in the last five years. But I didn't. That's not exactly a woman chasing her dreams, is it? And I may be a complete fuckup in a million ways, but I always chase my dreams. So, what does any of this even mean?"

Joe continues to silently listen and look sympathetic. "I'm serious," I continue. "What do you think is the answer? I'm thirty years old and I still don't know what I want. Why do you think I'm acting this way and what does it mean?"

Joe considers my question, then answers. "I don't know."

Not the answer I wanted to hear. I don't know why, but I was kind of hoping this miscreant, narcissistic, perpetual Peter Pan would say some magical sentence and everything in my life would suddenly all make sense and fall into place.

"You'll figure it out. And this," he says, waving his index finger back and forth towards him and me. "This is always a safe space while you do."

Ah, Joe. He's infuriating, vaguely belligerent and frequently in his own world. But he could always say exactly the right thing just when you needed to hear it most.

I put my hand over his and squeeze it. "Thank you."

And after debating a few moments, I decide to use the safe space. "I don't think I told you you were in my chair. I probably said you were in my Cerga."

"That's it!" he says. "You said chair and then Guh! Projectile vomiting."

And we're back. But I push on, "Cerga means family. I think I told you that you were part of my family."

Joe uncharacteristically looks away, smiles, and blushes. "You're mine too Samolina," he says.

He clinks glasses with me. We exchange smiles. Have a nice moment.

And then...

"Want to hear about the mating rituals of Pandas?"

"I do not."

Thirty

We get to the Van Nuys airport about twenty minutes later. Our limo pulls up to Isabella's Ferrari, giving us the pleasure of watching the two of them neck outside the driver's side of her car.

As our driver gets out, Joe and I can't help but watch them from inside the limo. "Makes a little vomit climb up to the top of your throat, doesn't it?" he asks me.

When the driver opens our door and we step out of the car, Dave quickly pulls away from Isabella. "Oh, sorry. Didn't see you guys."

"How could you?" Joe asks, asking in a tone of voice that could also mean, *How could you marry this awful woman?*

Dave appears properly chastised. "I'll be up in a minute."

As the driver retrieves our luggage from the trunk, Joe and I walk across the tarmac and up the metal steps to a medium sized white plane. Standing at the entrance is a stunningly beautiful blonde woman with what even I, as a straight woman, have to admit is a smoking hot body. Inexplicably, she is dressed in nothing but a black lace bra with matching black lace boy shorts and four-inch heels. "Good morning," she says brightly. "I'm Tiffany and I'll be one of your flight attendants this afternoon."

Joe looks her over lasciviously. "Nice outfit."

"Thanks!" Tiffany says cheerfully. "I have others I can show you during the flight."

"Do you have…" Joe begins.

I smack him on the arm.

"Ow!" He says, rubbing his arm as he turns to me. "You don't even know what I was going to say."

"No good can come from the end of that sentence," I counter.

"Awww…" Tiffany says, crinkling her nose. "That is so cute. How long have you two been together?"

"Oh, God! Never!" I blurt out, horrified.

Joe cocks his head at me, slightly offended. "Why the hate?"

"Oh don't tell me you weren't thinking the exact same thing," I mutter, then walk into the plane.

I have never flown anything but coach, so the decadence of the inside of this plane blows my mind. Everything is white: white wide leather seats, a white sofa designed for four, plush white carpet. In the back, there is a full bar on the right, where a woman in a French Maid's costume prepares drinks. To the left is a table draped in white linen, which appears to be housing a fruit and cheese plate, a caviar station, and a box of Krispy Kreme donuts.

As I decide which seat to take, I notice yet another beautiful woman, this one donning a red lace push up bra and matching underwear, red lace thigh high stockings and a red garter belt. She dances a sexy dance in front of Greg, Dave's old bandmate, who sits in a leather chair, talking on the phone, completely oblivious to her. Judging from his side of the conversation, he's talking to his wife. "Well honey, if you want me to come home, I'll come home…" he says in his Texas drawl. "Well, why would you call me to say she has a fever if you don't want me to come home?"

The woman tries to sit on his lap. "Can you hold on a sec?" Greg asks, then covers his phone to look up at Red Girl. "Darlin', you're quite the entertainer. But I'm on with the wife. Could you give me a few minutes?"

"Sure," she says. "Can I get you a drink?"

"A beer would be great," he says, giving her a thumbs up, then going back to his conversation.

"I'm not married," Joe says, quickly following red girl to the bar.

The woman in the French Maid's outfit takes a tray of drinks over to three guys, all about my age, who sit around a table, quietly playing poker. As she serves the drinks, she looks over at me. "I'm Genevieve. Can I get you a drink?"

"She's the wife," Tiffany tells Genevieve from the cabin door.

"I'm not the wife!" I say, maybe a little too defensively.

"She's my wife," Dave says calmly, walking through the cabin door.

Tiffany looks confused. "I thought you were the groom."

"I am," Dave concedes. "Sam's my ex-wife."

"Oh," Tiffany says, still mystified.

"And she'll get very upset if you give him any lap dances," Joe tells Tiffany from the bar as Red Girl hands him a beer. "She wants to give him all the dances!"

I wonder if I would make the front cover of the *New York Times* for killing Joe, or just the *National Enquirer?*

"Good afternoon," Tiffany says, taking a microphone from the wall. "I'm Tiffany. Your lady in red is Crystal, and your French Maid is Genevieve."

"So what French things can you do?" I hear Joe ask Genevieve as Tiffany continues, "Please take your seats, while we prepare for takeoff. Then...let the party begin!"

Joe applauds politely as the boys from the poker group give an unenthused cheer.

The poker group buckle their seatbelts, then continue to play poker. I sit across from Greg as Joe and Dave sit near the front. As we buckle our seatbelts, the flight attendants close the cabin door and make other preparations for takeoff.

"No, it's starve a fever feed a cold," Greg says into the phone, a little panicked. It's then that he notices me. His face lights up. "Sam! What are you doing here?"

"I…"

He puts up his index finger to tell me to hold that thought. "No, my friend Sam. She's an old friend from college," he says into the phone. "Oh well, I'm sorry I sound too happy. I only haven't seen her in five years." Greg listens to his wife a beat, then tells her, "Walk me through this… you're jealous of Sam, but the stripper trying to give me a lap dance me a minute ago, that you're comfortable with?" I buckle my seatbelt and continue to listen to him talk to his wife. "Honey, the girl's wearing a velour sweat suit, she's the only woman here who's even vaguely dressed… No, no, sweetheart. You're thinking of Stephanie. Sam was the wife, not the home wrecker."

I must have looked startled, because he covers the phone. "All water under the bridge, right?"

I shrug. "Sure?"

We hear the engine roar as Greg says, "I have to go now, honey. I'll call you when we get to Hawaii."

And he hangs up the phone.

Twenty minutes later, we are up in the air, and the party (at least from a sleazy guy's point of view) has begun.

Dave introduces me to the rest of the group: Pat, Mark and Ron. They're very polite. But, let's face it, I'm the girl in the tracksuit: who do you think they're paying attention to?

As Tiffany models a slutty cheerleader outfit for them, I head over to the catering table. "You're Sam, right?" Crystal asks.

"I am," I admit.

"These are for you," she tells me, opening the Krispy Kreme box to show me a dozen assorted donuts. I grab the chocolate glazed greedily.

Joe walks up to Crystal. "Any delights I can put in my mouth?"

Instead of smacking him, she giggles. "You are so funny," she says. Then she leans into him and whispers, "I love your work."

He ogles her. "Well, I love yours."

The two walk off together as Dave walks up to me. "I'm sorry about this," he says, watching the girls flirt with his friends. "This was Isabella's idea. I didn't even know planes like this existed."

"It's all right," I say. Then I lean into him and whisper, "Are they hookers, or just strippers?"

"I don't plan to find out," Dave whispers back. He takes my arm, and leads me towards a quiet spot next to the galley. "So, I want to thank you for last night."

Crap.

I smile. "No problem," I say, as though whatever I did were no big deal. (Please let it be no big deal.) "Anytime."

"It's just…" Dave looks down at his hands, struggling to find the right words. "I felt so much better afterwards. It was like this enormous tension was suddenly released."

Oh, boy.

"I mean, I'm sorry I was a little drunk," he adds. "It would have been better if I had been sober."

What the fuck?!

I nod and smile. "I was pretty drunk too, don't forget."

Dave shrugs. "Yeah, but you were mostly on the receiving end. Not that that doesn't require even more effort sometimes."

I nod, then take a huge bite of my donut. Now I'm so stressed, I'm tempted to stuff the whole thing in my mouth. But that may be the type of action that got me into this conversation in the first place. Who knows?

Tiffany walks up to us, carrying a silver tray with a bottle of Clos du Mesnil champagne, and three filled crystal flutes. "Would you like to have a glass of champagne with me?" she asks, handing us each a glass.

"I don't think I should," I say. "I'm supposed to be working."

Tiffany leans into me and whispers, "Yeah, me too. This takes the edge off."

Suddenly, the plane's lights dim, and the first chords of Prince's "Erotic City" start blasting over the sound system.

"Ooh, that's my cue. Gotta go," Tiffany says, quickly placing the tray down, then grabbing her champagne glass as she dance/walks over to the makeshift "stage" in the middle of the plane, where the other two girls are already dancing around in their skivvies.

Dave picks up the two flutes from the tray and hands me one. "I don't think you're going to get much work done on this flight."

I take the flute from him. "Just promise me no one gives me a lap dance, okay?"

The next five hours were a blur. The food was amazing. For lunch, we had something called Kobe burgers. They tasted like burgers to me, but I like burgers, so that was good. I also half a box of Krispy Kremes and an amazing chocolate fondue that fortunately I got to before the girls started using it for body paint.

Overall, it was a pretty tame party. Dave got one lap dance, where he sat stone faced, looking uncomfortable as hell. The other guys got tipsy and got dances, but no one got naked, and no one got laid. It was just a silly strip club atmosphere. The girls went out of their way to make sure I wasn't uncomfortable at any time, and if it weren't for the fact that I still didn't know what Dave and I did last night, I wouldn't have been.

We landed at a private airport in Honolulu, and split up into groups of four to take two pink limousines to the Royal Hawaiian Hotel in Waikiki.

Built in 1927, The Royal Hawaiian is one of the older hotels on the island of Oahu, and a landmark in Hawaii. Nicknamed "The Pink Palace of the Pacific", because of the building's coral pink stucco, it's the giant pink hotel located right in the middle of Waikiki beach.

Dave and I stayed here once, when his band played a festival at the Aloha Stadium. It's stunningly beautiful, and manages to be elegant, yet laid back.

The limos pull up to the front, and as the valets deal with our luggage, our group heads into the open air lobby. The lobby was designed in the 1920s, when old Spanish was the décor du jour. I take a moment to revel in the dark wood, textured walls, and arched doorways.

"Wow, it's just as beautiful as I remember it," I semi-whisper to Dave, slightly breathless as I inhale the smell of the Pacific Ocean just outside.

As we walk up to the front desk, a woman with the nametag Lelani greets us. "Aloha."

"Aloha," Dave returns. "Stevens. We have reservations for seven."

Lelani begins typing on her computer, as a beautiful young lady magically appears carrying purple pikake leis. "Aloha," she says to me, placing a lei over my head.

"Aloha," I say back happily. I love leis. They surround me with perfume and make me feel exotic.

She then repeats the lei greeting with each of Dave's friends, giving each of them a gracious, "Aloha."

"Can I see everyone's ID?" Lelani asks.

We all pull out our driver's licenses or passports, then she continues to type. A minute later, Lelani slides several envelopes over to us. "Okay, we have Mr. Stevens in the Kamehameha Suite," she says to Dave, slipping him a pink envelope with a hotel card key. "Mr. Smith and Mr. Winston are in Room 431," she says, handing Pat and Greg their card keys. "Mr. Robinson and Miss Evans are in Room..."

"Wait a minute," I interrupt. "I am not staying in Joe's room."

"Oh," Lelani says. "I'm sorry. Miss De Leon specifically requested particular rooms for particular guests. Is that not satisfactory?"

Of course she did. Why that little...

"What's wrong with staying with me?" Joe asks.

"Well for one thing, I'm too old to return to my room to see the knob draped with a tube sock."

"Woman, that was years ago," Joe says, dismissing me with his tone. "And it wasn't a tube sock, it was a condom."

I stare daggers at him.

"It wasn't a used condom," he points out.

"Oohh... that's much better then," I retort. Then I turn to Lelani. "I'm gonna need my own room."

Lelani types some more. "We're completely booked up this weekend. But we have a lovely room at our sister hotel, the Sheraton. It's just next door..."

"I'll take it," I say immediately, thrilled to be an entire hotel away from the bachelor party.

"Don't be silly," Dave says. "Knowing Belle, my room is probably huge. You can bunk with me."

"I'm not bunking with my ex-husband the weekend of his bachelor party," I insist.

Lelani looks visibly shocked by my statement.

I glare at her. "Oh, like that's strangest thing you've ever seen at this hotel."

Thirty-one

Ten minutes later, I am in a beautiful room with a breathtaking view of the Pacific. I open my window, inhale the wonderful scent of flowers mingling with ocean breezes and listen to waves pounding against the white sand beach.

Aaaahhhh…

I lie down on my beautiful bed and admire its Hawaiian themed, flowered bedspread and pink pillowcases and sheets.

Joe walks out of our pink bathroom, wearing nothing but a pink towel wrapped around his six-pack waist. His face is covered in shaving cream. "What do you think Samolina?" he asks, then begins singing to the tune of The Clash's *Should I Stay or Should I Go?* "Should I shave or should I grow now? Should I shave or should I grow now?"

I'm in no mood for this. I cross my arms and determinedly look away from him.

He keeps singing. "If I shave there will be stubble. But if I grow it will be double…"

"Must you always live your life like a Mentos commercial?" I snap at him.

"You're tense."

"Your powers of observation have never failed to amaze me."

"Listen, I'm just gonna grab a quick shower, I got Genevieve's perfume all over me, then we'll head to the Mai Tai Bar and get some drinks into you."

"What makes you think I need drinks in me?" I ask in irritation.

"Okay, sweetheart, if you throw one down the middle like that, you know I'm gonna have to swing," he says before retreating into our pink bathroom.

221

The moment Joe's out of hearing range, I call Dave's room.

"Hello?" he answers.

"We're going to the Mai Tai Bar in a bit. Wanna come?"

"Um...yeah," Dave answers, sounding stressed. "I'll meet you down there as soon as I can. Okay?"

"You okay? You sounds weird."

"I'm fine. Just on with Belle. I'll see you down here."

"Or we could..." I begin, but I realize he's hung up on me.

Fifteen minutes later, Joe and I are sitting at a pink table, under a pink and white umbrella, at a beachside table of the hotel's famous Mai Tai Bar. We have a view of Diamond Head and the white sands of Waikiki Beach, and there is not a cloud in the sky.

The bar is so named because it is reputed to be the place where the Mai Tai tropical drink was invented. (Trader Vic's makes the same claim.) I was planning to be traditional and get a Mai Tai. But I couldn't help myself. When I'm Hawaii, I want a Lava Flow: a tropical drink similar to a Piña Colada, but with strawberry puree mixed in that is supposed to resemble lava coming out of a volcano. The bartender garnishes the drink with a purple flower, which makes me almost giddy. I don't know why, but there's something about a flower in a drink that I just love.

Now if only the company was as wonderful as my drink.

"Come on," Joe taunts, sipping a pint of pink beer. "Weirdest place?"

"I'm not telling you," I say emphatically.

"It was a bed. I know it was a bed."

"This is a stupid game," I state, sucking the Lava Flow froth from my purple flower, then putting it behind my ear.

"Maybe once you were at the foot of the bed, which was really wicked..."

"Next question, please."

"Or maybe you're one of those button up freaks who has done it on a Merry Go Round..."

"Next question!" I snap.

A honeymooning couple turns to stare.

Joe considers changing the subject. "Spit or swallow?"

I stare at him, disgusted. He just stares back. I would say we engage in a staring contest, but it's more like I blink a few times, then give up.

"The Eiffel Tower," I finally answer.

At that, Joe looks both shocked and impressed.

"We were on the stairs, it was winter so no one was around. It was a stupid idea. What about you?"

"Dodger Stadium."

"Really?"

Joe shrugs. "They were losing by so much, I got bored. Car?"

"Huh?"

"Car. What make and model of car have you had sex in?"

I have to think for a moment. "1979 Honda Accord. You?"

Joe ticks off the answers one by one with his fingers. "1956 Chevy, 1962 Mustang, 1966 VW bug, 1976 Cobra, 1979 Jeep..."

"Okay, I think I get the point."

He leans into me and whispers, "I got a 1997 Porsche back in L.A.. Can I tempt ya'?"

I roll my eyes. "Remind me again of how talking about all of this is supposed to make us better friends?"

"It doesn't. But now every time I see a picture of the Eiffel Tower, I gotta real nice visual."

My cell rings. I see it's Dave, then click on. "What should we order you?"

"Can you come up to my room?" he asks me rather urgently.

I'm being summoned to his room? That can't be good.

He knows how I feel about expensive hotel rooms: they make me want to have sex. Why is he inviting me up? Does this have to do with whatever happened last night? I sneak a quick glance at Joe, casually sipping his beer and checking out the ladies in bikinis on the beach.

"When you say *you*, do you mean singular or plural?"

"I mean just you. Tell Joe to throw on a bathing suit and get a tan or something."

I cover the phone. "Dave wants to know if you want to go grab a tan for awhile?"

Joe shrugs. "He's the groom. We can do whatever he wants."

I put my tongue over my top lip, thinking about how to rephrase that. "No. I think he wants to see me...alone."

Judging from the eyebrow raise, Joe's interest is piqued.

He grabs the phone from me. "Dude, what's up?" he asks seriously into the phone. "Uh-huh...yeah...yeah, okay."

Joe presses the *End* button and hands me my phone. "Go. I'll take care of the check. We'll catch up with each other later."

So I do.

Thirty-two

I knock on the door of the Kamehameha suite, and Dave opens immediately, holding his cell phone and covering the mouthpiece. "I'm sorry. It's Belle again. Make yourself at home. There's a bottle of champagne on the patio if you want some."

"It's Sam," he says into the phone as he walks into the bedroom and shuts the door for privacy.

I close the front door, walk into the suite's living room, and just stand there ogling. Wow. His room is in the dead center of the hotel and his ocean front view is nothing but water from every window. The view alone makes me secretly wish I had bunked here.

And his living room is massive. I walk on the highly polished Koa floors and check out the plush white sectional sofa that would have easily been big enough for me to sleep on. I look at all of the Queen Anne furniture longingly and wish I could move in. He even has a dining room table for six and a work desk. I could totally move in. He might not even notice.

I walk through the French doors onto the lanai, which is large enough to throw a party. A bottle of Clos du Mesnil champagne is chilling in a silver champagne bucket next to the chairs. I pour myself a glass, marveling at how I got so lucky that lately I've been drinking champagne like it was Diet Coke.

"I'm off the phone!" Dave yells from the other room, sounding either tired, agitated or a combination of both. "Can you come into the bedroom?"

I pour Dave a glass, then bring our champagne flutes to the bedroom.

Double wow. The bedroom is cavernous. The pink marble bathroom is huge. There's yet another lanai outside with seating and a view of the ocean.

As long as I work for the rich and famous, it never fails to amaze me how well they get to live. How can you not be deliriously happy when you're staying in a place like this?

Of course, I'm probably about to have that question answered as Dave looks miserable. He has his hands on his hips and is glaring at his luggage, with most of his clothes sprawled out in piles all over his bed.

"What you think?" he asks angrily. "And give me your honest opinion."

I try to make a joke. "I think, as usual, you're not appreciating the hotel at all, and the fact that you have to have your socks in the top drawer before you even get a drink downstairs is ridiculous."

"I meant about the clothes," he says, pointing to the designer suits laying neatly in his unzipped garment bag.

I wish he could just tell me what I'm supposed to be mad about. "I'll admit, they're not the most appropriate clothes for Hawaii…"

"And look at what she had packed for me during the day," he rages, rifling through one of his Tumi suitcases to toss out several button-up shirts and a pair of nice white linen pants. "There isn't a T-shirt or a pair of jeans in here. It's like I was telling you on the phone last night: this is one of the multitude of ways Isabella uses to control me!"

On the phone last night. Okay, that's a good start.

As I stand there dumbly, Dave continues pawing through his things. "And I know that you'll defend her and say that she's only getting me clothes because she thinks I'll look good in them, But that's why you used to buy me clothes. I don't think that's why *she* buys me clothes. I think she does it because she wants to control my image; control the impression people have of me. You know, 'He dresses in Armani, he must be...'" Dave struggles to find the words. "Okay, I can't even think of what I'm supposed to be, dressing in a suit in Hawaii, but I can guarantee you, it's not who I am."

He looks up at me, just noticing the champagne. "It's like this champagne," he says irritably, taking his glass from me. "She sent it up without my even asking for it. Why? To impress the waiters? I'd never heard of Clos du Mesnil until two weeks ago, and suddenly it's all we're drinking. What's wrong with having a beer once in awhile? Or maybe a Pepsi while we just stay home one night, maybe grill something on the barbecue without anyone around snapping our picture."

I open my mouth to say something sympathetic, only to have him continue his tirade. "Or maybe it's not how we're seen – maybe it's all about control with her. I mean, what was up with that plane? Obviously since she's paying for it they're going to give her every detail about happened during *my* bachelor weekend! Plus she got reservations for us at some five-star steakhouse tonight, followed by yet another strip club. Exactly when do *I* get to decide what *I'm* doing with *my* bachelor weekend?"

I try to think of the perfect thing to say. Deciding actions speak louder than words, I head to the mini bar, pull out a bottle of Pepsi and hand it to him. "Here. For the road. Let's go to the mall and buy you some Levi's."

Thirty-three

While the boys were out lounging by the pool or hanging out at the beach, Dave and I spent the afternoon shopping.

The Ala Moana Center is a Mecca for Hawaiian tourists and natives alike. The mall is home to elegant stores like Neiman Marcus, Prada and Louis Vuitton. But we headed to Sears for jeans, then to a local shop for Hawaiian print shirts in crazy colors.

The twentysomething me would have been horrified. I didn't even know Sears sold jeans. And no one looks sexy in a Hawaiian shirt – it's just that simple. Dave never had, and never would have, any sense of formality. Which used to drive me crazy. Putting him in suits was like dressing a tiger in a peignoir set: the clothes would fool no one and it would just make the tiger angry.

But the thirtysomething me was a little embarrassed by my former self. So what if he proudly buys jeans on sale for twenty bucks? Clearly, they make him comfortable and they make him happy. Why was I never able to see that before? And he was really happy now. He had been cracking jokes and making me laugh all afternoon.

"What? You don't think this is sexy?" Dave says, modeling a red and yellow polyester Hawaiian shirt for me that he wears out of the store.

I laugh as he spins around.

"You know that's so unfair," Dave points out with a smile. "If a girl asked if this was sexy, a guy would not burst into fits of giggles. He would just say, 'Of course it is. You look insanely hot.'"

I keep laughing. "You're right, that was rude of me," I say, trying hard to suppress my laughter as I deadpan, "Wow, you're so hot in that. Take me now."

"Now, see? Was that so hard?" he jokes.

"You know what would make that outfit even hotter?" I ask.

"Dark socks with sandals."

I laugh again, nodding my head up and down in agreement. Then I ask, "So, is there anywhere else you want to go shopping? Maybe we can find some sweaters at Lowe's?"

"You are such a snob about clothes," Dave says as we walk past the Ala Moana stage, where a group of Kama'aina (meaning local) women perform the hula in traditional dress.

"I'm a girl," I point out to him. "We're expected to be snobbish about clothes."

"Not necessarily."

"Oh, please. It's part of that whole double standard thing. A girl goes to a party, she has to wear the right outfit, do her hair, get her makeup perfect, etc. A guy goes to a party, he has to take a shower. And sometimes not even that."

"True," Dave concedes. "But at least once the girl does all that and gets to the party, she can sleep with any straight, single man in the room."

"And wait by the phone the next day..."

"Here we go..." Dave says, having heard my monologue a thousand times.

"Filling ourselves with self-loathing when we're rejected yet again..." I continue.

Dave rolls his eyes. "I can't believe you're still on that after all these years."

"Because it's so unfair! Men still have all the power in the relationship. They get to approach the girl, they get to make the first call, they get to decide when the first kiss is going to be..."

"Wait a minute. Didn't you call me first?"

"I most certainly did not!" I gasp, horribly offended at his revisionist history. "I waited three days for you to pick up that phone and call me. And then I waited almost two weeks for you to kiss me."

Dave grimaces. "Well, you could have kissed me, you know."

"Why do men always say that? It's one their staples, along with, 'I would love it if a woman asked me out.' But in reality, if we ever do ask you out, you lose all interest. You need the thrill of the chase."

"That is so not true," Dave argues.

"Of course it is. You're genetically programmed..."

"I guarantee you of the six billion people on this planet, not one has ever shrieked in shock and horror, 'I'm sorry, Miss Berry, but did you just stick your tongue in my mouth?'" He walks up to a mall directory. "Are you hungry? Want to split a hot fudge sundae?"

"No, and always," I answer happily.

We spent the rest of our afternoon exchanging similar banter about the war between the sexes, mixed with filling each other in on how our lives have been these past few years. Although we weren't exactly flirting, I notice we were both careful not to mention our significant others unless absolutely necessary. (And since, over the course of the afternoon, I took a call from Eric once and Dave took calls from Isabella eight out of twelve times, sometimes it was absolutely necessary.)

That night, his friends and I skipped the steakhouse and anything else Isabella had planned, ordered room service, then hung out on Dave's lanai. Around eleven, Joe took the guys out barhopping while Dave and I lounged on the plushy white sofa in his room, watching reruns of "Mad About You" on cable.

"I'm telling you, they were us," I insist, taking a swig of Sam Adams from my bottle.

"They were not us," Dave says, shaking his head, laughing and looking adorable as he relaxes on the couch in his Hawaiian shirt and jeans.

"When they're at that party and she gives him the hair signal that she's talking to the most boring person on the planet?" I say. "We totally used to have signals at parties."

"All couples have signals at parties," Dave says. He takes a sip of his beer. "And, by the way, I don't think walking up to me and saying, 'If you leave right now, we can have sex,' really counts as a signal so much as a bribe."

"It worked, didn't it?"

"I was a twenty two year old man. Of course it worked. And they're not us."

I point to him. "Okay, what about the episode where they're planning their wedding? Doesn't him not knowing they registered for a gravy boat remind you of when we registered?"

"All right, that one I'll give you. Whatever happened to that gravy boat anyway?"

"Oh, I still have it. And six place settings of formal china to go with it. I think I've used it once in eight years."

I'm not sure what I said wrong, but Dave's face suddenly turns serious.

We share an awkward moment of silence as Dave goes pensive on me. "That was a pretty pattern you picked. No flowers. I liked it."

Boy, did that moment change. Here I was flirting, doing the giggling, leaning in, *touching him on the arm when I don't really need to* thing, and suddenly I'm dead in the water.

"You know who's like us?" Dave says, changing the subject. "Dave and Kate."

He's referring to my novel's protagonist and her ex-husband. "Well, I guess that wasn't really an accident," I admit.

Dave turns to me and looks deep into my eyes. "I really liked the book."

"Thank you," I eke out, turning my eyes away and feeling embarrassed.

Dave won't take his eyes off of me. "I would have liked the book even if I hadn't known you. It got me thinking."

I don't know how to respond to that. Finally, I screw up the courage to ask, "Thinking about what?"

As Dave opens his mouth to answer, his hotel phone rings.

It being almost two o'clock in the morning, I already know who it is before Dave answers. "Hey, Baby," he says into the phone, trying to sound loving, even though I recognize his, *I love you but how many times are you going to call me today?* voice. I point to the door to signal that I can leave.

He shakes his head no.

So I wait.

And wait. And for several minutes I listen to him agree to whatever wedding questions Isabella throws at him with answers like, "That's fine," "I don't know. What do you think?" and "I don't care. Whatever makes you happy. It's your day."

Then I hear my cell phone ring. I pull it out of my pocket to see it is Eric. I pick up. "Hello," I say, suddenly realizing how slurred my voice sounds.

"Well, you sound like you're having a good time," Eric says, clearly amused.

"What are you doing up?" I ask.

"It's eight in the morning here," Eric reminds me. "I just checked out of my hotel and I'm on my way to the airport. I was hoping you'd still be up. How's the raucous bachelor weekend going?"

"I had a Kobe burger today," I say, trying to sound happy to hear from him, when really I can't help but want to listen in on Dave's conversation.

"What's that?" Eric asks.

"I don't know. A cheeseburger? But it sounds exotic. Listen, can I call you back in a bit?"

"Oh," Eric whines rather uncharacteristically. "I've barely talked to you all week. Can't you call it a night with the guys and keep me company en route to the airport?

"Well…" I begin, looking at Dave on his cell.

Dave and I make eye contact. He mouths an "I'm sorry," to me, then continues to talk about his wedding plans.

Wedding plans. Right. Go home, Evans.

"Hold on," I say to Eric, then cover the phone and whisper. "That's Eric. I'm going to head back to my room."

Dave covers his mouthpiece. "Wait. I'll only be another minute."

"That's okay. I'll see you in the morning."

We exchange an awkward wave and I leave for the night.

Which is worse: that I would have preferred to stay up all night talking to my ex-husband, rather than my current boyfriend? Or that I spent the next few hours tossing and turning in my bed, wondering what my novel got Dave thinking about?

Thirty-four

The seven of us spent the next day frolicking on the beach (a word I do not use often, but with a beach this pretty one must frolic). And Dave just kept getting cuter and cuter. We were starting to fall back into our routine of finishing each other's sentences and answering each other's questions before hearing them: "Remember that cabin...?" "Oh yeah, with the..." "Yeah, and that weird..." "Right?!"

And at some point during the afternoon, I hate to admit this, but I started thinking about kissing Dave. Just for a minute. Just to see if he still kisses as well as he used to.

Which I know is stupid.

I know I could never compete with Isabella. Not long term anyway. Forgetting about the exquisite face and the flawless skin and the perfect body: I would never be able to give him hotels like this. Or limos and private planes and houses on the beach and the money and freedom to do whatever he wanted with his life. I just paid off my student loans two months ago. At this point, I might have enough in savings to put a down payment on a postage stamp.

So I put kissing him out of my mind and threw my energy into thoroughly enjoying a weekend with old friends.

It's now four in the afternoon and I am attempting for the third time to get through Ulysses, Eric's favorite book. I am up to Page 51 and bored out of my mind.

Joe emerges from the bathroom dressed in nice gray slacks, a matching jacket and...wait for it...a tie! "Go get ready," he tells me impatiently.

"I am ready," I say as I read.

Joe looks me up and down, appearing to be confused as he observes my J. Crew pencil skirt, flip flops, and 'Does Not Suffer Fools Gladly' T-shirt. "You're wearing that?"

I refuse to look up from my book. "No. I just put it on for your amusement."

Joe laughs. "Oh. Well, in that case, very funny. You had me going for a minute. Go change."

I look up and sigh. "What's wrong with what I have on?"

"What's *wrong* with it? Well, for one thing, you're a size four, not a size eight, so everything's baggy and you look like a slouch. And for another, we're going to a high-end gentleman's club. They require a jacket and tie for the men…"

"And a thong and a smile for the women," I retort.

"Work with me here," Joe implores as he walks over to my luggage and starts pawing through my stuff. "What else did you bring? Jeans, jeans…" He pulls out a pair of flannel pajamas. "Are ya' kidding me?"

"They're from Victoria Secret," I say, sitting up to grab them out of his hand. "Tyra Banks looks gorgeous in them."

"Tyra Banks would look gorgeous in a potato sack and mittens. Oh, here we go!" Joe says, his voice brightening.

He pulls out a small black dress, and puts it up against himself. "This could look hot."

I peer into my suitcase. "Where did you get that? I didn't pack that."

"Wait, there's a note," Joe says, pulling out a lavender sheet of paper, then reading, "I packed you this and black Jimmy Choos. Kitten with a whip. Meow. Love, Vanessa."

"Oh, for Fu…"

"P.S.," Joe continues, "I also packed some edible underwear. Don't do anything I wouldn't do, and by that I mean make him remember why he married you." Joe rifles through my things, then pulls out the pack of edible underwear. "Red raspberry and dark chocolate. Sweet."

I lie back against the pillow and try to focus on my reading.

Joe throws the dress and the undies onto my stomach. "She didn't pack a matching bra, but that's okay. You're still pretty perky. You can go commando in the dress."

I glance down at the dress, now piled on my stomach. "I'm sorry. Am I fucking you?" I ask in irritation.

"Excuse me?"

"Am I fucking you?" I repeat. "Because, if I'm not, you can't give me fashion advice."

Joe takes a moment to ponder my statement. Then he looks at his watch, starts to undo his tie. "Okay, but quickly. We have to be out of here in ten minutes."

"I just hate everyone," I pout, slamming my book shut and grabbing the dress. "Fine. I'll wear the dress."

"And the…"

"I draw the line at edible underwear," I say, marching into the bathroom and slamming the door shut.

"If you're not going to wear them, can I eat them?" Joe yells through the door.

"You ate all the candy in the minibar, and I'm kind of peckish."

Thirty-five

Thirty minutes later, I am seated at a table at one of Honolulu's newest hotspots from chef Roy Kawaguchi. Dave sits next to me, and while the other men talk amongst themselves, Dave and I continue finishing each other's thoughts and flirting like mad.

"You know what this restaurant reminds me of?" Dave asks. "That Japanese place in Hollywood."

"Oooh, that one with the sake and the sushi," I say, slightly breathless at the memory.

"Yeah, that we couldn't afford. I think that charge stayed on my Visa until...last Wednesday."

"Oh, but it was so worth it," I almost whine nostalgically. "I still think that's the best Ebi I've ever eaten. And do you remember that poor girl at the next..."

"I know, with her blind date..."

"That awful guy..."

Dave imitates the man. "But enough about me. Let's talk about my job..."

I burst out laughing.

We share a moment of silence. But's not awkward at all, it's comfortable. Another thing to crush on Dave about.

I remember I used to be slightly saddened watching older couples eat their dinners in relative silence. I used to think, "That's so sad. They've run out of stuff to talk about."

But now I think silence is golden. My goal is to be with someone I am secure enough with that I don't have to spend every minute talking or actively listening. Someone I feel secure and happy enough with to just enjoy my scallops without yammering on about my friend's engagement or listening to him yammer on about the Lakers.

Dave leans into me. "You look very nice tonight."

"Thanks," I say self-consciously. I tug at my mini-dress, trying to pull the hem down enough to cover my thighs better. "I feel a little underdressed."

Dave looks around the room. "There are people in Hawaiian shirts and sandals. How could you feel underdressed?"

I lean in and lower my voice. "I meant..." I look over at the rest of the guys at the table. They're whooping it up, not listening to our conversation at all. "I meant I don't have much clothing on. It feels weird. Like I'm trying too hard on a third date or something."

Dave slowly eyes me up and down and smiles lasciviously. "Man, if we were both single, I'd ask you out for dinner tonight, lunch tomorrow, and then room service tomorrow night. Get to that precious third date."

Wow. Is what he said wildly awesome or hideously inappropriate? The butterflies in my stomach would like to know.

"Thanks," I say shyly, looking away and taking a nervous sip of water.

Am I blushing? I feel like I'm blushing. Dave and I exchange awkward smiles, and if this were another time and place, I think he might lean in to kiss me.

So I fill that silence with yammering. "Which placemats did Isabella and you finally go with?"

Dave looks at me blankly. "What placemats?"

"The Pratesi ones," I say. "I think that was Isabella's eighth call of the day. She was debating between blue or black embroidery."

Dave sighs. "Oh, that." He scratches his ear self-consciously. "Can I ask you something?"

"Sure."

"Does Eric ever make you feel..." Dave struggles to find the right word. "Inadequate?"

"Ummm... maybe a little sometimes," I admit. "But not intentionally."

Dave nods. He sounds relieved when he says, "Okay."

"I mean, it's just that Eric is so perfect. Sometimes I feel a little awkward around him. It's nothing he's doing. It's more like I look at him and think, 'Why me'?"

Dave gives a quick laugh, shaking his head. "Why you? You don't honestly ever think that, do you?"

"Uhhh... yeah," I say. "Most women, when they really like a guy think, 'Why me?'"

"But that's ridiculous. You're beautiful, you're smart..."

"I'm insecure, I don't exercise enough..."

"You're really funny..."

"Yeah," I practically snort. "And guys notice that from across the room."

Dave smiles, clearly charmed. "They can. I did. That first night, I spent at least twenty minutes watching you and trying to figure out how to go up and talk to you. At one point, I overheard you make a joke to Liz about Gary Hart. And I laughed. And it made me want to talk to you twice as much."

I never knew that. I smile, look down at the tablecloth, and blush.

Crap. I am definitely blushing. Change the subject. "So...placemats."

"You know what? I'd really like to just *not* talk about the wedding. Just for one night. Is that okay?"

"Uh...sure," I agree, curious despite myself.

What does he mean by that? That he's tired of wedding plans or that he'd like to forget the whole wedding ever existed?

No, Sam. Don't do this to yourself. He's just flirting, he's not really interested in you. And, even if he is, it doesn't matter. He's getting married in a week to someone else.

Two servers come with our appetizers, giving me a minute to collect my thoughts. As one server puts a small plate of spring rolls in front of Dave while another serves me my salad, I decide it's just flirting. Everyone does it. Particularly people who are about to be married. Means nothing.

We thank them and everyone digs into their food. After a bite, Dave asks, "So, what will you do for your next wedding?"

"Vegas," I joke. "Figure wedding at the drive thru chapel, reception at an all you can eat buffet, then onto the lounge, where the first dance will be to *You're Having My Baby*."

Dave laughs. Then he gives me one of his languishing stares that always used to make me melt. "Seriously, have you ever given any thought to what you'd do differently next time?"

"Um... Yeah, I have actually. I'd like to get married in Kauai."

I can't tell from the look on his face if I've offended him or not.

"It would be something small, just Liz, her parents and a few friends. Quick destination wedding kind of thing."

Dave has this weird look on his face that I can't read. I shouldn't have told him the truth about Kauai. That's a giant can of worms. What was I thinking? Why not just answer, "No. Thought never crossed my mind."

Dave takes a sip of his beer, then asks. "What did you think of our wedding?"

"I loved our wedding," I answer immediately. "It was everything a wedding should be when you're twenty-two. But I'd feel kind of silly having four bridesmaids now." Remembering Isabella has twelve, I quickly add, "Not that there's anything wrong with that."

"Did we fight much about our wedding?" Dave asks, sounding like he genuinely can't remember.

"I don't think any more than most couples," I tell him.

Dave thinks about my answer as our waiter reappears to take our entrée orders. Dave gets the charbroiled short ribs, I opt for the Roasted Macadamia Nut Mahi Mahi. As the others give their orders, the two of us eat in silence.

The silence is getting deafening. Yammertime. "Joe says you're directing his next video. What's it going to be about?"

Dave's cell phone rings. He sighs loudly. "Hold that thought," he says, then walks away from the table as he answers. "Hello Belle," sounding tired and defeated.

I look around the table. Everyone is involved in a conversation except Greg, who sits on the other side of me. I smile at him and ask, "How's fatherhood?"

"Perfect," Greg says, his face lighting up. "Did I show you pictures of her on Halloween? We dressed her as a Hershey's Kiss."

"Not yet," I lie, letting him show me pictures for the third time today.

Dave stomps back to our table. "Look, we'll talk about this when I get home tomorrow. I gotta go," he nearly spits into the phone before snapping it shut. Then he stares at it like he's going to hurl it across the room.

We all notice.

"Give me the phone," Joe says calmly, putting out his hand.

Dave shakes his head. "I don't want you doing anything stupid."

"Wouldn't dream of it," Joe assures him, wiggling his fingers, waiting for the handoff.

Dave reluctantly hands Joe the phone.

Joe drops the phone to the ground, stands up from the table, and pounds his foot down several times in rapid succession. He picks up the phone, now crushed, and hands it back to Dave. "Sorry I broke your phone, man. I'm all thumbs."

Dave smiles. "You can't take care of anything nice."

"Well, it's one of my few flaws," Joe says, taking his seat.

As Greg passes the Halloween photo around the table, I ask Dave. "Want to talk about it?"

He shakes his head and smiles. "Nope." Then he reaches around me to envelope me in a light hug. Very sweet. Totally innocent.

And I have I catch my breath.

Thirty-six

Two hours, three courses of food, and many drinks later, our group gets into a limousine to be whisked away to Ruby, which is apparently *the* high-end strip club in Honolulu.

The limo pulls up to a red carpet leading to a bouncer guarding the door. Apparently Isabella has made reservations for us, because the moment Dave steps out of the limo, the bouncer runs up to him and deferentially says, "Good evening, Mr. Stevens. I'm Carl. We've been expecting you."

Carl quickly leads us up the red carpet and inside the club.

I've never been to an "upscale" Gentlemen's Club before and all I can say is... Ewww! I only know it's upscale because that's what Joe told me. I can't even imagine what the lowbrow ones look like. The place is covered in red velvet: the walls are red velvet, the carpet is red velvet. And where the red velvet ends, the mirrors begin: big mirrors, little mirrors, full length mirrors. It's enough to make a girl want to hide in a dark closet inhaling Mallomars and diet Dr. Pepper.

And then there are the stages. We have the main stage, a neon monstrosity enhanced with a silver pole on each end. On one pole is a girl dancing in a schoolgirl plaid miniskirt and unbuttoned Oxford shirt revealing her bare breasts underneath. The other pole has a dominatrix clad in a black leather thong and what I can only describe as a black leather nursing bra.

Then there are the mini stages located throughout the room. Each stage has a girl in a different ensemble: a cheerleader with a skirt but no top, a businesswoman in a miniskirt, heels, and again no top, and various your generic stripper outfits to show boob job, boob job, and more boob job.

"What do you think?" Dave whispers to me.

"Remember before, when I said I was underdressed? Now I feel overdressed."

Joe looks up to the ceiling and starts fingerbrushing his hair.

I look up to see the ceiling is covered in mirrors as well.

I pull out my lipstick to give myself a touchup.

A blonde girl wearing a bikini top and boy shorts walks up to us. "Good evening," she says cheerfully, flashing her bleached white smile at Dave. "Are you the groom?"

Dave looks around the place in mock fear. "Oh, I don't know if I want to cop to that."

She giggles like that's the wittiest remark she's ever heard. "I'm Tammy, and I'll be your taking care of you. Miss De Leon has reserved the entire club exclusively for you and your guests this evening. So if there's anything you want, or any girl you want to dance for you, you just let old Tammy know."

Old? She's eighteen if she's a day.

"I'd like a beer please," Joe says.

Tammy points to the bar, where two girls in teeny bikinis wait to serve us. "That's Joy and Treasure. They'll be happy to get you whatever you want."

"Gentlemen," Tammy yells to the group. Then she notices me. "And lady," she adds, flashing me a big smile, "we have a variety of girls here who can't wait to have fun with you. Miss De Leon has taken care of everything, so please don't be shy, and have a great time while you let us cater to your every whim. I just need to steal the groom for a few minutes. Have a blast y'all!"

As Tammy gestures with her index finger for Dave to follow her, I watch Greg immediately pull out his cell phone and speed dial. "Honey, you are not going to believe this..." he says, walking away from us as he describes the club to his wife.

Joe walks up to me and hands me a flute of sparkling wine. "You want to follow him to the champagne room now? Or wait until Tammy gets him nice and worked up?"

I take the flute. "Ew," I announce in one clipped sound.

"Let's check out the floor show," Joe says, heading to the main stage.

"Actually, I think I'm gonna take off," I tell him.

Joe turns to me. "Come on. They don't bite. At least not this early."

"I'm really not comfortable here…"

"I'll let you in on a little secret — no one is really comfortable at a strip club. It's a bizarre premise when you think about it. Like cookie dough ice cream. Or beer with pumpkin in it."

But those sound awesome I think to myself as I begrudgingly follow Joe to the main stage.

My cell phone rings. I pull it out of my purse. Isabella. "Hello?"

"Hey girl! It's Libby. I keep calling Dave, but it goes straight to voicemail. Is he with you?"

"Um…kind of. I mean, we're here at Ruby. I'm with Joe though."

"Oh," Isabella says, sounding worried. "Well, could you go find him and put him on?"

"Sure," I say awkwardly, starting to walk away from Joe. Joe quickly follows and grabs the phone from me. "Belle? No, Dave's in the men's room right now. He got really sick. I think it was all the Jell-O shots we did earlier. He's gonna have to call you back." I watch Joe as he listens to Isabella. "All right, I'll go get him," Joe says. He walks three steps, yells "Oh shit!" then presses a button to completely shut down my phone. He puts it up to his ear, listens a moment, then hands me my "dead" phone. "Damn, Samolina," he begins, no emotion in his voice, like he is reading from a telemarketer's script. "I dropped your phone in my beer. I am all thumbs. So sorry. I'll buy you a new one tomorrow."

"She's not going to believe I let you kill my phone."

"She's an idiot. Of course she will," Joe promises. "Now, let's wait for Dave to emerge."

I follow Joe to the table front and center of the main stage. We sit, then Joe gently clicks his beer bottle against my glass for a toast.

As the song *Rag Doll* by Aerosmith comes on, this little embryo of a thing excitedly screeches, "Oh my God!" then runs across the stage wearing nothing but an unbuttoned oxford shirt, a white thong and clear plastic heels so high, goldfish could live in them. "You're Joe Robinson!"

Joe flashes his smarmiest (I suppose he would say his sexiest) grin, "In the flesh, baby."

The girl starts waving her hands frantically in the air like a hyperactive child. "Sir! I love you! I've been listening to you ever since I was a little kid!"

I laugh so hard, I choke on my drink.

"Are you okay?" the girl asks.

Joe hits me twice on the back. "She's fine."

When I finish coughing, I ask her, "When were you a kid? When was that? Tuesday?"

"Oh no. I'm nineteen now," the girl tells me proudly.

"Oh, to be nineteen again," Joe says wistfully.

"I'd ask for ID," I suggest to him under my breath.

The girl turns around and runs backstage. Moments later, she runs back out to us, waving her driver's license in the air. "See," she says, handing it to me. "I'm legal."

I read her license. "Your real name is Candy?" I ask, furrowing my brow.

"A fine name," Joe he tells her. "And you're the most beautiful Candy stripper I've ever seen."

"How droll. I'm sure she's never heard that one before," I retort.

"Stop it," Joe mutters to me under his breath. Then he smiles at Candy. "How's your day been so far?"

Candy's eyes bug out. I think she's had a little too much Red Bull. "Oh my God, THE Joe Robinson just asked me how my day was! My friends in Sheboygan are going to die!"

"Sheboygan," Joe repeats. "So you're a cheesehead?"

"No," Candy says sadly. "I barely got my GED."

I laugh out loud again. Joe glares at me. As I hand Candy her driver's license back, Dave emerges from the champagne room looking incredibly uncomfortable. He walks over to us.

"So how was it?" I ask teasingly.

"I need a drink."

I leave Candy and Joe to head to the bar with Dave. He orders a pint of Sam Adams for himself and another glass of wine for me.

"No, no," I tell him, "I'm going finish this and head out."

Dave turns to me. "You're going to leave me here? Alone?"

I look up at a naughty nurse wearing nothing but a lab coat, stethoscope and thong. "Yeah," I joke, "Poor guy, being around all this. I'm sure you'll have nightmares for weeks."

"Well, at least you didn't say the memories will keep me up nights," Dave jokes, seating himself at the bar, then patting the seat next to him. "Back to our earlier conversation. Why me?"

"Oh that," I say, sitting next to him to finish our earlier conversation at the restaurant. "Well, I think I'm a pretty normal girl about this. When you like someone a lot, it's natural to feel like they could do way better, so when I met Eric I thought..."

"No, no. That's not what I meant," Dave corrects me. He leans in close and looks me deep in the eyes for the second time tonight. "I mean, why *me*?"

This is way too close for comfort. I try to breathe, but it doesn't work very well. "Um…well…you're handsome. And funny. And smart. Fun to be around. Why wouldn't Isabella want to spend the rest of her life with you?"

A smile creeps onto Dave's face and I think I see a tiny hint of blush. "Actually, that wasn't what I was asking. I told you before why I picked you. Why did you pick me?"

I don't know how to answer that question better than I just did. Dave and I continue to stare at each other. It's one of those moments where if we were both single, I would lean in to kiss him, and it would be the most natural thing in the world.

But I'm with someone. Someone I like very much. Love. Love very much.

"I already answered you. You're handsome, you're charming…"

"You already said that."

"Come on. You know why I picked you. You're…you."

Dave still doesn't take his eyes off of me. He's thinking about kissing me. I can tell by the way he leans…

Joe suddenly appears with Candy. "Hey, turns out there are a bunch of champagne rooms here. I'm taking Room One. You take Room Two."

Startled, Dave pulls away from me. He turns to Joe. "I don't think…"

"Actually, you think way too much. That's why *I'm* here," Joe says, then pushes Candy towards Dave. "Candy's already got the champagne chilling in there, plus she's keeping some things nice and warm."

Candy seductively whispers into Dave's ear, then crooks her index finger to lead him towards The Magnum. He follows, clearly intrigued.

"It's called the magnum?" I ask Joe in disgust.

"Yeah. Works on so many levels, right?" he jokes. Then Joe gently takes my hand and starts to pull me towards his champagne room. "Come along dear. I got a few moves of my own I want to show you."

I try to pull my hand away as he drags me towards Room One. "What are you doing?" I ask angrily.

"Hopefully getting my friend some action," Joe says cheerfully, still holding onto my hand. "I am the Best Man you know."

I watch Candy open the red velvet curtain of The Magnum and gesture for Dave to walk in. He does.

Damn it, I could fucking kill Joe right now. "You know, we were right in the middle of this intense conversation."

"Maybe you're not clear on why guys come to places like this. Trust me when I say it's not for the conversation." Before I can respond, Joe pops his head through Dave's red curtain. "Candy? Baby? Could you come out here for a minute? Sam has a question for you."

As I yank my hand away, Candy walks out, smiling at me. "What is it, honey?"

Joe leans in to Candy as though he's going to kiss her. "Sam was just wondering..." he begins in his seductive *I'm a famous rock star* voice. "Do you like me?"

Candy giggles. "Of course I like you."

"Well then," Joe says. "Clearly I chose the wrong girl."

And in one seemingly choreographed move, he pulls Candy towards him while simultaneously pushing me through the red velvet curtains of Dave's room.

I stumble into the room, trying to regain my balance after being pushed.

Dave stands at a wall, peering at a framed Playboy cover. At the sight of me, he smiles. "Say what you want about Joe. He did find a way for both of us to get away from the party without actually leaving."

"I guess," I agree, looking around at the room. More mirrors. Off to the side, a small stage with a pole. I walk up to it. "Seriously, what women find this empowering? Do you know there are actually aerobics classes that teach stripping and pole dancing now?"

"Huh. Maybe it's time I renewed my gym membership," Dave jokes. "So it turns out, there is champagne in the champagne room." He points to a silver bucket with an open bottle of champagne and two filled flutes on a table by the stage. "Care to hide out with me for awhile?"

I nervously walk over to him as he hands me a glass. "I don't want your friends to get the wrong idea."

Dave laughs. "What's the right idea?"

"You and I being friends," I say firmly. "Just friends."

Dave smiles at me, then lifts his glass in a toast. "To old friends."

We toast. Both of us take a sip and then, "Oh yuck!/Jesus, that's awful." We put the glasses down.

And then – silence. Well, relative silence: I can hear a Prince song playing just on the other side of the curtain.

Both of us nervously look around the room. I try to kick start the conversation. "So, what happened when you were in here before? Did one of the girls dance for you?"

"Yeah, but it was weird."

"Right. A beautiful woman dancing for you. Men hate that."

"Hate's a strong word. But...let's just say I had a different woman on my mind."

Okay, breathe.

Dave walks to the seat in front of the small stage. "So," he begins, smiling at me, "I dare you to dance for me."

I smirk. "Wow," I begin, trying to diffuse the sexual tension in the room. "Maybe you could double dare me, and I'd be so intimidated I'd really have to show you who's boss."

"Come on. You used to dance for me."

"First of all, I never danced for you like this. And, second of all..." I struggle to think. "Well, I don't have a second of all. But the answer is no."

Dave nods, resigning himself to my answer. "Second of all, I've got a fiancée. Who I love."

"Right," I remember, pained to hear him say it out loud.

We both glance around the room and avoid eye contact awhile longer. Then I blurt out, "You do love her, right?"

Dave narrows his eyes at me, "Do you love Eric?"

I'm unnerved by his question. "What? Of course."

Dave looks at me in all seriousness. "Because, you know, if you didn't, you still have a lot of options."

My mouth opens to say something, but I'm at a loss. As I think, *What Would Happen?* by Meredith Brooks begins blasting on the speaker system.

As Brooks begins to croon, Dave slowly takes my hand and gently pulls me onto his lap. I rest my head onto his chest, and the two of us lie together, his arms around me, in an easygoing hug. I take a deep breath to inhale the comforting scent of Dave's cologne. He smells amazing. Always has. I miss the way he smells. I miss the way he feels. I could stay on this lap, lying here doing nothing, for the rest of my life.

Soon Meredith begins the chorus, "What would happen if we kissed? Would your tongue slip past my lips? Would you run away, would you stay?"

I specifically avoid eye contact, turning to stare at the tacky neon strips of lights decorating the private stage as she continues singing.

Sitting there in his lap, I somehow manage to stay completely relaxed on the outside, while on the inside becoming jumpy as a teenager about to play spin the bottle. And for a moment, I desperately wish I could be twenty two again, sitting on his lap on his avocado green couch in his old apartment, confident that I could seduce him, because I had already done it so many times before.

The song seems to go forever, but neither of us moves. Eventually, Meredith fades out.

And we still don't move. I can feel him breathing, his chest slowly moving up and down. My stomach fills with butterflies. I hate myself for having these feelings, but I desperately want to kiss him. No, I want him to kiss me.

I ache for him to kiss me. Maybe if…

No.

I jump up from Dave's lap and take a few steps towards the exit. "We should get back to the group. Don't want to start any gossip," I say awkwardly.

Dave blinks, as though coming out of a trance. "Oh," he says. "Of course." Then his face gets serious, and he says something I have not heard in years. "Five more minutes?"

I laugh lightly. "Daaavvveeee," I sing-song warningly.

Mötley Crüe begins blasting over the speakers. Dave grins. He makes a joke of patting his lap twice and yells over the song, "Five more minutes!"

I debate. Then yell, "Is there any way they can turn this down?!"

And the volume magically lowers. We both look up at the speakers. "That's a little creepy," I say.

"That's a strip club for you. They might be filming too," Dave jokes. Then he smiles and pats his leg twice again.

I make a point of rolling my eyes as I walk back. "Fine. Five minutes, and then I'm leaving."

Dave smiles as I sit back down on his lap. We have a few awkward moments as I try to get into a comfortable position and try to relax again. I make an effort to control my breathing. Deep breaths Sam, deep breaths.

Dave takes my hand and gently begins to stroke my palm. His fingers might as well be shooting jolts of electricity through my body.

"What are you doing?" I ask suspiciously.

Dave smiles. "Nothing," he says, his finger drawing a circle around the palm of my hand. He definitely has the *I want to kiss you* look in his eyes. I've seen it a million times.

"We're not going to do anything," I insist, wondering how I have the strength to keep myself from putting my tongue in his ear.

"I know," he says.

Dave's finger begins to move up my arm. I watch as he slowly, agonizingly slowly, traces a path up my arm and onto my shoulder.

"You're getting married in a week," I remind him.

"You let me do this the week before I got married last time," he jokes, his finger now stroking my neck. "As a matter of fact, you let me do a lot more than this."

I shake my head. "This is a bad idea."

Dave pulls his head back a bit to look me in the eyes and asks me seriously, "Do you think getting a divorce was a bad idea?"

Before I can answer, Dave kisses me. And it is… the perfect kiss. As I part my lips to feel his tongue, I can feel my knees locking. Fortunately, I'm sitting. My lips feel like they've just touched an electrical socket. I return the kiss as deeply as I can, while desperately blocking out any thoughts of where this puts us in the future.

And, just like that, my future comes to a screeching halt.

"What the…?!" I hear Joe exclaim loudly from the other side of the curtain. "Belle, sweetheart, what are you doing at Dave's bachelor party?"

I immediately jump out of Dave's lap as I hear Isabella tell Joe from the other side of the curtain, "I missed him. And I thought it was bad luck to see the groom the weekend of his bachelor party, but it turns out I just can't see him the night before the wedding. Where is he?"

Dave quickly stands up, adjusting his pants.

"I think he may still be in the men's room," Joe continues at a decibel of eleven. "He's had way too much to drink. Poor guy can't hold his liquor anymore…"

"But Greg said he was in here with Sam," Isabella insists, sounding confused.

Dave bugs out his eyes at me, silently asking me what we should do.

I hate myself for it, but I can't think of any other option. "We're in here," I say, making sure my tone of voice implies that I couldn't be more bored. "Mr. Party Animal just threw up, but I think I got it all cleaned up."

Dave shoots me a look: *weakest lie ever*. I shrug as Isabella bursts through the curtains, Joe following quickly behind. "Oh Baby, you poor thing!" she says sweetly, racing over to Dave and giving him a big hug. "Let's get you home and into bed."

If only I'd have suggested that ten minutes ago.

Dave looks at me apologetically as Isabella continues to hug him. "I'm okay now," he lies. "Um…what are you doing here?"

Isabella breaks away from the hug just enough to pucker up her lips and begin kissing him. "I missed you so much, I couldn't stand it. Decided to surprise you."

"I missed you too," Dave says tentatively to her as he looks at me, his eyes full of apologies. "But I thought you still had a bunch of wedding plans to take care of…"

"Well, I did but…" Isabella pulls away from him, noticing our two glasses of champagne across the room and becoming visibly distressed. "Were you two drinking those?"

Uh-oh. Dave and I exchange a quick, "Now what?" glance.

"Uh…yeah," Dave manages to get out.

Isabella looks suspicious as she walks over to the silver bucket, then pulls the bottle out of the slushy water. "Just the two of you?"

Dave and I exchange a look.

"Candy and I were going to join them…" Joe begins.

Isabella throws the bottle back into the bucket. "Dave, this stuff is crap. What kind of beer are you serving your guests? Pabst Blue Ribbon?"

I'm not sure if our collective sigh of relief was audible or not.

Isabella takes Dave by the hand and drags him out of The Magnum. "Come with me. Before we go, I wanna see what a real lap dance looks like."

If only she had given me five more minutes…

Thirty-seven

I spend the next hour at Ruby, begging Isabella to let me take a cab home. But she insists that I stay, so I choose to dull my emotional pain in that time honored college way – the beer bong. (Sidenote: what a bizarre contraption. I wonder who the first person was to say, "Drinking isn't enough. You know what this party needs? A funnel and some plastic tubing.)

At two a.m., our group piles back into the limo and heads back to the hotel. Once we're in the lobby, Isabella invites us all to their suite, but I politely decline and tell everyone I'm going for a late night walk out on the beach.

As soon as I'm out of everyone's line of sight, I run out onto the beach and plop myself down on the sand. As I watch several happy couples walk hand in hand past me, I begin my descent into the vortex of self-pity.

How did I get to this point? I am a strong woman. I have consciously chosen everything I wanted in my life: where I live, what I do for a living, who I date. And I have worked my ass off to make things happen the way it needs to. How did I somehow fall in love with the wrong guy twice? I have a perfectly wonderful man waiting at home for me. Why can't I just want him? What the hell is wrong with me that I have to make my life this complicated?

A beautiful blonde in a sundress walks past me with her model-handsome new husband. I can tell they're newlyweds because their rings are so shiny. They look so happy. So…optimistic about how their lives are going to turn out.

Was I ever that happy?

Joe appears and sits down next to me. We're silent for a few moments, just listening to the waves. Finally, he announces, "If you want to talk, I'm a pretty good listener."

I'm so sad right now, I don't even know where to begin. So I shake my head a little. He nods in understanding.

More waves. Then Joe says quietly, "I was such a dog in college. Chased anyone who would give me the time of day. But you know why I never tried to sleep with you?"

I realize I've started crying. I quickly turn away from him to wipe my eyes. "Because I don't own a Hazmat suit?"

He laughs quietly. Then he gets serious. "Because you look at him the way I wish someone would look at me. And he looks at you exactly the same way."

"And yet, he's marrying someone else," I point out, sniffling back tears.

Joe shakes his head. "He doesn't look at her like that. And she sure as hell doesn't look at him like that."

If he's trying to make me feel better, it's backfiring. I just want to crawl into a fetal position and die. My eyes start to well up with tears again, and I really don't want Joe seeing me like this. "You need to go away."

"Sam…"

"No, seriously," I say quickly, as I begin crying harder. "Go get a new tattoo or a drink or a stripper or whatever, but please get away from me."

Joe pulls a handful of tissues out of his pocket and hands them to me. And I lose it. I cry for current me, I cry for freshly divorced me from all those years ago, I cry for the naïve bride me that thought it would last forever.

Joe strokes my hair. "Shhhh… It's all going to work out the way it's supposed to," he says, gently pulling me into his chest.

And I sob so hard I can't breathe.

Thirty-eight

An hour later, Joe and I are back in our room, watching a rerun of *Frasier*. My eyes are red rimmed, my makeup is smeared, but I'm actually feeling better. We are doing our version of a slumber party: both of us on Joe's bed, me in my cherished flannel pajamas, him in an old pair of sweats and a UCLA T shirt, playing "Truth or Drink": a game similar to "Truth or Dare," except that when the person asks you a personal question, you can either answer or drink.

I point to the top of Joe's head. "Toupee?"

Joe looks down at the beer he grabbed from the minibar, debating whether or not to take a sip. Finally, he admits the truth. "Hair transplant."

I burst out laughing. "You're dying hair that's not even yours?"

"Think of that insanity as the beauty that is me. My turn. How many guys have you been with?"

"Truthfully, six. But if Dave ever asks, say three. How about you?"

"Guys? None."

I roll my eyes. "Girls."

He gives me a weird look. "Doesn't leave this room?"

"Pinkie Swear," I promise.

Joe doesn't answer. Stares at his beer bottle again. Slowly starts to peel off the label.

"A million and four," I joke.

Just as I take a sip of minibar wine, he whispers the number in my ear. I choke on my wine, nearly spewing it out all over the hotel's flowered bedspread.

"Lower or higher than you thought?" Joe asks.

258

Eww, wine in my nose. I try to sniffle it back down my throat. I can see Joe looks ashamed of his number, so I try to make light of it. "Truthfully, I thought it would be a lot higher. You've been touring for eight years. I would have guessed you were up to at least seven hundred."

"Well, as far as the guys are concerned, I am," he jokes, smiling and clearly relieved I'm not judging him. "Biggest regret of your life?"

"Coming here this weekend. You?"

Another pause. "Liz," he says seriously.

"My Liz?" I ask.

"You sound surprised."

"Well, I mean, I know you made out with her a few times in college, but…"

"What I should have done the night I met her was what Dave did with you: marry her quickly, before she had time to figure out what a putz I was."

My heart is starting to break again. The problem with drinking is how quickly good times can get somber. "Is that what Dave is doing this time?" I ask Joe sadly. "Marrying the girl before she has a chance to change her mind."

"Nah. I think it's the other way around," Joe assures me.

I don't think either of us wants to continue this conversation, so the game stops, and we focus on *Frasier*. David Hyde Pierce says something hysterical. Both of us are feeling too serious to laugh.

"You could ask her out, you know," I finally say.

"Nah. Guys like me… girls like you only go out with us once. You want us on your resumé, want to be able to tell your friends you took a walk on the wild side. But to actually spend Christmas with? Bring me home to meet the parents, tattoos and all? Marry? Nah."

"That's not true," I insist.

Joe shakes his head, forcing a smile. "Of course it is. I've dated a long time. I know who's into me. And who isn't. Trust me. I know my limitations."

I have to admit, I doubt Liz would ever fall for him. She's known him too long, he's stuck in the friend zone. And if she heard his sex number... I shudder to think of the card she'd write.

And yet...

We watch *Frasier* again in silence.

"You healthy?" I ask, even though I know I'm being rude.

Joe cocks his head, confused.

"You know," I say awkwardly, bulging out my eyes. "Your partners, all of them have had partners..."

"Oh. That. I always use condoms. My uncle died of AIDS... So...yeah..."

I think about Joe and Liz as a match. I mean, who's to say? She did horribly with the straight-laced lawyer in the Brooks Brothers, or the V.P. of sales in the Ralph Lauren. Maybe shed be more suited to the rock star with tattoos and badly dyed hair. "You ever cheat on a girlfriend?" I ask.

"Never," he says emphatically and I can tell from the pride in his voice that he's telling the truth. "I've had one night stands, but only when I was single. Once you're in a relationship, you're in. Anything else is bullshit."

I think about that. Take another sip of wine. "Did Dave cheat on me?" I ask, my voice cracking.

"You mean before or after you sent him the divorce papers?"

Well, I guess that qualifier answers my question, but I persist. "Before."

Joe shakes his head. "Absolutely not. Not once. Not ever."

Hm. I'm not sure I really wanted to know that. If that's true, does that mean the divorce was all my fault? That if I had done things differently, I would be happily married right now? Maybe with a couple of kids?

"And after?" I ask, not really wanting this answer either.

Joe shrugs. "You hurt him pretty bad, Samolina."

I nod sadly. Yeah, I guess I did. Boy, it's amazing what we'd do over if we could.

"I think Liz kind of likes your Beatles tattoo," I tell Joe.

Joe smiles, then silently toasts my glass with his beer bottle.

Thirty-nine

I wake up later that morning in a strange man's bed.

By this I mean Joe, out cold next to me, snoring. I guess I never made the five-foot walk over to my own bed last night.

I nudge Joe. "Stop snoring," I demand, trying to go back to sleep.

He rolls away from me, then continues snoring so loud, I'm surprised the walls aren't shaking.

"Quiet!" I yell, shaking him awake.

Joe jolts up in bed. Then he looks around the room to get his bearings, his eyes glued shut. After a few moments, he announces, "I think we need to hit the pool."

"I don't want to move," I say, forcing my tired body to sit up.

"I think I need to drink the pool," Joe says. He scratches himself on the shoulder, then turns to me. "You okay?"

I shrug. "Been better. But I appreciate the all-nighter."

Joe smiles, then gives me a kiss on the forehead.

We hear an urgent knock on the door. "Sam?" Dave asks through the door.

Joe and I exchange glances.

I throw the pink hotel robe over my clothes, then open the door to Dave, who appears to have pulled an all-nighter himself.

Which, in the light of day, suddenly angers me. "Ah, the return of the prodigal husband."

"Okay, I know you're mad," Dave begins.

"Mad?" I repeat mockingly. "Why would I be mad? Because you kissed me, then went home with another woman?"

Dave looks down at the carpet sheepishly. "I did do that. And I'm sorry. It was a mistake." He looks up. "But it's not completely my fault. You always knew exactly how to seduce me."

"*I* seduced *you?*" I nearly spit, narrowing my eyes in disbelief.

Dave shrugs. "Come on Sam," he says weakly. "You were sitting on my lap. We had just listened to a song about infidelity. What did you think was going to happen?"

My jaw drops. Then, a complete mood change. "You know what? I'm going home. Have fun at your wedding. You two truly deserve each other."

I try to slam the door in his face, but he stops it with the palm of his hand. "Fine. I seduced you. How can we move past this?"

"Believe me, I've moved past it," I say, turning to walk to my open luggage, piled high with clothes, on my made bed. "I'm so far past it I can't see it in my rear view mirror anymore."

Dave follows me in, not yet noticing Joe. "If we could just talk about..." he begins. Then he sees the pile of clothes in my suitcase and can't help but ask, "You didn't unpack?"

"No! I! Didn't!" I spit out angrily, rifling through my stuff to find a clean T shirt. "I kept my clothes in a pile in the suitcase! Just like I always do! Because I'm not Miss Perfect. And I don't have a private butler to unpack for me!"

"Let's not bring Belle into this," Dave says warily.

"She certainly wasn't in it last night, was she?" I say, finally finding the red Hawaiian shirt I bought at the mall and a pair of jeans to go with it.

"Should I go?" Joe asks.

"No," I say, trying to brush past Dave so I can head into the bathroom to change. "I'm gonna throw on clothes, call a cab for the airport, and get the hell out of here."

Dave suddenly notices Joe for the first time, and does a double take. He looks at Joe, lying in a pile of pink sheets and blankets, then looks at my bed, completely made up and untouched. His jaw drops. "Are you fucking kidding me?"

I look at Joe and his bed, confused. "What?"

Joe rolls his eyes. "Dude, don't say anything stupider than you've already said so far."

"You always had a thing for her," Dave angrily accuses Joe. "You've just been waiting for me to fuck up so you could make your move."

Joe stands up. "Come on, man. If that had been true, don't you think I would have tried to fuck her five years ago?"

I stare at Dave incredulously. "You think I'm so messed up over you that I would sink to sleeping with Joe?!"

Dave turns to me. "Well, I wouldn't have thought you'd sink so low, but I think the evidence speaks for itself!" he points out, waving his hand at my unmade bed.

"Yes, Dave," I say dryly. "As you can tell from my slutty flannel pajamas, clearly we've been going at it like rabbits all night."

"Please, you wore flannel pajamas to bed plenty of times when we were married. It takes less than thirty seconds to…"

"Slipping into the *Too Much Information* territory, guys…" Joe warns.

"Oh, for God's sakes! It's Joe!" I point out, like that answer unequivocally explains my innocence.

"Plus she doesn't own a Hazmat suit," Joe says.

"So you like the joke now?" I ask as an aside.

"It grew on me."

Dave won't be distracted from the fight. "Because it's Joe? That's your excuse? Joe sleeps with everyone! If I hadn't grabbed my mother from the bathroom our senior year, he'd have slept with her."

"Ewwwwww..." I blurt out, turning to Joe. "You almost slept with Mrs. Stevens?"

"What?" Joe asks, shrugging. "She's hot."

"She's fifty-five years old."

"Back then, she was a very doable forty-something," he counters.

I shake my head in disbelief. "Ewww."

"Oh, so now you're going to insult my mother?" Dave asks me.

"You wanna stay on topic?" I counter. "I didn't sleep with Joe. But, even if I had, it shouldn't matter to you, because you're sleeping with Isabella. And what was that thing happening next week? Oh yeah, your wedding! You're marrying the little..."

"Language," Joe reminds me under his breath.

He makes a point. I stop talking and take a breath. "So," I continue much more calmly. "Since you have chosen this woman to spend the rest of your life with, she is the only woman you get to give orders to. I am free to kiss whomever I want. I am free to stay up all night with whomever I choose. I am free to not unpack when I'm in hotel rooms and I am free to wear flannel pajamas to bed in preparation for fucking whomever I want!!!!"

Point. Match. Game.

Dave bugs his eyes out at me. He balls his hands into fists, angry but trying to calm himself down. We engage in an angry staring contest, and I can tell that he's trying to come up with the meanest possible thing to say to me.

But, instead, he turns and stomps out of our room.

Joe follows him out and I follow both of them. "Dude, calm down," Joe begins.

"Don't follow me, man!" Dave warns, quickly marching down the hallway.

Joe grabs his hand to stop him. "You guys need to work this out. Just come back into the room…"

Dave turns around and punches Joe, knocking him flat onto the floor.

"That's for sleeping with my mother!" Dave yells, then turns on his heel and leaves.

I kneel down to Joe. "Jesus! Are you okay?"

"Meh. He barely grazed me," Joe says, standing up and rubbing his jaw. "It's just my chin. It'll be fine for pictures next week. I think he pulled the punch back, more trying to make a point than anything else. And in all fairness, I did sleep with his Mom. I had it coming."

"I thought he stopped you two from sleeping together."

Joe shrugs. "That was back in college. I nailed her a few weeks after graduation."

I stare at him. "What?" he asks. "Don't you know the term MILF?"

Forty

It took me only twenty minutes to check out of the hotel and get myself into a cab heading to Honolulu International airport, where I planned to get a Coach ticket for the next flight back to L.A. and forget all about the past week.

I turned on my phone for the first time since the night before to three messages from Eric and none from Dave. Which told me everything I needed to know.

Isabella called while I was on my way to the airport and begged me to stay, but I lied and said I needed to get back to work in L.A. She didn't push it, which surprised me, saying we'd talk about her book next week. She further surprised me by arranging a first class ticket on American Airlines, leaving at 1:25. Which was perfect. I would be able to spend tonight in my own bed.

"Or better yet, my bed," Eric says, talking to me on my cell phone.

I am now sitting on the plane, in a comfortable leather seat in first class, waiting for them to board the rest of the passengers. I didn't exactly want to call Eric yet, what with feeling horribly guilty about nearly cheating on him with another man. But I was also aching to hear his voice.

"I can't," I say to him. "I already called Liz to tell her I'd be home tonight."

On my way to the airport, my first call was to Liz, who I told about the kiss. The magically perfect kiss that I now hate myself for. I told Liz that I needed to go to Eric's. Needed to hug him, needed to tell him what stupid thing I'd done, beg his forgiveness, and move on.

But now that I am actually on the phone with him, I am too afraid.

"Call her back and tell her I'm picking you up instead," Eric insists. "Come on, we'll grab take out, come home, rent a video, open a nice bottle of wine... It'll be fun."

I hesitate, playing out in my mind exactly how he will react when I tell him I kissed Dave. He'll start pacing, not saying anything. I'll follow him around, apologizing profusely over and over again. Eventually, he'll blow up...no, Eric doesn't blow up. He'll calmly – preternaturally calmly – ask me why I would have done such a thing. What was missing in our relationship? And I'll say I don't know, and then we'll break up.

"Sam, are you still there?" Eric asks, jolting me back into the moment.

"Yeah, I'm just...very tired. I really want to go home tonight. Is that okay?"

Eric is silent. It is decidedly not okay.

"What happened?" he finally asks.

"Nothing big," I say. I try to get myself to say the words: *I kissed Dave.*

But nothing comes out. Just silence.

"Is it okay if we don't talk about it?" I finally ask.

Eric pauses. "Fine," he concedes, a bit angrily. "Will you call me when you land, so I know you got home okay?"

"I will."

"And can I see you tomorrow night?"

"Absolutely. And I promise I'll be in much better spirits then."

I can hear Eric sigh, mildly frustrated with me. "All right, I'll see you tomorrow then. I love you."

"I love you, too," I say.

And I do. Or at least I think I do. I mean, of course I do.

"Bye," he says.

"Bye," I say back.

And I click off the phone.

I stare at the phone and wonder how we can ever get past this.

I order a cappuccino from the flight attendant and unzip my carry-on to throw my phone inside. Three books taunt me: the red, brown and black diaries. I don't even know why I brought them. I'm glad I did though. Right now I want to remind myself, in vivid detail, of why I never want to see that jerk again.

I open up the black book to January 27th – the day my whole life unraveled.

January 27th

Dear Diary,

So yesterday was an eventful day. I quit school, gave notice on my apartment, and may have lost my husband.

I slip my key into the lock of my front door, but before I can turn it, Dave yanks it open. "Surprise!" he says to me, faking a bright and happy tone.

"What are you doing here?" I ask, startled. "Aren't you supposed to be in Cincinnati?"

"Cleveland. Well, the bus is on its way to Cleveland. But we don't perform for two nights, so I figured I'd fly in and surprise you."

"That's sweet," I say, maybe a little distractedly.

Awkwardness. Tension. Things I never thought I'd feel around my husband. Not to mention jealousy, rage…

Dave still stands in the doorway. "Are you okay? You look…weird."

I'm definitely not okay. I've been dreading this conversation all day. But I might as well get it over with. "I think maybe we should sit down," I suggest as I walk in and head to our living room.

Dave closes the door behind me. "Sam…" he begins, thinking he knows where this conversation is going.

"Just please…sit," I say, not knowing where or how to begin.

Dave takes a seat on the couch as I shrug off my winter coat and prepare to hunker down for a long night. He sighs. "If this is about Stephanie again…"

"I quit school yesterday," I interrupt.

Dead silence. I stand by the couch, watching Dave as he clenches and unclenches his jaw. "Yesterday?" Dave repeats. "Why didn't you call me?"

I want to say, *Because I knew you wouldn't support my decision.* Or *Because I'm tired of you emotionally blackmailing me into staying in a place I hate.* Instead I say, "I didn't want to bother you when you were on the road."

Dave purses his lips, looks down, plays with an imaginary thread on the couch. "You're making a mistake…"

"Dave, I hate it. I actively hate it. I lie awake at night dreading the next morning. Then in the morning, I don't even want to get out of bed because I can't stand the thought of going to school one more day."

Dave stares down at our beat up hardwood floors. "Okay," he says, sounding defeated.

"Don't say it like that," I say, beginning to pace, deliberately not making eye contact.

"Like what? I said okay," Dave repeats, making it clear it's definitely not okay.

"I hate it! I really fucking hate it," I say firmly, my tone of voice carrying a warning.

"I know you hate law *school*," he argues, emphasizing the word school. "You never gave *law* a chance."

"Wrong," I insist, my voice rising. "I gave law a chance every God damned day!"

"Fine," Dave says in retreat. "So what's next?"

I work up the courage to say aloud, "I want to have a baby."

"Yeah, because we're in such a great place right now," Dave says under his breath.

I feel like he just stabbed me in the lungs. Not because I think he's wrong. I'm not so delusional that I think we're okay. We're definitely not okay. It's just that neither of us has ever said it aloud before.

I stare at Dave a few moments, observing him. I have this terrible feeling in my gut that I know why he's home. "You slept with her, didn't you?"

"No!" Dave says for the umpteenth time, storming into the kitchen. "Jesus, what's the matter with you?"

I notice he didn't look me in the eye when he said no: he avoided me.

I don't follow him. Instead, I stare out our second story window and watch snowflakes blow onto the glass. "What happened in Cincinnati?" I ask, loud enough to be heard one room over.

Dave doesn't answer. The apartment is silent, save the wind blowing outside. Neither of us make a move to join the person in the other room.

Finally, Dave walks into the kitchen doorway. We make eye contact. And from the look on his face, I know all I need to know.

"Fuck you," I say bitterly, then storm into our bedroom.

Dave follows me. "It's not what you think."

"Get out! Just get the fuck out!" I scream, pulling a large suitcase from our closet.

"Sam, I love you…"

I throw my suitcase down on our bed and open it. "Schyeah, you've got an odd way of showing it," I say, yanking open my top drawer and grabbing a fistful of underwear and socks to throw into the suitcase.

Dave tries to take me in his arms. "Sam…"

"Don't touch me!" I yell, quickly stepping away from him.

"I didn't sleep with her!"

"You did something to get that look on your face."

Dave sighs, closing his eyes. "I kind of…sort of…have a crush on her."

I shake my head, confused. "Meaning?"

"Meaning…you're here and she's there. Meaning you're never happy anymore, and she's always happy. Meaning, she's thrilled to be around me, she thinks I'm great. You hate me. You blame me for everything in your life not going the way you want, and I'm tired of it. Meaning…"

I'm afraid he's going to say, *Meaning I want a divorce.* Instead he says something even worse. "Meaning she tried to kiss me last night."

My jaw drops. "She *tried* to kiss you? What does that mean…she *tried* to kiss you?"

Dave sighs. "That's not really the issue."

"Actually, it is. Because if you want this marriage to work, you're never seeing her again," I rage.

Dave shakes his head. "You know I can't do that. I'm not the only member of the band. I can't just kick people out."

"Sure you can. Just tell Joe and the rest of the guys what happened, and tell them it's you or her."

"Joe knows what happened. He's the one who sent me home to see you."

I open my mouth, about to say something, but I'm at a loss. Clenching my jaw and crossing my arms, I sit on the bed. "Fine. So what happened?"

Dave takes a deep breath, then begins. "We had just finished our show and we were back at the hotel. Joe had met this girl who came back with us and..."

"Were you drunk?" I interrupt.

"I had been drinking, yes," Dave concedes quietly. "Not a lot though. But Stephanie was kind of toasted."

"I'll bet," I mutter.

Dave chooses to ignore my insult. "Anyway, she and I were talking and... it just happened."

His voice drifts off. I wait for him to say more. "What just happened?" I finally ask.

Dave stares at the floor, unable to look at me. "She leaned over and kissed me."

I notice he went from "tried to kiss me" to "kissed me." Which means he kissed her back.

I think I might throw up.

"Baby, I'm sorry," Dave begins.

I start shaking my head. "I can't believe you did this to me," I say, walking in circles, trying to decide if I should leave or stay.

Dave tries to hug me but I shrug him off. "You can't see her anymore," I repeat.

"Sam, I told you I can't do that. Besides, she's not the problem, we are. I think we should consider therapy."

"Huh. Well, I would think the first thing a therapist would do is point out you don't need a drunk girl you have a crush on seeing you late at night when you're not with your wife."

Dave audibly sighs. "I told you, she's not…"

"The problem," we say together.

"Yeah, well, she's not the solution either," I counter. "And either she's leaving the band, or you're leaving the band, or I'm leaving you."

We talked all night. And maybe we made some progress? I don't know. It killed me when he left this morning to go back to Ohio. I told him, in no uncertain terms, that if she stays, I leave.

I look up from the black diary.

She stayed, all right.

Yup. It's good I left. And this little black book can keep reminding me of that. I turn the page to read more about why I hate him.

An elderly woman wearing a giant purple muumuu and matching purple lei and clutching a Bible, sits down in the leather seat next to me. "Hi. I'm Trudy."

"Hi," I say, moving my shoulder away from her, exuding clear body language that I want to be left alone.

I continue reading…

January 9ᵗʰ

Dear Diary,

Dave called me today from the road.

"Is that a good book?" Trudy says, scrutinizing my black book, looking for a title on the cover.

"Yes," I say tersely, trying to concentrate. I look down again to read.

January 29^{*th*}
Dear Diary,
    Dave called me today

"I should have bought a book from the airport gift shop before I left," Trudy says, looking down at her hands, then absentmindedly playing with a hangnail. She looks at her Bible, then looks back up at me. "I suppose I shouldn't have brought a Bible. Passengers look at you like you know something they don't."

I smile weakly at her joke, then try to go back to my reading.

"I'm going to Denver," Trudy says, looking around first class absentmindedly. "The flight is going to be more than nine hours if you include the stopover in Los Angeles. Are you going to Los Angeles?"

I look over at the woman. She's eighty if she's a day. Why is it the old people always find me? "Yeah," I say, forcing a smile.

She laughs nervously to herself. "Well, I mean, of course you're going to Los Angeles – you're on this flight. I just meant, are you going anywhere else?"

I sigh loudly, hoping she'll catch on that I don't want to talk to anyone. "Nope," I say, moving my eyes back down to read. "Just Los Angeles."

January 29^{*th*}
Dear Diary,
    Dave call

"Live there?" Trudy asks me.
Politely, but through a clenched jaw, "I do."
And back to my book.

But there will be no joy in Mudville. Trudy continues, "My husband Bill and I retired out on Kauai. That's the Garden Isle. Have you been there?"

Jesus, is she ever going to shut up? "A few times," I say, staring at the pages of my diary with feigned intensity. "My ex-husband and I were going to retire there actually."

"You say *ex*? Are you divorcing him now?"

"No. A long time ago."

She nods. "Still in love with him?"

"No," I shoot back rather angrily, amazed at this woman's chutzpah that she thinks she can just bulldoze her way into my life for the next five hours.

Trudy seems startled by my vociferous reaction. "Sorry. I'm always prying into people's lives. My husband Bill's always getting on me about butting into other people's business. You go back to your book."

"Thank you," I say, looking down to read *January 29th* for the fourth time.

Trudy looks around, trying to find a good place to rest her eyes. She turns back to me. "It's just that my husband Bill is actually my ex-husband too. We were married for two years before we divorced. Then we got back together a few years later."

"Well, there's no way in hell that's happening with Dave and me," I say, almost spitting the words out at her. I see her Bible and immediately feel bad for cursing. "But I'm glad it worked out for you."

Trudy stares at her left hand, then twists her gold wedding band around her finger. "It worked out really well," she says. She turns around to look back towards coach. "Bill is on this flight."

God is testing me today. "Well, Trudy," I say, about to lose it, "then why aren't you sitting with him?"

"I can't," she answers, and I realize tears are filling her eyes. "He's in the cargo area. He died Thursday. I'm taking his body home to Denver."

I am the worst human being on the planet. How could I have become so caught up in the stupid minutiae of my life that I couldn't see so much pain so obviously sitting right next to me? I close my diary. "I'm so sorry."

"Me too," she says sadly, looking down and taking a balled up tissue she's been holding to wipe her tears. "We've been married fifty four years. Well, including the first time. Weird thing about life – I almost didn't marry him again. Thought he was more trouble than he was worth. But he was the one I thought about when I had good news. And he was the one whose arms I needed to crawl into when I had a bad day." She looks off into space and I realize she's reliving a memory: giving him happy news, or crawling into his arms. Who knows?

Trudy blows her nose and wills herself to stop crying. "Oh, I told myself I wasn't going to cry again." She takes a deep breath, then turns to me. "So tell me about this boy who wanted to retire in Kauai."

I toss my diary onto the floor. Eh, I can remember why I hate Dave anytime. "Why don't you tell me more about Bill?"

Forty-one

After we land in L.A., I keep Trudy company while she waits for her flight to Denver, then I stand at her gate until I know she has boarded safely. After she disappears down the carpeted hallway and into the plane, I turn on my cell phone and call Eric.

He answers after the first ring. "And she's safe," he says to me softly.

"Can I come over?" I ask, exhaustion and sadness in my voice. "I need to come climb into your arms."

Forty-five minutes later, a cab drops me off in front of Eric's house. It's pitch black out as the driver unlocks the trunk and helps me with my bags.

"Let me get the cab!" I can hear Eric yell from his front door.

"Don't worry! I got it!" I yell, but he's already racing down his steps in his pajamas and slippers.

He gets to the driver as my last bag is pulled out. "How much is it?"

"Thirty-eight," the driver says in his foreign accent.

Eric hands him two twenties and a ten. "Keep the change."

As the cab driver slams the trunk shut and makes his way back into his car, I wrap my arms around Eric and burrow my head into his chest. I don't stop hugging him until the cab pulls away.

"I have never been so happy to see you in my life," I say, my voice muffled in his shirt. "How was New York?"

"Pretty uneventful," Eric says, softly stroking my back. "I didn't go to a champagne room with my ex, I didn't sleep with a man I can't stand and I didn't try to quit my job."

I look up at Eric. "You talked to Isabella."

"When you said over the phone that you didn't want to talk about what happened, I figured it had to be pretty bad."

"I didn't have sex with Joe," I state emphatically.

Eric nods. "Of course not. And the other things?"

I shrug, trying to make a joke of it. "Eh, whatcha gonna do?"

Eric smiles, kisses my forehead, then takes my bags. We make our way up his stone walkway and into his house, a beautiful old Tudor home nestled amongst the trees in the Hollywood Hills. I relax the moment we enter. Even though his house is less than three miles from Sunset Boulevard, it was built at the end of a cul de sac, and it's so quiet up here, you'd think you were in the middle of Connecticut.

Eric drops my bags at the door, gently takes my hand and leads me into his gourmet kitchen. "I made decaf," he tells me. Two coffee mugs are already out on the counter, waiting for us. "So what happened?" he asks, pouring coffee into the mugs.

I sigh. "I did end up in the Champagne room with Dave, but nothing happened."

"Well, duh," Eric says, his voice a little smug as he opens the refrigerator to pour half and half into my coffee.

I must admit, I'm a little thrown by his smugness. He's acting so superior to Dave, like there's no way anything could have ever happened with someone so clearly beneath him.

"I didn't do anything with Joe either," I say, my voice rising.

"I never said you did," Eric reassures me, putting the half and half away.

As he hands me my mug, I complain, "Yeah, well Dave thought I did. We had a big fight over it."

"Because he's still in love with you," Eric declares.

That came out of left field. "He's not still in love with me," I insist.

"Right," Eric says dryly. "That's why he was so upset when he thought you slept with his best friend."

"I didn't sleep with his best friend!" I reiterate, raising my voice again. "We spent the night watching *Frasier* reruns!"

"Hey," Eric says softly, giving me a hug. "Calm down. I'm on your side, remember?"

I hug Eric back and breathe in his scent. I missed the way he smells. "I'm sorry I'm yelling. It was just a tough weekend." After a few moments, we break the hug. "So Isabella told you I quit."

"No. She said you tried to quit, but she wouldn't let you."

"Shit," I sigh. "Well, I'll quit again next week."

Which makes me sad: No big check. No novel published. And... oh right, I'm fired. So no career.

"Before you do that, hear me out," Eric begins. "I understand the last ten days have been ridiculous and the weekend sounds awful. But you've already done most of the really hard stuff: you done the interviews with Libby, you have a lot of material, and you'll have even more once we get through the wedding."

We get through? Oh shit. I totally forgot I still have to go to the wedding as Eric's date.

"This is book means A LOT of money," Eric continues. "Life changing money. Now how many more interviews would you still have to do before you'd have enough material to write her book?"

I shrug. "I don't know. Two or three maybe?" I answer weakly. Then I quickly add, "But it wouldn't just be interviews. I'd probably still have to be in her wedding."

"Paris is worth a Mass," Eric says, referring to Henry IV's quote about having to convert to Catholicism in order to become the King of France.

"Have I mentioned how much I love that you know quotes like that?" I ask him.

"Yeah. And let's not forget, doing so allowed him to pass the Edict of Nantes. Just like how you doing this will allow you to publish *Edict of Edith*."

I sigh. How dare he be so logical and correct?

"It's a great book, Sam," Eric continues. "Reading it was one of the reasons I fell in love with you."

Huh. I didn't know that. That's actually very sweet.

"You mean it wasn't because I'm so low maintenance?" I ask in mock disbelief.

"Well, of course that was the other reason," he jokes, then pulls me into a hug. "That and our mutual distrust of Koalas."

Forty-two

The next morning, I wake up to Eric kissing the back of my neck. I smile. "Watch yourself," I joke as I turn around to face him.

Eric leans in to kiss me and... oohhh... his kiss is so sexy. What is it that makes some men such phenomenal kissers? Eric begins caressing my thigh as he pulls me onto him. "I missed you," he tells me seductively.

"I'm right here," I giggle, moving in to kiss him again.

As our make out session begins to heat up, I kiss his neck, then move down to his chest and perfectly toned stomach.

I stop at his stomach to examine a surgical scar he has on his belly. It makes me smile. "I love your scar," I say contentedly.

Eric opens his eyes. "What?"

"I love your scar," I repeat, touching his scar lightly with my finger. "It's very sexy. It's like you're perfect, but you're not perfect. And I'm the only one who gets to see that."

As I lightly caress his stomach, I can not help but get more serious. "Why me?" I ask.

Eric looks confused. "Why you... what?"

I shrug. "You're gorgeous, you're smart, you're funny: you could have any woman in the world. So why me?"

Eric smiles. "Were you always this insecure?"

"Absolutely. Whenever I've liked a guy, I've never known what he sees in me. I mean, I wish I could be like Isabella and think I'm fabulous and that everyone's lucky to know me. But I've never been like that. I'm just this geeky girl who somehow managed to get a guy like you to like me, and I have no idea why. So why me?"

Eric looks sad listening to my confession. He intertwines his fingers with mine, and answers, "Because you're perfect, but you're not perfect. And I'm the only one who gets to see it."

And that was the right answer. We begin kissing again. And for the first time in weeks, all is perfect in my world.

Until his beeper goes off.

We both stop kissing to turn and look at it. "Is that work?" I ask.

"It shouldn't be. I'm not on until noon," Eric says, picking it up from his nightstand to read the phone number. "Libby."

Of course.

Eric picks up his phone and dials. Then, "Hey, it's me. What's up? Of course Sam is with me. It's six o'clock in the morning."

He gives me an apologetic look. "You did?" he says into the phone. "You did...? Does Dave know?"

Does Dave know what? I think to myself as Isabella monologues on her end of the line.

"No, we'll come over," Eric says. "Just sit tight... I love you too. Bye."

Eric hangs up the phone and sighs.

"What happened?" I ask.

"Libby wants to call off the wedding," he says as he gets out of bed. "I told her we'd go have breakfast and talk about it."

"Oh," I say, slightly surprised that he's just going to take off and leave me. "Can you drop me off at home first or should I have Liz pick me up?"

"No, not 'we'd' go have breakfast, Libby and me," he clarifies. "'We'd'" on that word, he gestures his index finger back and forth between me and him. "Go have breakfast with Libby. You and me. We're meeting her at the Polo Lounge."

Forty-three

Half an hour later, Eric and I walk into the Polo Lounge to see Isabella sitting alone at a table, wringing a lace handkerchief in her hands, then dabbing at her wet eyes melodramatically. The moment she sees us, she gets up from her table and runs across the room dramatically. "Oh, thank God you're here!" she says, grabbing me in a tight hug.

As Isabella hugs me, I make eye contact with Eric and raise my hands as if to ask, "What the Fuck?"

Eric shrugs.

The three of us return to her table and order breakfast: a ham and cheese omelet for him, eggs benedict for me, and a very tearful order for a crepe filled with rare filet mignon and steamed broccoli for the drama queen, with a scoop of vanilla ice cream on the side.

As the waiter pours our coffees, Eric tries not to sound gruff as he asks, "Okay, what happened this time?"

Isabella shakes her head and wrings her handkerchief. "You think you know a person and then he winds up being a totally different person."

I refrain from explaining to her that she just summed up marriage.

"You were right," she continues to Eric. "I never should have agreed to marry Dave."

Eric said that? Why?

"I didn't say you shouldn't marry him. I said I thought you were rushing into things."

"You also said that you weren't coming to the rehearsal or the rehearsal dinner. That's not exactly a rousing vote of confidence."

"You're not going to the rehearsal or the dinner?" I ask Eric.

"I have to work," he explains calmly.

"You can't take a day off from work for your best friend's wedding?" I blurt out, surprising myself just as much as everyone else at the table.

"I *am* taking the day off for her wedding," Eric tells me rather sternly. "I'm just missing the rehearsal."

"Because you don't approve," Isabella whines.

"Nooo," Eric says, dragging the word out several syllables. "Because you gave me all of five weeks notice and my hospital makes my schedule months in advance. Do you have any idea how much finagling I had to do just to go to your wedding?"

Sensing that she's getting nowhere with him, Isabella turns to me. "You're still coming to the rehearsal, right?"

A pit begins forming in my stomach that's about the size of the rolling rock from the Indiana Jones film.

"I'm pretty sure Dave wouldn't want me there," I say to her diplomatically.

"Because you slept with him?" Isabella asks me in a nonjudgmental tone of voice so confusing I couldn't read it with a magnifying glass.

I take a quick glance at Eric to gauge his reaction before I assure Isabella, "I have not slept with Dave in many years."

Isabella turns away from me and shrugs. "Well, someone is sleeping with him. Which is why I have to cancel the wedding."

"Jesus, this is engagement three all over again," Eric mutters, shaking his head. "All right, I'll bite. What makes you think he's having an affair?"

"I can't tell you. It's too personal."

Then she turns to me. "But I can tell you. Because you're a girl." Isabella leans into me, then says in a stage whisper, "Dave and I haven't had sex in…"

Cue dramatic tone.

"…three days."

I have no idea what to do with that tidbit of information. Several times, I open my mouth to fashion a response, but words escape me.

Fortunately, Eric comes to my rescue. "On what twisted planet do you live that three days without sex constitutes an affair?"

Isabella glares at him. "Okay, I know *you* don't find me irresistible, but most men do. My sexuality is all I have over them. After that, they want conversation, moral support, things I can't give. When the sex is over, the relationship is over."

Eric tells her sympathetically, "Libby, you're selling yourself short. Dave wouldn't be marrying you if he didn't love you. If all he wanted to do was have sex, he would have had it by now and moved on."

"You know nothing about men," Isabella states to Eric, then turns to me again. "How many days did you and Dave go without sex before he dumped you?"

"Thirty seven," I lie, immediately and without hesitation.

"Really?" she asks, eyes wide.

"Maybe even forty," I continue.

Eric smiles at me. He knows I'm lying and he thinks it's funny.

"Was it because of the weight thing?" Isabella asks innocently.

My pride gets the better of me, forcing me to ask, "*What* weight thing?"

"Dave said you gained a lot of weight during your first year in law school. Is that what started the forty day dry spell?"

"Dave sai…" I begin. But life's too short. "Fine. Let's go with that."

Isabella beams as she stands up and grabs me in a big hug. "Oh my God, then that means everything's okay," she says cheerfully.

"Enjoy your breakfast. I have a fiancé to seduce. Eric, I'll see you at the wedding. Sam, I'll either see you at the rehearsal dinner, or before. I love you both! Bye!

And she's off.

Eric and I decide to stay and enjoy our breakfast. Which was delicious. Then return to his to enjoy some other deliciousness.

But, despite myself, throughout the morning I couldn't help replaying what she said in my mind: *Three days.*

That means they didn't do anything Saturday night. Or last night.

Why am I so happy to know that?

Forty-four

Eric drives me home late that morning, on his way to work. He offers to help me bring my luggage in, but I tell him I've got it. He pulls my suitcases out of his car, then sends me off with an incredibly romantic kiss goodbye. I watch him get into his car and pull away. I smile, feeling so lucky.

I roll my suitcases down our walkway, unlock the door and yell, "Honey, I'm home!" as I walk in.

"Hey, I'm on the phone with Joe!" Liz yells from her room. "Be right there!"

Then I hear her giggle.

Liz giggling? Liz up in the morning?

I leave my luggage at the door, then head towards her room just as Liz opens her door, takes my arm and pulls me towards the kitchen. "Let's get some coffee on. I want to hear all about Dave and everything that led up to that kiss. Then I want to ask you some questions about Joe."

"Don't want to ever think about that kiss again," I tell her. "It's so over. I will happily talk about Joe though. I think he likes you."

"Well, I figured that. I've been on the phone with him since noon."

"How is that possible? It's only 11:30."

"No, noon yesterday. He called me from your room in Waikiki. We just got off."

"You mean you guys were talking for over twenty-three hours?!" I ask her incredulously.

"No. We took bathroom breaks every few hours. Plus we fell asleep around four a.m. my time"

My eyes widen. "You mean, you didn't hang up to sleep?"

Liz shakes her head. "Nope."

"Oh yeah, we're so having coffee right now. I need to hear everything."

Liz and I talk for the next few hours about Joe and Dave. Liz decides to give Joe a shot and excuses herself to call him to accept his invitation to be his plus one for the rehearsal dinner on Friday night. Which is a relief, as I figure I'll need all the moral support I can get when I see Dave again.

Dave.

I am so mad at him and so mad at myself. There is just no way to win here: we tried the *in love* thing, it didn't work. We tried the *friends* thing, it didn't work. I guess now we'll try the *Yes, I know you're on the same planet as me, but other than that, you're dead to me* thing.

Hey, it worked for much of my twenties.

Late that afternoon, I call Isabella and arrange to see her Tuesday for one of her last interviews.

Then I unpack, and suddenly realize I have lost my black book.

The diary of our breakup.

I remember exactly when it happened. Trudy and I were talking so intensely that we barely realized the plane had landed, and when we disembarked, I quickly grabbed my black book from the floor and threw it in my bag. Turns out, I accidentally picked up Trudy's black Bible instead.

I open the front cover of the Bible. Thank God (no pun intended) she wrote her name and phone number in the front left corner: Trudy Masterson. (808) 555-1617.

I call her home in Kauai and get her machine. A man's voice: "Hi, Trudy and Bill can't come to the phone right now. Please leave us a message." Beep.

"Hi," I begin. "This is Sam. From the plane flight? Listen, I accidentally took your Bible by mistake and I'm wondering where I should send it..."

I hesitate. "And, um, I'm pretty sure that means I left something with you. A...diary? It's kind of important to me, so if you could call me at..." I give her my number, "maybe we can find some way for me to get it back..."

And I hesitate again. I never know what to say to people when they're grieving the loss of a loved one. "Listen," I continue, "I just want you to know that I've been thinking about you, and about what you said about true love and that you're in my thoughts and prayers. Okay, take care."

And I hang up the phone.

Forty-five

Dave never called to apologize. Not that I thought he would.

Okay, maybe I thought he would.

Or maybe I wished he would.

The following morning, I head out to Isabella's Malibu compound, pass some paparazzi setting up across the street from her gate, drive through the gate and over her crunchy gravel drive and parked in her driveway built for twelve.

As I am pulling my briefcase out of my car, I see Dave duck behind one of Isabella's Ferraris.

He's hiding from me? Oh, Hell no.

I toss my briefcase back in the car and storm over to the Ferrari, where Dave is trying to slowly open the driver's door and sneak in. "Dave!" I say loudly.

Startled, he accidentally bumps his head against the door.

Good.

"Hey," he says casually, forcing an awkward smile as he stands up.

I put my hands on my hips and jut my chin towards him. "Are you fucking kidding me? You're just going to avoid me for the next five days? Really mature."

"Well I tried talking to you in Hawaii," Dave counters in his *You're a raving lunatic and I'm the only sane one in this relationship* tone of voice. "And your response was to leave the state."

"After you accused me of sleeping with your best friend."

"I didn't say I was trying to *rationally* talk to you," he blurts out. Then he realizes what he just said, and backtracks. "All right. I apologize for accusing you of sleeping with Joe."

As he lets that hang in the air, I think maybe we have a shot at salvation here.

Until he says under his breath, "But after you kissed me…"

"You kissed me," I correct him, then turn on my heel and march back to my car.

Of course he follows me. Why do men never chase us when we want to be chased? Why do they always chase us when we're dying to have the last word?

"Why can't you just admit that Eric is wrong for you?" Dave asks in a patronizing tone.

I shake my head as I trudge back to my car. "Yeah, Eric's the problem. Your powers of observation never fail to amaze me."

"What's that supposed to mean?" he asks, clearly offended.

I flip back around and seethe, "It means that no one in the world knows you as well as me." And then I pause for effect, staring him straight in the eye. "Which means we both know what you're thinking about right now."

Dave's jaw drops. He's floored. Which is awesome. I win! (The fact that in reality I have no clue what he's thinking is beside the point.)

Isabella walks toward us, her nine hundred dollar Jimmy Choo boots crunching on the gravel. "You're here!" she says excitedly to me. "Perfect timing. I need some help with the seating chart."

She takes Dave by the hand and drags him towards the main house. "I need your help too, baby. Sam told me you have an aunt who drinks."

We walk into Isabella's palatial Subzero kitchen, where Britney is setting up a huge, light green felt board with dozens of numbered purple felt circles stuck onto it.

As Isabella walks up to the board, Dave says. "You've been at this for three hours. Aren't you done yet?"

"Shyeah," Britney laughs under her breath as she pulls out little pink felt names.

We all look at her, surprised at her outburst.

"Sorry," she says to Dave. "I thought you were kidding."

"Baby, we've only done the seating for the main tent," Isabella croons, doing her best fake baby talk. "That's guests one through five hundred. Now we have to do the seating for the auxiliary tent."

Judging from the look on Dave's face, I feel a fight coming on. "If we don't care enough about someone to have them in our tent, why do we care who they have dinner with?" he asks Isabella pointedly.

"Um…if you guys need a minute," I begin.

"Don't be silly," Isabella insists to me. "I need your help. I want to know where to seat your friend Liz." She turns to Dave. "A perfect example of someone we care about who, unfortunately, didn't make the final cut into the main tent."

I hear my cell phone ring and pull it out of my purse. As Dave and Isabella continue to argue, I check the caller ID. James Evans.

Dad.

I let it go to voice mail.

"You can't put Liz in the auxiliary tent!" Dave insists. "She's Joe's plus one."

"Fine," Isabella says, ripping off a piece of pink felt from the green board. "You want her in the main tent, I'll just move the mayor…"

As Britney and Isabella put Liz's pink name on the light green felt board, I hear my phone beep that I have a message. "Can you excuse me for one sec?" I ask, leading myself out of the kitchen.

I check my message. My Dad is yelling into his phone, convinced he's about to be disconnected. "Hi honey, it's Dad.

Listen, we just got Dave's invitation. I'm still on my lecture tour, but I'm moving stuff around so we can be there. We're landing at LAX at four o'clock Thursday. I'd love for you to come meet us at the airport. Good for you for going to your ex's wedding. You're keeping a fine family tradition alive. Love you, Bugaboo."

And he's off. I stare at my phone in wide-eyed alarm. My eyes continue to look like an owl's as I walk back into the kitchen.

"What's wrong?" Dave asks, concerned about the look of horror on my face.

"Did you invite my Dad and his brood to the wedding?"

Dave looks confused. "Why would I do that?"

Indeed...why would he? I turn to his future wife. "Isabella," I say, taking a deep breath and struggling to keep myself calm. "Did you invite my father to your wedding?"

Isabella puffs up her chest, clearly proud of herself. "Yes, I did. And I had a devil of a time getting him an invitation. He was in Paris one day, London the next, then he was off to Rome... So you're welcome." She looks to Dave, acting like I've just helped her make her point. "See. Sam's father. There's someone who can be in the auxiliary tent."

My eyes flare up.

That's it. I'm done.

Dave can sense the volcano about to erupt and immediately changes his mood from snippy to conciliatory. "Sam..."

"How the hell could you do something that STUPID?!" I explode at Isabella, my voice booming so loudly that if I were on stage they could hear me in the back row... of the theatre down the street.

"What?" Isabella asks me innocently. "I figured that it might be hard for you to watch your ex-husband get married. I thought having family around might ease your suffering..."

I start hyperventilating. Britney turns to me. "Are you all right?" she asks, looking concerned and leading me to a chair.

I continue to hyperventilate. "Fine. What does a stroke feel like?"

Dave grabs a paper bag from a drawer and hands it to me. "Breathe deeply."

As I inhale and exhale into the bag, trying to get my blood pressure lowered to three hundred over two hundred, Dave turns to Isabella. "What have you done?" he asks, his voice threatening.

Threatening to everyone except Isabella, who just tsks. "I invited Sam's only living ancestor to our wedding. What's the problem?"

"Oh, and the fact that he's a Pulitzer Prize winning, internationally known novelist never crossed your mind," Dave responds in an even tone that is both angry and eerily calm.

"He's still her father," Isabella points out.

"You didn't care about him being her father," Dave insists. "You wanted to class up your wedding by having *the* James Evans as your guest."

"Our wedding..." Isabella reminds him.

"No. Your wedding," Dave corrects her. Then, "Your goddamn wedding with its nine hundred guests, and five-thousand-dollar soup tureens and its gophers!"

"Groundhogs..."

"Whatever!"

Isabella looks genuinely shocked by Dave's outburst. I must say, I'm a bit surprised myself. She turns to me. "I'm really sorry," she says, starting to shake a little. "I just assumed you'd, I mean, he is your father..."

I take the paper bag away from my lips. "My father and I haven't spoken much since he married a woman four days younger than me, then had three kids with her."

"That bastard had more children?" Dave quips. "At his age?"

"That *bastard*?" I say, suddenly defensive. "Whoa...you did *not* just call my father a bastard."

"I'm sorry, but what would you call a man who's so selfish he has kids in his sixties?"

I would call him a bastard. But he's my Dad, and I'm allowed to do that. Dave, not so much. "Oh, and like you come from the perfect family," I say sarcastically. "When was the last time your mother was sober? 1983?"

Dave's jaw drops, then he points at me. "Do not bring my mother into this. She adores you."

"She adores her?" Isabella blurts out. "But she hates me."

"Then take back what you said about my Dad!" I yell at Dave.

"I'm trying to be on your side!" Dave yells back, exasperated. "If it weren't for him and his four wives..."

"Five," I correct him.

"...and his plethora of mistresses and his being completely incapable of ever holding together any kind of a real relationship, you wouldn't have..."

Dave abruptly stops himself. Isabella, Britney and I are silent, waiting for him to continue. He doesn't. Instead, he collects his thoughts, and says to me very calmly, "While this is an unfortunate turn of events, I'm sure, in the long run, we can find a way to turn what would normally be an uncomfortable situation into an opportunity for growth and maybe a little healing."

Wonder what self-help book he got that from. I'm silent, trying to think of a way to have Isabella killed without it getting traced back to me.

Isabella then makes things ten times worse. "He's really proud of you, you know," she says weakly.

I shrug, look at the ground, don't answer.

Isabella continues. "And he loved *Edict of Edith*. Said he always knew you were an amazing writer."

I look up at her, my eyes widening into saucers. "You gave him my novel?" I ask as I stand up from my chair and come right at her.

Dave blocks my way. "Sam…"

Isabella doesn't seem to know she's in mortal danger, judging from the innocence of her answer. "Absolutely. I was telling him about the book you're writing for me, and how everyone loves your other book, so he asked if I could have Britney mail him a copy…"

"I'm going to kill you," I say levelly, trying to push Dave out of my way to get to my victim. I wonder where they keep the knives.

"It's occurring to me that maybe I overstepped my boundaries," Isabella concedes.

And I keep coming at her as Dave continues to try to stop my progress. "It's time for Ron to magically appear," I say, now staring at her over Dave's shoulder with the eyes of a madman. "Because I'm going to kill you."

And I lunge, only to have Dave pick me up and throw me over his shoulder. "We're gonna go outside and talk," he says calmly to Isabella and Britney.

"I don't want to talk," I say just as calmly. "I want to kill her."

Ron appears just as Dave carries me out of the kitchen.

Britney yells toward me, "I'm sorry I sent it. I just loved the book so much, I thought you'd be proud."

"Britney, you're closer to her," I yell as Dave carries me away. "Grab her boot, and stab her carotid with its spike heel!"

Forty-six

Dave carries me out towards the cliffs. At first, I smack his back with my fists and scream for him to put me down. But then the whole fight just seems futile. Isabella wins. Isabella always wins. Giving up, I lay over his shoulder limply in defeat. When he gets near the cliff's edge I give him my new plan. "Just throw me over the rocks and into the water. I had a good run."

"If I put you down, do you promise not to kill anyone?" Dave asks.

I shrug.

"I need to hear words," Dave says.

I sigh, "Fine. If you put me down, I won't kill anyone."

He slowly puts me down. I take a moment to look out over the Pacific.

Dave stares out at the ocean with me. We both stand there in silence, thinking.

"I'm sorry Belle invited your Dad," Dave begins.

I don't say anything. Just continue to look out at the water.

"I'm sorry I kissed you," Dave continues.

I silently contemplate what he means by that. "You're sorry you kissed me, as in it was a mistake? Or you're sorry you kissed me, as in you're sorry Belle showed up?"

Dave sighs. Looks at pretty much anything around him but me. Debates how to answer. "I'm sorry I kissed you, because it was a mistake. It'll never happen again. Is there any way you can accept my apology and we can move on like it never happened?"

I shuffle my feet on the grass. Then I squint as I look up at the sun.

Dave sweetens the pot. "Would it help if I came with you to get your Dad?"

I shrug. "Maybe. I just hate...I mean, I love him and all but..."

Dave slowly pulls me in for a hug.

And I go limp. I just have no fight left in me.

"So, are we friends again?" he asks me softly.

"Sure," I tell him.

While all the while thinking, *At least until our next fight.*

Forty-seven

Two days later, Dave goes with me to the airport to pick up my Dad, my latest stepmom, and their three little rugrats.

I stand in the area of LAX where you greet international passengers and debate leaving the country before anyone spots me. Dave walks up, carrying two venti lattes and a paper bag from the airport Starbucks. "I got you this," he says, handing me the drink.

"Thank you," I say, then take a sip. Caramel.

"And this," Dave says, handing me the bag.

I look inside. There are two giant cookies. "Thank you," I say, pulling out the chocolate chip one. "Can I have this one?"

"They're both for you," Dave tells me.

I smile. "If you weren't already engaged, I'd propose," I joke, taking a big bite of cookie. "Thanks for coming with me. I'm not ready to introduce him to Eric yet, but I don't think I could have handled this on my own."

"No problem," Dave says, breaking off a piece of my cookie, and tossing it into his mouth. "When was the last time you saw your Dad?"

"About a year ago. He was doing a book signing. Took me to dinner just to tell me baby number three from wife number five was on its way."

"I'm sorry," Dave says.

I shrug.

Dave tries to find something comforting to say. "You know, a lot of guys have babies late in life. It doesn't mean they don't love their first kids."

I shrug again. "Tell that to Kate, Johnny, Marisa and Melissa," I say, referring to my siblings from marriages two through four.

Before Dave can answer, I hear a boisterous, "Bugaboo!"

And there's Dad, a six foot four bear of a man with a white beard and gray hair. Running ahead of him is Jack, his four year old. "Sam!" Jack yells, running into my arms.

"Hi, Munchkin," I say, smiling as I hug him. (Okay, yes, I hate my Dad for spreading his seed all over the world. But, come on, who can resist a hug from an adoring four year old?)

As my Dad shakes Dave's hand, booming, "David, good to see you." their two-year-old daughter Priscilla quietly walks into my arms to get a hug as well.

"Good to see you as well, sir."

"Dave, this is my wife, Diane," Dad says, pointing to a thirty-year-old blonde yoga instructor carrying a sleeping six month old in her arms. As Dave and she shake hands, Dad continues with the introductions. "My son Jack, my daughter Priscilla. And the latest addition to the Evans brood is David."

Dave looks a little startled by this revelation. I forgot to warn him in advance. He turns to me for clarification.

"Yeah," I say to him dryly, wrinkling my nose. "He named his son after my ex-husband."

"It's a fine name. And it's not like you're ever going to use it."

"You don't know that, Dad," I insist as I take the luggage cart from Dad and start wheeling it towards yet another limo Isabella has sent for me to use.

Dave and Dad divide up the rest of luggage to wheel and carry as the group begins to follow me out.

Then Dad decides to bait me. "So… what? You're going to name your firstborn after your ex?"

"I could marry another guy named Dave," I counter.

"I thought you were marrying this Eric guy," Dad responds.

"That's not the point. You didn't even know about Eric when you..."

Dad tries to squish me with a tight bear hug. "Let's not fight. I love you and we flew halfway around the world to get you through your ex-husband's wedding. I want points for that."

I purse my lips together, shutting down emotionally. "Fine. Points."

Dad smiles and pats my shoulder. "Thank you. Speaking of Davids, I read *Edict of Edith*. You might want to change the name of his character."

"Already on it," I say, already counting the minutes until they go home.

"It's really good. Proud of you, Bugaboo. Of course, chapters fourteen through nineteen need work, but you know that. I brought my copy with me. We'll go over it when you have time."

How many minutes to go?

That night, at what Isabella called her "pre-rehearsal dinner" for guests who had come in for the whole wedding week, I introduced Dad to Eric (they hated each other, but were polite), Dad to Isabella (they hated each other, but were polite), and Dad to Vanessa (they loved each other, and I had to keep my eye on him all evening to make sure he didn't start cheating on his wife with my client).

After dinner, Dad invited me back to his suite at the Beverly Hills Hotel so that we could go over chapters fourteen through nineteen. Nothing like seeing your work slashed with a red Sharpie to put you in a good mood.

We were up all night – literally, all night – going over his notes, fighting about his notes, fighting about why I had made the choices I had with certain characters, rewriting when I couldn't justify why I had made those choices, then rewriting again when he suggested other choices that were either better or made more sense within the context of the characters.

When we had room service the next morning (because he didn't want to bring three kids under five into the Polo Lounge for breakfast and who could blame him?) my book was better.

Much better.

And I hated him for that.

Forty-eight

Friday afternoon, after a three-hour nap, Liz and I drive out to Isabella's Malibu compound for the wedding rehearsal, which will be followed by a rehearsal dinner for two hundred at the Crystal Ballroom back in town at the Beverly Hills Hotel.

As I pull up to the compound's front gate, Liz talks softly into her cell phone. "We're here now. Gotta go... No, *you* hang up... No, *you* hang up."

"Someone hang up before I throw that phone out the window in a tantrum," I warn.

"All right, I'll hang up," Liz says, then clicks off her phone. "You're in a mood."

"Yes, I am, and I plan to continue to be until Sunday morning," I say, waiting for the party rental truck in front of us to be let in by the guard. "You're with each other practically every minute of the day. And when you're not, you're on the phone. Why the sudden 180?"

Liz shrugs. "Maybe it's not a sudden 180. Maybe I've been thinking about driving in that direction for years, and just now saw the right moment to make a U turn."

Fair enough.

The gate slowly swings open to let the truck through as Reggie, the front gate guard, walks to my window with a clipboard in his hand. "Hey, Sam," he says to me pleasantly. "I'm sorry. But I gotta check everyone's ID. Security orders."

We pull out our driver's licenses and hand them to him.

"Wow," Liz says, letting out a low whistle as she observes the paparazzi setting up at a press booth to our right. "People live this way."

Reggie makes a note on his clipboard, then hands me back our licenses.

"Thanks," I say, taking them. Then I lean in to ask him confidentially, "What kind of a mood is she in today?"

Reggie shakes his head. Not good. I give him a grateful smile. "Thanks for the heads up."

He presses a button in the guard booth to open the metal gate. As it slowly swings back, several photographers run behind my car and madly snap photos of what they can see of the inside of the property.

"Guys," Reggie almost whines. "She's gonna let you in tomorrow. Just chill."

"Thanks for coming with me," I say to Liz as I drive down the gravel path and over to Isabella's driveway. "I'm not sure I could have handled Isabella on only three hours of sleep without moral support."

"Or Dave," Liz reminds me. "How is that going, by the way?"

My eyes widen a little as I ponder that question. "Fine, I guess," I say, in a tone that tells her it's anything but fine.

"You sure about that?"

I shake my head "no" as I pull up to a group of cars parked in Isabella's driveway. "It meant a lot to me that he came with me to pick up Dad. I don't know, sometimes I feel like I'm developing a crush on him again, then other times I'm totally comfortable being just friends." I turn off my car and we unbuckle our seatbelts.

As Liz and I get out of my car, Isabella races up to us. "Oh good, you're here!" she says excitedly. Then she grabs my hand and starts dragging me towards her backyard. "Come on. I want to show you how it's going."

Liz follows us as we walk through the house to the backyard.

I am astounded at how quickly a backyard can be transformed into the perfect wedding venue. While a slew of construction workers hammer, screw and bolt in the altar, two dance floors and ice rink, others put up white tents and lattices. To our left, people stand on ladders, decorating a thirty foot tall Christmas tree with ornaments and bows. To our right, an animal trainer stands on a fenced off mound of dirt, coaxing groundhogs out of their manmade holes.

"I've included anything I can think of that happens during winter," Isabella says happily, walking us past a machine that shoots light airy flakes of snow over us as we pass. "We're testing the snow machines now. When the reception begins, there should be snow everywhere."

Isabella brings us into the main tent, where Paul's design team has begun putting out tables and chairs. "This tent will house me, Dave, and five hundred of our closest friends." She walks up to the bride's table in the middle of the room, the only table completely decorated with linens, china, crystal and flowers. "This is how all of the tables will look tomorrow. We're doing six layers of different linens, starting with a burgundy red on the bottom, and finishing off with a beaded and embroidered silver linen on top. The china's Christofle, as is the matching flatware," she says, referring to the silver and white china on the table, accessorized with nine different silver utensils. "The crystal's Waterford," she continues, referring to the red wine, white wine, champagne and water glasses, "and for the center piece, I went with mirrored paillettes, balls and Venetian glass boxes, mixed with vases of red and white roses."

"It is stunning," I admit.

"I know I'm stunned that someone could spend so much on a wedding," Vanessa says cheerfully from somewhere behind us.

We all turn around to see Vanessa, putting out her arms in a diva pose. "Darling," she says, wrapping her arms around me in a maternal hug. "The minister is here," she tells Isabella. "Paul sent me to get you. He wants us to get started so we can be out of here and back to Beverly Hills before traffic snarls."

"Yay!" Isabella squeals. She looks at me, glowing. "Tomorrow, I'll be a married woman!"

Then she runs out of the tent, expecting us to follow like Geishas.

"You'd think after five times, it would lose its allure," Liz says to us.

"Nah, I've done it four times. It's always fun," Vanessa assures her, putting her arms around our shoulders as she leads us out of the tent.

We walk over to the altar, built next to the cliffs overlooking the Pacific. Though not yet decorated with the requisite roses and orchids, it still looks spectacular.

Dave and Isabella are chatting with Joe and some of the others in the bridal party, as the minister asks people questions, then makes notes on his notepad.

Okay, I ask myself, *How do I feel seeing Dave standing there, preparing to get married?*

Weird.

Bad weird? Good weird?

I don't know. But I wish Eric was here.

As Liz runs into Joe's arms, I take a seat at one of the white chairs in the guest area, waiting for the rehearsal to begin.

Dave notices me, smiles and waves. I wave back.

Bad weird.

"You know, I could have thrown a wedding like this for you," I hear from behind me.

I turn around to see Dad taking the seat next to me.

"What are you doing here?" I ask, barely disguising my annoyance.

"Diane wanted to take the kids to the zoo, so I tagged along with Vanessa so I could see you. And maybe talk you into a fancier wedding the next time around."

I cross my arms and pout. "I liked my wedding."

"I did, too," Dad concedes. "Of course, it would have been nice to walk you down the aisle."

I stare straight ahead at the altar, refusing to look at him. "It also would have been nice if you hadn't invited your current wife *and* your mistress. How is Elsa, by the way?"

"She's fine," Dad answers as though my question isn't the least bit offensive. "Became a grandmother last year. The kid's gorgeous. Smart as a whip, too. When I saw him last month, he was already trying to talk."

"Last *month*?!" I repeat, alarmed. "You mean you're still seeing her?"

Dad looks confused by my question. "Why wouldn't I still be seeing her? She's an old friend."

I let my jaw drop. "You're having an affair on your thirty year old wife with your sixty-two year old mistress?"

"Sixty-one."

"Oh, well, that's very different then," I say in a huff.

"I never said it wasn't unorthodox," Dad admits.

"Unorthodox is writing your ex-husband's fiancée's autobiography. What you're doing is just plain weird."

Dad has no retort, so the two of us briefly watch the minister give instructions to Isabella and Dave.

Dad leans into me and whispers, "I made a mistake."

I keep my eyes on the altar, refusing to look at him. "Which time?"

"I never should have cheated on your mother. When she divorced me, I should have done everything I could to get her back."

Dad looks at Dave, holding hands with Isabella, listening to the minister. And he shakes his head. "Don't make the same mistake I did."

He pats me on the shoulder, then leaves to explore the grounds.

Paul calls those of us in the bridal party to the back of the staged area, behind the guest chairs. We go through the rehearsal, where we are given explicit instructions for walking down the aisle ("Don't go until I point." and "Step once with the left foot, stop. Step once with the right foot, stop."), as well as once we get up to the altar ("When the minister asks, 'Does anyone know any reason why this couple can not be joined in holy matrimony?' Shut the hell up.")

The whole shebang takes all of twelve minutes, and then we are excused to go home and get ready for the spectacular rehearsal dinner, which will begin promptly at seven.

As everyone disperses, I walk up to Dave. "You looked good up here," I say, trying to keep things light.

"Thanks. Let's hope I do okay tomorrow."

"You did pretty well last time," I joke.

He looks at me in all seriousness. "You think?"

I nod my head. "Yeah, I do."

"I've been thinking a lot about that night the last few days."

I furrow my brow. "You mean the night of our wedding?"

"Yeah."

I don't know how to take that. What am I supposed to say? "Aaaand...?" I finally ask.

"Aaaand…" Dave begins. "Do you ever think…"

Isabella runs up to us, grabbing Dave's hand. "Oh, baby," she purrs, "You have to see the ice rink. It looks so romantic."

Seeing his betrothed seems to jolt Dave back to reality. "Huh? Oh yeah, I'd love that. Let's go see."

I watch Dave silently wave goodbye to me, then allow himself to be pulled towards the rink and away from me. Halfway there, he turns around to look at me, mouthing the words "sorry" as they leave.

Sorry.

Yeah, me too.

What was he going to ask me? Do I ever think…what?

Forty-nine

The Crystal Ballroom of the Beverly Hills Hotel is a stunning space to begin with: fifteen foot high ceilings, gorgeous art deco design, glittering chandeliers floating above the guests. And everything in the room looks sparklingly clean. Like a stunningly beautiful dream brought to life, with no dust or clutter to get in the way of perfection.

And tonight, it is even more spectacular: Isabella had the entire room decorated in black and white, with silver accessories dotting the landscape. The tablecloths are bright white, laid with black and white china, glittering silver flatware, and sparkling crystal stemware. The chairs are outfitted in black lace studded with silver beads. The flower centerpieces are a sea of black and white roses mixed with white orchids and hydrangea.

Everything is exquisite.

I couldn't be more miserable. "You could at least show up for an hour," I whisper to Eric on my cell.

"When?" he asks, exasperated with me. "I'm covering for Marty until ten. I'd have to go home, clean up and put on a tuxedo. I wouldn't be there until at least eleven and it will be over by midnight."

I grab a glass of champagne from a silver tray at the front entrance. "How exactly did it work out that I'm at your friend's rehearsal dinner, but you're not?"

"Look, I said I was sorry," Eric says. Then his voice softens. "Why can't you just come see me afterwards?"

"Because you should come to me. Has it even occurred to you that I might be freaked out watching my husband get married tomorrow?"

Eric is silent on the other end. Then, "I thought you were okay with that."

"I am. It's just...I don't know...it's still hard to know he got there first."

"Got where first?"

"Got married first. Got to fall in love first. Got to move on with his life first. And it would have been nice if during this week I could have had my boyfriend around, reminding me that I've at least come in a close second. I mean, you're not only not here tonight, you've been working extra shifts all week covering for people."

"Because I took a week off to go to New York, which was planned months..." Eric stops himself to consider my point. "Never mind You're right. I could have put more effort into getting more days off. But look, the week is almost over. Can I make it up to you some other way than going to the rehearsal dinner an hour before it ends?"

I sigh. "I guess," I lie.

Another moment of silence between us.

"Buy you a car?" Eric jokes.

I chuckle ever so slightly.

"Maybe a piece of jewelry?" he asks in the same light tone.

"Yeah, just try not to make it more than three carats. It weighs down the ring finger," I joke back.

"How about two?" Eric asks.

"Two what?" I ask, now laughing.

"How about a two carat ring?"

I stop laughing. "Wait, what?"

"You know what? That was the wrong way to ask you," Eric says. "But let's just put it on the table as an option. Okay?"

Put what on the table? Did he just propose? What the hell just happened here? "Sure," I say tentatively.

"Good," Eric says and I can hear a smile in his voice. "They're calling me over the intercom. I gotta go. I'll see you tomorrow. I love you."

"Love you, too," I say, still trying to figure out Eric's question.

"Bye," Eric says.

"Bye," I say.

And I hang up the phone.

I definitely need a second opinion.

I run over to Table Fourteen, where Liz and Joe are sitting, laughing, and doing all that other happy couple stuff that's making me want to puke.

"Okay, I need you both on this," I say urgently. "I'm going to tell you word for word what just happened and then you need to tell me what he meant."

I quickly recount my conversation with Eric, then wait for the girl and guy opinion.

"Oh, shit!" Liz exclaims.

"He's not fucking around, " Joe says.

I struggle to sit down in my tight, long black evening gown. (Tuxedos were mandatory for men, black or white evening gowns for women.)"So what does it mean?"

"Means he just proposed," Joe says. "And badly."

"Shit, that's what I thought," I say, feeling like I'm going to hyperventilate.

"What are you going to say?" Liz asks.

"I don't know," I answer honestly. "I mean, I love him. But we've been dating less than four months. This came out of left field. I just... I don't know."

"That's fair," Liz says calmly. "So, what was your gut reaction when you first realized he was proposing?"

Good question. I try to go deep and honest. "Fear."

"Fear of commitment or fear of committing to him?" Liz asks.

"I don't know," I answer back truthfully.

The band begins to play Isabella's #1 ballad "Something" as Dave and Isabella make their grand entrance. He looks amazing in a tuxedo made just for him. But Isabella looks even better, resplendent in a blood red, bias cut, sleeveless velvet dress.

Everyone else in the room is in black or white, so she stuns in red. I should have known.

"Ladies and gentlemen," the bandleader begins, "Miss De Leon and Mister Stevens request the honor of your presence on the dance floor."

Dave leads Isabella onto the dance floor. As the two of them begin a waltz, other guests fill the floor and begin to slow dance.

Our table stays firmly rooted in our seats.

I love Liz and Joe for that. They are my Cerga.

We can't really hear each other over the band, so I have time to watch Dave while contemplating what Eric has just asked me.

Why am I feeling such fear? Is it fear of marriage or fear of marriage to Eric?

It could be either. I've already shown I'm no good at marriage. And, frankly, I think Dave has shown he's no good at it either. I don't see him holding hands with Isabella on a porch in fifty years. I see hot sex with her for a few months, followed by her cheating on him.

But maybe I'm being cynical.

The next few hours are filled with dinner, dancing, the compulsory toasts to the bride and groom where people talk way too long, and, at our table, me talking too long as we discuss every detail of my conversation with Eric over and over again. I brought Dad, his wife Diane, and Vanessa into the conversation, and they all agreed with Joe's assessment: yes, it was a proposal.

For the most part, no one gave an opinion on my answer until around 10:30, when Dad suggested I say yes to Eric, but, and I quote, "Keep Dave on ice." (Dad's way of saying to have a thirty-year affair with Dave, much like his affair with Elsa.)

For that remark, I told him he had had too much to drink and sent him back to his suite.

Isabella left around eleven, citing that age-old superstition that the groom can't see the bride the night before the wedding, which gave me a chance to see Dave for the first time all evening.

As the guests begin to clear out (despite the band still playing and the bartenders still serving), Dave walks up to our table.

Liz, Joe and Vanessa quickly vacate, ostensibly to find more drinks or to dance.

And I love them for that.

Dave puts a glass of scotch, neat, down on the table. "Well, if it isn't my first wife," he jokes.

I smile, despite myself. "How ya' doin', first husband?"

Dave thinks about my question. Then he smiles. "To tell you the truth, I'm not really sure." He leans down to look at my dress. "Stand up," he says, suddenly realizing something.

I stand.

What Dave is noticing is my dress, a sparkly black number that was way too expensive at the time, but which I've worn for years. It is my favorite dress in the world.

Because Dave bought it for me.

Dave shakes his head slowly. "It's so unfair. I've gotten old and fat, and you still look exactly the same as the day I married you."

"Oh pleeeease!" I nearly squawk as we take our seats again. "I've got lines around my eyes now, I've gained at least ten pounds, I found my first gray hair last month…"

"Shut up," Dave says, smiling.

I smile back. "Sorry. I still don't know how to take a compliment."

We look at each other in silence, both smiling awkwardly. I finally work up my nerve to ask, "So what were you going to ask me before?"

Dave cocks his head, not comprehending.

"Earlier…at the rehearsal…you asked, 'Do you ever think…?' but then Isabella pulled you away. What were you going to ask me?"

"Oh that," Dave begins, then shakes his head dismissively. "Nothing important."

Damn.

"Joe tells me Eric proposed," Dave says, taking a sip of scotch.

"That seems to be the general consensus," I say noncommittally.

"Gonna accept?" he asks.

Gonna accept? How is he asking me that? Gonna accept? As in, "Good for you, you've moved on." Or Gonna accept? As in, "Please don't."

"I don't know," I answer truthfully.

Dave doesn't say anything more.

While the two of us drown in our awkward silence, Joe walks onto the stage, taking the microphone from the bandleader. "Good evening everyone. I'm Joe, the best man, and I'd like to thank you all for coming."

The few people left in the crowd applaud politely.

"Thank you," Joe says, walking over to the piano. "Now if you will indulge me, with the help of my man Alejandro on Sax, and the rest of the band, I would like to play one my favorite songs for my best friend Dave."

Uh-oh.

Suddenly feeling unsettled, I lean in to quietly ask Dave, "What is he doing?"

"Being Joe," Dave says matter-of-factly.

"Dave, I hope this brings you back to college," Joe tells him.

Joe sits down at the piano, and begins to play a few bars.

I know that song.

Oh crap.

Joe looks up and smiles at Alejandro, the sax player. Alejandro puts his lips up to his saxophone, and begins to play the instrumental version of *Against All Odds* – the first song Dave and I ever slow danced to. No one sings, we just hear the melancholy saxophone as if it sings:

How can I just let you walk away? Just let you leave without a trace...?

"Well, that's not very appropriate..." I exclaim.

"Name a time when Joe has ever been appropriate," Dave says, standing up, taking my hand and leading me to the dance floor. He slowly dances me around the room as we hear the saxophone continue to seduce the crowd, while Joe plays piano, and I think back to that night at Red Herring so many years ago.

When Dave asked me to dance. And we slowly hugged and swayed to this song. And at the end of the dance he kissed me, and suddenly we were a couple.

I relax into Dave, and as the band plays on, I forget about the past, I don't worry about the future, I just enjoy this moment:

So take a look at me now...

As a tribute to me, Dave's band covered the song as part of their demo album, which later became their first album. I remember the first time we ever danced to their version of the song. Dave had decorated my apartment roof with white lights and sprinkled white flowers all over the ground.

May 26th
Dear Diary,
 Tonight I became a fiancée...

"What are we doing up here?" I complain, scrunching my arms together in the college girl scrunch, already shivering as we emerge from my building's elevator and onto the rooftop. "It's freezing."

"I know. I just want to show you something," Dave says, dragging me by the hand out of the elevator. "Someone decorated the whole place. Check out all these flowers."

As we walk around the roof, I see white Christmas lights twinkling around the rooftop fence and all over the shrubs. Someone floated candles and gardenias in the pool, and there is a hidden sound system playing soft music that floats in the breeze of the fifth-story rooftop.

"It's magical," I say, walking around to look at all of the decorations. "What is that song playing? Is that from your demo?"

"No. It's from my *album*," Dave says, beaming with pride. "We got the record deal today. It's definitely a go."

"Oh my God!" I yell, jumping into his arms. "I am so proud of you!"

He takes my right hand in his left and we start slow dancing to the song. I am blissful. My boyfriend has a job doing what he really wants to do. I am going to law school next year to do what I really want to do. Life can not get any better.

"Wait," Dave says. "That's not my only news. I have a present for you."

He pulls a black velvet box from his pocket and gets down on one knee. I cover my mouth, in shock. Dave opens the box to reveal a small, vintage, half-carat diamond ring, with tiny diamonds surrounding the bigger stone.

I gasp. "Oh my God!" I scream, moving my hands to my cheeks and starting to bounce up and down.

Dave smiles, placing the ring on my left ring finger. "Now if you take this, you have to agree to marry me."

Could a moment have ever really been that perfect? Or did I somehow imagine it all?

My head comes back to the Crystal Ballroom, listening to our song and wishing time back then could have stood still forever.

The memory quickly changes from magical to painful.

I can't do this.

I think I'm still in love.

Damn it.

I gently push myself away from Dave and turn to leave. But Dave pulls me back to him. As we continue to dance, I'm back on that rooftop in Westwood eight years ago.

Dave spins me around the room faster as the horns and saxophone continue, and the drums go crazy. I can hear the final lyrics in my head. Then all of the other instruments go quiet, and we hear nothing but the mournful saxophone play its tragic finish. The music is so beautiful, I want to cry.

Dave pulls me into a tight hug. I hug back, wishing I could go back in time and fix everything.

And then the music is over. Dave lifts my chin with his finger and our lips almost touch. And I'm twenty-two years old again. If this were a movie, we'd kiss. And you wouldn't have to see the messy breakup with the fiancée or the boyfriend. The audience would magically jump ahead to the protagonist in a wedding gown happily reclaiming what once was hers.

But I already know how this movie ends. I've seen it before.

I push Dave away sadly and shake my head. "I can't," I whisper, turning away from him and racing off the dance floor.

Dave follows me. "Sam, don't leave."

"I have to," I say, grabbing my purse from the table and quickly making my exit. "I'll see you tomorrow."

As I hurry out of the Crystal Ballroom and into the lobby, Dave runs after me. He grabs my hand and flips me around to face him. "Look. Okay, I almost kissed you again. I'm sorry. I had a moment where I..."

"Where you started longing for your past," I say, my eyes getting wet as I interrupt him. "I get it. I did too."

"I don't know what to do here," Dave tells me in frustration. "Do you want me to tell you not to marry him?"

I guess that is what I want him to tell me. Huh.

"I don't know," I say, realizing my voice is cracking. "What do *you* want to tell me? What do you want? What do you want the rest of your life to look like?"

That last part startles him, and I can see him debating. He shakes his head and throws up his hands. He doesn't know.

Or he knows and doesn't have the balls to fight for it.

Either way, I have my answer.

I slowly turn and walk out of the lobby to the valets up front.

And Dave lets me go.

Fifty

I quietly put my key into Eric's lock. Getting to his place took longer than it should have, mostly because I had my cell phone turned on and kept waiting for Dave to call, declare his undying love for me and beg me to come back.

It didn't happen. In real life, men never do anything that romantic. That's why *Pretty Woman* did so well at the box office and running through an airport has become such a romantic comedy cliché.

I open Eric's front door, flip on the front hall light and yell out, "I hope it's not too late for a booty call!"

Eric calls out from his bedroom, "Whoa! You startled me! No, never too late for a booty call! I'm just jumping into the shower. Make yourself a drink and I'll be right out!"

"I'll join you!" I say, heading towards his room. "You would not believe the last few hours I've had!"

Eric pops out of his room wearing nothing but a towel. He seems a little jittery. "I can't hear you with the water running. What?"

I smile at him as I walk over. "I just said I'll join you," I repeat, giving him a big hug.

He hugs me back lightly, a bit jumpy. "No, no. I'll only be a minute. I reek of ER."

And my Spidey sense goes up. Something's off.

I inhale deeply. He smells like Jasmine and musk. I pull away from him, eyeing him suspiciously.

Then I turn towards the unlit living room. "Is Isabella with you?" I ask, trying to collect my thoughts.

"Noooo," Eric says, dragging out the word as though to ask *Why would she be?*

"Then why is her purse here?" I ask, noticing her sparkly red Chanel clutch on his coffee table.

Eric pauses. Debates. Sighs. "Actually, she is here. She's in the bedroom. She's having second thoughts about her wedding."

Man, when I was eighteen, I would have wasted so much time trying to figure out how to *not* catch him in that lie. "Huh. She's in the bedroom. And you're in a towel."

I wait for the ensuing barrage of excuses. Instead, Eric is silent.

Finally, Isabella walks out, fully clothed. "I can explain."

I put up my hand, and she stops talking.

They both wait for me to… what? Explode? Lecture? Give one great one liner she can quote in her next movie?

Instead, I turn and silently walk out the door.

The moment I close his front door, I quickly hustle to my car, hoping for a quick getaway. But he runs out after me. "Sam, come back inside."

"Why?" I ask, oddly zen. "I'm not the one. You're having sex with someone the night before her wedding. I'm not the one. And I think deep down I already knew that."

Isabella runs out a few seconds after him. "We made a mistake. Please don't tell Dave."

And at that moment I realize, "You didn't hire me to write your book so you could keep an eye on me and Dave. You hired me so you could keep an eye on me and Eric."

And then another thought occurs to me. I look at Eric. "You weren't in New York last week, were you? And you haven't been working all of this week. You just wanted the time to be with Isabella before she got married, didn't you?"

Busted. Eric looks down at the pavement.

I shake my head, and start laughing. Bitterly, but laughing, nonetheless.

I laugh as I get into my car. I laugh as I turn it on. I laugh as I pull away from Eric's house, and I laugh as I make a right onto his street.

Then I drive half a block, pull over and cry my guts out.

Fifty-one

I head back to the Beverly Hills Hotel and make my way to Room 249. I knock on the door. As the door opens, I think to myself, *"What the hell am I doing here? This is stupid. I don't need..."*

"What's up, Bugaboo?" Dad asks, sounding concerned and a little confused as he ties his pink bathrobe shut.

"Don't call me that," I snap, feeling the tears well up in my already red rimmed eyes. "I'm thirty years old. My name is Sam."

"Okay," he says carefully, almost apologetically. "What's up, *Sam?*"

"I'm mad at you," I say, sniffling back tears. "I'm mad at you for cheating on Mom. I'm mad at you for getting married five times. And I'm mad at you for having more kids at your age, because you weren't done raising me. I'm mad at you for teaching me never to trust any man in my life. Because I think I found the love of my life, not once but twice, and I let him get away."

And then tears flood my eyes again.

"Why don't you come inside?" Dad suggests sympathetically, trying to pull me into his room. "We'll work it out."

"No!" I yell, yanking myself away from him so that I can stay outside. "You don't get to talk to me like that. You don't get to be nice to me now. This is your fault." I take a breath to calm myself, then continue, "You shouldn't have cheated on Mom. And you should be able to stay in a marriage for more than six years."

Dad takes a deep breath. He looks back into his room to make sure I didn't wake anyone, then walks out, closing the door behind him.

"You're probably right," Dad agrees.

"About which part?" I ask through a stuffed nose, brushing tears off my face with my hand.

"All of it," Dad says somberly.

I've been waiting for him to say that for years. To admit that he was wrong, that I was right, that he has spent decades acting like a narcissistic asshole.

And now that he finally has admitted it, I don't feel any better.

"Can I ask you a question?" Dad asks me.

I shrug and nod my head yes.

"How much longer are you going to be mad at me?"

"I don't know," I say, sniffling.

We're both quiet for awhile. "Would it help if I said I'm sorry?" Dad asks.

I can't bring myself to make eye contact. "I don't know."

"Would it help if I told you that your Mom and I made peace at the hospital before she died?"

"You know what would help?" I say, wiping my nose with the back of my hand. "It would help if you told me not all men act like you."

"Not all men act like me," Dad promises me. "Do you want to come in?"

I shake my head. "I don't want to wake the kids."

He opens his door. "We'll be fine. We have a living room. Everyone's asleep in the bedroom." He takes my hand to lead me in, but I stay planted in my spot.

Dad sighs. He kisses my hand lightly, then asks, "What's it gonna take to get me into your Cerga?"

I shake my head and shrug.

"Come inside. Let's talk."

As I let him pull me in, I ask, "I don't have to go to this stupid wedding tomorrow, do I?"

325

"I can't decide if it's funny or sad that that's not the first time you've asked me that the night before a wedding."

"Your stupid fourth wife put me in a tiger costume for that ceremony."

"In retrospect, neither of us should have gone to that wedding."

Fifty-two

The next morning, I open my eyes and look around. Well, I'm in my own room and no strange man is with me. I guess that's something.

I look at the clock. 9:58.

Saturday.

Fuck.

The doorbell rings. I don't move to answer it.

There is no fucking way I am getting out of bed today. I am not going to this wedding. There is nothing anyone can do to make me go.

The doorbell rings again. No one answers.

"God damn it!" I exclaim, pulling myself out of bed.

I open my bedroom door, walk through the hallway, and open the front door to see Fred and Zac, ready for the Saturday morning drop-off.

"Hey, beautiful. I'm here to see your roommate," Fred says with his requisite smarmy seductive grin.

Yuck.

"I can take Zac," I nearly spit, holding out my hand for Zac's leash.

Fred pushes his way past me. "Liz, get your cute little butt out here," he yells out cheerfully.

Joe emerges from Liz's room, wearing the white Four Seasons robe Fred got her when they went to Maui last year. He's giggling like a schoolgirl as he turns his head back to tell Liz in her room. "I got it! You keep the bed toasty."

And Fred's face falls.

Joe closes Liz's door, then happily walks up to us. "Morning!" he says brightly. "Sam, I'm sorry I don't have the coffee started yet. Liz and I were kind of…uh…" He scratches his ear self-consciously, smiling. "Well, sorry."

I try to restrain my smile. "No problem. Joe, have you met *Fred* yet?"

"Fred!" Joe exclaims sunnily, putting out his hand. "Good to finally meet you, man."

Not knowing what else to do, Fred shakes hands with Joe. "I'm sorry," Fred says, puzzled. "And you are?"

Joe throws out his hands in presentation. "I'm Joe!" he says enthusiastically. Then he crouches down to pick up Zac. "Now you, old rascal, are getting one hell of a run today. We have got to get into better shape so that we can keep up with Mommy. Nice meeting you, buddy," Joe says to Fred, slapping him twice on the back, then subtly pushing him out the door.

"Uh… good meeting you too," Fred says, still confused.

Joe pushes Fred out the door completely. But before he can shut the door, Fred blocks it with his hand. "I'm sorry," Fred says (not sorry at all), "Just one quick question… How long have you and Liz been dating?"

"Celebrated our six month anniversary in Hawaii last weekend," Joe lies. "Bye now." And he shuts the door in Fred's face.

"How…" I begin.

Joe puts his index finger to his mouth. I tilt my head, wondering what he's up to. After about thirty seconds, he opens the door. Fred is still standing there. "Can I help you, buddy?" Joe asks him.

Since Fred and Liz only broke up five months ago, I'm sure there's a part of him that wants to punch Joe dead in the face. However Joe is 6'4". Fred is 5'10". You do the math.

"I guess not," Fred answers, dejected. We watch as he slowly gets into his Escalade, then drives away.

Joe closes the door, then turns to me, beaming. "That was fun."

Liz emerges from her bedroom, taking Zac from Joe. "You rock, dude," she tells Joe.

"Didn't oversell it?"

"Nope. It was perfection." She gives him a quick peck on the lips, then tells me, "Sam, some flowers came for you this morning."

Flowers. Hmm. "What color?" I ask.

"Purple and white. They're gorgeous! I put them in the kitchen."

Purple! That means they're from Dave. I race into the kitchen.

The bouquet is stunning. A combination of white and purple orchids, hydrangeas, roses, and lots of big and little flowers I can't name. I read the card.

"What's it say?" Liz asks as she walks in with Joe.

"I'm sorry. Please find it in your heart to forgive me," I read sadly.

Joe and Liz exchange a look. "Are they from Dave or Eric?" Liz asks.

"Neither," I answer, throwing the card down. "They're from Isabella."

"Why would Isabella be sending you flowers?" Liz asks.

"Well, I caught her in bed with Eric last night, so I guess she's a little nervous about what my next move is going to be," I say dryly.

Liz audibly gasps as Joe reasons, "Great! Now you can be with Dave."

"No, I can't be with Dave. We broke up last night. Or whatever it is we did."

"But that was before he knew Isabella was cheating on him," Liz points out.

I shake my head. "No. If he had wanted me, he would have picked me. What happens next in their relationship isn't my business or my problem. Besides, I wouldn't want to be his or anyone else's consolation prize. Now, if you'll excuse me," I say, padding my way out of the kitchen, "I'm having a bed day."

"Wait," Liz says, confused. "So do *we* still have to go to the wedding?"

"You can do whatever you want. Personally, I'm going to curl up in bed, watch sitcom reruns and binge on cookies all day."

Our home phone rings.

"Let it go to machine," I tell Liz.

She picks up. "Hello."

As I silently mouth, "I'm not here," she listens to the person on the other end. "Yeah, she's right here."

Before I can madly wave my hands in the air to signal that there is no way I am taking that phone, she hands it to me. "It's some woman named Trudy. She says she has your diary."

I grab the phone. "Hello?"

"Is that you, Sam? It's Trudy. I'm so sorry it took me this long to track you down. I have your diary."

"I know," I say, relieved. "I have your Bible. I left a message at your home in Kauai."

"Oh dear," Trudy says. "I don't know how to check my messages remotely by phone. They must be piling up. Listen, I know it's really short notice, but I just landed at LAX and I'm on a layover for the next three hours. I was wondering if you wanted to come pick up your diary?

Fortunately, traffic on the 405 freeway isn't too bad on Saturdays, because I am in the American Airlines terminal of LAX in less than forty-five minutes. I see Trudy waiting in baggage claim, race up to her and give her a big hug.

"It is so good to see you," I say. "How are you holding up?"

"There are good moments and bad moments," she answers, her voice a little faraway. "But overall, I'm doing okay." She pulls out my black diary. "Did I tell you I used to be a minister?"

I sit down next to her, repressing the urge not to rip the diary out of her hand. "Yes, you did."

Trudy seems lost in her own world. She traces the diary's black leather cover with her finger. "The Lord really does work in mysterious ways," she says, staring down at my little black book. She looks up at me. "I have a confession to make. I read your diary. Cover to cover."

A minister read my diary? What do you say to that?

"Um, well, give me ten Hail Marys?" I weakly joke.

"You love that man so much," Trudy says. "Almost as much as he loves you."

"Well, loved," I correct her.

She looks down at the diary. "Bill and I loved each other that much. Every page I read, it was like you were writing about Bill and me."

"During the breakup?" I ask, surprised by her positive emotions. I mean, after all, the black book is the breakup book.

"No, no," Trudy says. "I mean, I know you two split up when you wrote this. But he didn't sleep with that trollop. She wasn't anything more than a footnote in his life. She's at the singles table."

Trudy must see I look confused.

"Oh, sorry. Many moons ago, I used to perform weddings," Trudy tells me. "And at almost every wedding, there's an ex-girlfriend who the groom felt obligated to invite because she loved him so much and he was tempted by her at one point in his youth.

But she's not the bride. She's off at table thirty-seven somewhere near the kitchen."

And suddenly it hits me like a bolt of lightning. "She's in the auxiliary tent," I say, almost to myself.

Trudy thinks about that. "Yeah. That's a good analogy. But you? He loves you more than anyone or anything in the world," Trudy's eyes start to well up. "I lost mine once. I got him back. Don't lose yours."

Fifty-three

I say goodbye to Trudy, race to my house to change into my bright red hooker/bridesmaid's dress with matching heels and feathers, then speed down the Pacific Coast Highway towards Isabella's wedding.

Dave's wedding.

Unfortunately, halfway to Malibu, traffic slows to a crawl. Then about a mile before the turnoff to Isabella's house, police stop cars completely. Motorists either make an illegal U turn, or pull over to the side of the road to wait out the closure. Helicopters hover overhead, giving an area normally considered paradise a dark, almost insidious feel.

I manage to pull over and park before hitting the worst of the snarled traffic ahead of me, then run in my five-inch heels and micro-minidress over to a traffic cop.

"So sorry to bother you," I say politely. "I have a wedding to get to. Do you mind telling me what's going on?"

He eyes my outfit up and down before answering. "I'm afraid the road's closed for a bit. Press covering the Isabella De Leon wedding has blocked everything. We're clearing it up as fast as we can."

I pull out my wallet from my matching red feathered bag. "No problem. I'm in the wedding," I say, showing him my driver's license. "See, that's me. Samantha Evans. I'm on the list."

"Maybe, but you're not going to make it to the wedding. According to my walkie, the guests are taking their seats, and the press is being let in to photograph the event."

I think fast, then point to my car. "I'm the Blue Civic. Am I allowed to be parked over there?"

He looks past me, to my car. "Yeah. That's fine."

"Great," I say, quickly taking off my high heels. "Thanks officer!"

And I run like a bat out of Hell. Turns out that when I tried jogging before, all I really needed was the threat of losing the love of my life to get me moving.

I sprint past small beach house after small beach house, then take off into grass and mulch by the side of the road as the houses become larger and larger estates. I run so hard, my lungs are burning.

But I keep running.

When I make it to the metal gate, open for cars, I dart past Reggie's booth. "Hi Reggie!" I yell as I race past. Reggie leans out of his booth. "You forgot to show me…"

"Later!" I yell back, running barefoot in my now shredded nylons down the uncomfortable gravel path.

Ow, ow, ow, ow, ow…

I circle around the outside of the house, losing steam. I pass the Winter Wonderland backyard make it to the guest house, where Isabella and her gaggle of bright red bridesmaids wait, preparing to make their dramatic entrance.

"I made it," I announce, then stop, double over and grab my stomach as I begin gasping for air.

"Sam!" Isabella exclaims. I can't tell if she's startled or scared to see me.

And I don't care.

"Hey there," I say, lungs on fire as I greedily gulp up all the oxygen around me. "Got your flowers. Thank you."

Paul looks at me like he's going to have a conniption. "You're late. And what on Earth happened to your nylons?"

"There was traffic on the PCH…" I begin.

"Never mind," he says. "You need new hose. Here," he magically makes a plastic egg of L'eggs nude pantyhose, size B, appear in his hand.

I lift up my skirt and tug down my nylons.

"And you have pit stains!" Paul nearly screeches, handing me a can of Secret antiperspirant.

Vanessa leans into me and whispers, "Might improve the look of the dress."

I smile to her as I shimmy into the pantyhose, then spray some deodorant under my arms. Paul hands me my bouquet: maroon striped lady's slipper orchids paired with feathers interlaced with fake diamonds and rubies.

"All right, ladies!" Paul announces, clapping his hands. "You're going to follow me to the back of the seating area, then form the line you did yesterday. When I give each of you the signal, I want you to walk down the aisle like we practiced."

As we follow Paul out of the guest house and onto the grounds, I whisper to Vanessa, "How do I look?"

"Like Big Bird's wet dream," Vanessa whispers back. "Maybe for the reception she'll ask us all to do a rendition of *Hey Big Spender*."

The bride and bridesmaids walk up to the back of the seating area. Our waiting area has been covered with white lattice, so I can not see Dave, or anyone else for that matter.

Not that I even know what I'm going to say to him once I see him.

As a string quartet plays *Hello* by Lionel Richie, Paul waves his index finger to bridesmaid #1.

Go.

She does. And the parade of bridesmaids walking down the aisle begins.

As I wait for Paul to point to me, I can barely breathe. I feel like I'm about to throw up.

Butterflies. It's just butterflies. That's a good thing.

Paul signals me.

Go.

I emerge from the lattice, and begin my journey down the aisle.

I see Dave, standing at the altar, looking achingly handsome in his tuxedo.

I slowly continue down the aisle, searching for friends and family: There's Dad, smiling and winking. Liz, smiling and giving me a thumbs up. And Joe, up ahead, standing next to Dave.

My Cerga. For better or for worse. My rock. My family. I can do this...

And then I see the look on Dave's face.

No, I can't. His jaw is clenched so tight you'd have to pry it open with pliers.

I try to smile at him as I take my place standing with the bridal party. But his eyes are laser focused, keeping his sights on the back of the lawn, behind the hundreds of seated guests, waiting to see his future wife emerge.

Britney walks down the aisle as the maid of honor, takes her place, then turns to watch her sister make her grand entrance.

The quartet begins Mendelssohn's *Wedding March*. The crowd stands up. And Isabella appears.

She looks radiant in her jewel covered gown, cathedral length train and stunning veil. Absolute perfection.

I may burst into tears.

She and her father slowly make their way down the long aisle, waving and smiling at onlookers as they pass. Eventually, Isabella's father hands off his daughter and he and Dave shake hands. The crowd sits. We have a few moments of silence where I listen to a combination of ocean waves, photographers snapping away, and my beating heart trying to jump into my throat.

The minister begins, "Dearly Beloved, we are gathered here together to join this man and this woman in holy matrimony, a bond which is commended to be honorable, and therefore is not to be entered into lightly, but reverently, discreetly, advisedly and solemnly. Into this holy estate these two persons now come to be joined. If anyone can show just cause why they may not be joined together, let them speak now or forever hold their peace."

Joe coughs loudly. Both Dave and Isabelle turn to him. Joe looks to the audience. "Anyone?" he asks hopefully. Then he gives me a pointed look. I glare back. "No one?" he asks breezily. "Okay, then continue."

There are some nervous titters in the audience, then the minister continues. "Marriage is the union of husband and wife in heart, body and mind. Through marriage, David and Isabella make a commitment together to face their disappointments, embrace their dreams, and accept each other's failures. We are here today, before God, to witness the joining in marriage of David and Isabella."

Joe coughs loudly again. We all turn to him. "I'm sorry. It's just... Isabella? Are you *sure* you can't think of a reason you might not want to do this?"

I can't see Isabella's reaction from where I'm standing, but Dave does a Chandler Bing bulging of his eyes at Joe, who shrugs. "I'm just asking."

Joe turns to look at Eric, standing next to him as a groomsman. "What about you sir? Any thoughts?"

Eric looks down sheepishly, refusing to make eye contact with Joe or me.

The minister's eyes are scanning the room like a speedreader. Isabella pushes on. "Father, why don't we just move ahead to the vows?"

"Good idea," the minister says, closing his Bible and smiling as he asks, "Do you David William Stevens take Isabella Josephine De Leon to be your lawfully wedded wife? Will you love her, comfort her, honor her and keep her, in sickness and in health, for richer, for poorer, for better, for worse…"

I slowly raise my hand.

Dave looks over Isabella's shoulder. He shakes his head *no*.

But I think *yes*. "This is a mistake. Don't do it."

Isabella turns around to stare daggers at me.

You got one shot, Samolina. Plow ahead.

"I know," I say quickly to Dave, the words tumbling out of my mouth. "She's gorgeous, confident, rich, wildly successful, driven and really nice to you. And I'm neurotic, unsure of myself, barely treading water in my career, and I'm still fighting with you about things that happened years ago."

Despite the horrified silence from the crowd, I continue. "And, as you know, the worst thing about me is that I avoid confrontation as long as is humanly possible, and then I find the absolute worst time to bring up a subject: like that time I turned off the TV and told you I might be pregnant with two minutes to go in the NBA Western finals. I mean, that was bad. I was wrong to do that. But here's the thing: you're in love with me. You're not in love with her. She's a Stephanie: a girl in your auxiliary tent. So forget about all the people here, forget about the press taking pictures, forget about all the crap you're going to have to deal with in the next twenty four hours. None of that is going to matter when you're on a porch in Kauai in fifty years. What's going to matter is whose hand you're holding."

Aaannnnd scene.

I wait.

Everyone is frozen, waiting for someone else to say something.

Joe breaks the silence. "Plus, it'd be nice if the hand you're holding hasn't been touching some other guy's…"

"That's enough, Joe!" I interrupt.

Dave furrows his brow and turns to Joe. Joe nods once. Only once. But with that one signal, they have an entire unspoken conversation. Dave turns back to Isabella. He takes her hand gently. "I think we need to talk."

"No!" Isabella snaps, stomping her feet up and down like a two year old, and causing the crowd to gasp. She yanks her hand away from Dave, then turns to me and growls demonically, "You…"

Uh-oh. I try to back away from the gazebo and make my escape as she throws down her bouquet, coming at me like she's about to cut me. I back away more quickly. "Isabella, I can see how you might feel that I was out of line…"

"I'm going to kill you!" she yells, then tackles me.

"You have every right to be angry… Ow!" I squeal, trying to claw my way out of her clutches. For a second, I manage to pull away, but she tackles me again, and the two of us start rolling around on the ground, the paparazzi snapping like crazy. "Stop pulling my hair!" I yell.

"Belle, get off of her!" Dave commands. "You're causing a scene."

I manage to push her off of me and crawl backwards on the ground. "Listen, I don't want to hurt you," I say weakly.

"I knew you were a threat!" Isabella screeches, pouncing on me and grabbing my neck to throttle me. "No matter what I did, employing you, being nice to you, constantly keeping you in my sights, I knew he still loved you."

"Isabella," I say through a muffled voice, "Don't make me..."

Having no other option, I punch her dead in the face. Isabella flies backwards. I stand up into a crouch, balling my hands into fists to begin Round Two.

It's then that I feel Ron's hand mysteriously appear on my shoulder.

Shit. I turn to him.

And watch a dainty hand gently land on his shoulder.

Ron turns towards the hand. Vanessa smiles at him like a Cheshire Cat. "Ronald, please don't put me in the awkward position of having to call your wife to tell her what we did in my suite last night," she warns amiably. "Or to give her details about the awkward positions you liked so much while we enjoyed each other's company."

A wave of fear crosses Ron's face. He slowly lets go of me. Vanessa smiles, gives me a thumbs up.

Isabella gently touches her bleeding lip. "You punched me," she says, surprised.

"You were trying to strangle me," I point out.

"Belle," Dave says, apologies in his voice, "Can we have a minute?"

"Don't Belle me, you asshole!" she nearly spits at him. "I spent over a million dollars on this wedding, and you are going to marry me!"

"But I'm in love with another woman," Dave points out gently.

"So what?! I've been in love with another man for years. You think that stops me from getting married?!"

Gasps emerge from the audience. Isabella glances over at them. "Oh, give me a break! How many of you are really in love with your spouses?" Then her jaw clenches as she sticks her index finger in Dave's face. "You have been a complete jerk the entire time we've been dating. Not wanting to have sex that first night. Not wanting to get married. I don't need this shit. I am the most beautiful woman in the world. I can have any man I want. So you get over your little college crush. You've traded up. Deal with it!"

"Libby," Eric begins quietly.

"And you!" Isabella screams, spinning around in anger and pointing her index finger at Eric. "You of *all* people don't get to talk to me right now!" She thrusts her thumb back at me. "Tell me she's the love of your life," she seethes. "Was she your first kiss when you were eleven? Was she the first one you called when you got into college? Or Med School? No! *I'm* the one you called, *I'm* the one you love! So don't you dare tell me what I can and can not say at my own wedding, or who I get to choose! I will get over you if takes me ten weddings to do it!"

"Libby!" Eric's voice booms. "You're being a jackass. Stop it!"

She puts her palm up at Eric. "I'm not talking to you anymore."

Eric rolls his eyes. "Oh, for God's sake," he mutters to himself.

And here's something I didn't see coming: Eric walks to Isabella, picks her up, and throws her over his shoulder. She starts pounding her fists on him as he walks her away from the gazebo. "What are you doing? We're not five anymore! Put me down!"

"Ladies and gentleman," Eric says calmly. "Miss De Leon will be indisposed for the next few moments. Please stay seated."

And he carries her into the house.

A stunned audience turns to Dave, who stares back at the nine hundred guests like a deer caught in headlights. "Good afternoon everyone!" he stammers. "As you know, Isabella has become very superstitious about this wedding. She wanted to make sure that the wedding was special…that nothing happened in this wedding which had already occurred in her previous five weddings…"

All eyes, including mine, are on Dave who I'm sure has no idea where he's going with this. "So… we decided to follow an old family tradition where the couple has to have a big fight right before the ceremony. I believe it was Shakespeare who…"

Eric and Isabella hurry out of the house, holding hands and smiling as they walk back to us. "There's been a small change of plans," Eric announces to the crowd. "There will still be a wedding. It's just that the part of the groom will now be played by… me."

I tilt my head. I can not wait to watch the videographer's film of this when everything is done.

"Of course, with my ex-fiancé David's best wishes," Isabella interjects, looking over at Dave. "Right, honey?"

Dave puts up his palms to show *no contest*. "Absolutely."

Isabella and Eric walk back to the altar, then take their new places as the bride and groom. Isabella looks over at me. "Can you get back to your spot, sweetie? We're on a tight schedule."

I silently walk back over to my position in the gaggle of bridesmaids as Dave silently takes a seat next to Dad.

The freshly engaged couple get through their vows in just under four minutes. The string quartet plays, then the newlyweds make their way back down the aisle and towards the reception. I watch as Joe takes Britney's arm, then follows Eric and Isabella.

Next, it is my turn to walk down the aisle. I begin to head down solo.

Until Dave runs up to me, grinning, and puts out his elbow for me to take. "I will get even with you for ruining my wedding day."

I smile back as I interlock my arm with his. "Really? How?"

"I'm not sure. But we've got the rest of our lives to think about it."

Epilogue

March 14th

Dear Diary,

What a month it's been. I lost my job writing Isabella's autobiography (can't say as I blame her for canceling the project), lost my book deal, and got fired.

Yup, 'Edict of Edith' didn't get published in exchange for writing a twenty-nine-year old's life story. Instead, I sold it completely on its own merits. Vanessa read the book and loved it so much that she called one of her ex-lovers, a publisher she nicknamed, "that old guy with the paunch, the thirty-something wife, and the toddlers running around" and told him to buy it.

He said no. So Vanessa invited his thirty-something wife out to lunch and over Champagne and niçoise salads said, "Read this."

The wife loved it.

It will be in bookstores next year.

And what happened to that Dave guy? We decided on a ridiculously short engagement. One month to the day. My engagement ring wasn't a million dollar pink diamond, but the tiny vintage piece that cost Dave nine hundred dollars so many years ago.

We flew out to Kauai, telling all of our friends that no one had to feel obligated to go, but that there'd be a small beach ceremony in Princeville if they wanted to join us. And twenty people did.

Liz was the maid of honor. Joe was the best man. Priscilla was the flower girl and little Jack served as ring bearer. Trudy served as minister. My half brother John and half sisters Marisa, Melissa and Kate were in attendance. And this time my dad walked me down the aisle.

There were no four hundred-dollar invitations, no thousand-dollar stilettos, no half million-dollar dresses. The wedding cake had two tiers, not six. The car we drove to the ceremony wasn't a limousine or a horse drawn carriage, but a rented Ford Mustang convertible. And Isabella may have managed to get Dave into a tuxedo, but I got to enjoy my fiancé comfortable and happy in a white button up shirt, white linen pants, and dark green lei.

And it was the best day of my life.

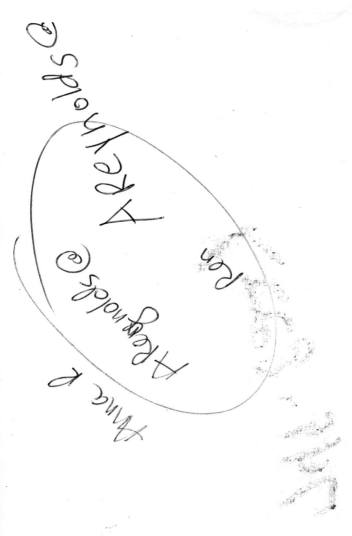

Made in the USA
Middletown, DE
21 October 2021